I0595042

CONTENTS

Towards the end of her arduous and wonderful life, my grandmother was propped up in a tiny twin bed. Her wooly, white hair was placed in a low bun. She looked at me with her wrinkled face and smiled. "If you can, try to fall in love at least once. I never got to."

This book is for her, and anyone who feels that they are too sick to deserve love. I aim to prove us all wrong.

CONTENT WARNING

This book covers heavy topics such as: severe mental illness, life in an asylum, electroshock therapy, bigamy, suicide, and death. There are also a couple of spicy bits. Gird your loins, and read on if you dare.

Chapter One

Samya ground the chili peppers she'd nicked from the commissary with the heel of her shoe.

"What if he catches you?" Aisha whispered. The waif-like nurse's trembling flashlight illuminated Samya's delinquency in the otherwise pitch-black office.

Samya waved the shoe in the air. "Let him! I wouldn't have to do this if that donkey with a stick up his ass didn't ogle you and the other nurses. Men like him must be taught."

Aisha's nerves did not seem to ease.

Samya smiled. "Besides, I didn't have time to buy you a goodbye gift, so this will have to do."

Aisha was horrified by this little stunt, but it was standard for Samya. At age five, Samya had purposely stuck gum in little Talia's silky blond hair (in contrast to Samya's unruly black curls) because the girl had called Samya ugly. After Samya had taken the gum out of the girl's hair with a pair of scissors, Talia had walked around with a bald spot for several weeks. At age seven, Samya had stabbed a boy's hand with a pencil after he'd made fun of her friend Omar for being an orphan. When a El-Qasr El-Ainy Medical School Professor protested women being enrolled in the school, Samya had painted his imported mahogany desk pink. Yes, she was vindictive but it was always justified...in her eyes.

That morning, Samya had found Aisha crumpled and crying at the nurses' post. When she finally calmed down, Aisha told her how Dr. Foad had grabbed her rear and laughed in front of two orderlies. When Aisha had confronted him, Foad had told her she was too sensitive.

So, tobacco. Chili. Justified.

Samya gathered up the crushed peppers, poured them into the tobacco tin placed on Foad's desk, and blended them in with her finger. Her mouth curved upwards. Foad consistently chewed tobacco from that very tin at least five times a day.

Thud.

Both women whipped their heads around toward the closed door and froze. When no further sound was heard, Samya replaced the tin on the odious man's desk. "Turn the light off," she told Aisha.

Samya peeked out of the door and into the dark hall that reeked of rusted metal. When satisfied that the coast was clear, they slipped out covertly.

"Thank you, *habibti*!" Aisha hugged her tightly.

"You are going to choke me, woman!"

They heard muffled voices around the bend. Samya squeezed Aisha back and then took off in a sprint, leaving Aisha to return to her post at the nurses' station. Samya ran through the hallway, her lifeless hospital gown making a swishing sound. She prayed that she could manage to avoid the orderlies that checked up on patients every fifteen minutes to make sure they didn't kill themselves with a toothbrush or some such thing. Being caught by one of them would mean an elongated stay as a patient in the Alexandria Asylum—the premiere mental hospital in 1958 Egypt. *The booby hatch for crazies w*as what the patients lovingly called it.

For six long months Samya had called this place home. The first floor contained patients' rooms (for those that had means), the doctors' offices, and nurses' post. The second floor housed a cafeteria and treatment rooms. And the third floor contained patients who were less financially fortunate, apparently thrown about and chained to hospital beds in the hallway. Screams emanated from that floor followed by complete silence, which she imagined to be their tranquilizer shots working. Samya had never been called a coward in her life, but she knew that the third floor was one place she couldn't bear to go. The thin line between her and the third floor was family money.

So when Samya slipped into the windowless room she had occupied for the last six months, she didn't complain. Packed suitcases sat at the edge of her cardboard-like bed. It was a miracle she'd convinced one of the orderlies to release her belongings early. Tomorrow, Samya would be released into the world again. Though she wouldn't miss her fabulous accommodations at the booby hatch, she wasn't ready to enter back into highfalutin 1950's Cairo society. Honestly, it wasn't clear which one was worse.

Tomorrow came with a loud scream.

"AAAYYY!"

Ever so elegantly, Samya opened her door and strolled out towards the hallway that led to the doctors' offices. She was glad to be wearing the high-waisted pants, white shirt, and Italian leather shoes she'd come in with when she'd checked in. She pinned her curls back in a quick twist as she followed Dr. Foad's screams.

Dr. Foad ran towards the kitchen next to the nurses' station. Samya took a look at her handiwork. Foad was a sniveling little shit in his twenties, newly graduated from Alexandria Faculty of Medicine, no doubt a degree paid for by his parents, who wanted to throw his weight around like an *effandi*. The man's potbelly was jiggling as he frantically shoved water from the sink to his mouth.

Foad spoke between gurgles. "It's burning! It's burning!"

Samya handed him a cup that he slammed against his mustachioed lips without looking. He took one swallow and then sprayed it all over the sink. "What the hell was that?" Tears were streaming down his red eyes.

Samya did not hide her amusement. "Oh, no, it's cooking oil. I could have sworn it was water. My mistake."

He brought his hands up towards her, paused, and then puked into the kitchen sink.

Samya made a 'toodleloo' gesture and let Foad's GI tract torture him.

As she walked back towards her room, she saw Aisha biting her lip and trying to hold back laughter. Aisha came up to her and surreptitiously slipped Samya two Melachrinos cigarettes, her favorite. Samya had been forced to "quit" when she arrived, which meant she'd bribed orderlies to let her smoke in the tiny garden behind the hospital at night.

"We don't approve." Aisha nodded toward the other nurses in their white uniforms with high white socks. "But we thought our savior deserved a little gift on the way out."

It was uncommon for the staff of an asylum to hug and see a patient off on their last day. But each nurse and some of the orderlies hugged Samya as she walked towards the exit of the asylum. She was informed that her father would be waiting for her outside. It was always easy for Samya to make friends. The trouble was keeping them.

Before she turned to leave, Foad caught up with her. "I know it was you."

"What was me?"

"You poisoned me!"

"What nonsense, Foad."

He bared his teeth. "Doctor! It's Dr. Foad!"

"Where?"

Aisha, bless her, though no doubt frightened, stepped towards them.

Samya shook her head slightly and winked at her. Samya didn't need help with little boys like Foad.

Foad invaded Samya's personal space. "You think because your baba's rich you can do whatever the hell you want? This is a respectable establishment—"

She cut him off. "I agree with you. And a respectable establishment needs respectable people who treat others respectfully. And when they don't treat each other respectfully, well, there are consequences."

"You crazy bitch." He gritted his teeth but then rapidly stopped fuming and grinned wildly. He grabbed her arm in such a hold that would surely leave marks. "No matter." He whispered, "You'll be back in a couple of months anyways."

Staring daggers at the man whose breath smelled of fresh vomit, she shoved him off.

Although her arm hurt, she was secretly thankful for the distraction the fool had provided. After months of being in the booby hatch, the outside seemed a scary, unknown place. Yes, inside there was screaming, shots, being dazed and confused, and the occasional humiliation via some corrupt orderlies, but Samya had been given a routine. She knew what to expect every day. There was no one to judge her— no one that mattered anyway. And now she felt like she was being thrown out on her ass to fend for herself.

Taking a long breath, Samya swung the exit doors open and then stepped outside the building. The noises that had sounded muffled inside her hospital room for so long were now at full volume. Cars honking, kids playing soccer, waves from the beach crashing onto the shore, shopkeeps yelling their fruit prices in hopes of enticing customers. The fresh air stung her skin.

"*Habibti.*" Samya's father hugged her as she stepped out onto the sidewalk. Dr. Mahmoud Roshdi was ever the same, sporting a gray mustache, his slight belly protruding from his gray suit. A gold watch chain swung from his lapel. "Are you ready, you think?"

Her mind went right back to automatic survival mode. The facade she had so carefully lived behind rose in front of her. Samya kissed her father on the cheek. "Who knows? But I'm craving macaroni béchamel, and the cook here is shit."

Her father laughed. "Good. Because Zoo Zoo prepared you a feast fit for kings."

"There haven't been any of those since the revolution, for shame." Samya smiled at her amused father.

Truth be told, the hospital food hadn't been all that bad. It was more that the shock treatment Samya had been taking made her lose her appetite. Her weight had dropped significantly (her mother would be elated). But give it a couple of weeks, and her ass would grow back to its normal, rotund size (to her mother's inevitable chagrin).

Dr. Mahmoud must have sensed his daughter's anxiety. He put his arm around her and spoke sotto voce. "How do you really feel this time, *habibti*?

She looked up at her father, who was only a couple of inches taller than herself. This gift and curse of being able to fake stability and hide inner chaos came from him. But his body betrayed him. His eyes were puffy. Lines that hadn't been there months ago had found shelter on his pale face. He was worried. Oh, so worried because of her.

"Better, *Baba*, really."

He scrunched his eyebrows a bit and had a hopeful look in his eyes. "Really?"

She gave him the smile she had practiced so much in her windowless room. The smile that said "There's nothing wrong here!"

"Really." She hugged him. "Now off to the train station we go." She interlocked her arm in his and started skipping.

"Not in public, you silly child." Her father faux-chided her with a chuckle.

They walked down the street with the competing smells bouncing around them of fresh roasted corn from the street vendors and *bokhoor* from the incense sellers. The Egyptian sun was beating down on the populace, dismissing the cool wind from the sea. At the Alexandria train station, Samya's father bought her a sesame candy just as he had when she was a little girl. Never mind she was all of twenty-nine, a medical school dropout, and a mental case. With her father beside her, she settled into a seat in first class and chomped on the candy on their way to their family home in Cairo.

The Alexandria landscape flashed by as the train started picking up steam. She was fine. She was breathing. She could think clearly: the minimum. Samya tried to focus out the window of the train. The sand-colored buildings of the city disappeared one by one, giving way to Egypt's rural terrain. Farmers in their traditional long frocks were scattered around picking cotton in the long, swaying grass. Women were beating clothes with rocks at the edge of the Nile River. A tied group of donkeys sought shade from the punishing sun underneath swaying palm trees. Soon the landscape would change into the concrete metropolis she called home.

Still, the words she was trying to suppress kept echoing within her.

"You'll be back."

Chapter Two

Aaaah!" Samya's sister bolted out of their family's grand villa in Cairo towards Samya, who was frazzled after the three-hour train ride. Despite the fact that the petite Hend was 5'2 to Samya's 5'7, Hend's hug about crushed Samya's organs.

Hend was gorgeous inside and out. Long, silky auburn hair cascaded down her back. Her hazel eyes sparkled in the sun, and her white organdy Dior dress emanated sophistication.

It was difficult to tell the two were sisters. But where they lacked physical similarity, they shared identical senses of humor. Samya was the only one who truly understood Hend's genius. In polite society, Hend portrayed the image of an empty-headed, pretty girl. Samya wasn't entirely sure why Hend disguised herself.

Hend grabbed her sister's face. "How was Greece, dear?"

Dr. Mahmoud and Samya had agreed that it was best to tell everyone she was visiting relatives in Greece to cover up her long absences in the hospital. Society didn't take kindly to any illness, and didn't take at all if that illness was of the mind. Samya was especially protective of her younger sister and didn't want to burden her, so she gave Hend the same story as everyone else. In fact, before leaving the hospital, Samya had concealed the bruises on her temple with makeup so that Hend and her mother wouldn't see them.

"Their cheese is stinky, but their beaches are gorgeous."

"Both of you come in now, or did you forget we are amongst civilized people?" their mother, Madame Magda, chided.

Once they were inside the family's villa, Samya's mother kissed her and wrapped her in a warm hug. "I've missed you, *habibti*. Oh, Samya!" Her mother pulled back and looked at her in horror. "What have you done to your hair?"

"I washed it, Mama."

"Your hair was never like this growing up. It was so soft and straight. You've ruined it."

"Mama!" Hend said.

"Yes, Mama, I wake up every day at five in the morning and use a pencil to curl every individual strand in order to upset you." Samya rolled her eyes.

Madame Magda responded to her unruly daughter. "Make fun of me all you want, but it is true. You used to have such beautiful hair. Come, let's eat."

Samya's mother was obsessed with her daughter's looks. Madame Magda swore up and down that the girl had been fair-skinned straight from the womb. Apparently, Samya had ruined her skin from too much sun, turning it into (unfortunately, according to her mother) a warm bronze.

Ironically, Samya looked most like her mother. Madame Magda donned a slightly darker skin tone, coily—but always chemically relaxed—black hair, and an ample bottom. Her mother, however, dressed in the latest fashion for her age group: gold, furs, sequins, anything that was blindingly shiny, really. And put full makeup and half a perfume bottle on every day. Samya opted for simplicity. Sartorial happiness came in the form of cigarette pants and a tied white blouse.

No one could likely tell, but this homecoming was overwhelming to Samya. She hadn't seen a soul out of hospital uniforms or gowns in months. Now, she had to interact with the main population as if she hadn't recently been jolted with electricity for her recurring depression and bouts of catatonia. She was like a newborn fawn, awkwardly taking her first steps back into real life.

Despite the off-kilter feeling, Samya had her outward mask of calm on tight. She headed to the dining room with Hend, arm in arm. That was the maddening thing about being...well...mad in the way she was. As long as she wasn't in the middle of a breakdown, she could often pretend all was normal. She could laugh and joke and gossip and look merry. All the while, her depression was chipping away at her mind, and the catatonia, now dormant, was lurking in the shadows. Even if she told anyone she was sick, it would be difficult to believe, given her behavior. Fortunately, no such confessions were ever going to happen. Her dad was the only one who had to know, and she was racked enough with guilt that he had to handle that burden.

The dining room had drawers with glass cases housing little ceramic cherubs, figurines of eighteenth-century European men and women, silver and gold cutlery, and fine china. The drawers surrounded a large beige marble table that seated twenty and was encased in a plastic covering. Allah forbid they get the table dirty with food. Up above, a bloated chandelier illuminated the room.

Samya's mother sat down and started piling Samya's plate with macaroni béchamel, stuffed grape leaves, grilled duck, *molokhaya*, and rice with *sha'aria*. All of which were Samya's favorite foods. Samya dug into them like she was on an expedition.

"Now, you are just in time! The Gamals will be over on Friday for a small, intimate gathering. Your father also invited a strapping young man." Madam Magda strived for nonchalance. "You and Hend will dress gorgeously, of course."

Samya mussed her hair so that her curls went in all directions, widened her nostrils, and with chicken grease on her mouth, smiled in an odd way. Using a rural accent, she exclaimed, "Do...you...think...he'll... like...me... Mama?" She walked over to her mother's chair and kissed her on the cheek with grease still on her lips.

Her mom screeched and hit her while Hend, Samya's father, and Samya burst out into laughter.

"Nonsense. That's what you're good at. This is your fault, Mahmoud."

"What have I done?" Samya's father asked.

"You've allowed her too much freedom. Now she thinks she can walk into a room with wild hair, no makeup, and live her life as a spinster." She turned to Samya, who was patting her hair back into a coiffure. "Do you want to end up like your Auntie Khadiga? Puttering around in her apartment, raising pigeons, and twiddling her thumbs waiting to get an invitation to a family dinner?"

"I'm not going to end up like Khadiga. I'm going to raise ducks."

Her mom huffed.

"She'll have time for that yet, Magda." Her father interjected and patted her hand. "For right now, she is going to focus on getting back to medical school. Her exams are coming up, and she'll be too busy studying to worry about any of these silly young men you scrounge up."

Samya sidestepped her father's hopeful glance and turned to her mother. "I'm not going to see the Gamals, *habibti*. But don't worry. I'll go to every gathering you will me to after."

Madame Magda squinted her eyes and then relaxed. "Fine. But after that, girl, you are going to get your hair straightened and be a proper young lady. If it takes me to the ends of the earth to find him, I am going to get you a husband."

Samya would never let that happen. But for now, she let her parents live in their delusions.

Chapter Three

"Last call for the train to Tanta!" A porter announced.

Jacques sat in first class looking out the window at the Cairo train station's Ramses Square. Men with sandals and long frocks sat cross-legged by the newsstand, sipping traditional tea with cardamom and Turkish coffee. A little further, posh families in westernized clothing patronized a modern patisserie, "La Monde." They drank that same tea and coffee for likely ten times the price as the newsstand's. All the while, an eighty-three-ton, three-thousand-year-old statue of Ramses II watched over this clash of old and new.

Egypt: this was his father's homeland. The first time Jacques had ever set foot in it. Jacques had lived in France all his life. His father, Abd El-Hameed—or "Abdo" as he'd affectionately been called by his French neighbors—had been a traveling businessman with a big personality and an abundance of humor. Jacques remembered the lines on his father's face. The deep brown skin that accompanied them. The big, all-encompassing smile. The green eyes that had been just a shade lighter than Jacques's. After an absence from Jacques's life for over a decade, Jacques's father had died in a train crash on his way to Paris to see his son.

Now, Jacques just had to make it to his father's hometown, Tanta. Finish business and head back to Paris. "Business" was a callous word for it. He was bringing his father's body back from France to be buried in the family's catacombs. Ironically, the plane ride from Paris to Cairo had been the longest Jacques had spent with his father in years.

Since his father's death, Jacques had been seeing images, snippets of memories. Reminiscing, he supposed. Isn't that what you're meant to do in these situations?

For instance, he remembered being five and running into his father's arms.

Abdo would laugh while trying to ease his son's cobra-like grip on him. "I'm here, *habibi*."

Buried in his father's crisp, three-piece suit, Jacques would inhale the familiar scent of coffee, tobacco, and spiced cologne. His father was often away from home for months at a time in the name of business, so Jacques soaked up every second he had with him when he would come back to their little town outside Avignon.

Back in the present, the train started "chugga-chugga'ing;" smoke clouds ripped from the chimney, and the iron wheels moved it slowly out of the platform and onto its destination.

Jacques ran his hand through his wavy, obsidian-black hair and asked for whiskey from a train attendant, his second one of the day. Out of the corner of his eye, he saw two women staring at him and whispering. Not an uncommon event, Jacques smirked. He took a sip of his smooth, fiery drink. Then Jacques got up from his seat and adjusted the kerchief in his gray, bespoke suit.

The two whispering women in hoop skirts (wasn't that passé now?) sat across from one another. One was a curly-haired redhead with a pink bow in her hair, must have been in her mid-twenties. The other, similar in age, seemed quite tall, even sitting down, and had a sober black bob with bangs.

Not one to be shy, Jacques approached them. "Ladies, I may have spilled coffee on my suit. Would you be so kind as to tell me if it is noticeable?"

The redhead squeaked. "You speak Arabic?"

Jacques was grateful to the old man for that, at least. Abdo had made Jacques learn Arabic from a young age. Also, spending time with an Egyptian family in the neighborhood had helped him keep the language fresh in his head. From Jacques's understanding, the majority of the upper class in Egypt spoke French, but post-revolution there was a trend to migrate back to Arabic. So, his proficiency came in handy.

The sober bob whispered to her friend. "I told you he wasn't a foreigner."

So many Egyptians were mixed with different ethnicities that there wasn't a monolithic look per se. With his green eyes and fair skin, he could have blended in. But the way Jacques carried himself made him stand out amongst the crowd.

The three made empty conversation, with the women laughing every couple of minutes at jokes even Jacques didn't think were that funny. Nonetheless, they were sweet and kind enough to entertain his antics. It didn't take much for Jaques to convince them to join him at the bar in the middle of the train. Not that he was completely focused on their company, but he needed a distraction. Distractions would get him to Tanta and then right back to Paris as planned.

There were small booths alongside the windows up and down the bar area of the train. The bar itself was humble. Some imported beer, whiskey, nuts, and other small bites. The shelves that housed the alcohol were as dusty as the bartender. He looked a hundred if he looked a day. Whenever he poured a drink, the man splashed liquid everywhere with his shaking and tremors.

Jacques sat across from the two ladies in a booth by the bar, the terrain passing them by through the window.

"Jacques?" The redhead (how awful, he didn't even know their names) bit her lip. "Entertain us, will you? We're bored."

"Hmmm. Entertain you, eh? How about some magic?"

Jacques struck the right chord as the women wriggled in excitement. He bummed a deck of cards off of another passenger and placed four face down on the table. "Now pick one and show her. Don't let me see it." He looked away dramatically as they giggled.

When the redhead finished picking, Jacques reshuffled the cards. He picked one up. "Is it this one, Mademoiselle?"

"Oh, no." Sober bob said.

"Of course not, because it must have been this one." He pulled up another card.

"It is closer, Monsieur. It did have hearts. Uncanny," the redhead said, her eyes wide.

He kept pulling cards and waiting for them to get the joke. That he didn't know a damn thing about magic, and he was just teasing them. But nothing was landing quite right these days.

The monotony of holding the cards, and getting them wrong, encouraged Jacques's mind to drift again. Today, Jacques was in first class on a train. His younger self wouldn't have believed it. Jacques's childhood had been less than idyllic.

His father's visits home had become less and less frequent as Jacques grew up. Whenever Abdo was home, he and Jacques's mother, Vivienne, would go at each other like cats and dogs.

"I love her, but your mother is making things difficult for herself. Another man would have left her by now."

And then, when Jacques was a teenager, Abdo left.

A now-grown-up Jacques understood that his mother had been more than merely difficult. Hell, his father likely knew that, too, what with all the visits to the hospital and Jacques's grandmother yelling that Abdo needed to take care of his wife. But it was easier to blame a person for being difficult than to be responsible for their care.

So, why, if Abdo had turned his back on his family, had Jacques agreed to see him before he'd unexpectedly died? He wasn't sure. It may have been curiosity. It may have been loneliness. Since his mother's suicide, he'd been on his own in Paris. It may have been a yearning for the idealized version of a man he loved.

Expressions of awe brought Jacques back to the failing card trick.

"*Monsieur*, that's the one! The queen of hearts!"

Look at that. And it had only taken him ten tries to get it right. *Mon dieu*, he was a depressing bore today. These moments from the past had previously been repressed for good reason. Jacques shuffled the playing cards, smiled at the women, and resolved to be cheery. Well, at least tolerable. He got the table another round of drinks, and some other passengers joined them. They also were intrigued by Jacques's ability to speak the language.

A passenger asked him about his background.

"Jacques Ali Abd El-Hameed. A pleasure. I live in Paris, *oustaz*. My mother's French, but my father is Egyptian." *Was* Egyptian, Jacques reminded himself.

"Wait, *the* Jacques Ali Abd El-Hameed? Are you the mystery author?"

Jacques's cheeks pinkened. By all measures, Jacques was successful. At only thirty-one, Jacques had two published novels to his name. The first, *The Fastidious,* was a hit and the second, *The Decrepit,* had broken the curse of the sophomore slump. In fact, the success of the second book had been the catalyst for Abdo reaching out to congratulate his only son. Abdo had telegrammed that he wished to see Jacques and would be visiting Paris if he was so inclined to oblige.

Jacques worked hard but would never stop holding his breath when someone talked about his books.

"I haven't read your work, but now I plan to!" the man said, and Jacques let out a sigh of relief.

Changing the subject, he regaled the passengers with tales of his travels and musings on Egyptian culture as an outsider. A captive audience was a refreshing change of pace.

"Tanta!" The voice of an attendant served to shake the passengers out from under Jacques's spell, and they dispersed back to their original seats.

When the train came to a slow stop, Jacques hesitated before getting off. His complicated journey with his father was coming to an end. Shaking his head, he gathered his bearings and made the step on to the concrete runway. The Tanta station was not as populated as Cairo's had been. There was more old than new here. But the heat remained consistent throughout the country. The sun was setting on street vendors making their last bid to sell sesame candies, Coca Cola, and cigarettes. Little kids in dusty sandals ran after each other, screeching, dangerously close to the train tracks.

Jacques took a deep breath and gripped the trinket in his pocket. It was the only thing he had to remember his father by. Abdo had given him the little, black, wooden beetle when he was young. Jacques used to hate when his father left for work.

"This is a scarab. A long time ago, the old, old Egyptians used to wear them for protection," his father said to him at Gare d'Avignon-Centre, the train station where his family was seeing him off.

Jacques remembered feeling the grooves in the wood.

"Did you know what they thought of the scarab? It was lucky and unlucky. Good and bad."

"Why would they wear bad things?" Jacques sniffled as he was coming off a particularly bad fit.

"Because they believed that was life. It is up and down. Bad and good. When I leave, how do you feel?"

"Sad."

"What about when I'm here?"

"Happy."

"You see? Bad and good. When you are feeling sad, *habibi*, remember there is also happy in the world. When you are feeling happy, remember there is also sad in the world. It is okay to be both. We all need both."

Jacques felt the grooves of the scarab now as he had back then. There was a lot of bad lately. He wasn't so sure about the good.

Chapter Four

Jacques and a three-man crew took his father to the family catacombs. No matter how many times Egypt had been conquered, the people hadn't changed their burial process since the days of the Pharaohs.

They drove off from the train station with his father's casket strapped to the top of the car by flimsy ropes.

"Don't worry, *basha*. It won't fall off," one of the men said to a hesitant Jacques. With a salt-and-pepper mustache and a long traditional frock, the man drove with one hand and held the side of the casket on top of the car with the other.

When in Rome, Jacques supposed.

Instead of the headstones Jacques was used to seeing in a graveyard, there were large gates every couple of feet. Behind each gate was what looked like a cement garden. Together, Jacques and the men carried the casket down the long hall of gates and stopped at the one with a huge sign announcing "KAMAL." Jacques unlocked the gate with the keys he'd been given in Cairo by his father's former porter.

It had turned dark outside. The men carried flashlights so as not to trip on the stones and rubble of the unkempt grounds. At the back of the cement garden, Jacques opened a wooden door that led to the catacomb. He was assaulted by thick air and the smell of rot. Braving it, the men carried the casket down the stairs.

They finally went deep enough to find rows and rows of the dead. They were all wrapped in cloth that was tattered but had likely once been beautiful white cotton. The men opened the casket where his father had been wrapped in white in accordance with tradition. Jacques had requested that his father's face be covered also.

In that moment, Jacques expected to feel something rise in his chest. A howl, a dropping to his knees, yelling "Baba!" Maybe cursing God for taking such a young soul too soon. All he felt was the sweat trickle down his neck and the urge to leave as soon as possible.

The men carried Abdo's body and rested him in the row below the one Jacques understood to include his grandmother.

***

Jacques stayed in a hotel in downtown Tanta. It was the first accommodation he'd seen when he got off of the train. Not at all like the luxurious stays he was now used to, this place had cracks in the concrete stairs leading to his room. The room smelled of freshly cut meat from the butcher on the first floor. There was more dust than there was furniture. Far from the best, but it was shelter. Besides, he wasn't staying long. After a full two hours of restless sleep, Jacques left his gussied-up prison and saw the town in daylight.

Tanta, with its population of 100,000, was a rural city transitioning into a metropolitan one. The ambitious architecture made it seem like a younger sister copying its older sister, Cairo. Sand covered the new sidewalks that were outlined by black and white paint. Newer buildings were built in the European style with baby palm trees covering some of the unfinished bits. There were women wearing traditional *galabeyas*, headed to the market while balancing pounds of corn on their head, and others in hoop skirts clutching their embroidered purses.

Jacques didn't have to walk too far to a building filled with law offices. Apparently, his father's neighborhood in Tanta had held an enormous funeral procession the week before, so bringing the body back had been more of a formality. Jacques felt a relief in having handled the burial and was looking forward to returning to Paris.

But first, Jacques had been summoned to the office of his father's solicitor, Solayman Kabir, to tie up any supposed loose ends. While walking up the dusty concrete steps, he was stopped by an elderly man. The man had kinky white hair peeking out of a red fez hat with a swaying black tassel. Wild eyebrows appeared undecided as to whether to stay on his face or escape.

"It can't be! Oh, but it must be Jacques! *Ahlan wa sahlan*, my nephew!" the man exclaimed in greeting.

Jacques shook the man's hand. "Sir?"

"I'm Abdo's brother. Your *Amo* Mostafa. How grateful I am to see you. Such a strapping young man, you have your father's height."

"*Amo* Mostafa." How odd it was to meet an uncle you hadn't known existed. "What a pleasure. My condolences."

"Mine and yours, son. Mine and yours. He told me of you."

"I wish I could say the same, but alas, that was Abdo." Jacques smirked while putting his hands in his pockets.

Mostafa chuckled awkwardly. "He was a good man, that Abdo. Well, I don't want to speak ill of the dead...but he abandoned your *Amo* Mostafa. There is time to talk of that yet. You must come over for dinner after you are done with Solayman. That is who you are going to see, isn't it?"

"Yes, sir."

"Good man, but I wouldn't trust him to be honest with you. Your father, poor man, relied on him for everything. His finances might have well gone to dirt! Would you like me to go in there with you, son?"

"I wouldn't burden you with that, *Amo*. I will be sure to visit you another time."

"I'll hold you to it, now! Be careful with Solayman, will you?" Mostafa patted his shoulder.

Jacques waved the man off and went into an office on the third floor. Solayman's office was decorated with modest wood furniture. Slightly worn carpet covered the concrete floor. Solayman, a lean balding man in his early sixties, was bent over a large wooden desk. Mountains of paper stood on either side of him, the floor next to him, and on the bookcase behind him.

He smiled and rounded the desk to shake Jacques's hand. "*Salam*, Jacques. You must look like your mother, but you certainly have hints of your father in you. My condolences, son."

Solayman called for tea and motioned for Jacques to have a seat.

"What do you know of my father's brother, Mostafa?" Jacques asked while sipping tea. Good stuff, the mint tea here.

Solayman pinched the bridge of his nose. "The less said the better."

Though Jacques and Mostafa were apparently related, he understood better than most that blood did not mean much. Given his interactions with the two men, Jacques trusted Solayman's unsaid side of the story.

"Well, there you have it." Jacques said with an exasperated sigh. "What's up, Solly?"

Solayman gave a lopsided quivering smile at the new nickname. But then darted his eyes, refusing to look at Jacques.

Taking a deep breath, Solayman finally blurted it out. "We must go over your father's will. Abdo left you fifteen properties spread throughout Tanta, Cairo, and Alexandria."

Jacques looked at his father's soft-spoken solicitor, incredulous. "You're joking."

"It is written in his will, son."

"I haven't seen the man in nearly two decades. I can't imagine he would leave me anything."

Jacques read over the paper slid to him. There in plain black letters, it read:

I, Abd El-Hameed Kamal, bequeath to my son, Jacques Ali Abd El-Hameed Kamal, the remainder of my possessions...

Solayman cut in. "With the exception of a villa in Tanta and money to Mostafa, he has given his assets and property to you."

Without a beat, Jacques said, "I don't want them. I'm headed to Paris tomorrow."

"You can't reject them. They're yours."

"I give you permission to sell everything and send me the sum or, better yet, donate it to an orphanage. My father would have finally provided for someone's children."

A memory washed over Jacques. A deep ache in his belly and worry over where he would even find a morsel to fill himself and his mother. Without income from his father, and given the severity of his mother's illness, they were left in a precarious position. When all the while Abdo had been sauntering around with fifteen properties! The man was not merely negligent, he was malicious. Any sympathy Jacques may have had for his father disappeared.

Solayman sighed. "He was going to Paris to talk to you about it, but then, unfortunately... Well, you know."

That damn bastard. Jacques had struggled for years, uncertain of his future, and nothing from his father. The moment Jacques amassed some modest success, he was all of a sudden worthy of Abdo's attention.

"It is reasonable to be upset at him," Solayman said. "But he built an empire here, Jacques. He was a shoeshine boy from the poorest district and built something out of nothing. He wanted to pass all that along to you."

"Let Mostafa have them, then."

Solayman jerked up. With a defiant confidence unlike his character so far, he said, "Your uncle…well, I will let you have your own relationship with him. Your father and Mostafa had a complicated history. Suffice it to say, your father would not have wanted Mostafa handling any of this.

"There are many people that call these properties home. If you give away your birthright, these people will be in danger of getting kicked out and having their lives upended. You are a good man, son. I know you will do right by them."

"You give me too much credit." Jacques couldn't believe the amount of destruction and mess Abdo had left in his wake. "I am my father's son, after all."

Solayman looked at him with kind eyes. "You are your own man. You decide how you behave. Besides, if you did want to sell, it would take me a couple of months to do a valuation, find buyers, and so forth. I'd need you for that."

"I have a life of debauchery and drunkenness to get back to. I don't know a thing about real estate and business. I'd bankrupt the properties in a month!"

Solayman gave Jacques a pat on the back.

"I will help. Besides, it is not so different from debauchery and drunkenness, you know. They all require a strong stomach."

Jacques quirked his eyebrows and gave an imperceptible smile.

"Stay in Egypt. This is your country, too, after all. It will be an opportunity for you to get to know this part of your culture, eh? And who knows? You may find a good wife and want to stay." He wiggled his eyebrows. "On second thought, Egyptian women may be too turbulent for you. Stick to the food. You will love it."

All of Jacques's internal logic screamed for him to leave Egypt as soon as possible. He had a third novel to write, and he was two months past the deadline to submit his first five chapters to his editor. Though he spoke the language, he was still an outsider in his father's home country. Fifteen properties and the tenants that went along with them were too much responsibility for the likes of him.

Though Jacques was a bastard, he wasn't a cold-hearted one. He didn't want to oust people from their family homes, for God's sake. Besides that, though he wouldn't admit it, there was a deep loneliness looming inside of him at the thought of going back to Paris. Being alone and being lonely were two surprisingly different things. And after everything that had happened, Jacques was both. What did he really have to go back to?

He sighed. "Since I don't have a choice, why not?"

Together, they planned for Jacques to stay in Egypt for a couple of months to acquaint himself with the properties and give Solayman enough time to finish all the paperwork necessary for a transfer of assets (a surprisingly long process in Egyptian courts). Over the next two months, Jacques paraded all over his father's country, checking out properties, signing off on maintenance of said properties, checking on tenants, and doing a slew of other things that a novelist such as Jacques had no business doing. With the help of Solayman, he became a bit more acquainted with land ownership.

In the meantime, Jacques decided to make Cairo his headquarters. He stayed at the Mena House Hotel just outside Cairo with accommodations befitting his current lifestyle. It didn't take long to fall in love with Egypt, most especially Cairo. The city was always vibrating, always awake. It was a mix of modern, European-style buildings, medieval Islamic architecture, and ancient Egyptian artifacts and landmarks. The people were a treat. They were funny, welcoming, irate, over-sharers.

Jacques's Arabic was impeccable, but he would give himself away occasionally. One time he mentioned to a store clerk that he had an *ishr*, a shark fin, as opposed to an *irsh*, a coin. The storekeep laughed enthusiastically for five minutes straight.

He met many interesting personalities during his travels, and one such personality was Dr. Mahmoud Roshdi. The doctor was intrigued with the chemical properties of aspis, a snake poison. He was all too pleased to have Jacques as an audience. Jacques's first novel contained a nefarious assassination, so Jacques had spent an exhaustive three weeks interviewing the most boring group of people known to man: forensic toxicologists. When he finally held an understanding of the cursed subject, the plot changed, and the knowledge he'd acquired went down the drain. Apparently, it hadn't totally been useless, however, as it fascinated Dr. Mahmoud to no end.

"My boy, you must come dine with us. My wife is having a gathering tonight at our villa. Say you will grace us with your presence?" Dr. Mahmoud asked.

Even though he was spending a lot of time traveling across the country, Jacques hadn't had much time to really get to know anyone aside from Kareem, the new friend he'd made on the plane over from Paris. Kareem was a successful horse-trader who hated the upper echelon of Cairo society, widely known as the "Cairo elite." But Kareem hated most people, so really Jacques didn't give much weight to Kareem's ire.

"It would be a pleasure, Doctor," Jacques replied.

Chapter Five

Jacques arrived everywhere fashionably late if he could manage it. There was a certain panache in waiting as long as it took for a healthy crowd to gather, so they could all gaze in admiration as he made a grand entrance. He also detested small talk and thought the first hour or two of a party were best shaved off from his life experience. He employed this practice when visiting Dr. Mahmoud's villa.

"Welcome, *basha*." An older man, wearing a traditional Arab, blue-and-white frock and a neatly trimmed mustache, took Jacques's coat and motioned him through the door. From context clues, Jacques had gathered that *basha* was a respectful title for a man of rich consequence.

"They are expecting you in the salon."

Jacques walked the long, ceramic-ridden hallway in front of him. The whole place was the very picture of a wealthy Egyptian's home in the 1950s. Spanish in style, covered with warm maroon walls, golden silk curtains, and with small potted palm trees every couple of feet. A roar of laughter erupted from the end of the hallway, "HAHAHAHA." As Jacques turned the corner towards the laughter, Dr. Mahmoud greeted him.

"Jacques! How are you, my boy?"

Jacques returned the greeting with his most winning smile. "Good evening, Dr. Mahmoud. Thank you very much for inviting m—"

Not entirely listening to Jacques's response, Dr. Mahmoud pressed on. "But of course you have to eat proper food and be exposed to some good conversation. Come in, my boy. Come in."

They walked into the salon that housed furniture with European figures embroidered on the cushions. On a table in the middle of the room were trays of bananas, mango, strawberries and a plethora of pastries. The air smelled of baked goods and cigar smoke.

The laughter erupted again, "HAHAHAHA." Sitting in the European, gold encrusted furniture were the culprits of the laughter.

"Friends, let me introduce you to a very exceptional young man whose acquaintance I had the pleasure of making yesterday at the café. Jacques Ali Abd El-Hameed."

Jacques chimed in. "You can call me Ali if you prefer."

Dr. Mahmoud continued. "Ah, yes, Jacques *or* Ali. Let me introduce you to our cackling hyenas over here…"

More laughter erupted from the group.

"The distinguished gentleman to your right is *Oustaz* Gamal." Jacques had learned that Oustaz was a respectful title for a business man. "This stunning lady to his left is his wife, Madame Hoda."

A fair-skinned woman in her late forties smiled brightly. She wore red lipstick and a long sleeved, low-cut dress.

"Stunning?" Another woman at the very center, yet to be identified, spoke in an agitated manner, and another eruption of laughter ensued.

Ignoring the retort, Dr Mahmoud carried on. "Gigi and Hatem, Madame Hoda's children."

A girl in her early twenties, a younger version of her mother, giggled mischievously at Jacques. A surly, lanky teenager, presumably Hatem, barely registered his existence.

"My daughter, Hend." Dr. Mahmoud continued, motioning over to a girl with fair skin and long, reddish-brown hair. She batted her hazel eyes at Jacques.

"And of course, her mother, and unfortunately my wife, Madame Magda."

A truly striking woman, likely in her mid-fifties, snapped back. "Yes, just his wife. Not his '*stunning*' wife, mind you."

Madame Magda had a birthmark over her lip *ala* Marilyn Monroe and wore a brilliant, dazzling tan dress with a not-so-understated gold colored shawl.

"Ignore her." Dr. Mahmoud tried to comfort Jacques. "The boy has French sensibilities. He is not used to the typical Egyptian woman: aggressive and uncouth."

Madame Magda fired back. "Oh, yes, the poor Egyptian male has to deal with the vulgar Egyptian female. Why do you think we are like this? We have to put up with all your nonsense!"

"Well, Madame, it is a pleasure to meet such a fine example of sophisticated Egyptian femininity," Jacques assured her as he kissed her hand.

Madame Magda smiled. "Now, that is how an Egyptian man should behave. Take note, Hatem. You don't want to be like these old farts." Her eyes darted over to Dr. Mahmoud and *Oustaz* Gamal.

"What did I do?" *Oustaz* Gamal asked while laughing.

"Guilt by association," Madame Magda retorted with an infectiously charming smile.

"Now, Jacques or Ali—you know, I will call you Jacques, actually. Have a seat, *habibi*. Yes, right there next to Hend."

"I think he wants to sit next to Gigi, Magda," Madame Hoda said sweetly.

"Yes, *habibti*, but he is already halfway to Hend, and I don't want to run our guest ragged back and forth."

Jacques, amused, sat down. There was an understanding amongst certain classes in Cairo. A woman went from her father's house to her husband's house. As "good" men were scarce, a little competition brewed amongst the marriage-minded mothers for their daughters' coveted futures. Of course, many cultures had the same practice. But Jacques was a vagabond of sorts. He only really ran with artist collectives, revolutionaries, and on his own. This was a new world for him, and he was having a hell of a time learning about it. It would potentially provide inspiration for the novel. If he ever got around to writing it.

"Hend, go pour our guest some whiskey. Actually, what do you drink, dear?" Madame Magda asked.

"Whiskey's fine, madame, thank you." Jacques would have drunk gasoline to get the chance to study this cast of characters. Hend looked sheepishly at Jacques, walked up to the golden roll-out cart at the side of the room, and started pouring him a drink.

"What is this French business, son?" Madame Magda asked.

"My mother is French, madame. My father is Egyptian. He came over to France in the twenties."

Hend brought him the whiskey on an overly decked-out golden tray.

"For you, monsieur." she said.

"Thank you, Hend. Yes, madame, I grew up in a small village outside Avignon."

From seemingly nowhere, Dr. Mahmoud gleefully brought up an off topic. "Do you know that France possesses the most rare sort of honey? It has antibacterial qualities and was used in the World War—"

Madame Magda lit her cigarette with heavy-lidded eyes. "Mahmoud. For Allah's sake, no science talk."

"Why not?" Dr. Mahmoud snapped.

Leaving them both to bicker, Madame Hoda continued the interrogation. "So your father is Egyptian?"

She looked over at her daughter Gigi, who was way ahead of her. Gigi had already crossed over and wedged her way in between Jacques and her brother.

Madame Hoda continued. "Is that what brought you to Cairo? Your father?"

"Yes, madame. Unfortunately, my father had to die in order for me to visit his homeland."

Madame Magda came out of her bickering match for a second. "You poor dear. And deprived of culture for so long. Our condolences."

Jacques chuckled. "Thank you. Not all is lost. I now have a chance to learn about my father's homeland a bit more. I have inherited properties that will keep me in the area for a couple of months."

Gigi leaned in towards Jacques. "Do you have anyone to show you around, *monsewer.*"

Jacques had to control his cringe at hearing such awful French.

Hend took advantage and grabbed Jacques's still-full glass. "Let me get you something else to drink, monsieur."

Gigi got up. "How about *I* get you something to eat? You look famished."

"Oh, don't worry about it, Gigi, I am—"

Suddenly, this character study became less fun. Like a zebra caught between two lions, Jacques grabbed the opportunity to flee while the predators were distracted.

"Dr. Mahmoud, may I use your telephone?"

Coming up for air out of his bickering with Madame Magda, Dr. Mahmoud obliged. "Oh, of course. Zoo zoo!"

A portly maid showed up. In her early sixties, she couldn't have been more than five feet tall. She wore a tan and pink bandana wrapped around her graying hair.

"Zoo zoo, show Monsieur Jacques to the study."

"Yes, Doctor." She replied.

Zoo Zoo led the way from the cackling group and down the hallway with Jacques following behind. She stopped short of a doorway and motioned with her hand for

Jacques to wait. With all the sign language she was deploying, it was clear Zoo Zoo assumed he didn't speak Arabic.

"Girl, the doctor's friend, a foreigner, needs to come in and use the telephone," Zoo Zoo said as she stepped into the study.

"Alright, let him come in and use it, then." A female voice said.

"Leave so he can come in. It's not appropriate."

The voice responded, "It's very appropriate for foreigners to use telephones."

Zoo Zoo huffed and puffed, while Jacques stepped towards the doorway.

"Wait, why are you red? Are you in love, Zoo Zoo?" The voice asked.

"Girl..."

Bashfully, Zoo Zoo looked at Jacques and then back into the study. Not so quietly, she whispered, "He looks just like Gregory Peck. If only I was a bit younger."

Though he couldn't see into the office, for some reason he imagined the unknown figure smiling.

"Oh, very well."

A tall figure, at least compared to the height-impaired Zoo Zoo, slid past her out into the hallway. The only light was the afterglow of the study. All Jacques could make out were wild black curls and wide hips that swayed like a newly rung bell within an unflattering dress he could only describe as a blue potato sack.

The maid scowled at the retreating figure and motioned with aggressive sign language for Jacques to use the office.

"When you are done with lover boy, bring me some grape leaves," The girl said from down the hallway.

Zoo Zoo left the office, and Jacques could hear their banter fade. "So demanding, Samya, you are a copy of your mother. Little Magda, I swear."

"That is about the most disturbing thing you have ever said to me," Samya said. "And a slice of chocolate gateau, woman!"

Jacques sat down in the office and crossed his legs, never having intended to use the phone. He only sought a reprieve from the infighting back at the gathering. On the gaudy marble desk in front of him was a copy of *One Thousand And One Arabian Nights*. He leaned over to look at the page to which it had been opened. Closer inspection showed some of the text partially crossed out with pencil:

Sultan Shahryar: Look into my eyes. What do you see, Scheherezade?

Scheherezade: Me. Looking at you, my love A bloated jackass with an inferiority complex, my love.

He smirked. Why would Dr. Mahmoud and Madame Magda's newly discovered daughter not be with her family and guests? Curious. He didn't let himself dwell on it for too long and instead flipped through the book. Taking out his black scarab, he threw it up in the air a couple of times. After letting a few more minutes pass and assuring himself that the lionesses had calmed, he left the office.

He spent the next thirty seconds getting lost, and then all the bulbs lighting the hallway suddenly went out, accompanied by loud groans. Another fact Jacques had learned about Cairo. Blackouts here were frequent and inevitable. Figuring he would let the moon peeking from the large glass windows light his way, he carried on. Down the seemingly never-ending hallway, paintings of golden-haired, cherub-like European children lined either wall. This was an odd yet common theme in rich Egyptian households. One painting, however, was a bit different from the others. He stopped to observe. The scene depicted lush palm trees and long, swaying cotton plants. An Egyptian woman in traditional black clothing was reaching for a translucent head wrap that was floating away with the wind. Her body was forever frozen in time seeking the wrap that made its ascent to the heavens. It felt out of place with the rest of the pieces that were no doubt imported from Great Britain. Somehow this very simple painting seemed the most valuable thing in the overly decorated house.

There was a commotion, interrupting his thoughts. A few feet from him, he saw ringlets of hair leaning out an open window.

"Boy. Psst, psst, psst. Boy." He heard who he assumed was Samya, the mysterious second daughter, whisper-yell out into the street.

Jacques walked over and looked above her head, out into the street, and whispered. "Who are we looking for?"

He heard a gasp, and before he could block it, she backhanded his face.

"Ow!"

"Sorry." She cupped her mouth in regret. Then, without a beat, slowly relaxed and raised her chin defiantly. "Your own fault for sneaking up like that."

He grinned. "Fair point."

The moonlight spilling from the window revealed dark, almond-shaped eyes and beauty spots that seemed to be placed strategically across Samya's face, tempting one to connect the dots.

Samya took a step back from him. "You speak Arabic? Zoo Zoo is going to kill me. Actually, you should speak Arabic in front of her. It'll give her a heart attack."

"I think I'd rather spare the poor woman. She was only stating the obvious." Jacques shrugged. "Though I've always thought of myself as more of a Brando than a Peck."

The woman was stone faced. Apparently, her sense of humor was only reserved for few, and he was not among them.

"Well. The party is that way. *Salam*." She turned abruptly back to the window, dismissing him. "Psst...psst...psst." Her body slumped as she exhaled a loud, frustrated sigh.

Samya's dismissiveness did nothing but intrigue Jacques further. "Why are we harassing Cairo youth at this hour?"

"*I* want the kid to get me cigarettes from the store." She dismissed him with a wave. "You'll want to be getting back to the gathering now."

Jacques put two fingers in his mouth and whistled loudly, a trick he'd picked up quickly in the dense expanse of the country terrain he'd grown up in.

A young boy of no more than twelve in a dusty white kufi looked up at the window.

"What's your name, kid?"

"Hussain, *oustaz*."

Jacques chucked a piaster out the window for the kid to catch. "Hussain, go to the corner store and get *Abla* Samya here a couple of ..." He looked at Samya.

"Melachrinos," she said to Jacques.

"Melachrinos. And get yourself a cola."

The kid jumped for joy and ran off.

She clicked her tongue and screamed out into the night. "Boy! If you cheat this man and don't bring my cigarettes, I'm going to sic the coyotes on you!"

She crossed her arms. "If you throw money at him up front, he could just run away with it. How have you survived in Cairo like this?"

"Through the kindness of strangers like yourself."

"Here." Samya shoved a piaster in front of Jacques.

He declined it. "Amends for sneaking up on you."

"Suit yourself."

For a second they were both quiet. The noise of a stray dog's paws pattering on cement and very faint *tabla* music from the café a street over filled the space.

Samya broke the silence, "What's your name, then?"

"Jacques…actually, it's Ali, if you prefer."

"If I prefer? You Europeans are very accommodating. Sometimes people say, 'Hi my name is Zainab, but you can call me Zizi' but never 'Hi my name is Zainab, but you can call me Ginger.' My point is what do you prefer?"

"Ginger."

Caught, Samya smiled. Her entire face lit up, and at the left corner of her mouth, a dimple appeared. He had to stop himself from reaching out to press the indent.

"Who'd you call on the phone?" she asked.

He put his hands in his pockets and shrugged. "No one. I wanted to get away for a bit."

She smiled. "So they're fighting over you already."

"How'd you know?"

"You are male and likely single. Those are the requirements." She looked him up and down, assessing him. "So you chose to hide."

"You are making me sound pathetic. It was more like a dignified avoidance."

Seemingly absentminded, she tucked some of her unruly black hair behind her ear, revealing a circular bruise at her temple. Jacques could just make out a second half of the matching set on the other side. His lingering must have alerted her, and she pulled her hair quickly back to cover the bruises.

"*Abla* Samya!" Hussain's little voice sounded from below, breaking the awkwardness. Samya caught a package carrying the cigarettes the boy tossed up.

She nodded at Jacques before walking away from him.

Bewildered, Jacques yelled after her. "Mademoiselle Samya."

Samya turned around.

"There's a café around the corner that has a superb selection of gateau. A little bird told me you are a fan. Would you like to accompany me tomorrow? I'll allow you to insult my manhood some more."

Her reply was measured. "No."

"No?"

As if he weren't there, she opened the package to pull out a cigarette and placed it in her mouth while she fumbled in her dress pocket.

"I don't see the need." She spoke through her teeth, balancing the cigarette.

"Does there need to be a need? It may be fun to get to know each other."

"This was enough. I got the gist."

She pulled out a lighter in triumph, lit the cigarette, and exhaled in relief. As she turned around and walked down the dark hallway, Samya yelled behind her, "Make sure you speak Arabic in front of Zoo Zoo. It'll give her hell."

Chapter Six

When she had enough distance from the mysterious man, Samya sprinted around the corner, up the stairs, and straight into her bedroom. She almost burned her fingers as she clumsily attempted to put her cigarette out in the ashtray lying on a small table across from her bed. That done, Samya took a deep breath.

In a year where she'd oscillated between extreme anguish and resigned numbness, she hadn't expected this new sensation. Her heart was pounding, her face flushed. His black hair, his warm green eyes that seemed to crinkle upwards when he grinned at her, his very broad shoulders. Closing her eyes quickly and tightly, she reminded herself that she hadn't seen a soul aside from medical staff for a while. It was logical that a stranger would confuse her. As she slipped back into the fold of society, her reactions would become more tame. She was sure of it.

Besides, judging by his sharp suit, cocky stride, and arrogant smirk, he was a copy of Dr. Foad and all the other pampered jackasses she'd ever encountered. To top it all off, he was a handsome foreigner. No doubt all the females of Cairo were fainting at the sight of him. It was a cruel thing that Allah put the most awful people in the most beautiful packages.

In the vanity mirror, she caught sight of the bruises at her temple. Dammit, she'd forgotten to put makeup on them. But he'd seen them and hadn't looked away. The threat of shame crept up on her, but she pushed it down. It was none of his business to look at her, judge her. Still, it was strange he'd invited her out after that. Perhaps to ridicule her? It didn't seem that way, though. Samya was glad that her cold exterior cemented from years of hiding and survival had done its job. He wouldn't have seen any weakness, she thought. She lit another cigarette and inhaled. It was done with now. In any case, she'd likely not run into the man again.

***

Samya's mother wasted no time. They only had a week to prepare Samya for her reentry into the Cairo elite. Madame Magda insisted that after a year of being in seclusion in "Greece," her eldest daughter would get married. That and prayer would be the solution to Samya's "behavioral problems," as Madame Magda put it. So off to the modiste they went.

"Yellow," Madame Magda said. "Pink or white, even. Just no more black!"

Madame Magda and Hend huddled in the tiny dress shop while Samya was measured by the modiste. The shop's modest exterior was in contrast to the expensive products it housed. The store had the best silks, fabrics, and accouterments you could find in Cairo. Inside, it was an explosion of textures. To her mother's annoyance, Samya preferred to dress in a minimalistic style, so all the variety was wasted on her.

"What are you? A seventy-five-year-old woman in mourning? No, I will not have it. Bright colors!" Madame Magda shoved the modiste to the side as she inspected Samya's waist.

"You are getting portly, *habibti*. I'll have Zoo Zoo fix you tea and honey for the next couple of days."

"Mama!" Hend snapped. "There's nothing wrong with her!"

Samya laughed. "Mama would rather have the Brits recolonize than have folks see the curves of my belly."

"I can never say anything to these girls," Madame Magda addressed the modiste and then turned to Samya.

"You know I think you have the most beautiful face. If you could only give a bit more effort to your body, you would be perfect."

"Mama, really?" Hend said.

Samya never loved her sister more than when she was sparring with their mother on Samya's behalf.

Samya turned to the modiste as Hend and Madame Magda continued to duel. "Dark blue. It's a compromise," she said with a fiendish smile.

"It's on your head, then, mademoiselle." The modiste left to get fabric.

Samya's mother had a certain standard of beauty that the men of Egypt apparently did not subscribe to. Samya had often gotten attention for her looks. It was her great personality that scared them off. Although she told herself her mother's words were harmless, the "well-meant" criticism did not help the anxiety she felt about seeing the elite. Especially since the only companions she'd recently had were the nurses and the rats that scurried down the hospital floor. Her first appearance would be at Madame Hoda's cocktail party in five days' time. It wasn't a soiree but a small gathering, if you could call fifteen prominent families small. The event was the perfect dip in the water before Samya dove off the cliff.

"Alright, you stubborn girl," Madame Magda yelled at Samya over Hend's shoulder. "Give me at least one pastel pink dress."

Samya nodded, and Madame Magda rushed to her and kissed her cheek.

Hugging her daughter tightly, Madame Magda looked in the mirror they were facing. "Now if we could only do something about this hair."

"Mama!" Hend yelled.

***

Oustaz Gamal and Madame Hoda's villa was located in the well-to-do district of Maadi. Samya walked through the doorway with an air of outward confidence that masked the cowering little girl she was inside.

The sandy exterior of the villa hid the garishness inside. Each room featured bold colors. Their salon was a stark pink, the hallways were chick-yellow, the kitchen bright orange, and on and on. Madame Hoda proudly credited a "European" designer for her mismatched mansion. Samya was convinced they had been scammed by some charlatan by the way they doubled down on their pride over the decor.

The deep red ballroom Samya stepped into was carpeted in an even deeper red and brightened by several chandeliers glittering above. Cliques of fabulously dressed guests clustered throughout the space. Women wore a variety of full-skirted swing dresses with all sorts of colorful patterns and matching jewelry. Men showed up in sharp tailored suits and mustaches. Some wore maroon fez hats. There was plenty of champagne, tea, Turkish coffee, and hors d'oeuvres handy, but what Samya needed was a cigarette. Unfortunately, it was unbecoming of a lady to carry her own, especially in front of company.

Her family strode before her, led of course by Madame Magda. To her mother's begrudged satisfaction, Samya wore a royal blue, narrow sheath dress with little fuss or muss, something short sleeved, silky and that hugged her waist. Her curls were somewhat tamed and molded into the Katherine Hepburn style that was all the rage. Samya's lips were painted in her signature scarlet.

After all introductions were made, she slinked back to the side of the wall near some refreshments. The air smelled of expensive *bukhoor* and fresh flowers. As Samya exhaled, she felt a hand tap her on the shoulder.

"Oh, thank Allah!" She beamed.

In the empty hallway nearby, Omar, a lean and very handsome fellow with glasses and thick eyebrows, motioned her to leave the ballroom and join him. When she did, he tried to shake her hand. Samya batted his hand away and jumped up to hug him. Making sure no one was looking, he lifted her up off the ground. "Ay, *captain*! Life has been so dull without you."

Omar Khaled Nabil, an up-and-coming prosecutor, was one of her very best friends. They'd grown up, fought, and laughed together. He was the complete opposite of Samya in many ways. He put propriety and social contracts above all else, but he was still one of the only people she trusted. He pretended to be above all her nonsense musings, but he would always indulge her and, when no one was looking, would sometimes join in. Omar was the epitome of a strong, well-bred, well-mannered Egyptian male, sometimes stuffy to a fault. But as he'd been adopted by his uncle under scandalous circumstances, he was, deep down, an outsider. Elegant, haughty, and sometimes arrogant, but an outsider, nonetheless.

"I've missed you." She squeezed his hand.

"Me, too. I've had no one to stress me out with their antics. It's been abominable." Omar motioned to the balcony. "Shall we go to the balcony, so you can save me from my misery?"

Samya tilted her head at him, and he rolled his eyes. "And smoke, of course."

She grabbed his arm and laughed "Who is saving who now?"

They headed out towards the balcony overlooking the buzzing street below with cars, lights, and people. She smelled the fresh, crisp air. The balcony railing invited her to lean back on it with one bended knee in what her mother would deem a very unladylike manner. Although they were outside, they could hear the faint sounds of a female singer crooning lyrics about how dark and sweet the world was. A small band including a *rababa*, violin, and cello parroted back her words, affirming them to their audience.

Omar, tutt-tutting Samya's unseemly posture, handed her a cigarette and fished in his breast pocket for a lighter. Before he could find it, a hand, cupped over fire, rose to Samya's cigarette-clad mouth.

"May I?"

Jacques emerged from the shadows. His crooked smile heated Samya's cheeks. And yes, he was as devilishly handsome as he'd been all those days ago. Irritating man.

"Merci." Samya spoke steadily, refusing to lower her eyes from his gaze.

Though the balcony was only dimly lit with red and yellow stained lamps strung across the railings, she was close enough to see him clearly. His black hair was swept to the side and back, leaving room for a hair or two to rebel and float across his eyebrow. Those eyes looked like he was in on some joke that no one else knew about. And he had a little beauty mark underneath his right eye. It was so slight, one would have to really focus in to see it. Like she was doing now. Dammit, she was ogling. But apparently, so was he. They were having a veritable staring match. Neither one wanting to relinquish power. Those dreamy eyes of his may have felled many a woman before now but not Samya Mahmoud Roshdi. She just had to tell that to the traitorous butterflies multiplying in her stomach. Truly, she couldn't figure the man out. And she needed to label him as soon as possible and put him on a shelf deep in her mind where no one visited. A charming Lothario he most certainly was. Really, nothing more than a face and a body, she concluded. Uncomplicated. Just a simpleton. All this information she decided could be gleaned from looking into his eyes.

"Monsieur Jacques." Omar gave him a firm handshake that Samya was sure was intended to disrupt the interaction. "Hiding, are we?"

Jacques took his time leaving their little game and then raised both his hands in defeat. "Well, there is nothing so emasculating as hiding from Egyptian mothers. And I am resigned to becoming a coward only fifteen minutes into this gathering."

"Hmmm." Omar frowned. "Albeit an annoyance to some, the mothers play an important role in our ecosystem. They only want a good match for their daughters and to create a strong Egyptian family."

Blocking Samya's view, he continued. "You can kindly indicate to them you are not a player in the game, and your stay in Cairo will be a bit more to your liking."

Samya stepped from behind Omar and addressed her old friend. "I would be proud of you for protecting the reputation of Egyptian women if you hadn't complained about the very same mothers at least three times since we've gotten here."

Omar grabbed Samya's shoulders and squeezed as he would when they were kids. "I've been dealing with this for thirty years. I've earned the right to complain. He…" Pointing at Jacques. "…hasn't."

Scrunching her face, Samya laughed.

Jacques looked at the two of them quizzically before Omar noticed his faux paus. "My manners. Jacques, this traitorous woman is Mademoiselle Samya, Dr. Mahmoud Roshdi's eldest daughter. Samya, this is Monsieur Jacques. We met earlier this evening."

Jacques kissed the back of Samya's hand. "A pleasure, mademoiselle."

She snatched her hand out of his. "This is our second meeting, monsieur. No need for false pleasantries."

Omar raised an eyebrow while taking in a puff of cigarette smoke. "You know each other?"

"Yes. In fact, if memory serves me, Mademoiselle Samya informed me that I wasn't worth talking to." Jacques smiled.

Samya turned to Omar. "Do you suppose all French people are this dramatic, or is it a trait unique to Monsieur Jacques?"

Before Omar could respond, a voice greeted them. "So this is where the real party is."

A tall, slender man walked towards them, accompanied by a raven-haired beauty.

Adam. Samya's temper started climbing, threatening to flare.

Adam, you foppish, fribble, half-witted, white-livered, nincompoop. Samya didn't much care that her face reflected her thoughts.

With a coldness befitting the arctic caps, Omar continued. "Adam. May I introduce you to Jacques Ali Abd El-Hameed? Jacques, this is Adam Waqab and his wife, Sara Ali."

Adam looked pointedly at Samya while Sara hastily grabbed his arm tight.

You weasel-faced, chicken-hearted son of a bitch.

"Lovely to see you out and about, Samya. Last time I saw you, you were pudgy and surly. You look…" He paused, looking directly at her. "…less surly."

CHAPTER SEVEN

Samya wanted to lunge at Adam.

Omar looked tense and clenched his jaw.

Controlling her breathing, Samya schooled her features. "You looked like a pompous jackass the last time I saw you." She looked Adam up and down. "Nothing's changed."

Adam chuckled awkwardly and turned towards Jacques. "Samya and I *were* in medical school together. I managed to graduate a couple of years ago. As for Samya, I heard you were puttering around in Greece was it?" He spoke in a faux sweet manner. "Too bad you couldn't cut it in school. Jacques, you know Allah grants the prayers of the unfortunate before anyone else's, don't you? Samya, would you pray for me and my wife? Allah is sure to hear your prayers the loudest."

Samya raised her hands up high in the air. "Oh, Allah, please give Sara the wisdom and strength to withstand a spineless snake and eunuch of a husband. Oh, Allah, protect her from his greasy hair and even greasier personality."

"Alright, Samya." Omar tried to keep a straight face.

Adam broke free of Sara's grip and stepped towards Samya. "You disrespectful..."

Not giving Adam time to follow through, Jacques turned to Samya. "I'll need a bodyguard if I'm going back into the arena. Mademoiselle Samya, are you up to the task?"

She put out her cigarette on the balcony railing and left with him.

Entering the ballroom, they were immersed with sounds of laughter, talking, and clinking glassware. The songstress had moved on to singing about the pain and beauty in her lover's eyes. Samya, meanwhile, was deep in thought.

A couple of years ago, Hend had been head over heels in love with Adam. He would write her love letters and lavish her with sweets and flowers. Samya and, reluctantly, Omar would devise rendezvous for the lovers under the guise of group outings. One spring day, a wedding procession came through Hend and Samya's street. Hend looked in shock. The groom-to-be was Adam, and his betrothed was not Hend, but a pale, raven-haired woman, Sara. There had been no prior warning or indication from Adam that he was moving on from Hend. Hend went inside her room and cried. Samya suspected that she only allowed herself that night to lick her wounds as she never spoke of it again.

Unbeknownst to Hend, Omar and Samya had separately confronted Adam. He'd been aloof, cavalier, and had accepted no fault in the matter. According to him, Hend should have known it was a mere tryst and nothing else. He'd never offered her promises of marriage.

Samya could have killed him out on the balcony but had held back out of respect for her younger sister.

When they were out of earshot of company, Jacques whispered. "If it is any consolation, I hate him already. Loathe him, really."

She scrunched her face so as not to smile.

"Really, really, horrible snake." He grabbed two glasses of *karkadeh*, a roselle flower drink, from a server and passed one to Samya. "Petulant. I don't trust his mustache either."

She laughed.

"Should I stop?"

"Go on." She smirked.

"Annoying, horrible man. Ugly inside and out."

She chimed in. "A bad dresser."

"That, I must object to. You can criticize the man for anything else, but his suit was exemplary."

"Alright, his voice, odious."

"Nails on a chalkboard, mademoiselle."

She chuckled and then sighed. "I suppose you can drop all this 'mademoiselle' business. Call me Samya."

"So I'll have the opportunity to talk to you again?"

"You are apparently a part of the Cairo elite circles. We're bound to run into each other at these tiresome gatherings."

"I've been bumped up to unavoidable acquaintance, then? Oh, happy day! How about Sam? Or Sim Sim, instead?"

"Don't push it, Ginger."

Beaming, Jacques said, "Alright. Samya, when you're behaving. Fred, when you're not."

She rolled her eyes.

After a beat of silence, Jacques cleared his very handsome (Samya was trying very hard not to think this) throat. "Will I be privileged enough to know what that..." He pointed to the balcony. "...was about?"

Samya raised her eyebrow.

"He isn't exactly an upbeat fellow, is he? Though I will say you are not the easiest to get along with."

This near stranger seemed to revel in poking at her.

"I'm sorry, that was badly done. My Arabic is fragmented," Jacques apologized.

"I would consider one who knows how to say 'fragmented' in Arabic to be quite fluent," Samya said.

"Well, then, I meant..."

Feeling devilish, she hooked her arm in his and moved them across the ballroom without a word. Soon enough, they reached a group of women who were so engrossed in conversation they looked like they were plotting a coup. That is, until Jacques entered their line of sight.

"Samya, darling!" One of them, Lobna Ayoub, welcomed Samya with a kiss on each cheek, all without taking her eyes off of Jacques. Lobna, Hend's best friend, had the air of a ringleader. She had the rich brown skin common amongst those in upper Egypt and donned a mishmash of pink, from her feathered headpiece down to her bejeweled heels. Lobna's family was new money, which garnered disrespect from some in the Cairo elite. Though they couldn't buy respect, her family did earn entrance and reluctant acceptance from them. Samya suspected Lobna was eccentric even amongst those in her hometown. But most geniuses were. Either way, it didn't seem to matter to Lobna. She wore what she wanted, when she wanted. The one societal trap Lobna did fall victim to was the illusion of the happy ending. Lobna loved American movies and couldn't wait to fall in love with the man she would call her husband. She wanted it so badly she wasn't above forcing a connection.

Lobna spoke to Samya while fluttering her eyelashes at Jacques. "Welcome back. How was Europe, darling?"

"It was wonderful." Samya responded. "Speaking of Europe, may I introduce you to Monsieur Jacques? He's from France, you know." She turned to Jacques with the biggest smile. "Jacques, before you are three of the most fabulous of our society. Mademoiselles Lobna, Kareema, and Mandy."

All three beamed at him.

Kareema and Mandy were identical twins who were rarely seen apart. Both girls' posture resembled that of a mouse eating cheese. Their hair was pulled back into tight updos. They did prescribe to some variety, though. Kareema wore orange to Mandy's yellow.

"Very nice to meet you all." Jacques smiled back, looking a bit unsure, which was exactly what Samya wanted.

"You speak Arabic so well." Lobna said, grabbing, more like clawing, at his arm. "Oh, my, oh, my, you are positively dreamy, Monsieur Jacques."

Samya, still on his other arm, squeezed it and said, "Jacques has been looking for someone to acclimate him to Egyptian culture." She tried to concentrate on the task at hand and forget about the firm muscle she had her hands on. "And I thought and I thought...of course there is no one better than Lobna to take on the task!"

"Oh, you thought right." Nudging Samya out of the way, Lobna almost pushed Jacques against the wall. "Monsieur! I can't wait to show you around. I must, must, have the pleasure of being your personal guide. Oh, you lost little bunny. You are likely to be taken advantage of by the hustlers and crooks, aren't you? Probably have been already, poor thing."

Jacques couldn't get a word in as Lobna continued on about how he was a lost lamb, and she was his shepherdess or some nonsense.

Samya left Lobna with her new toy. A bit later, she saw a bewildered looking Jacques scanning the ballroom, no doubt realizing that Samya had managed to extricate herself from the scene. When his gaze finally found her, Samya smirked at him in satisfaction from the safety of the other side of the ballroom. He feigned shock and betrayal, making the Egyptian gesture for "just you wait" with his hand, in turn making Samya laugh.

Samya hadn't realized how much of an awkward shock it was going to be to get thrust into society after a year of isolation. It felt good to play. It felt good to have someone play back.

The rest of the party went by fairly smoothly. When people inevitably asked, Samya regaled them with made-up tales of her "extended trip" to Greece. She also occupied herself with the food. She had four pieces of baklava. She was chided by her mother for eating the four pieces of baklava. Then she ate two more out of spite, which made her a bit queasy. At one point, she cackled with the matriarch of the Gamal family, who was getting close to ninety, blunt, and who had cherished a soft spot for Samya since she was little.

"Who is that delicious man looking at you, Sim Sim?"

Across the room, Jacques was away from Lobna and in the midst of men smoking cigars. He squinted his eyes at Samya and gave her a knowing grin.

"Why do you want to know?" Samya poked at her. "Are you in the market for a husband?"

"Who said anything about a husband?"

Warmth filled Samya at making the old woman laugh. There were some good things about being back in the real world. But it was odd trying to camouflage herself while in society. Samya had always enjoyed cutting up with others, well, with certain people. It felt lonely, though, when she was constantly hiding parts of herself.

When it was time for the guests to leave, and the crowd was busy giving their traditional goodbyes, Samya walked into the empty hallway towards the kitchen to sneak in one more *atayif* pastry. Without warning, she was swung around and kissed on her left cheek, scandalously close to her mouth.

Jacques's eyes bore into hers as he gripped her waist. "Did I shock you, Fred? I'm just a lost bunny and am not used to Egyptian culture."

Samya could hear her heart beat in her head. And Jacques's self indulgent smirk dropped as he looked towards her lips and back into her eyes.

"Oh, Monsieur Jacques!" Lobna's voice, which carried no matter where she was, sounded close to them.

Jacques smiled once more, let Samya go, and was off without another word. The cheeky bastard.

Despite Lobna's voice nearing, no one was around, thank Allah. Frazzled, Samya abandoned her mission to steal food and went towards the exit with the rest of the guests.

Samya spotted Hend and linked their arms to take her towards the door.

Hend raised her eyebrows at her sister. "How was it, *habibti*? Not so bad, right? I would have stolen you away, but I saw you were rescued by the charming Jacques."

Samya turned her nose up decidedly. "I rescued him. He was at the mercy of scheming mothers. Had no choice but to jump in. I'm nothing if not charitable, you know."

Then looking at Hend's face, Samya leaned in closer. "I saw *him* today. Did you know he'd be here?"

Hend gave her a small smile. "Oh, yes. It was all very cordial."

Samya knew better than to trust her sister's facade of calm but didn't push her. They walked to their car, and their father drove off. Samya rolled the window down so the cold wind could hit her face. Her eyes watered from the force of it, but she didn't mind.

Truth be told, she was glad Jacques had been at her societal comeback. Not just because he'd saved her from pummeling Adam, but because he was a comfortable yet excitable presence. His presence pushed her nerves to the back of her mind. He was unexpected. Though she wasn't sure if unexpected was good or bad.

CHAPTER EIGHT

In Cairo, Jacques felt, dare he say it, at home. In his actual home, Paris, there were times he stuck out like a sore thumb. Though his complexion allowed him to blend in with his French compatriots, his raven hair, thick eyebrows, and full lashes always betrayed him. Here in Cairo, there wasn't really a consistent look. The people were of all different shapes, sizes, colors, and yet...Yet, they were all bonded by this intense sense of nationalism. If you were born in Egypt, or by way of an Egyptian in his case, you were Egyptian. Not that he was treated better or worse for being an Egyptian and not that he fully belonged, as he was French by birth and culture. But that it didn't really matter what he looked like. He was welcomed for better or worse. Once they knew you were Egyptian, you were a part of the collective.

Jacques walked into a room filled with dust-covered artifacts. The Egyptian Museum in Cairo. Mon Dieu, he had never seen anything like it. There were statues, jewelry, and tools from the Pharaonic era stored in glass cases. Large stone walls with hieroglyphics and scenes etched in were stacked on top of each other with small tags, yet to be catalogued by archaeologists. The air smelled of sand as if the artifacts had been freshly dug out from the ground. Though the building was the size of a bloated castle, it could not begin to accommodate the treasures that were being unearthed by the minute. How would it feel to be resident of a land where you were quite literally walking, living, and breathing on top of untold history beneath you?

Finding a bench, he sat in front of a statue of a small man sitting next to his immeasurably taller wife. Jacques opened his notebook and started to sketch, a habit he had when he was too anxious to write. He told himself it was to soothe his nerves and not just a form of procrastination.

The plaque next to the statues told the story of the small man and his wife. The man was a dwarf by the name of Seneb who'd lived around 2520 B.C. The son of a farmer, Seneb had originally been destined for mediocrity. However, while attending school, he was able to show extreme ability in mathematics. The Pharaohs immediately capitalized on his talent, and he moved up the ladder, becoming one of the highest ranking court officials of his time. There he met his wife, Senetites, a high-ranking priestess, and had three children with her. Apparently, Seneb was an example of how dwarves and those with disabilities were highly respected and revered in ancient Egypt.

He sketched the natural hairs peeking out of Senetites's wig on the sculpture. With her hand resting on Seneb's shoulder, she wore a serene and dignified expression. One of contentment and support for her husband. One that ladies around the world were taught to don when in society. It reminded Jacques of one woman who would never pose like that. He smiled to himself.

Jacques loved women, and there wasn't one he'd met who hadn't proactively welcomed him to her bed or, at the very least, to a quick kiss. Egyptian women were no exception. A couple of widows, baristas, and store clerks had already thrown themselves at him, and he'd allowed himself to sample one or two. After all, he did want the full Egyptian experience.

But the charming, ornery woman he'd met at Dr. Mahmoud's villa was proving the exception to the rule. Perhaps her rejection of him was the main source of the intrigue. In any case, he loved a challenge.

"Why are you grinning like an idiot?" A harsh statement invaded his thoughts.

"A class greeting," Jacques chided.

Kareem Ahmed Waqab was the first friend Jacques had made since he'd come green as grass to Cairo three months ago. Jacques had met him on the flight from France to Egypt. Kareem had been traveling from Belgium, where he had visited his sister and nieces. The man was often disheveled, with overgrown hair and a full beard. He was so brawny he looked like he'd worked on a farm his whole life. Never mind that he was a self-made millionaire and owned the most profitable horse-trading business in North Africa. Even though his attitude rivaled that of a disgruntled eighty-year-old man complaining about rowdy youth, he was younger than Jacques by a couple of years. Kareem never showed distress of any kind. He was most often stone-faced. Though many cowered in the face of Kareem, few knew what a generous person he was. He'd helped Jacques find his way around and had provided no end of support.

"What do you know about the Roshdi family?" Jacques asked.

Kareem clicked his tongue. "If they're part of that highfalutin society you are so fond of, then shit all."

Kareem came from one of the richest families in Cairo, but received none of the perks of that connection. He and his sister had been shuttled from relative to relative while growing up and had never truly been allowed to participate in society. Jacques didn't know all the details but knew Kareem detested the elite.

Kareem looked up from his drink. "Why? Do they owe you money?"

Jacques laughed. "No. Just met their eldest daughter. She's...interesting."

Kareem smacked Jacques on the back of the head.

Jacques winced. "My hair!"

"Stay away from all the girls you meet at those bloody things. All it takes is you looking in their direction, and they'll expect an engagement ring."

"I didn't say I would do anything. She just seems an interesting subject is all."

Kareem heaved a sigh. "Mark my words, friend, you don't want to get caught up in all of that business. You'll find yourself at the end of a gun shackled to a brat for the rest of your life."

"How do you know she's a brat?"

"They all are. They grew up with a sense of entitlement and have only one target: to marry the wealthiest sucker they can bag." Kareem shook his head in disgust. "If you want 'interesting subjects,' there are plenty of *real* Egyptian women for you to 'study.'"

"Alright. Alright."

"Enough gossiping like old women. Let's go. I just came home from Poland, and I am not wasting my free time at a museum."

Jacques clapped his friend on the back as they got up to leave. "You know, I'm suddenly in a very studious mood."

Chapter Nine

Samya wiped away the remnants of her eyeliner as she sat in front of the pearl colored vanity in her room. The bedroom was her sanctuary. It had blue and gold curtains framed on either side by fresh flowers, an intimidating four-poster bed, white drawers, and a blue settee. The smell of her favorite *bukhoor* permeated the air. Her vanity, with all its lights surrounding the mirror, made her feel like some dramatic actress backstage getting ready for her third or fourth lover to arrive. Alas, hers was a far cry from such a glamorous life.

Samya had just come back from dinner with the Amirs, whose son was twenty-nine going on thirteen. The poor boy, Ahmed, had a landscape of pimples cascading down his cheeks and a voice that broke.

And still, Madame Magda announced in front of all the guests, "What a delight that you are so close to your mother, *habibi*! You know what a wife would do? One that can take care of you just as good as mama does? Samya, would you clear Ahmed's plate for him?"

It was one terrible outing after the other where her mother happened to "accidentally" run into a family friend, who somehow always conveniently had a son of marriageable age.

After a month of this, Samya's mother threw the pretense of subtlety out the door. Against tradition, Madame Magda bypassed the family and openly discussed an alliance or marriage directly with the prospective man. As if Samya would change into a white dress and veil as soon as the bachelor agreed. With the way her mother was acting, everyone would think Samya would take anything she could get. Having men ogle her, particularly her ample bottom, forced Samya to deploy evasion tactics. She talked a lot, laughed overly loud, made faces at them when no one else was looking, and found other creative ways to scare them off.

Part of her understood that her mother wanted Samya to have a family of her own and be a normal girl and have what normal girls had. Another part of her was furious at being paraded through the city as a desperate, aging spinster. Even if Samya's medical circumstances had been different, she wouldn't have wanted to get married. In her experience, men tended to be bastards. Aside from her father, of course.

Another part of Samya, a tiny hidden part, was hurt. Though her mother hadn't been told about Samya's illness, it was difficult to think she didn't know. Samya had been nineteen and in her bedroom the first time her body had seized up and betrayed her. She'd been stiff as a board: couldn't walk, couldn't talk, couldn't move. Madame Magda had screamed and got her husband to check on their ailing daughter. Her father, being a doctor, had been quick to take her to a discreet psychiatrist. Her father was at a loss, a bit out of his depth, but he was supportive and with his medical expertise, could consult intelligently with any doctor she encountered.

Samya came up from her painful woolgathering and stared down at the explosion of clothes on her floor. Although she could be a brat and wait for Zoo Zoo to come in and clean, she didn't like to bother her. Zoo Zoo was getting older, and though she would never admit it, she had a hard time moving around like she used to. Sighing loudly to no one, Samya started picking up dresses and hanging them.

As she fluffed up the tulle on one of her skirts, she thought of the multiple hospital visits she'd been through before she was eventually told she had catatonia. It was a temporary paralysis of the body that was likely connected to her depression. Samya had struggled with sadness all her life. The sadness was like a shadow that followed her but wasn't overly invasive. When leading up to the bouts of catatonia, however, that shadow would consume her mind and body.

After a decade of suffering with the syndrome, Samya recognized a pattern. A bout of catatonia would start by each episode lasting a minute to an hour. Though the episodes were frightening, during these early stages, she could still function and carry on living life. That was the maddening part. Samya could be laughing and the life of the party one minute, and break down in tears in private the next. People would never have believed her if she'd told them what was going on.

As the days grew into weeks, however, each episode would eventually escalate to the point where it lasted up to eight hours, and she would then need medical intervention. Finally, after a couple of months, the episodes would peter out. Samya had experienced this cycle and had been hospitalized three times in her life. Twice, when she was in medical school. Doctors theorized that stress may have induced the condition, but there was little to no information to confirm that. She was told she was lucky, though. Others with the ailment had more extreme presentations. They were frozen for weeks or even months at a time.

They never spoke about that night when she was nineteen, but Samya knew her mother had never forgotten it. Her mother's denial of the illness meant she never had to take Samya to different hospitals or look for solutions to the episodes or witness the extreme depression that clouded Samya all her life grow and grow and grow. Her mother never had to see her daughter anesthetized and given shock treatments for weeks at a time. She was never there when Samya was in a haze and would lose memory as a result of the treatments.

Though she didn't involve herself with Samya's illness, Madame Magda had still gone through various stages of emotions over the years. First, it had been anger. She'd yelled at Samya for anything and everything. For being contrary and not the perfect darling she wanted her to be. Then, it had been denial. Samya should pray more to get rid of her "quirks." Someone had certainly given Samya the evil eye since she was such a smart girl and had gotten into medical school. Even though her mother, ironically, had originally fought her about going to medical school. Either way, the damned curse of the evil eye had made her daughter act oddly; her mother was sure of it. Nowadays, the emotion was more denial mixed with an iron will to rid Samya of her strange ways. Samya needed to get married. Her mother wanted her to fit in, and this was the only way she knew how to accomplish that goal. Her child was falling apart. What was a mother to do? It was easier to focus on a tangible goal, to get Samya married.

And Samya understood all of this. But what she wanted her mother to understand was that Samya had accepted her lot in life. She was sick. They'd tried every treatment. Some had been promising at first, but none so far had lasted long enough to cover the next crescendo of catatonia. The best she could do was take barbiturates that were supposed to curb the episodes, though the drugs were terribly unreliable. In essence, she was resigned to her fate. She accepted her life was difficult. But what she did not accept or want was to drag someone down with her. And that's what having a husband would do. He would become a person she would imprison. Someone she would drain the life out of. The hospital visits, the yelling, the crying, the madness. It was bad enough that her father had to deal with it. She would be damned before putting that on one other soul. No one deserved that.

So she would put up with her mother's desperate matchmaking and would even have fun warding off each and every male thrown at her. Her mother would tire of it, eventually.

A knock on her door brought Samya out of her tiresome thoughts.

"Sim Sim. I'm coming in." Zoo Zoo opened the door, followed by a petite young girl who looked terrified.

Samya looked questioningly at Zoo Zoo.

"This is my niece, Ruqquyah." About the only characteristic the aunt and niece had in common was their short stature.

The girl tucked behind her ear some of the silky brown hair that peeked out of her pale pink bandana and finally met Samya's eyes. "*Salam*, Mademoiselle Samya."

Ruqquyah had the biggest brown doe eyes Samya had ever seen.

"*Salam*, Ruqquyah. Please have a seat." Samya cleared a space for them on the settee near her bed.

Hesitating some, Ruqquyah eventually adjusted her traditional black frock and sat.

Zoo Zoo looked grave, which was not a look she sported often. Dramatic, yes, but never grave.

"What brings you here, Ruqquyah?" Samya said.

Ruqquyah looked helplessly at Zoo Zoo, who put her arm around her niece. "She's a good girl, Samya. She is. She works in a factory on the weekdays and then cleans the villas with her mother and sister on the weekends."

Downcast, Ruqquyah looked at her feet as Zoo Zoo went on.

"The girl got in trouble, and she won't tell me who or how it happened. Her mother, my sister, found out and won't let her return to the house."

Tears fell from Ruqquyah's cheeks onto her sandals.

"She can stay here, obviously." Samya said, but Zoo Zoo waved her off.

"No, no. She is staying with my friend. We need to hide her until the child comes. People will talk if she is seen with me. That is not the trouble. She's been bleeding, and we don't know what to do."

A thousand questions flooded Samya's mind, but she slowed things down so as to not overwhelm an already frightened young girl. Ya Allah, she looked so young.

Ruqquyah continued to avoid looking Samya in the eye.

Samya needed to help this girl. To her surprise, her rusty mind kicked up medical knowledge she thought she'd filed away for good. Samya got a bit of background on how long the bleeding had been going on for and how far along Ruqquyah was. She knew instinctively it was likely nothing to worry about, but she would take them to Dr Nadia, her former professor, who would certainly have the expertise to confirm Samya's hypothesis.

"Oh, *Alhamdulilah*!" Zoo Zoo exclaimed, thanking Allah as she reached for her niece. "See? I told you all would be well, *habibti*. Samya is a pain, but she is a smart girl."

Samya threw a dark look at Zoo Zoo. "Who do you think taught me to be a pain? You helped raise me." Then she winked at Ruqquyah, who finally began to relax.

After they left, Zoo Zoo returned to Samya's room with a big slice of chocolate gateau.

Samya narrowed her eyes at the feisty woman. "What is this for? The other day you told me my ass was getting too big for my pants."

"Why do you speak like you come from the streets, girl?" Zoo Zoo retorted and then patted Samya on the hand. "I'm proud of you, Sim Sim. The poor lamb has been shaking for days, and you eased her spirit. May Allah bless you and your future husband and children. I can't wait until you graduate medical school, and we can celebrate 'Dr. Samya Roshdi'."

Allah could save the blessings. Nothing in that sentence would ever happen.

Samya was surprised that she even remembered anything she'd learned in medical school. But it had come to her as easily as breathing. A faint warmth blossomed in her chest when she thought of it. In that small window of time, she felt right. But she would never admit that much to Zoo Zoo or anyone else, for that matter.

Samya mulled Ruqquyah's predicament over in her mind. "How old is Ruqquyah?" she asked Zoo Zoo.

"She just turned nineteen."

"What about the father? You have to get it out of her, Zoo Zoo. He needs to take responsibility. Think. Her reputation. What her child will go through because of it."

Zoo Zoo sighed. "The silly girl will not say a word about him. She refuses. I will get it out of her. A little bit of patience is all."

Samya hoped Ruqquyah would open up soon. Whenever there was a scandal, the man was never held accountable. It was always the woman who suffered.

51

Chapter Ten

The next morning, Samya put on her tennis skirt and shirt and grabbed her gear. She then convinced Ali, the family's driver, to drop her off at the *nady,* on his way to run errands. She had barely been outside, and going to the country club would be her first public outing. The *nadys* had been erected all over Egypt by order of the government to promote athleticism, family, and a sense of community. The *nady* was a club that had tennis courts, cafés, a track, restaurants, and multiple parks and gardens. Though the nadys were meant for all, due to their pricing, only the rich were able to attend.

Samya expected to feel nervous or embarrassed at being so exposed out in public, but all her fears melted away as soon as she stepped onto the rust-colored tennis court. Omar always picked the earliest of times, so they were unbothered. Even the ball boys didn't get up this early. Samya thought Omar's timing had a lot to do with her insistence on playing in a skirt. Omar was a stickler for propriety, so she took it as a win that he played with her at all.

"Ay, captain!"

She swiveled to meet the person who'd just greeted her.

Omar came forward in a crisp white shirt and shorts, bouncing a tennis ball on his racket.

"Prepare to be decimated!" Samya bellowed as the desert sun exuded heat.

Omar quirked up the side of his mouth. "Have you suddenly gained athletic ability in Greece?" Then he stopped. "Samya, why must you wear that skirt and not the regulation women's wear? Really, do you need to throw all sense out the window?"

"Oh, shut up you old ninny, and let's play!"

Omar tut-tutted as he bounced a tennis ball with the racket and then served. Whack. Samya swung and missed. "That was a practice swing."

"Mmm." Omar picked up another ball and served. "You never told me about your time in Greece. How are your cousins?"

She hated lying to the man she considered her honorary brother. But she wouldn't be able to stand the look on his face if she ever told him the truth.

"They like cheese, wine, and togas. What's to tell? Serve! I'm feeling good about this one."

"Ever the conversationalist," Omar said. "Speaking of which, are you going to dinner at the Gaber's tonight?"

Samya missed and hit her own face. "Ay!"

Omar looked unaffected. "I'm going. Ergo, you are. By the by, how do you know Jacques?"

Samya swung angrily and missed again. "I met him a couple of weeks ago while he was visiting my parents."

"Hmm."

Sweat was dripping from her face, her curls were popping out of her ponytail, and they were only five minutes into the game. "Hmm, what? If you have something to say, Omar, say it."

Omar put one hand on his hip, stopping a volley with his racket. "Are you interested in him?"

"In what way? Of course not."

He lobbed a serve, not a curl of his out of place. His glasses weren't even fogging up. "Well, you would be the exception, I guess. The rest of the silly female population is practically dizzy for him."

Samya swung hard and missed again. Through heavy pants of breath, she managed to singsong, "Ay, captain, you jealous?"

"He can have them all as far as I'm concerned."

This wasn't a shocker. Omar was practically engaged to a society darling, a Mademoiselle Sawsan, or was it Zobaida? Samya couldn't remember but did recall that she wasn't all that impressive. Their relationship was kept a secret due to his lack of pedigree. Being a premiere lawyer didn't count for anything, apparently. He constantly assured Samya that the secret was just for now until they could get his would-be fiancée's family on board.

"But you, you be careful." Omar said.

Samya was growing a bit irritated that Omar was lecturing her when his own love life wasn't exactly a model of perfection.

"Keep serving," Samya grunted. "Careful of what?"

Omar smacked a ball that Samya finally got over the net, only for her to miss upon its return towards her.

"Him. He is aware of you as a woman."

Samya scowled to cover up her flushed cheeks. "Well, how else would he be aware of me? As an alley cat?"

"Aware, meaning he wants to play with you. Well, not just you. He would gallivant with anything in a skirt."

Samya scoffed. Never would she admit it, but she was insulted. So, she wasn't special, then. Just another plaything. Of course, she'd known Jacques was a playboy and likely flirted with anything with two legs. Only a fool would expect consistency from a man like that. Oof, but she was angry with herself for even caring. To top off her frustration, she was annoyed that Omar saw fit to draw any attention to the subject at all.

"Samya." Omar lowered his tone and came up to the net. "He's not like us. Europeans are loose. He'll misunderstand, and you'll be out of your depth."

"Omar," Samya said in a dulcet tone.

"What?"

"You don't need to worry. I can handle myself, him, and any other bastard who dares cross my path."

"Yes, yes, you are so strong and menacing. If only you could aim a tennis racket with the same accuracy as your barbs."

"Serve, dammit!"

Chapter Eleven

S amya was cajoled into attending an "intimate" dinner at the Gaber's three-story villa located in the Old Cairo district. "Intimate" dinners were lavish affairs that consisted of no less than five families. And families meant unmarried sons, which meant an evening of Samya's mother throwing her at said unmarried sons. But Samya always enjoyed the food at these things, so she wouldn't find it a total loss.

The Gaber's dining room housed a long marble table surrounded by gold-encrusted chairs with depictions of gods and goddesses as an ode to the family's Greek roots. The room was lit solely by the candelabras that lined the long table, which seated no less than thirty. Samya was ushered into the room along with the other guests and saw there were assigned seats via placards with everyone's name written in elegant calligraphy.

The placard next to hers had Omar's name on it. Good. That ensured a welcome escape from the desperation her mother was intending to exhibit on her behalf. Samya smoothed out her slim, belted, pale blue skirt, which she'd paired with a white boatneck top tucked in. Hend had complimented her on looking Sophia Loren-esque. Samya had only heard of the up-and-coming Italian actress, but she assumed the comparison was a good thing.

As she sat down, she felt a prickle of awareness shoot through her. Someone threw Omar's placard a couple seats down and put another next to Samya's. It read *"Jacques Ali Abd El-Hameed."*

"Don't you dare complain. You got me into this trouble with that young lady." Jacques motioned his head towards Lobna at the corner, who was fluttering her eyes rapidly at him. "And though I enjoy a woman's adoration, her conversation is exhausting."

Samya threw her head back and laughed. "What makes you think I won't be just as exhausting?" She whispered, "Because I have every intention of being so."

Jacques leaned in closer. She could feel his warm breath tickle her ear as he whispered, "I am very much looking forward to *you* exhausting me."

Her cheeks flushed at the innuendo, but she'd be damned if she'd let him rattle her. Samya started to motion Lobna over when she was interrupted by a jab to her thigh.

"So help me, I'll poke you with this fork and change seats with *Oustaz* Amir. He'll talk your head off about the good old pre-revolution days.

No, Samya did not want to endure an old man hearkening to a time when Egypt had been suppressed and under another country's rule, just because his family had benefited from it. As if in a delicate hostage situation, Samya retreated her hand slowly, and Jacques, equally paced, brought his fork to the proper setting in front of him.

Molokhyia and pita bread were served.

Jacques leaned over after a couple of seconds. "I'm ignoring you by the way. In case you didn't know."

"Ah, I was wondering why it was so peaceful." She took her first sip of the hot dish.

"You have more bread than I do. Give me a slice."

"I thought you were ignoring me."

"Yes, but I can't stay silent when an injustice is being done." As Jacques picked up his fork to try to pick at her plate, she covered the plate with her arm, looking like a child trying to prevent another from cheating off her during a test.

Jacques paused. "Are you ticklish?"

Before she could answer, he tickled her ribs. She jerked her hand away and accidentally banged the table. Everyone looked in her direction. Jacques joined the procession and acted appalled.

"Decorum please, Samya," he said before spearing a slice of bread and placing it on his plate.

She glared. "Are you even going to eat it?"

Jacques shrugged. "No, but it's the principle of the thing." He tore a piece of his original slice and popped it into his mouth.

His lips looked soft, set against such a sharp, cutting jaw. This close, she could see a shadow of a beard and didn't know if she wanted to slap him or gently run her hands across the bristles on his face.

He caught her looking at him and licked the corner of his mouth slowly.

Definitely slap him.

"What is this anyway?" He pointed to the hot, green dish in front of him.

Thankful for the opportunity to break his piercing gaze, Samya answered. "*Molokyhia*, Jew's mallow leaves ground up and mixed with chicken broth. It's a national dish, you fraud of an Egyptian."

He chuckled.

"It's delicious," Samya said. "Just taste it."

He looked perturbed. "What will you give me if I do?"

"Absolutely nothing."

"How ever will I learn about my culture if good samaritans like yourself don't educate me?"

Faux irritated, she looked at him. "What do I care what you do? Eat it. Don't. Choke on it, for all I care."

Normally, when Samya was sarcastic with a man, he would shrivel, retreat, and move on to a sweeter, more docile audience.

"Alright. You've convinced me." He took a mouthful of the soup, winced, and swallowed.

Samya raised her eyebrows. "Well?"

"I feel as if I've inhaled crocodile snot."

She laughed and said in a hushed tone, "Don't let anyone hear you say that."

As if encouraged by her laughter, he switched their bowls, and spoke loudly to their hostess, Madame Wafaa. "Madame, the *molokhyia* is unparalleled."

Several guests nodded in assent and congratulated Madame Wafaa on a successful start to the dinner.

"Samya, please finish your bowl. You're being incredibly rude. This is the premiere Egyptian dish, don't you know."

She glowered but bit her lip to keep from smiling.

The servers cleared the table and brought in plates of food: grilled pigeon and pheasant, rabbit, rice with vermicelli noodles, stuffed grape leaves, cucumber salad, *tzaaki*, and a host of other delicious food that Samya couldn't wait to rip into.

They both started piling their plates up with food.

"So, Jacques. How are you finding Egypt?"

He tsked. "Small talk? You are better than that, Fred."

"What do you propose we discuss then, *Ginger*?"

"Hmm, tell me about medical school."

Her breath hitched. Such a painful subject she didn't want to discuss. But he was not a serious person, and this was a nonsense conversation that would go nowhere. So she decided to play along. "What would you like to know?"

"Why'd you get into it?"

"My mother told me I couldn't."

He raised an eyebrow.

Samya laughed. "She and I fought constantly about everything. She loathed that I got my clothes dirty, played pranks, and preferred running around with the boys in the neighborhood rather than playing house with the girls. I couldn't tell you the number of times she was called into school because I...well, I fought a lot."

"How unlike you," he said.

Ignoring him, she continued. "Anyway, my grades weren't all that great, and my mother insisted that I was better off going to trade school and getting married quick because I couldn't cut it anywhere else. I was a delinquent, destined for failure, you see. Naturally, I looked for the most difficult challenge to prove her wrong. There are very few women who become doctors. So, I worked hard and got in to El-Qasr El-Ainy, all thanks to spite. But when I got there, I found myself falling in love with it." She'd never told anyone that.

"Why is that?"

She shrugged. "The body is a paragon of truth. If something is wrong, let's say your kidneys are failing, well, your face turns yellow from jaundice. Your body's communicating to you via a physical reaction that something is wrong. It is undeniable honesty. Made a lot of sense to me." Samya was letting herself ramble.

Jacques looked intensely into her eyes. She had to gather all the strength in her not to be unnerved and look away. This man had a way of making you feel that the only things that mattered to him were the words coming out of your mouth. The best thing to do was clamp that mouth shut, which she was having a hard time doing when floating in a trance-like warmth.

After a bit, he shook his head slightly and cleared his throat. "What sort of medicine would you like to practice?"

Nonsense conversation, nonsense conversation, she kept repeating to herself, so she wouldn't get invested. *This is all play for him.* "I wanted to be an obstetrician."

He paused. "Wanted to?"

She sighed. "I got sick."

She wanted to nail her mouth shut immediately.

Surprisingly, he didn't look away from her.

Awkwardly, chuckling, she said in a lower voice, "Actually, I've had to drop out two times now. No one knows this, but I'm not going back."

Before he could retort, which she felt in her bones he would do, she quickly blurted out. "You saw my bruises the night we met."

She meant it as a question, but it came out as a declaration.

He nodded. "I did."

Her heart was hammering. It was on her mind every time they talked, but she hadn't had the courage to ask him. The thing was that talking with him was so easy. As if she could say anything, and he wouldn't judge her. "Do you know what they are?"

He drank a swig of water as the sound of people chatting carried on in some faraway universe they were no longer a part of. "Yes, my mother received the same treatment."

It was as if a giant rock plummeted in Samya's stomach.

Jacques continued, seeming careful. "How are you?"

"I'm fine now." Why in the hell had she brought it up in the first place? She tried to change the subject. "Is your mother alright now?"

"She passed when I was seventeen. Oh, it's fine. She was in a lot of pain. I often didn't know what to do. I've always felt like such a failure when it came to her. I am ashamed to say there was some relief mixed in with the sorrow."

"And now your father. I'm sorry."

"I didn't really know my father. At least, not that well. I hadn't really seen him since I was younger. We were going to reconnect before all that death business came into play."

How can someone be so charismatic and lighthearted and yet have endured an endless wealth of pain? She wondered what support he had, if any. *Do not get invested,* she thought to herself as she simultaneously asked, "With your father being away, who did you stay with?"

He smirked. "No one. I left for Paris."

"By yourself? At seventeen?"

Jacques motioned over to a waiter, and after grabbing a couple of champagne flutes, placed one in front of Samya.

"I lived in a communal studio, worked at a printing press and as a shop boy until I could enroll in the Sorbonne. Scrounged a bit until I wrote my first novel. I remember when the first check came in from the novel's sale." He smiled as if reminiscing. "I bought a bottle of whiskey, Merguez Frites, and sat in the middle of my empty and newly bought shoebox apartment overlooking the Eiffel tower. Gleeful as can be."

Leaning back in his chair, he put his hands at the back of his head and eyed her. "You must be wishing you could take back every time you've ever insulted me. You are likely thinking, 'That Jacques is so strong, so resilient. What an honor that he bestows such attention on me! How handsome he is! What strong arms he has!'"

"I'm actually thinking, 'The devil was an angel that fell from heaven, but he's still the devil.'"

He laughed and slung his arm on her chair. Several people around them stilled and seemed to look over. Jacques lowered his arm.

"No family there and none here?" she said, all the while feeling Omar's inevitable disapproving gaze.

"You look adorable when you are pitying me." He sighed. "It's been just me for a while, anyway, so I'm used to it. I did find out recently I have an uncle in Tanta. Though it is not likely we'll be that close. To top it off, the bastard—my father, that is—left me all these properties across the country that I now have to manage." Jacques shrugged. "But at least it's given me the chance to get to know Egypt. I'm enjoying learning about the culture." He bit into a roasted potato with tomato sauce. "The women aren't too bad, either." He winked at her.

She rolled her eyes. "I don't pity you. I pity the women of Egypt—and France, for that matter. So you are an author of some sort?"

He snorted and looked down at his plate, fussing with his food. "Of some sort."

"The one time I'd like for you to actually talk, and you have nothing to say."

Jacques sped through his speech. "I'm writing my third novel. It's going swimmingly. It's confidential, and that's all I have to say about that. Now I have a question I've been dying to ask you."

Samya tilted her head in anticipation.

He took a breath. "If a train leaves Damanhour at 3:00 p.m. at 65 kilometers per hour and another train leaves Tanta at 2:00 p.m. at 45 kilometers per hour, when does the first train overtake the second..."

Samya laughed. "Shut up."

The guests were then ushered into the salon for coffee and dessert. She looked down at her plate, which seemed untouched, but somehow she felt full.

Chapter Twelve

T he minute Jacques entered the salon with Samya, a gaggle of pastel-dressed, heavily perfumed girls swarmed him. Meanwhile, Omar took Samya aside and argued with her in hushed tones. Jacques made a note to look into what relationship Omar had with her.

Statues of Aphrodite and Artemis bookended the open, cream-colored balcony doors, ushering a breeze into the stuffy room. Over the girls that crowded him, Jacques saw a table full of sliced mangoes, plums, dessert wine, varieties of gateaux and baklava. The elders of the party had full plates and drinks in hand and were lazily engaged in conversation.

"*Damak khafeef awy*, Jacques!" Lobna, one of the swarm, said to him as Samya and Omar approached the group.

He looked over at Samya. "My blood is light?"

She smiled. "It is a saying. It means you are charming and funny. Obviously, Lobna is having some sort of stroke."

"You are so naughty, Samya, darling!" Lobna said.

Samya's eyes were dancing with mischief. In that moment Jacques wanted to take her against the wall and bite her because kissing those red lips just wouldn't be enough. It was incredibly difficult to concentrate on conversation or anything else when she was around. He barely knew what the hell he'd eaten at dinner or if he'd eaten at all if he was being honest. All he wanted was to know more about this woman who had been through so much, who hid all that suffering, and who'd come out the other side. An intelligent, funny siren with a biting sense of humor. And that ass, mon Dieu. Today it was wrapped in a pale blue that hugged the slopes of her hips and showed off her waist. Those curves flowed defiantly in opposition to the frail thin frames of Parisian women. The things he would do if given the chance.

As if he could read Jacques's mind, Omar spoke through gritted teeth. "Jacques, let's leave the ladies and head to the balcony for a cigar."

"I'll go, too," Samya said.

"Is your name 'Jacques?'" Omar retorted.

The girls all screamed, "We want a cigar, too!"

There was an explosion of giggles.

Omar pinched the bridge of his nose. Jacques took the opportunity to steal Samya while Omar was preoccupied in scolding the girls on their lack of propriety.

"Meet me in five minutes at the far end of the balcony," Jacques whispered to Samya.

"Why should I?" She crossed her arms in mock protest.

"Didn't you hear them? My blood is light."

She shrugged.

"Alright, I'll scrounge up cigarettes, you heavy-blooded woman."

She chuckled, threw him a nod, and left.

Jacques slapped Omar's shoulder, interrupting his fight with Jacques's fan club, and shook his hand with the other. "I'm off."

Omar held on to his hand. "I need a word before you leave."

Jacques saw Samya slip out to the balcony. "I'm afraid I don't have time."

"You'll make time." He motioned Jacques toward an isolated corner that had a couple of red velvet chairs facing each other, removed enough that no one could overhear their conversation.

Jacques sat across from a seething Omar, who snarled, "I know what you are about, and I don't like it."

"What is that, then?"

"I saw you talking with Samya at dinner."

"You're very observant."

"You looked like a wolf eyeing a lamb."

Jacques laughed. "Samya? A lamb? The woman makes grown men cower. I don't think she needs you censoring who she can and can't talk to."

"Samya comes off like a bull, but she is soft inside. But for the blood running through our veins, that girl is my sister. I won't let anyone hurt her."

Ah, so this was Omar's role: the overly protective big brother. Jacques wouldn't be cowed. "You underestimate her. Besides, I don't intend to hurt her."

"Are you planning to marry?"

"I thought I could at least get through coffee first before grabbing a sheikh to officiate."

Omar's lips tightened. He clearly didn't think Jacques's blood was light. "These girls here, they come from good families. If a man is talking to them the way you are, the expectation is the man is courting to marry. Anything less, and her reputation will be tarnished in this society. If you are not looking to marry, stop playing with her."

"Omar, I've had a handful of conversations with her. It's hardly a proposition."

"Yes, and I've watched you during those 'conversations.' Harmless flirtation is one thing. But you are laying it on thick, my man, and in public, no less." Omar sighed. "Play this out. She will get attached, you'll get bored, leave, she'll break, and then I'll have to break you."

Jacques set his jaw.

Omar continued. "I have nothing against you. But if you are a man with honor, you'll back off."

Omar stormed off, and Jacques was left staring at the floral pattern of the wallpaper in front of him. Omar was an uptight ass, but he was a correct one. Jacques was surprised at how easy it had been to get sucked into Samya's gravitational pull. But he wasn't offering anyone marriage. He wasn't looking for anything complicated. Samya was complicated. Her culture was, her situation was, her personality was, and Jacques wouldn't be able to handle any of it. He wasn't a man of honor, but he liked Samya too much to hurt her. Resolved, he stood up, thanked his hosts, and promptly left the villa. He didn't trust himself to tell Samya he was leaving.

CHAPTER THIRTEEN

"One ticket to Tanta, please." Jacques paid for his transport at the counter of the Cairo train station. The night before, a letter had arrived.

Jacques,

Please come to my office at your earliest convenience.

There is an urgent business matter to attend to.

- Solayman Kabir

"What's wrong with you?" Kareem accompanied him. He was headed to meet a potential buyer who was vacationing in Alexandria. Kareem would be on the same train until Jacques deboarded in Tanta.

That was a question with many answers, but Jacques gave his friend the easiest one. "Oh, nothing. The management of the properties is going surprisingly smoothly with Solayman at the helm. It's a bit odd that he asked to see me."

Kareem clapped his shoulder. "Be prepared for the worst. That way you won't be shocked."

"Thanks for the comforting advice."

They boarded the train with Jacques carrying a suitcase housing little more than his sketchbook.

He smiled at a woman who was carrying a basket full of sesame sweets on her head. Vendors from the train station would hop on a train quickly before it left, sell what they could, and then jump off right before the train left the station.

"Two please. Keep the change."

She smiled so widely it warmed his roguish heart.

Kareem was busy looking over contracts, leaving Jacques to his thoughts as the train ran across the landscape.

Odd or not, Jacques thought the trip to Tanta was perfectly timed. He needed to get away from the Cairo scene and a certain young lady. Yes, she was gorgeous, and funny, and playful, and a whole lot of other things. But she was an innocent, a member of a respected family who would be expecting a commitment that he could not give.

There was the matter of those bruises he'd noticed when he first met Samya. He felt a guilty familiarity with such bruises.

Though infrequent, Jacques's mother would leave him for weeks at a time.

"Where is maman?" a young Jacques once asked his grandmother, who took care of him during those absences.

"She is tired, mon petit, and must take a little vacation to get better for you."

"Why can't I go with her?"

"Little boys are not allowed to vacation."

When he was twelve, Jacques's grandmother took him to see his mother during one of her "vacations."

They took the train to Paris and arrived at a huge, white building with the moniker "Sainte Anne Hospital Centre." A woman in a white uniform and blond hair pulled in a bun so tight it rearranged her facial features walked them down a hallway. The place smelled of stale vomit. The walls were a blinding white. The air carried muffled screams from behind closed doors. Jacques looked at his grandmother, unsure.

"Mon petit, you are a man now. You must be brave for maman."

The tight-faced woman took out a circle of several keys and opened a small door. Inside, a hollowed-out shell that resembled his mother looked at him with glassy eyes.

Vivienne was in a white hospital gown, her lips were chapped, and she had circular bruises at the sides of her head.

"Jacques," the shell said.

His grandmother motioned him forward, and he hugged his mother hesitantly.

Too scared to speak, he sat in a chair by the corner for the rest of the visit while his grandmother talked to his mother. He had a death grip on the scarab in his pocket. Finally, to his relief, they left the hospital.

His grandmother looked at him with a frown. "She has to come here sometimes when it gets bad. If I am not here, you must remember this place, yes?"

He remembered his mother coming home docile, lifeless, but calm. Then his grandmother passed, and he had to take care of his mother on his own because his father was away on business. Jacques had to forgo playing outside with other kids and, for days at a time, even going to school. He gave up any sort of childhood he could have had. All the while caring for a person who didn't seem to have a cure.

Mon Dieu, Jacques felt the deepest pang of guilt, regret, and shame. If he would have just been more attentive. Sought more help. Forced her to the hospital when she didn't want to go instead of giving in. Things would have been different. It was a pain that could not be reconciled in his heart. Her disease had poisoned her mind and their lives. He had never seen someone so tortured in his life so that he felt a bit of solace that at least now she was at peace. And, oh, the guilt he felt over that relief.

He vowed that he would never do that. Be a caregiver. Be a husband. Have a family. Clearly, he was not equipped. He would certainly not take on a woman like Samya who had a similar affliction to his mother. Sure, she was all smiles, teasing, and laughter now. But that reminded him of his mother and the months when she was 'good' and laughed and played with him and frolicked in the country. But they were always followed by horrid, dreadful months where she wouldn't leave her room days on end. Wouldn't take a shower. Wouldn't eat. Samya would likely have the same issues. He couldn't take that on. He couldn't disappoint another woman.

It wasn't selfish now because he didn't owe her anything. He never wanted to owe her anything he couldn't give. He could get pretty smiles, inviting curves, and a boisterous laugh elsewhere with less complication.

A bit of distance was just the thing.

Upon reaching Tanta, Jacques said his goodbyes to Kareem and stepped off the train and onto the sandy streets. Jacques waved off a man who tried to sell him a ride on a curricle, opting to walk through El Khan market to Solayman's office instead. El-Khan was filled with merchants selling rich fabrics, cotton, spices and anything else the heart desired.

"Perfume, *basha*?" asked a portly woman who looked to be in her sixties. She had two braided pigtails cascading out of a transparent black scarf adorned with coins. "A handsome man must have a sweetheart to buy a present for."

"None so lovely as yourself, mademoiselle," he said, making her giggle like a schoolgirl.

Continuing on his way, he heard yelling. "She's being unreasonable! She would be taken care of by the family!"

Jacques heard Solayman's voice respond. "Lower your voice, Mostafa. We are out in public."

When he rounded the corner, Jacques saw his uncle hysterically confronting Solayman, who was guarding a rather elegant middle-aged woman.

The petite, blond woman threw her chin in the air and moved past Solayman. "I will not allow you to threaten my family, Mostafa..."

Mid-speech, her eyes happened upon Jacques. She whispered something in Solayman's ear and floated from the scene with her head held high.

"Where are you running off to, woman?!" His uncle made to lunge in her direction but was stopped by Solayman's arm.

"We will discuss this matter at a more appropriate time and venue."

Jacques's uncle harumphed. "I want to trust you, Solayman. I really do, but you've wavered as of late."

Ignoring the jab, Solayman herded Mostafa away from the front of his office building. "I will call on you tomorrow morning for tea and discuss the matter calmly. Don't let your nerves get the best of you, my man."

Mostafa stayed, arms crossed, rooted in place for a long moment before making a move to leave. "I wake at noon. I will see you fifteen minutes past. Not a minute later, mind you. I'm much too busy. *Salam*."

After Mostafa stomped off, Solayman motioned to Jacques and shook his hand. "Welcome, son. Welcome."

"And what a welcome it is. Does this have anything to do with the urgent business matter you mentioned in your letter?"

Solayman shook his head and motioned Jacques towards his office. "Come inside, now. The people out in the street have had enough entertainment for the afternoon."

When they were safely inside and away from prying eyes, Solayman collapsed in the chair behind his desk and looked at Jacques.

"I have told you before that your father was quite clear in his will."

"Is there an issue?" Jacques asked.

The solicitor gave a most pitiful look and then let out a resigned sigh. "Your father, as I said, was quite explicit in his will. He had very specific instructions. One of those was to ensure you were taken care of, of course. As the sole male heir, you were given rights on top of those assets your father saved for you. But..."

Jacques sought to ease the man's obvious discomfort. "I can handle it. What of it?"

"He expressly forbade me from revealing this next bit, but I could not in all conscience deny you this information. Your father bequeathed a house here in Tanta and a small sum of money to a widow and her two daughters."

Jacques wanted so badly to interrupt but let the man continue. He grabbed the scarab in his pocket and felt the etchings.

"When you arrived a couple of months ago to take management of the properties, your presence was investigated, and it was confirmed that you are your father's *legal* son. He was originally married to your mother. However, your Uncle Mostafa took this information to the courts to repeal your father's bequeathment of the house and funds to the family in Tanta. That family is your father's recorded wife and children, whose legitimacy is now being questioned. The children are your half-sisters, then. I'm assuming you did not know of their existence until this conversation."

Jacques held his breath.

Solayman continued. "While they are being questioned, their house and settlement could be taken away and given to Mostafa. He would be entitled to a percentage of the property as a recorded family member and by the fact that you weren't specifically named to the deed of that property. The family needs a male witness to the union, or they need you, their default legal guardian, to strike the case."

"I am their legal guardian? Of my father's abandoned children? How do I even know this woman's claims are correct?" He answered his own question. "Of course, they are correct; he left money for them."

"It is a lot to take in. However, the situation stands. Your sisters..."

Jacques winced at hearing that word.

"They need you. They can lose their home. I implore you as a man, an honest man, to handle this. At least meet them, son."

The blond woman fighting with his uncle was his father's *second* wife. His father certainly had a type.

"How long has my father had this second family?" Jacques inquired.

Solayman hesitated but then said. "They got married when your father was still married to your mother. His oldest daughter is eleven and the youngest is nine."

If Jacques wasn't so dazed, he'd be livid. He couldn't muster a coherent thought as he was spinning out of control.

"If you just meet them..."

At that Jacques raised his hand. "It would be uncomfortable for both me and them. How much income did my father leave them?"

"Approximately five hundred pounds total."

Jacques shook his head and looked to the heavens. At least his father had been consistent in his negligence.

"Please draw up whatever petition you need me to submit to attest to their rights to the property and sum. Funnel one hundred pounds a month to each of their bank accounts. If they don't have accounts, please create them. You can use the profits from the Alexandria properties." Jacques pushed off the table to leave.

Solayman stood up. "That is good, my boy. I knew you would do the right thing. But I am sure they want to meet their brother. Please think on it."

Jacques smiled at the old man and shook his hand before darting off. "Thank you for everything, Solly. I'll await the paperwork in Cairo. *Salam.*"

And with that, he went right back to the train station to get the first train out of Tanta.

***

Jacques looked out the train window at the different colored cement apartment buildings passing him by.

Pieces of the puzzle of his life were falling into place rapidly. His father would leave for long stretches at a time for "work." Now he knew what "work" had been. His father had left Jacques and his ill mother to travel across the globe and be with his normal family, his whole family. And leave the damaged one behind. Jacques wasn't at all surprised that his father hadn't planned a future for his second family since he hadn't done so for his first while he was living. Why were the children so young? Shouldn't they be closer to Jacques's age if his father's marriages had overlapped? Why hadn't his father provided more for his young children? Had he been planning to tell Jacques on the visit to Paris? Jacques wasn't sure he wanted the answers.

At one point, Jacques had idolized his father. He couldn't reconcile the man he'd once worshipped with the man who'd shirked all responsibility and thrown his mother and him to the wolves. Had his mother known? Did the other family know about all of this? He couldn't imagine showing his face to those two girls who somehow shared his blood. Would they look like him? *Enough*.

He would do what he always did when he received disturbing news: push it down.

"Madame?" He motioned to an older woman pushing a drink cart. He proffered his most charming smile. "Whiskey neat, please."

Chapter Fourteen

"There is light bleeding, sometimes pink, sometimes brown." Samya found herself speaking for Ruqquyah, who was too shy to say a word. They were at El-Qasr El-Ainy Medical School in Dr. Nadia Ghali's, Professor of Obstetrics, office. It had been difficult walking up the steps of the school. Though Samya was not exactly shy nor did she give in to humiliation, she'd thought being back on campus would make her hide for cover to avoid seeing anyone she knew. Instead, she'd felt a little light inside of her turn on. She even got lost staring at the students in the main lecture hall, remembering how eager she'd been when amongst them a year ago.

Dr. Nadia was Samya's favorite professor, which had nothing to do with her nonexistent bedside manner. She was around seventy and had been educated in Canada before returning to practice in her home country of Egypt. Her coarse, white hair was in a low bun, she hunched over into a slightly pudgy 5'2 frame, and her leathery brown skin was crinkled in a way that etched her facial creases into a permanent frown.

Dr. Nadia's office looked and smelled much like a hospital room. She occasionally took patients, so she had a hospital bed and some medical equipment. The only personal touch was a picture of her shaking hands with Nelson Mandela and her medical degree mounted on the desolate white wall behind her desk. Given her qualifications, the whole damn wall should have been covered in certificates and prizes from the medical community.

Shaking, Ruqquyah lay down on the hospital bed in the office with Zoo Zoo holding her hand and looking concerned.

"How long has this been going on?" Dr. Nadia asked as she pressed into Ruqquyah's lower abdomen with both hands.

Ruqquyah flinched and looked at Samya, who squeezed her shoulder in response. "It started about eight weeks into the pregnancy. It's been five days."

Without looking up at Samya, Dr. Nadia asked, "And what do you conclude?"

Samya clutched her chest. "Me? No, no. That's why we came to you, Doctora."

"Come on, girl," Dr. Nadia said. "You were in my class; I know you haven't forgotten everything I've taught you."

Samya's cheeks flushed, and she fought the urge to start shaking harder than Ruqquyah was.

Pushing away nagging thoughts of incompetence, she took a deep breath. "With the frequency of the spotting and the fact that it is getting lighter after five days, I would think..."

"Not think. What do you know?" Dr. Nadia interrupted.

"I know it is likely implantation bleeding, probably scarring around the endometrium." Samya looked at Ruqquyah and Zoo Zoo. "Meaning the bleeding will go away in a couple of days, and your baby is fine."

Dr. Nadia put her stethoscope back around her neck. "What do you need me for? The girl knows what's going on."

"Thank you so much, Doctora." Zoo Zoo said. "You have no idea how much comfort this gives us. May Allah bless you and your family! May he grant you the highest place in heaven! May Allah provide you with wealth and health in this world and the next—"

"Enough already." Dr. Nadia interrupted. Zoo Zoo's face dropped and immediately tensed.

"If the bleeding goes past a couple of days, or it gets heavier, have the girl bring you back here." Dr. Nadia grabbed her ebony cane and hobbled over to her desk.

"Rude old woman." Zoo Zoo murmured under her breath.

Dr. Nadia eased into her humungous leather chair that seemed to swallow her up. She adjusted her white lab coat and took off her shoes. "Girl. You stay. The rest of you may leave." She cocked her head at a shocked Zoo Zoo and Ruqquyah. "Do you need your hearing checked, as well? The door's that way."

Ruqquyah sprinted and Zoo Zoo rebelliously walked slowly out the door. Samya stayed back as instructed. No one crossed Dr. Nadia. If she said jump, you didn't say anything because you would have already jumped.

Dr. Nadia started in on her bag of sunflower seeds. It was known on campus that where there were sunflower seeds, Dr. Nadia was not far behind. "Sit down."

Samya obeyed and sat down on the wood chair in front of Dr. Nadia's desk. "Thank you, Doctora. For everything."

"Pssht." Dr. Nadia frowned even more, if it were possible, and waved her hand in dismissal. "You've gotten plump. Good. Last I saw you, you were withering away."

Samya had never heard "plump" described in a positive context, but she'd take it. "Greece has done me some good, Doctora."

"Don't insult my intelligence, girl. How long ago did you stop treatment?" Dr. Nadia spit out a seed shell onto a pile that was ever growing on her desk.

"Um." It was no use lying to her, but Samya did start to get worried. How did she know? Who else knew?

"I'm friends with your father. You think that geezer would lie to me? I got it out of him in seconds. How long have you been out, then?"

Samya held her temper back with what felt like a fraying string. Calling her father a "geezer" didn't help the situation.

"A couple of months."

"Your bruises must have healed. So you've been out in the world doing what for months?" Dr. Nadia crunched open another sunflower seed.

What was this, the Spanish Inquisition? Yes, Dr. Nadia was a genius and one of the most respected professionals in her field, but that didn't mean Samya owed her anything.

"I've been spending time with my family."

"So nothing, then."

Samya's anger was competing with her shame.

"And the first time you step foot in this school after a year, and it is for some trite reason."

"Respectfully, Doctora, I didn't know you and I had a standing appointment."

"You left my class abruptly, without explanation. You had a reason, I suppose. I don't see an excuse now."

"Dr. Nadia, I'm not coming back to school. I don't think they would even let me in for a third time if I tried."

The door noisily swung open, and a handsome man with slicked-back hair, wearing a suit entered the office without permission and announced himself. "Dr. Nadia, I presume. I'm Hamdy, a medical sales representative for Hamdy Pharmaceuticals." He approached the desk with his hand extended out for a handshake. "I wanted to talk to you about a brand new medication."

Without hesitation, Dr. Nadia got up, walked over to the gentleman, pushed him out the door with her cane, and then shut the door in his face. She opened her door once more and shouted at a student teacher. "Didn't I tell you to keep the riffraff away?" She then slammed the door again and waddled back to her desk.

She sank back into her chair. "No school, then? And what will you do instead? Find a poorly kept, middle-aged man to drive you up the wall, have children, and hate your life? I've already done it. That life is for some. You are not some."

"You'll be happy to know I don't need a man. I can drive myself up the wall all on my own." Her cheekiness was only met with a harumph from her former professor.

"So, you're giving up. I see you've chosen to be dead amongst the living."

Samya couldn't handle it any longer. "With all due respect, you have no idea what I have been through or what my life is like."

"You were sick, maybe still are. What of it? Did you expect sympathy? I'm too old to give you any. There are too many people like that sassy maid of yours and her kin that need skill and talent. They don't have time for sickness and dramatics."

"I hardly think I'm being dramatic, Dr. Nadia."

"Listen here, girl. A woman is not skirts and smiles and simpering like you are doing at those blasted soirees with the ignorant. A woman rolls her sleeves up, gives life, takes care of the house, protests the Brits with pride, and works the hospital to feed the babes. A woman is not farting around waiting to die in her twenties. A woman lives and takes shit and lives and takes more shit and lives again. That is a woman, girl. That's the kind of woman you could be if you chose to be."

She didn't give Samya the courtesy of a response. No matter, Samya was left speechless by Dr. Nadia's words. Speechless and unworthy.

"Now, you owe me a favor for seeing your mouthy maid and her unfortunate family member. There is an open clinic a couple of months from now. I need an assistant. You'll be there." It wasn't a request; it was a demand.

The old woman went back to chewing on her sunflower seeds and reading papers off of her desk. She looked back up at Samya, expressionless. "That is all."

Before Samya could thank her again, Dr. Nadia pulled out her cane. Samya hightailed it out of there before she could get whacked with it.

Chapter Fifteen

"Samya!"

Samya awoke from a deep sleep. Her eyes fluttered open slowly.

"Samya!" She recognized the voice to be her mother's.

"Samya, why aren't you dressed already? Who sleeps until noon?" Madame Magda removed the covers from her daughter.

Samya looked at her mother. "Someone who has nothing better to do."

She flipped and buried her head face down in her pillow as her mom opened the curtains to let the harsh sunlight come in. A certain professor had called her out yesterday for being a big zero. Sleep was the best escape for all that humiliation, she thought.

Madame Magda continued on. "We are going to the *nady* in half an hour for a family outing."

"Why can't we just have a family in-ing and be done with it?"

Madame Magda ignored Samya and rifled through her closet. "Where is it? Here it is! This will do." She pulled out a pastel pink dress with tiny white bows and pearls sewn throughout, her own creation.

Madame Magda pulled her daughter out of the bed by twisting her ear and then pushed her towards the bathroom while smelling her hair. "Oof, your hair. Take a shower immediately, girl. And wrap it!"

"No straightening. It takes too long."

From the other room, Samya could hear her sister crying out. "Mama! What is Samya wearing so I can match?"

Her mother rolled her eyes and ran out of the room to attend to her youngest daughter.

After everyone was dressed in their finest day wear, the family made their way to the *nady*. They sat on the patio in a chic café called Rainbow. They were surrounded by umbrellas to shield them from the unbearable Egyptian sun. The café patio was not so much a patio but an outdoor space that could house one hundred people. Of course, it was too early in the day for all that. There were no more than a handful of people drinking tea and stray cats looking for scraps of food. Samya had ignored her mother's request to wear that hideous dress and instead had opted for a short-sleeved, white-collar blouse tucked into a simple, mid-length green skirt.

"Mahmoud, order us lemonade," Madame Magda ordered.

"A Turkish coffee for me, baba." Samya said. There was still sleep crust in her eyes. She needed to wake up to handle the day. As the pathetic layabout she apparently was.

"She'll have a lemonade, Mahmoud."

Before Samya could object to being denied caffeine, three figures practically ran up to their table.

"Magda, *habibti*!" The woman, who was long, thin, ruddy cheeked, and dressed in silver (a bit inappropriate for the daytime, Samya thought) stretched her arms out to Samya's mother and gave her two kisses on each cheek.

"Nora! Oh, it's so good to see you!" Samya's mother exclaimed.

There were two men behind Madame Nora. One man, a bit older, balding, and shorter than Madame Nora, was hiding behind her. The other was a young man who was about Samya's height and age, from the looks of it. He was corpulent, with blond, curly, receding hair, fair skin, and green eyes.

Madame Magda turned cheerily towards her family. "This is my husband, Dr. Mahmoud. And my two beautiful daughters, Hend and..." She pushed Samya towards Madame Nora. "...my eldest, Samya."

Beaming, Madame Nora said, "Oh, charmed, and this is my lot. My husband, Khalid Basha, and my gorgeous only son, Louay. But we call him Lu Lu." She gave Lu Lu a big kiss on his cheek.

"Well, sit down, sit down." Samya's mother said.

Madame Nora pushed her husband out of the way and guided her son to the empty seat next to Samya.

Like angels dropped from heaven, on the horizon, behind the trees lining the road, Lobna was walking with some of Hend's other friends. Samya and Hend looked at each other.

"Mama, may I join my friends on their stroll? I rarely see them anymore," Hend said.

"Of course, *habibti*." Madame Magda replied.

"May Samya come as well?"

Samya made to get up from her chair. Her mother slammed her right back down onto her seat. How ridiculous. To be almost thirty and still be ruled by your mother.

"I need her here, my love. Run off and have fun."

Hend gave Samya an apologetic look and escaped. Samya made a note to kill Hend when they were back home. She quite honestly wanted to add her mother to that list.

With no effort to conceal his gaze, Louay looked Samya up and down.

Their parents continued to converse while he turned to Samya. "Mademoiselle Samya, how old are you?"

Samya's eyes widened, "What?"

"Oh, excuse me. I wasn't aware you were hard of hearing. How...old...are...you?" he asked.

"*Oustaz* Louay." Samya attempted to tamp down her infamous temper.

"Ah, Lu Lu." He corrected her.

"Louay." She doubled down. "I'm not sure I've ever heard anyone come out so quickly with that question."

"Well, you look..." He motioned to her. "Older. I just need to know how much older. You don't need to be embarrassed. I normally wouldn't mind at all. As I want a son as soon as possible, I do need to know if a woman of your years can provide that for me."

"Ah, I see."

Samya understood now. Madame Magda casually sipped lemonade while clearly eavesdropping. Her mother had arranged this little gathering ahead of time. She had the subtlety of a *zafaa* band. Louay, or Lu Lu, seemed to share that trait.

"A man who likes to get down to business. To hell with compatibility or desire to marry, for that matter," Samya said with a sigh.

He fairly glowed. "Thank you, mademoiselle."

Before she could continue the very odd, uncomfortable nightmare she was in, her mother practically jumped up with glee. "Jacques. Oh, he is absolutely charming. Jacques!"

She turned to her friend. "Unfortunately French mother, but Egyptian father. Now an orphan, poor child."

A lean, athletic man turned around. There he was. Annoyingly attractive, in a white, button-up, short-sleeve shirt, sunglasses placed in his shirt pocket. He had one hand casually placed in his tan slacks and a notebook in the other.

"Jacques, my boy. Come here and say hello!" Dr. Mahmoud joined in.

His presence, as it always did, brought a mixture of dread and anticipation. Nervousness and calm. Always a paradox that left Samya thrown.

Jacques walked up to the table. Samya's mother introduced their guests and insisted he sit between herself and Samya's father.

Jacques was calm, cool even. He didn't look at Samya. She had no words anyway. Samya, who was not the least bit reticent, couldn't muster coherent conversation in that moment. The last time she'd seen him had been at the Gaber's. They were supposed to have met on the balcony, but he'd never showed. It was for the best, she thought. Begrudgingly, Samya knew Omar was right in that Jacques was trouble.

Lu Lu, meanwhile, looked quite pleased. "It is confirmed, Mama. I must have European blood. Monsieur Jacques and I have the same green eyes and fair skin. Though I have blond hair. I may be even more European than you, monsieur." He chuckled.

"Must be, *Oustaz* Louay." Jacques assented.

"Lu Lu." He corrected and then turned back to his dratted conversation with Samya, ignoring Jacques.

"I would have hoped that my children would inherit my looks, of course. But I was told your sister with the fair skin was not available. You do have good bone structure, however. In some circles you would even be considered pretty, I suppose. Pity you are a bit dark."

Panicking, she saw both sets of parents get up to leave, her mom pulling Jacques with them.

"No, you stay, *habaybi*." Madame Magda said to Samya and Lu Lu, throwing Madame Nora a conspirator's look.

Normally, Samya would have had no qualms about putting the idiot in his place and storming off. But her mother was on a crusade, and Samya had promised herself she was not going to embarrass her family with a fight in front of company.

When the group abandoned them, Samya addressed Lu Lu. "You are right. It's unfortunate, isn't it? I could never match up to your standards. It would be a shame for your children not to bear and carry on your beautiful genes. I guess we are done here."

"Don't be so hard on yourself. All things you cannot control. Your figure works in your favor, you know."

"That it does." Jacques pulled up a chair next to Samya. "I can't say the same for yours, Louay."

Lulu smiled, showing off his underbite. "Call me *Lu Lu*. You are too kind, monsieur."

"And, why, may I ask, are we discussing anyone's figure on this fine day?"

"Samya and I are discussing our compatibility. Mama and I think it is high time that I settle down and gave her grandkids. Have to stop running around, if you know what I mean." He winked and jabbed Jacques in the ribs.

"Of course, Louay."

"*Lu Lu*." He corrected.

Jacques placed his hand underneath his chin as if he was giving something serious thought. "Yes, and what is it that you are looking for in the lucky lady who will finally shackle a rebel such as yourself? Aside from a fine figure, that is."

"Well bred. Good family is a must. Feminine. Quiet. Shy."

Jacques gave a tight smile, no doubt to hold in laughter. Samya narrowed her eyes at him.

"Quiet and shy? Why, that's Samya! I hadn't even noticed she was here until just this very second! Educational requirements, *Oustaz* Louay?"

"No, no, it's *Lu Lu*. Secondary school is fine. A couple years of college, if she must. But her family must be her priority. That and she absolutely must get along with mama."

"I went to medical school and don't get along with my own mother," Samya said.

Still not looking at her, Jacques retorted, "Samya is awfully cozy with those of the middle-aged persuasion and was a dunce at school. The other day she was walking in circles for an hour because she forgot how to make left turns."

Samya's blood boiled. She should have gotten up and left. She really should have, but she couldn't resist responding to his ludicrous provocation. "Like you said, I'm dark. You prefer fair skin."

"As I've told you, Samya, I am open-minded," Lu Lu said.

For the first time since his appearance on the scene, Jacques looked at her. He held Samya's hand under the table and rubbed his thumb over her knuckles. Her body worked hard to contain its reaction to his touch.

Locking his eyes with Samya's, he said to Lu Lu. "You have a preference for fair skin? But who would not luxuriate in such a tone as this, hot tea with just the right amount of milk, I think?"

"Well, yes. She misunderstood. I only meant my child would have a better chance of keeping my family's handsome looks if my wife was also fair. It's a plus, not a must."

Samya tried to yank her hand out of Jacques's, but he held fast. "Her skin is quite smooth, as well."

She dug her nails into Jacques's hand until he winced and let go.

"I have eczema." Samya said.

"She has very soft lips. Though I must warn you, they do house an incredibly sharp tongue," Jacques continued.

Exasperated, Samya snorted. "First I'm quiet and shy, now I have a sharp tongue. What kind of nonsense..."

"Samya's type is all the rage in Paris right now, Louay."

"*Lu Lu.*" Louay corrected. "Really?" His eyes went wide.

"Mmmm, wild curls."

"Filled with dandruff," Samya chimed in.

"High cheekbones."

"They are uneven."

"Long legs."

"Like tree trunks."

"A laugh to die for."

"What sort of odd list is this that Paris has a type of?"

Lu Lu slapped his knee and giggled. "You are selling her quite well. I knew when I saw the girl that she was just for me. Tres chic."

"Tres, tres chic! And she's very obedient. She'll march to whatever command you give her."

Samya found Jacques's thigh next to her, discreetly pinched it, and twisted extra hard.

Jacques instinctively batted her hand away but not before contorting his mouth to hold in a yelp, which satisfied her.

"You must be quite acquainted with her, Monsieur Jacques! To know all of these details. I must say I am lucky to have run into you. Samya does not represent herself that well. You are right. She is quite shy." Lu Lu made dreamy eyes at a horrified Samya.

"This is splendid. You shall do. Samya, I'll make the arrangements."

That was about enough. Samya bolted up from her chair. "Please excuse me, I have to use the restroom." Not bothering to let anyone know when or if she would return, she marched off.

Chapter Sixteen

"Then I had to enlist in the army. But of course mama bought me an exemption. I'm made for positions of authority, you know. Then I..."

Jacques thoughts were drifting as the dummy pattered on. He needn't even nod or acknowledge the conversation as it was clear that Lu Lu needed to talk and didn't really need anyone to listen.

Jacques smiled to himself. He'd almost hesitated to join the group when Madame Magda had called his name. After their last meeting, he'd been resolved to cool his interactions with Samya.

But he hadn't been able to help himself after seeing the clear attempt to match Samya to an overly pompous and oblivious ass. What was her mother thinking? Samya would steamroll a man like that. Wild and untamed, she was a soul no one on earth could keep up with.

Yes, she could have handled herself. Still, he couldn't resist poking at her. Goading her. He'd been doing just that until he'd held her hand. It had been smooth and warm.

Halting Lu Lu's soliloquy, Jacques said, "I'm going for a smoke. It was a pleasure meeting you."

And with a firm handshake, he left the fool.

Jacques wandered off around the exterior of the café, wondering where Samya was hiding. Probably begging some unsuspecting busboy for a cigarette.

A loud rumble of people from a bocce court nearby grabbed his attention.

"Fight!"

"Ya Allah, someone get help!"

"Yes, finally some action!"

Jacques pushed his way to the front of a mob of people encircling something. What he saw next would have been laughable if it wasn't so terrifying.

Two burly men, had to be over 250 pounds, 6'5 feet each, were hurling towards each other. Fists in the air. Screaming epithets he had never heard before. And in between them, arms outstretched separating the two, was a woman half their size: Samya.

"You idiots!" She was screaming over their grunts. "Stop, damn you!" The collar of her shirt was askew, her hair was escaping its bun, and she was being ping-ponged around by the two men.

Jacques smacked his palm against his face. The crowd he was caught up in was swaying him to and fro. "Samya!"

His voice was drowned out by the collective.

Behind one of the bullish men was a petite brunette who looked like she could be blown away if the wind was at the right angle.

The crowd yelled. "The girl! She pit them against each other!"

Jacques finally caught Samya's eye while trying to push himself out of the drove. She waved at Jacques as he elbowed a well-dressed man taking bets. Samya had the audacity to motion Jacques over so he could help and get crushed alongside her.

Meanwhile, the petite brunette faced the crowd, slapped her hands on top of each other, and popped her hip to the side like he'd seen many an irate Egyptian woman do.

"People. One of them has been claiming to be my fiancé since we were five. He took my cousin to the club behind my back. Is that the kind of man who deserves respect?"

"No!" A chorus of women said.

"This other man bought me chocolates. Was I supposed to refuse?"

There was a less convincing assent from the crowd.

"You, girl!" Samya yelled as she somehow avoided being crushed by the brute sandwich. "Get your man, whoever the hell he may be!"

"Neither of them. Let them kill themselves for all I care."

The brutes slowed a bit.

"This is the girl you are fighting over?" Samya addressed the men. "I thought to myself, she's not cute, but maybe she has a good personality. Now that theory's gone to hell."

"What did you say about me, heifer?" The petite brunette yelled.

"You heard me, bitch!"

Before the wispy girl could properly lunge at her, Jacques finally broke free from the horde and yanked Samya from the scene. He didn't stop running until the crowd was no more than bobbing little dots in the distance.

He ushered her under the bleachers of a running track that was currently occupied by seventy-year-old women walking and gossiping. Jacques and Samya were hidden in the shade but for lines of light sneaking through the gaps in the benches above.

"What are you doing?" she asked him in between pants of breath once they were outside of the war zone.

"What am *I* doing?" Jacques was similarly catching his breath. "Not only were you going to be crushed by two thugs, but jumped by a baby banshee!"

"So?" Samya popped her hip.

"So? *Je suis au bord de la crise de nerfs*! How is their argument any of your business?" He put his hand on his face and then peeked through his fingers. "My heart stopped, woman."

"Good. You deserve it. Talk about minding my own business. What do you mean by selling me off like cattle to that idiot, Lu Lu?"

Jacques lowered his hand and looked casually at his nails. "Oh, you would be such a swell couple, really. He would stare at the mirror all day. You would be trapped in his house doing his mother's bidding. That should keep you out of trouble."

Grimacing, she pinched his ribs and tried to twist. Still facing her, he intercepted her hand and swiveled it behind her back.

"You really can't do such vulgar things. Lu Lu would be disappointed," Jacques said.

She tried to break free with her other arm, which he quickly grabbed and similarly, but gently, brought back behind her.

"To...hell with you...and Lu Lu." She tried to wriggle out of his hold, doing her best to glare but failing to hold back giddiness.

"Bad form, Samya," he said, half grunting, half smirking. "You'll have to show more of your docile side soon."

His straight face cracked as she burst into laughter. Mon Dieu, she was soft.

That feeling brought him to where they were and what position they were currently in. Their thighs touching. His arms wrapped around hers. Her skirt resting on his legs. Her breasts, pressing against his solar plexus, and heaving in and out to match her quick breathing. The smell of night jasmine engulfing him. The laughter and playfulness turning into want and desire. Her head was tilted down, so he couldn't tell what she was thinking. Perhaps he should let go. But then, tentatively, she turned her head and placed it on his chest. So lightly. So sweet. So timid. So unlike the exterior of the woman he was coming to know, despite himself. The realization hit him that he was holding something precious, delicate, and private. And for the first time in a long time, he felt...shy.

She looked up at him, and he could feel her heart pounding. Or was that his? He was going to forget himself very soon.

Unfortunately, like a sharp needle, the voice of the senior chatterboxes who were on another lap around the track pierced through their orb. A stark reminder that the world still existed.

An unspoken conversation passed between them, and he knew to let go. He loosened his hold, and she eased off of him.

After the minute they both took to cool off, he cleared his throat and made an attempt to act normal. "Where are we?"

"And you were supposedly leading the way. Come on, then." "Irritated Samya" was back and he was trying to be glad for it. They'd been very close to making a mistake.

She stomped out from under the bleachers. "Lu Lu will want to know where you went."

But his body overrode his brain. It wasn't enough to merely verbally spar and leave it at that. He wanted more. He really thought, maybe, she did, too. Jacques caught up with her and carefully interlaced his fingers with hers. Samya looked up at him.

He shrugged. "Hold me close, or I may get lost."

It was a gamble with Samya. He braced himself for a slap that would ripple across the universe. But she didn't respond or object. His hand felt a light squeeze.

They walked side by side for a while, holding hands, in silence, not in a particular hurry to get back to wherever they were supposed to be getting back to.

The path was covered by trees on either side of them. The lane was empty, as if some force knew they needed the solitude. A slight breeze blew Samya's hair across her face. Jacques decided to be a bit more bold and leisurely pulled her into him. She smiled and then seemed to scold herself for it. "I do that when I'm nervous."

Normally, he would have had a retort ready to go. But his mind wasn't allowing any thoughts in. He was acting off of pure instinct. Moving her hair, he swiped her velvety bottom lip gently with his thumb. His pulse was rising again. He didn't care about mistakes, propriety, right or wrong. There was just this moment with the woman with the wild curls and wilder personality. The woman who made him ache.

Samya didn't wait for him. Hesitantly and softly, she bit his thumb.

Excitement coursed through him. He had not been expecting that. He whispered a: "How dare you?" before lowering his face to hers. Yes. Consequences be damned.

Chapter Seventeen

"Samya!" A voice startled Samya and Jacques, breaking them apart.

Hend and Lobna ran up to them with Omar storming behind.

"Thank Allah. You escaped, *habibti*." Hend kissed her sister's cheek.

Though Jacques was disappointed, he knew that he should be thankful. Once he calmed down, he would fully comprehend that.

Hend and Lobna flanked either side of Jacques. Samya fell back to walk with a seething Omar. The walk helped orient Jacques. There were people around. Time to come back to earth.

Through eavesdropping and the fact Omar didn't deck him, Jacques gathered that the group hadn't seen what Jacques and Samya had been about to do.

Lobna and Hend were bombarding Jacques with giggles and questions. He was starting to suspect, however, that Hend was only playing the part of an empty-headed pretty girl. All in all, Jacques didn't mind the attention, but in the undercurrent of his mind, he could still feel the imprint of Samya on him. Those lips were silky as satin. What had he been about to do? Every time he was around that woman he lost a bit of sense. Ironically, he was thankful to see Omar. Omar had the opposite effect. Like a bucket of cold water splashed on him. A reminder that Samya was not for getting close to. She was complicated. He couldn't handle that. He could only handle uncomplicated and fun.

Though she *was* fun.

So much fun.

Stop, he thought to himself concentrating on Omar's frown. *She's complicated, complicated, complicated.* Jacques resolved to ignore Samya for the rest of the day.

The gang of five walked and then settled on benches in a garden with lush pink and white flowers. It made one forget that all of this land was once desert. The sun was making its descent, and more and more people filled the *nady*. Pulling out his sketchbook, Jacques started drawing.

"What are you doing, Jacques, darling?" Lobna asked sweetly and leaned into him, placing her hand, not so subtly, on his arm. Gleaning that Samya rolled her eyes, he smirked.

"I'm structuring an outline for the novel that I've been commissioned to write," Jacques said.

"I love books. What is this one about, Monsieur Jacques? Oh, do tell us." Hend's eyes fluttered, and then she flashed a smile at Samya as if letting her in on a private joke.

Samya smiled broadly. Jacques frowned at her. How was he supposed to be rid of her when she did things like that? Like smile. Like laugh. Walk. Breathe. He refocused his energy on the other girls.

"It is highly confidential, of course. But if I could give you a hint, it is full of twists, turns, drama, and lust."

The girls squealed with pleasure. Samya retorted, "Oh get a grip the both of you."

Hend and Lobna laughed. Even Omar cracked a smile.

Eventually, Samya wandered off to get a cigarette, and the rest of the gang, sans Jacques, went to get sweets. Jacques was the only one left in the garden when Samya returned a half hour later. Not looking up at her, he noodled in his sketchbook. "They went to get fit...fit..."

"*Fiteer bil sucar*." Samya corrected the term for the sweet flaky pastry. "Haven't you been in Egypt long enough to pick up the language?"

"And they said Egyptian women were the sweetest, gentlest creatures," he mused. "Well, there are exceptions to every rule, I suppose."

"No one has ever said that about Egyptian women in the history of time." She lit her cigarette.

He should have won an award for the restraint he showed. To be close to her. She could have won a couple of awards herself. It was as if the last couple of hours had never happened. *Complicated. Complicated. Complicated.*

He continued doodling as if he was cracking a complex cypher. She walked over to him. As she came closer, he slammed the book closed.

"I should add nosiness to your list of vices, then?"

"Tsk. Tsk. Tsk. Protective of our work, are we? Let's see it."

"No." He kept a firm grip on the book.

Samya looked to the right and left of her, likely to make sure no one was looking and then, with her cigarette in her mouth, grabbed at the book.

"Woman. I. Said. No," he grunted.

When she couldn't get him that way, she stepped back. "Why?"

"The woman wants to know why," he said to no one in particular. "Because it is not yours, that's why."

She nodded. "Fair point. Are you ticklish by any chance?"

His eyes widened, and before he could object, she tickled under his arm. He laughed with a jerk, giving her enough time to grab the book.

She opened it and flipped through with her cigarette in one hand.

Of course, she was seeing his procrastination in full force. The book was filled with drawings. A young boy offering tea on an ornate tray. Women on the street with baskets on their heads. Nude women with lines around their hips indicating they were shaking. Nude women who somehow had oversized pyramid shaped breasts. Then just incomprehensible scribbles. Mon Dieu, he needed to be concentrating on getting pages in and stop messing around.

"It's not done yet. Obviously," he snapped.

She smirked, taking another puff of her cigarette, and closed the book, keeping it behind her back. "You haven't even started yet, have you?"

He looked sideways at her. "I've been busy."

She waved the book around. "Clearly."

He snatched the book out of her hand and sat back down on a bench. After a minute of silence, he rose with his nose in the air. "I'm ignoring you, by the way."

She shrugged her shoulders. "You talk a lot for one who consistently ignores me."

"I know how you can make amends." What? He was playing. Play was permissible, wasn't it? Yes, he played with everyone. He was just being his whorish, playful self.

She ignored him and put out her cigarette. "You are stuck. My friend Mena had the same issue."

"Who the hell is Mena?" He snapped.

"You know what gets him out of it? A change in scenery."

Omar and the gang came back, wiping the powdered sugar off of their mouths and hands.

"Omar." Samya said. "I think we should show Jacques downtown."

"What's in downtown?" Jacques asked.

Ignoring him, Omar responded to Samya. "I have a case coming up I have to prepare for."

Hend encircled Omar with her arms around him. "Please, Omar! We want to go shopping."

"Or you can let us three defenseless girls get ruined by going on our own," Samya said.

Omar made an audible tsk.

Samya put out her cigarette. "Alright then, Jacques. I'll have to take you by myself. Alone. At night."

As always, she seemed to know just the right button to push.

"Fine. I'll bring the car around to your villa at 1:00 p.m. to pick up you three empty-headed blockheads." Omar turned to Jacques. "You can meet us downtown, if you wish."

Samya beamed and hugged Omar, who continued to be irritated. Then she moved to Jacques, and it looked like she stopped herself short. She slowly put her hands behind her back and grinned.

"Should I even ask where we are headed?" Jacques inquired.

Samya's smile grew tenfold. A smile that only served to pull him further into the depths of her orbit.

"Bring your notebook."

***

The day after the *nady* fiasco, a taxi, who no doubt charged Jacques double the price he would charge a native Cairo-ite, dropped Jacques off in downtown Cairo. Downtown Cairo, deemed "the middle of the city," was a commercial center. It was lined with gray cobblestone and the tallest buildings one would see in all of Egypt. It was home to Tahrir Square, an historic site for protests and the biggest changes in Egyptian history. Downtown was a mix of Islamic, Moorish, and early twentieth century European architecture. Apparently, the rich who lived there had fled after the revolution. They left behind them lavish buildings that were crumbling from lack of repair. It was beauty, decay, and rebirth all at once.

Jacques was surprised to find Omar, Hend, Lobna, and Samya already waiting. It was perhaps the first time in Cairo history that anyone had been on time to anything. Omar was frowning and made it a point to stare at his pocket watch and then back at Jacques. Lobna and Hend rushed Jacques with welcoming smiles and giggles.

Samya hung back. She looked exceedingly sharp in her white blouse with both hands tucked into smart cigarette pants. Her lips were cherry red. He had only ever seen her in skirts and dresses surrounded by families. This new look somehow suited her.

"*Sharaftina*. Thank you for gracing us with your presence, Ginger." Samya said over the girls' cooing.

He couldn't help but smile like an idiot, ignoring Omar's pronounced tight lip.

"I can show him the street while you girls shop," Omar said.

"No, Omar. We need you to protect us from hagglers." Hend tugged at Omar.

Lobna started strolling over to Jacques before Hend caught her arm, too. "No, *habibti*. You are coming with us. We need to both shop for the soiree next week."

Hend dragged Lobna and Omar, both sour faced, towards the city center.

When they turned a corner, Samya put both her hands behind her back and strolled in the opposite direction. "Come on, then."

Jacques hustled to catch up with her. "Without a chaperone? I need to be sure you won't push me into an alley and take advantage of me."

She rolled her eyes. "I'll try to restrain myself."

"I wouldn't ask you to do that. Do what you must." He continued, whispering into her ear, "How do you know you're safe with me?"

As close as they were, he could smell the familiar scent of night jasmine. It immediately conjured up the memory of her warm body pressed against his.

Samya pushed him playfully. "I've seen the women in your notebook." She made an obscene gesture indicating large breasts. "I'm not exactly your type."

Before he could annoy her further, they stopped in front of an open-air café. As if filled to the brim, buzzing energy spilled out of the place onto the street. The air smelled of cigars and Turkish coffee. The sounds of the legendary songstress, Umm Kulthum, were an undercurrent to the laughter, yelling, and general chatter from the café occupants.

And what occupants! Writing on napkins. Flirting with waiters. Waving their hands around in intense debates.

"Have Ismail Yaseen crashing into the hospital door. Now, that's brilliant!" said one very short man with a cigar between his teeth. Yaseen was a famous comedic actor, Jacques had learned.

Another man with a heavy mustache and pants tucked up to his chest snapped back. "How cliche! No, no. Make him crash into a man being ushered in on a stretcher!"

"It's a comedy. No one wants to be reminded of the sick!"

"The entire movie's set in a hospital!"

Samya ushered Jacques past a woman in a gray men's three-piece suit and dark red lipstick, holding a small dog with one hand and painting on a canvas with the other. Opposite her was a man before a typewriter talking to himself, completely swept up in his own world.

Samya shook Jacques out of his overwhelm and directed him to a decent-sized dark wood table with a simple wood chair. "Sit."

She left without a word, allowing him to get lost in a nearby group's in-depth conversation about Aime Cesaire's *Discours sur le colonialisme.*

After a couple of minutes, Samya returned with a small *fingan* of Turkish coffee and a metal cup with sugar cubes. A pre-teen boy with blemishes followed her and set up a water-based *shisha* next to Jacques. Samya gave the boy a squeeze on the shoulder and a piastre tip before he trotted off happily.

"Welcome to Zahrat El-Bustan. The café where writers craft revolutionary literature. Where the funniest plays are concocted. The gut-wrenching songs are composed. The dramatic movies that make you weep are born." She grabbed his notebook and placed it on the table. "And where Jacques Ali Abd El-Hameed Kamal will write his third novel."

Jacques shook his head. "I don't know about all that."

"No thinking, if you please. You aren't particularly good at it anyways. You currently have zero pages and ten bawdy women in that notebook of yours. I want to see at least one page of writing and, I suppose, six more sketches of bawdy women within the hour."

He looked around for another chair to pull up for her. Raising a hand, she pointed toward a crowd near the baristas. "I will be over there with the rest of the non-creative ignoramuses. I'll come back in an hour."

Swaying her hips like a metronome, she walked off without another word.

At first he stared at the page and started drawing large breasts. An eruption of laughter broke his anxious spell. He saw Samya surrounded by a raucous crowd. She was laughing, sitting on the lap of an older woman who was pinching her sides while Samya was giving a hard time to what looked like the woman's husband.

He placed his scarab on the table for luck, closed his eyes, picked up his pen, and let it flow.

Chapter Eighteen

Jacques slammed his notebook down on a table near Samya, waking her up. She had fallen asleep in a corner of the café. "There." He crossed his arms and legs and leaned against the wall.

Truth be told, she'd initially been worried that Jacques wouldn't last more than ten minutes in the chaos of the artists surrounding him. But when she'd checked in on him after a while, he'd been engrossed in his work. As the hours passed, she'd let him be while keeping an eye on him. He hunched over with furrowed brow and a fierce scribbling of his pen. This was Jacques in his element. It was the most attractive he had ever looked. No doubt Omar would scold and holler at her for being so late. But considering Jacques was in such a groove, it was worth it.

"Fifteen pages and ten nude women," he said smugly.

Thumbing through the notebook, she saw it had writing on the front and back of the pages. Towards the end was a sketch of a giant man flexing his biceps, smiling with ten mini women each hanging off an appendage.

"And one nude man. Well, I'll be."

"And you doubted me." Jacques walked out of the café with Samya once she'd bid farewell to the barista. "One page, you said. Ha!"

"Yes, yes. I told you good job," she said flippantly.

"No, you didn't. Despite the fact that you were horrid, I managed to push through and start an outline and the beginnings of a chapter. That's what a professional does. It's in my blood."

Samya snorted. "I said good job, already!"

"I don't believe you." He stopped to turn to her. "Your non-existent belief in my abilities is truly abysmal, Fred."

"I said…"

Samya didn't finish her response because he pulled her away from the people on the busy Cairo street and into an alley. He put his hands on her shoulders, looked her in the eye, and then crushed her into a hug.

"Thank you," he whispered in her ear. "I needed the push. Thank you."

She relaxed into him. How nice it would feel if everyone hugged this way. Hugging was nice. Ya Allah, what was that cologne that he wore? She wanted to pour it all over her pillow. She tried to keep her mind focused on his arms engulfing her and closed her eyes tightly to imprint the memory. It was all right to collect memories, she reasoned with herself. Memories for lonely nights. And this memory would accompany those she had of him at the *nady*. Touching her with his sturdy hands. Treating her in a way no one ever had. Foreign, yet welcome. It didn't surprise her that he wanted to touch her but that she was yearning for him to do so. She also wanted to run her fingers through his hair. To kiss him without being interrupted. Of course, she knew that for every caress he gave her, he was whispering sweet nothings to hundreds more other women. Nothing would ever come of this, thankfully. For now, though, it was all right to collect harmless but warm memories she would keep with her when he was long gone.

"Samya!" Omar yelled from a distance, and she pulled from Jacques.

"Anytime, you foreign bastard," she whispered. "You better leave before Omar chops both our heads off."

Jacques smiled that lazy smile he had and took off with his hands in his pockets. The darkness, thankfully, did not prevent a good view of his backside.

"Samya!" She heard Omar yell again.

"Yes, yes. I'm here."

Omar stalked through the cobblestone street with fists clenched. "Where were you?"

Samya looked at her nails nonchalantly. "The café, where else? Do you have a cigarette?"

"The café? Do you know how many cafés there are in downtown? We said we'd meet by the yellow-front patisserie at Qasr El-Nil hours ago! I've been up and down streets looking for…where is he?"

Omar erratically looked past Samya's shoulder as if she was hiding Jacques behind her.

"He left a bit ago. I lost track of time. Calm yourself. You'll have an aneurysm." She didn't know why she was lying to Omar. It struck her that she was acting as if she was guilty of something untoward. When in truth, nothing had happened.

Omar sighed. "You are being reckless. Your reputation."

"He wrote his book, and I sat tables away from him. I don't need to explain a thing to you. Just because I'm not always doing the 'proper' thing in your eyes doesn't mean I did anything egregious."

His eyes seared into hers. "You act like I'm being an unreasonable brute. I do not make these rules up. If you are caught in a precarious position with this man, your entire life will be at stake. Our society is not easily forgiving. Especially not to women."

"I'm not going to be caught in any situation. You misunderstand our intentions."

Omar scoffed. "His intentions are pretty damn obvious."

"We have become friends. You and I are friends."

"It is not friendship he wants. The man acts so unabashedly brazen in public with no regard for discretion or formality. And the fact that you *still* do not understand what he wants only shows how naive you are."

"Ya Allah! Omar, you are becoming tedious!"

"Let me enlighten you. All men want one thing, and they don't care how they get it or who they hurt along the way. Without exception. No matter how charming or French they may be. You are just a means to an end for him."

"Stop! Enough!" Samya yelled and walked away from him.

Omar tsked. "You just don't want to listen. That bastard didn't, either."

She stopped in her tracks and turned back to Omar. "You spoke to him?"

"Of course I did. You weren't listening. So I had to do something."

The sound of footsteps accompanied by feminine chatter entered the scene. Hend and Lobna were no doubt simpering away about their shopping trip, completely unaware of the storm they were about to enter.

Samya came close to Omar and spoke in a soft but menacing tone. "This is the last time I say this to you. It is none of your business who I associate with or how I associate with them. Don't you dare speak on my behalf again."

With that, she shoved him to the side, and stormed off past a confused looking Hend and Lobna.

Chapter Nineteen

What Samya had done for Jacques the day before, at Zahrat El-Bustan, well, she likely didn't know how much it meant.

He'd been off since the accident. His father's death begat death all around Jacques. Death of family. Death of creativity. Death of caring. He no longer had a reference point on this earth. Even if he hadn't seen his father in all those years, he'd still had someone he came from, belonged to. A tether, so he wasn't completely alone. Now, Jacques was tetherless. And learning his father had a second family all the while only made Jacques feel even more so.

All of the pain of his past and present had to mean something, didn't it? Otherwise it was for nothing. He was nothing. So he'd turned to the thing that gave him a sense of purpose in the first place: his writing. He had to be a writer's writer, someone worthy. The problem was he didn't know if he had it in him. There was a fear deep inside that his writing was formulaic and rote. And that thought and many others brought him to numb himself by going out, drinking, flirting, even handling the Egyptian properties. Anything to distract himself from what it meant to lose everything, and have nothing to show for it.

But that sacred artists' hub had broken open a rush of inspiration. Life itself was weaving and bobbing in every corner of that café. Waiting for any brave soul to harness a bit for themselves. And harness it he had. In the past two days, he had finished four chapters of his novel. A valiant beginning to a story deliciously unfolding from his brain, heart, and gut.

He loved the café so much that he took Kareem to it. It was satisfying showing someone else around for a change.

Kareem looked around the place. "Nice."

"That's it? Nice?"

"Well, the place sells coffee. What do you want from me?"

Jacques put his palm on his forehead. "The place itself is a muse worthy of the best artists. Look at all the creation that is occurring around us."

Kareem shrugged. "Do they have good tea or something?"

Aghast, Jacques scoffed. "You are making me regret bringing you here."

"Okay. It is very nice. Is that better?"

"Let's just get you coffee, you ignoramus."

Kareem laughed.

Jacques motioned to a waiter. "You should have seen me when Samya and I came here yesterday. I couldn't contain myself."

Kareem stilled. "Who's Samya?"

"Oh, she's someone I met at one of those gatherings you hate so much." Jacques was hoping the heat he was feeling wasn't transferring onto his cheeks.

"The same woman you thought was *interesting* a while ago?" Kareem appeared as though he wanted to say something Jacques wouldn't like.

"What?"

"This isn't good, my man." Kareem rubbed his face. "So, when's the wedding?"

"What?"

"You should see yourself when you say her name. Just saying it makes you light up like a fool."

"No, no. You're misunderstanding. We're friends, that's all. Nothing more."

Kareem raised his eyebrow.

"Yes, I find her attractive, but she is. I can't help that."

"This is more than that. It is all over your face."

Jacques made to wipe whatever it was off of him.

Kareem shook his head. "Just be careful and remember what I told you about guns, weddings, and being shackled to brats."

"Yes, yes. Fine, fine."

Jacques ordered Turkish coffee and *shishas* for them. Though he was careful not to mention her name again in front of Kareem, she was stuck in his mind, begging to come out of his mouth. These days, Jacques saw her wherever he went. He would see a sliver of red in the sunset and think of her painted lips. Jasmine flowers seemed to pop up everywhere. The reflection of the moon in the Nile reminded him of the moon lighting her face when they'd first met. He was disgusted with his own sappiness. But the obsession went deeper than her body. When he was around Samya, he was awake. Laughing became so joyful. Sorrow became visceral. Touch couldn't take place without electricity. There were colors to living that she was introducing him to, and he didn't know if he could stop wanting more.

***

When Dr. Mahmoud invited him to a soiree at the Roshdi villa later that day, he could hardly refuse. He was being polite, he assured himself. It had nothing to do with a chance to see a certain spirited, curly-haired minx.

The soiree was packed to the brim. Fashionable (and some gaudy) people were talking to each other and hand gesturing wildly. He loved that quality in Egyptians. Jacques had seen that in his father many times.

"Jacques!" A familiar and unwelcome male voice entered the fray. "How serendipitous to have found you, my man! When did you get here?"

Lu Lu's blond hair was parted the same as Jacques's, and he was dressed in a black suit with a white shirt, the buttons of which were doing God's work by hanging on for dear life.

Before Jacques could answer, he was cut off by Lu Lu who, true to form, only cared about what Lu Lu had to say.

"Oh, Jacques. I must thank you for the excellent recommendation you gave me in Samya. Though I have had some trouble locating her tonight, the stubborn girl. Every time I find her, she seems to disappear." Lu Lu sounded exasperated. "She's exceedingly shy."

Do not engage. Leave it alone, Jacques kept telling himself.

"Being coy is quite attractive, in a sense. Though if she is too much so, she is in danger of losing me. Hopefully, her mother has the good sense to warn her. She would be devastated if someone like me slipped through her fingers."

Jacques blocked out what the chatterbox was ranting on about when he saw a couple of familiar curls peek out of a balcony corner, followed by their owner. Samya put her

100

pointer finger to her lips, apparently pleading with Jacques not to expose her. He gave her a reassuring nod. Sighing in what looked like relief, she retreated back into hiding. Jacques should have left it alone. Really he should have. But this was just too sumptuous.

"You are in luck. I've found your lady. She's on the balcony," Jacques said.

"Is she? Then I'm off!" Lu Lu chirped.

"Tell her I said hello. She'll want to know that we spoke."

Ah, it was harmless. But her impending reaction to Jacques's betrayal made him grin. Just a bit of fun, that was all. They were friends. Completely appropriate for friends to play jokes on each other. And dream of how each other's bare skin would feel. Yes, absolutely normal.

He got closer to the balcony to eavesdrop. Lu Lu was assaulting Samya with, no doubt, a foolish jabber about his favorite topic: Lu Lu.

Samya sighed heavily, trying to get a word in and failing. Looking away from Lu Lu, she locked eyes with Jacques. She put her hand up in a gun motion, pointed towards him, and pulled the trigger.

Jacques put a hand on his heart as if wounded and smirked. He was rewarded with a smile. Warmth shot through his bloodstream, traveling through every part of his body.

Lu Lu turned away from Samya to see who she was paying attention to instead of him. When he spotted Jacques, he waved hello. With Lu Lu looking away from her, Samya took the opportunity to stomp on his foot with her heel. As the idiot yelped, she made her escape.

Jacques was on his way to go find her when Hend approached. "Monsieur Jacques. How do you do?"

"I'm well, thank you. How about yourself?" He needed to get the girl out of the way so he could get to Samya.

"Very fine. And it is so very good to see you, monsieur!" She fluttered her eyelashes. Samya's younger sister was in a white dress embroidered with flowers, her long hair was loose around her shoulders, and she wore satin gloves. Demure. Put together. Calculated. It was hard to see the resemblance between the sisters. In fact, Hend was exactly the type of person Kareem would absolutely loathe. She seemed to know this society inside and out and subscribed to it wholeheartedly.

"You see, my friend has a dilemma, and I would love some advice from a wise man such as yourself."

He couldn't discern if there was slight sarcasm that accompanied the word "wise."

"Happy to help. What seems to be the problem?"

"Well." She motioned for him to sit in a European, embroidered couch in the salon. "My friend is a bit taken by a young man who is as smooth as butter. With him being so suave, I have been having a hard time deciphering his intentions."

Jacques stopped looking at the balcony and brought his attention to Hend.

"You see, my friend is so dear to me. She is highly intelligent but quite sensitive. I do not want to see her hurt. Would you happen to know how one can tell what a man's real intentions are? I bring these silly troubles to you because you are a man of the world and know so very much."

Hend looked up at him with what he knew now was feigned innocence.

"Hend!" A voice rang out through the villa.

"Oh, that's mama. I better go." She held both Jacques's hands in hers as she got up. "Would you think on my friend's dilemma, Monsieur Jacques? I do value your esteemed opinion."

Apparently, the young man was not as smooth as butter. Jacques was being obvious. So much so, it was headed towards recklessness. He wasn't sure where his interactions with Samya were leading.

Nowhere. Not in this society. Not in this environment where the younger people dated in secret. Where they did no more than hold hands or kiss behind a tree if they were really feeling raunchy. The older generation expected any romantic involvement would lead to marriage within a few months. Jacques was inclined to think Samya didn't agree. She marched to the beat of her own drum. And although he didn't, Samya *did* have a reference point. She belonged to this society with all of its customs. Though he wasn't familiar with all of the culture, nor did he plan to follow any rules that deprived him of sex for a long period of time, he did respect the local traditions. And a woman like Samya deserved to be respected.

He did not agree, however, that Samya was so fragile. None of her actions supported that contention. But then his mother had been a pillar of strength, and look what had happened there. Eventually, her illness had overtaken her, and she'd fallen apart. And he'd been useless to her.

Someone like him couldn't give a woman like Samya the support she deserved during tough times. So, what was the use of entering into a relationship that he wouldn't be able to handle? He was unreliable. Besides, he was going back to Paris soon and Samya's life was in Cairo. For all those reasons and more, he didn't want to give Samya false hope for a real attachment.

He could tell himself for the hundredth time to stay away from her. To leave the city or avoid society gatherings. But he knew that sooner or later he would be drawn back to her. Despite trying to steer away from it, the line Samya and he were trying not to cross was getting closer and closer.

Chapter Twenty

A lanky Jacques walked home with his hands in his pockets, thinking smugly about the awkward yet passionate kiss he'd enjoyed with Raquel behind the school building in between classes. His friends teased him relentlessly, but he didn't mind. He was the one with a girlfriend. The open front door to his house broke his daydreaming haze. He jumped the fence, stumbled through the front door, and ran up the stairs to his mother's room. Vivienne lay on her side in a white nightgown. A yellow liquid poured from her mouth. Jacques shook her to no response. On the nightstand he found a small note in her handwriting.

Live beautifully now, mon fils.

When Jacques turned to look at his withered mother, she was sitting up and pale. "Why did you leave me? No one wants me! Not even my own child!"

Jacques, terrified, was unsure if he should run away or hug her. Slowly, an empty darkness crept up behind his mother and swallowed her bit by bit. That same black nothingness crawled its way toward Jacques and started to engulf his body. Squeezing his heart. Refusing to let go.

"Tea or Coffee?"

Jacques startled awake.

"Pardon me, *basha*. I didn't realize you were asleep. I will come back around." A man pushing a drink service cart spoke apologetically.

Jacques wiped the sweat that had built up on his brow and sat back up in his chair.

He had memorized every aspect of the train car as it had been his constant companion during the months he had been in Egypt. Once more he was headed to Tanta, this time at the behest of his uncle Mostafa. He had invited Jacques for dinner so they could get to know each other. Though Jacques was on his guard with the man, he thought the dinner might be a good opportunity to convince Mostafa to pull the court petition. The less Jacques had to do with that, the better.

When he arrived at his uncle's home, he found a lavish apartment building. The decor was unlike what he'd seen of the Cairo Elite. The apartment door was large mahogany with a round, gold knocker. A mirrored plaque announced: *House of Mostafa Kamal Morssy* in ornate Arabic calligraphy. Inside, intricate Persian rugs covered dark wood floors. Delicate, green geometric shapes were painted on white walls. Beautiful Arabic-style furniture gave the place an air of refinement. The fine home was in direct contradiction to the man that it housed.

Jacques took knife and fork to a grilled pigeon at a large dinner table.

His uncle, who sat opposite him, droned on about the "good old days" when he'd been young, strong, and irresistible. "I was quite handsome. More so than your father. He was too tall. Women don't like that sort of thing. No offense meant, son."

The piece of pigeon Jacques bit into was tough. "None taken."

"I could have any woman I wanted. But I fell in love with one in particular."

Mostafa looked from side to side and twitched his mustache. "Solayman told me that you now know of Lena, Abdo's...err...widow." He did not allow enough time for Jacques to respond. "That was badly done of him, Jacques. Very badly done to leave you and your poor mother like that. But wait until you hear what he did to me."

"*Amo*, I think I've heard enough of my father's misdeeds, thank you."

Mostafa clicked his tongue and took a big gulp of Stella Beer. "You must. You see, Madame Lena was originally betrothed to me. She was madly in love with me. And your father stole her."

Though Jacques had been around his uncle enough to know the man had a skewed perception of reality, he did not doubt his father could have behaved in an underhanded manner.

"And now with this business of Lena and her kids." Mostafa clicked his tongue. "They are illegitimate, you know. The court will take their property away from them."

Jacques set his fork down. "I thought you were the one who petitioned the court to do so."

His uncle ignored him. "I told Lena that I would marry her. Then this whole business of the villa will be done with."

"How romantic."

"Exactly my thinking, my boy. I would treat those kids as my own, of course. They would be sent to the best schools in England. But the woman is being damn stubborn. And Solayman is getting in her head. Talking poorly about me!"

Mostafa started chewing aggressively, and tiny pieces of poultry leapt from his mouth as he spoke. "I highly suspect he wants her for himself. He does! He acts respectful and proper, but he has a sneaky side to him. He almost led your father to financial ruin, you know."

Jacques didn't want the old man to have a heart attack, so he let him swallow before speaking. "*Amo, Oustaz* Solayman has been nothing but helpful in the time I've known him. My father's properties would have been in disarray without him."

This broke Mostafa out of his anger, and he smiled. "Yes, yes, the properties. How many did he leave you with, son? You should have really gotten me involved early on. I would have taken care of them for you."

"No need." Jacques gave a polite smile. "All's well in hand."

Mostafa stiffened. "Well, yes. Of course. Your father left me with nothing, which is not your fault at all, my boy!"

That was a lie. Solayman had confirmed that Mostafa had been given a hefty sum of money. It had been cruel of his father to give his only brother, with an apparently big gambling problem, a sum of money he knew he would likely lose in a week. Nevertheless, Jacques listened on.

"The rent for this modest apartment is high. Oh, but Lena and I were sweethearts, we really were. I think that you can talk to her and persuade her to reconsider my proposal. It would be best for all, really."

Jacques remembered a time when he'd been twenty-five and had to have a tooth extracted. It had shattered into pieces and taken the dentist four painstaking hours to get out. That encounter had been much preferable to this dinner, Jacques thought.

"*Amo*, I do not know her or the situation close enough to weigh in. I should tell you that I will be countering the petition in court. I know you care a great deal about her and her kids, so you won't object to having their assets protected, I'm sure."

Mostafa became animated. "But, son, who better to protect their assets than family? She is a woman alone in Tanta. She needs protection that I am more than happy to provide!"

"The material point is that she does not want that sort of protection from you. So best to leave it alone." Jacques was wholly unconvinced that Mostafa would indeed leave it alone. "Now, I can help you with this apartment. I'll set it up with Solayman."

"Yes, yes. I would be so grateful, my boy," Mostafa grumbled and then bit into a piece of bread looking anything but.

CHAPTER TWENTY-ONE

The Roshdis attended dinner at the Waqabs' villa. Every piece of furniture in their aristocratic villa had been imported from a western European country. All their clothes, the same. The Waqabs were the highest of the high class. They did not exhibit their affluence loudly, however. They were the sort of rich who were reserved. They didn't need to prove a thing to anyone.

They'd amassed the majority of their wealth during the monarchy and occupation by the British. The Waqabs were old money that the Brits had allowed to stay that way. To prevent Egyptians (and the rest of occupied Africa) from revolting, they'd allowed families like the Waqabs to thrive, to a point, both financially and educationally. For these families, the benefits of colonization outweighed the desire to rally for an independent nation. The colonizers, however, hadn't counted on the will of the poor to take on the task of freeing their country. The Waqabs had survived the turnover to democracy, but it was clear they weren't fond of associating with riffraff. This, however, was a very unpopular opinion to have in the new, free Egypt. Samya suspected that the Waqabs kept their prejudices to themselves.

The Roshdi family was acquainted with the Waqabs since the fathers often consulted on each other's cases. Though the fathers were close, the families weren't. Many a time Madame Magda had called Dr. Amr, the patriarch of the Waqab family, a humorless bore. So Samya was truly puzzled as to why her mother would agree to visit them, given her mother's position and the fact they hadn't done so in years. Madame Magda had no way of knowing, but the visit would prove doubly awkward for Hend since Adam, Hend's former intended, was Dr. Amr's nephew and may attend the gathering.

After a multi-course dinner, the families retired to the salon. Several servants came forth with trays of tea, Turkish coffee, fresh juice, sweets, and a plethora of delicious gateau. The families chitchatted about the weather, summer trips to Alexandria, and new films.

"How is London, Doctor?" Madame Magda asked Dr. Amr's forty-two-year-old son, Dr. Hosseni.

Dr. Hosseni was an Oxford medical school graduate. He lived in Great Britain and was married to a stiff, "bone dry" (as Samya's mother would so rudely say), English woman.

"It's rainy all day, the food is horrid, but that is where my work takes me, Madame Magda. Though I will always remain a Cairo boy at heart." Dr. Hosseni spoke firmly, with conviction and a deep baritone.

His masculinity was intimidating. Dr. Hosseni's presence made Samya feel like a child. He had elegantly long fingers, a lean but muscular build, and a clean-shaven face but for a well-groomed, full mustache, as was the fashion. His black hair had white sprinkled in, giving him a polish of distinction. He was classically handsome in a noble type of way.

Assessing him, Samya concluded that he was likely the same height as Jacques. Though the two men could not have been more different. Jacques was handsome in a *flirty-troublemaker-that-is-forgiven-for-all-sins-the-moment-he-flashes-that-smile* way. Jacques was the type to chat up a washerwoman, a businessman, and the Queen of England with the same deference and finesse. Jacques's spirit was so young compared to Dr. Hosseni's. Samya wondered if she actually preferred a younger spirit and ignored a niggling thought as to why she cared how Dr. Hosseni stood up to Jacques in comparison. And how she privately repeated that exercise with every male she'd met since. She was also ignoring the fact that she hadn't seen the confounded man in a while and was slightly (just a tiniest bit) missing him.

"And your wife, Dr. Hosseni? How is she enjoying London?" Samya's mother asked as she flashed a quick look at Dr. Hosseni's stepmother, who smiled.

Madame Zainab had married Dr. Amr shortly after his first wife passed. She was in her late forties and mother to the second Waqab son, ten-year-old Hatem.

"Sadly, we've separated. The divorce was finalized a couple of months ago." Dr. Hosseni took a sip of his tea, not looking very sad at all.

"How unfortunate." Samya's mother was a horrible actress. "But I'm sure it is for the best. Between you and me, I never liked her much at all."

Madame Zainab seemed to be part of the same failing acting troupe as Madame Magda. She patted her auburn coiffure and pursed her elegant, pink painted lips. "She was rude and didn't deserve Hosseni. He's better off with one of our girls, anyways. No more foreigners, *habibi*!" She smiled at Samya.

Ah, and there it was.

Dr. Hosseni gave the women a polite smile and nodded before joining his father and Dr. Mahmoud, who were deep in conversation about some new medical technique.

After tedious conversation about how the younger generation's latest fashion trends were abysmal, Madame Zainab motioned to Dr. Hosseni. Samya thought it was a bit odd that, although Madame Zainab was only a couple of years older than Dr. Hosseni, she acted like he'd come straight from her womb.

"Hosseni, *habibi*, I was just telling Madame Magda about my new floral garden. Please take Samya out there to show her. Hend can stay here and play with Hatem."

If Hosseni was annoyed to be taken away from his conversation with the other doctors, he didn't show it. Instead, he extended his arm to Samya and walked her out of the villa and to the garden.

At this point, Samya would normally act like a crazed maniac or do something absolutely ridiculous to scare a potential suitor away. She felt like she couldn't do that with Dr. Hosseni. He was too substantial. Someone to be respected. Too much of an adult.

"They're ridiculous in there. Completely obvious, don't you think?" Samya allowed herself to settle into a relaxed smile.

Hosseni looked ahead calmly with the same serene, cool face he'd worn previously.

She pressed on. "My mother's been dragging me from potential to potential. I'm sure yours is doing the same now that you are back."

It was as if he'd barely registered what she'd said.

Confused at the silence, Samya looked out into the bountiful garden. They were surrounded by a kaleidoscope of flowers. Though the sun was setting, there was just enough orange-tinted light to see the colors: pink, red, white, yellow. They were all arranged in elegant, uniform hedges. The smell was intoxicating. Past the large garden was a lawn of tall grass that ran for acres and swayed to and fro. Samya hadn't known this much greenery even existed in the city.

After a long pause, Hosseni finally spoke. "My stepmother does not deserve your ire nor your insolence."

Samya was caught off guard; she wasn't sure what to say.

"You seem pleased with yourself, that your mother is inflicting you onto others. Clearly she has no respect for this family if she thinks bringing you here as a potential for me is anything but insulting."

He seemed all too happy to continue in the same even, deep voice that now seemed so spiteful. "Your mother took advantage of my stepmother's naïveté. She doesn't know what you are. Weak in the mind. I know your...history, shall we say? Someone like you should be locked away, not traipsing around and getting flung at some innocent, unlucky man. One who would be stuck with you, resigned to a life with an invalid. It's a shame I'm bound by an ethical code as a doctor. Otherwise, I would warn the poor sods."

There was no mercy in his eyes. He kept digging into her with his knife-like words.

"A shame...your sister is very pretty. She could have her pick of men but has been scorned by many. It's bad enough you are mad, but your abysmal behavior reflects on her as much as it does on you. She has lost *prospects* because of you." And he emphasized that last bit as he stared her dead in the eyes.

"You can see the rest of the garden by walking out towards the field. *Salam*." With that, he left.

And Samya's world crumpled.

Hend. Her beloved sister.

The person she loved most in this world. Samya hadn't considered how her actions would affect her sister.

She didn't care about the jackass Hosseni because she would be sure to take care of him. But she did care about crushing the dreams of her cherished sister.

Hend's stock was going down because of Samya.

Her greatest fear had been confirmed. She was an anchor dragging her loved ones down under with her. Drowning them in her madness. Sometimes she thought they'd be better off if she was gone. Moments like these made those thoughts a tempting solution. What would it look like if her father was free from constant worry? If her mother didn't feel it was her sole obligation to make Samya into a normal girl? If Hend could truly shine without the blemish that was her older sister? But what would it do to the family to have a daughter who'd committed the ultimate sin of offing oneself? She was stuck.

Then there was the fact that she'd been audacious enough to act out when she couldn't afford to. She didn't know why she couldn't change her personality. Lower her voice to an appropriate tone. Rein in her temper. Stay away from mentors who gave her hope that she could one day practice medicine. Stay away from men who made her feel that certain things were possible. Things Samya had abandoned years ago.

And how the hell had Hosseni known about her being in the hospital? She suspected that rat Foad must have told him. Clearly, *he* didn't give a damn about an ethical code.

Hosseni's reveal put her entire situation in perspective. Her despair that seemingly came from nowhere had been increasing. She had not acknowledged it until this moment. It was harder to get out of bed in the morning. Harder to shower. Harder to move through life smiling. And now her fears about her family would only serve to accelerate her situation.

She took a couple of steps into the field and went as far away from the villa as possible. Then holding her arms tight, she buckled onto the ground. The tall blades of grass closed in on her, providing sanctuary. Finally, after months of holding herself together, she wept.

Chapter Twenty-Two

Jacques waltzed up to Dr. Hosseni Waqab's family home. He'd met Hosseni and his father at the café that Dr. Mahmoud frequented. Hosseni seemed a solid man, if a bit stiff.

Hosseni greeted him at the door and brought him into the salon.

And wouldn't you know it? The Roshdis were there. Because with his luck, why wouldn't they be? Jacques shook Dr. Mahmoud's hand heartily while trying not to blurt out, *"Just so you know, I'd like to take your first daughter over my shoulder, drag her into the first bed I see, and pleasure her until she screams."*

As for the aforementioned daughter he wanted to dishevel, she wasn't present. *Good,* he thought.

Hosseni and Jacques fell into an easy conversation, catching up on the latest cigars, life in London, and the like.

"So, how do you know the Roshdis?" Jacques asked.

"Old family friends." Dr. Hosseni then changed the subject.

Jacques couldn't help himself, so he redirected the conversation once more. "I met them through Dr. Mahmoud. Charming family. Hend, Madame Magda and, oh, where is Samya?"

Hosseni leaned back in his chair. "Don't go down that path, my man. Let me get you another whiskey."

"Ah, keeping all the best for yourself, then?"

Hosseni took a puff of his cigar. "What a truly depressing thought that she would be the best I could do." He paused momentarily. "Don't get me wrong. I wouldn't mind fucking her one night, but she's not anyone I would claim during the light of day. I don't say that as an insult to her family. More of a friendly heads up to you. She's wild. Who would go through all the trouble when there are plenty of fresher and prettier cunnies to be had?"

Jacques felt heat climb up his body. Blood rushed to his cheeks. He was not a violent person. He would never even swat a fly, though that was less kindness and more laziness. But he felt rage like he'd never felt before. "Hmm," was all he managed to get out.

"Hosseni, *habibi*, where's Samya?" Madame Zainab called out.

Hosseni took his time sipping his tea. "She's probably still admiring your floral garden."

Madame Zainab and Madame Magda exchanged indecipherable looks and carried on a private conversation.

Jacques didn't wait long before excusing himself to use the restroom. Of course, he marched to the back of the villa and looked out into the expansive garden. Off in the distance, a dark figure sat on the ground partially shielded by grass. As he walked closer, he could see curly hair escape the bun it was in, flapping in the wind. Samya.

He wanted to lift her up and hold her. Instead, he sat on the ground next to her.

"Are you following me?" he asked in mock horror.

Samya turned to him and playfully but weakly pushed his head with her hand. But then he saw her face. Her eyes were watery, the tip of her nose red, and her lips swollen.

He trapped her hand before she could pull it back and held it to his chest.

She looked away and made a feeble attempt to pull her hand free. She didn't resist when Jacques kept it tugged firmly, still looking at her with concern.

"What did the bastard do?"

She looked down at a tiny blade of grass she was pulling out in front of her. "Not sure which bastard you are referring to."

Stubborn, stubborn woman. He dropped her hand and tilted her head towards him, "Hosseni. What did he say to you?"

She didn't look him in the eye. "Nothing of consequence. No need to fight any duels on my behalf. Don't worry."

"Fight any duels? He's safer with me than he is with you, Fred. Though it would be amusing to take him on together, don't you think? You can punch his gut, and I'll pull his mustache hair."

She chuckled, and he relaxed a bit. "Just like you to make me do all the work."

"I'm not used to hard labor, like the likes of you." He smiled and rubbed her cheek.

He intertwined his hand with hers and joined her in looking forward into slivers of the abyss through the grass. "He's a prick. A lot of men are, but him especially."

"He's ill mannered, but not so bad, I suppose. I just heard some truths I didn't want to really hear today. It is good to be reminded, though," Samya said.

"What did he say?"

"Nothing I didn't already know."

"Dammit, Samya." He looked at her again. "Tell me, please."

She cast her eyes downward. "My mother and his were plotting to get us together. He was insulted that anyone had offered to pair me with him, given I was crazy. Of course, I don't care about any of that. He's right. It's just that I'm messing things up for Hend."

Jacques felt simultaneously livid and empathetic.

Samya continued. "She deserves the moon and the stars, that girl. Hosseni's cousin was courting my sister, albeit privately. He broke it off with her so abruptly. It destroyed her. I suspected it may have been because of me, but today I received confirmation. I don't care what happens to me. But Hend." Tears flowed from Samya as she whimpered.

Jacques couldn't help himself. He tugged her into him, allowing her to bury her face in his chest to muffle her cries.

He kissed the top of her head, and his heart ached. "It's not your fault, cherie. He's an ignoramus. And that twat who left your sister is one, too."

Jacques tightened his hold on her. "And you may not care about the shit he's said about you, but I do. Do you know how wonderful you are? You are smart, funny, maddening, and have a swaying ass that haunts my dreams."

She mumbled a laugh that sounded gargled against his chest.

"And besides, there are so many other valid reasons not to like you. You're stubborn, you're annoying, you laugh like an asthmatic old man."

She pinched him.

A bit softer, he continued. "Any one of these fools would be awestruck for the opportunity to be near you. And one lucky/unlucky bastard will one day make you very happy. And I already despise him.

"Besides, Hend is a big girl. You underestimate her, you know. She can handle more than you give her credit for. Have you seen the girl work a room? I've never seen a woman hunt men as stealthily as your sister does. Trust me, nothing anyone can do can affect her standing."

She relaxed a bit in his arms, let go, and then looked up at him. "She is that, wonderful."

"Like someone else I know."

"I hate when you are like this. It makes it very hard to hate you. It's annoying"

"Annoying you has become a beloved hobby of mine."

She smiled widely at that, her left dimple making a rare appearance.

How he wanted to lick that dimple. Mon Dieu, he was in trouble. They locked eyes for a moment. Then she broke it by backing out of his embrace and punching him rather hard on the shoulder.

They settled into silence.

After a while, Samya spoke. "I don't want him, you know."

"Who?" Jacques asked.

"The lucky/unlucky bastard you mentioned. I don't want him. I don't plan to marry, ever."

Jacques contemplated that for a moment. "Well, I'm sorry for him, then."

Silence eclipsed them once more.

"Jacques?"

"Hmm."

"What do you want from me?"

Jacques paused.

She looked at the darkness ahead. "You are very friendly. I would consider us friends, I suppose. But I've never had a friend like you before. If what you are looking after is...well, I'm not marrying ever.

Jacques chimed in. "I won't offer you marriage, ever. Honestly, I'm not planning to offer anyone marriage. That's not what I want."

"Then what do you want? Be honest. I cannot handle anything less after today."

Shut up, Jacques, he thought to himself. *Shut up. Leave. Make a stupid joke, chuck her under the chin and leave. Now.*

Instead, his stupid mouth took over. "As much as you'll allow."

She turned towards him, expressionless.

"Yes, I'm a bastard." He swept a ringlet of her hair behind her ear. "You are from a good family, and what's more, you are a damn respectable individual. But I want to touch you whenever you are around. It has been with extreme restraint that I have not."

She looked at him incredulously.

"Granted, I've not been subtle. Though what I've done so far is only the beginning of what I'd like to do. And I don't think I'm the only one who feels something."

Samya turned away from him silently and stared ahead. He picked up a blade of grass, toyed with it, and continued.

"I offer you no permanency. There is no future for us." He paused. "I have one more month before I leave for Paris. I know very well how I wish to spend that month, with you, in my bed, preferably. And after that, I'll be gone."

Samya fumed, her brows furrowed. She was back to the woman he knew, and he was grateful that she was heading back to normal even if it was in rage. She went to slap him with her right hand, but he caught it.

"I probably deserve that, but quick reflexes and all that. We *are* friends, you know. Probably my closest friend here if I'm being honest." He released her hand. "I, too, have never had a friend like you. I'm very attracted to you, and maybe it is because I've forbidden myself from you, and I've never forbid a woman from myself. And you should know that. I'm an utter whore. But for whatever reason, plain and simple, I want you. And the feeling is overwhelming."

He was babbling a stream of consciousness, but he was so tired of resisting he simply didn't care to be careful anymore.

"I didn't plan to ever tell you this. I should be flogged and hung, especially for telling you this today after what just happened with that weasel. I think we shouldn't see each other anymore. Because I can't stop annoying you, and wanting to touch you, and wanting more than you'll want to give me. And you should slap me and never talk to me again. As a friend, I urge you to do that. But the devilish part of me wants you for the time I have left here."

He waited to see if she would react. If she slapped him again, he'd let her.

"Was that too honest, perhaps? So be it. Think about it."

With that, he left. Away from everything he'd just laid bare.

Chapter Twenty-Three

It was dark. The only things truly visible were the lights from the villa. Samya pushed herself up off the ground and shook her semi-numb legs. Brushing the dirt off the back of her dress, she tried to register her shock.

"*I want you.*"

He had verbalized it. He wasn't supposed to speak it into existence. They could have just kept stealing moments, a couple of kisses, and not talked about it. Samya's shock turned to hate. Well, now he'd ruined it. He'd taken the one thing that had been an escape for her, dammit.

Preoccupied, she walked back into the villa. She thought she and Hosseni had passed a kitchen earlier on their way out of the villa. Sure enough, down the hall she heard clinking and clanging of pots and pans. As she got closer, she could hear whispers.

"Don't tell him," a soft female voice said.

"What will you do?" another replied.

"I'll figure it out. *Salam.*"

Samya stepped into the kitchen and saw the back of a petite woman with a pink bandana exiting the servant's entrance. She could have sworn it was Ruqquyah. It couldn't be, though. She was hiding out with Zoo Zoo's friend. Before she could follow the mystery woman, Samya was stopped by a maid in her teens.

"Madame?" The maid was peeling potatoes, likely for tomorrow's lunch.

Great. Just great. Now, she looked old enough to be mistaken for a "Madame."

"Do you have a cup of bleach I might borrow?" Samya asked.

"Bleach, Madame?" The thin maid wiped her hands on her apron. She was fair with dark brown hair.

"Yes. And here's something for your trouble." She winked at the girl.

The girl, looking confused, took the money being offered and tucked it into her apron. She left for somewhere outside the kitchen and came back with a cup of bleach.

Samya took it, thanked her, and then asked a couple of questions about the layout of the villa.

As Samya walked up the red carpeted stairs, careful not to spill the liquid, she chided herself for not giving Jacques a good punch in the face. The impudence that man had.

Up ahead she counted "one, two, three" and stopped at the fourth door to the right of the stairs. She looked left and right to make sure she was alone before pushing the door open. Closing it behind her, she walked into a room lined with ceramic floors. There were black drawers, a black-framed king-sized bed, a desk and, ah, the bathroom. The room was as cold as its owner.

It was impressive how little time Samya needed to come up with these plans.

As she moved through the room, the thought crept up that she wouldn't see Jaques again. How could she? After he'd propositioned her like that? So, it was all-in or nothing with him, huh? *Why did he have to make everything so damn dramatic?* she thought as she walked into the bathroom and looked in the bathtub.

Maybe Jacques's bold, highly inappropriate proposal was a good thing. A little escape hatch from the mess she would inevitably be walking towards if she'd gotten involved with him.

She found a bottle labeled "Tawn Shampoo." Pausing to make sure no one would come in, she poured a tiny bit (she didn't want to burn the jerk) of the bleach into the shampoo, put the lid back on, and placed it back where she'd found it. As she left the room, she saw a monogrammed "Dr. Hosseni Gameel Waqab" pen on the desk. She was very tempted to break it. But thinking better of it, she closed the door behind her.

"Are you alright?" Hend asked Samya when she sat on the couch next to her sister in the Waqab salon. Samya must have looked a fright.

Thankfully, the men were long gone, having repaired to Dr. Amr's study, likely to smoke, drink, and talk politics.

Samya nodded her head and started piling sweets on a plate. She didn't want Hend to crack her open. She was ashamed to be sitting next to a sister whose life she was actively ruining. Hend raised an eyebrow but settled back into playing jacks with Hatem.

Ignoring her mother's disapproving looks, Samya stuffed a large piece of chocolate gateau into her mouth.

No more sulking and raging. It was time for problem solving.

What she had to control was her behavior. Yes, it would kill her inside, but she could and would change herself. She would be her mother's and society's darling. No, she wouldn't get married, but she would be a model citizen. Straighten her hair, wear pastel dresses, speak in whisper tones. Though that wouldn't last for long. She'd give it a month. A month to rehabilitate her image and secure Hend's future. Then off to the hospital, Greece, or somewhere far away from Cairo. Out of sight, out of mind, hopefully.

Her anger subsided with the knowledge she now had somewhat of a plan for Hend. It allowed some clarity to come in. One month. The same amount of time Jacques wanted to do...whatever with her. One month. With him. Ya Allah, Omar would have a fit and tell her "I told you so" if he found out what Jacques had proposed. Never mind him; what did she think of the whole thing?

As much as you'll allow.

As annoyed as she was that Jacques had let his feelings be known, she couldn't hide hers anymore. Here in the privacy of her mind, she could admit it. She wanted him. Every caress, laugh, and prank brought her closer and closer to him. To wanting to be near him. What if he could jump out of her mind, where he'd been all these months, and come to life? What if she could live for once?

The trouble was they weren't in Paris, where all of this could be done without society batting an eye. They were in Cairo, where holding hands in public was as good as a declaration of love. A torrid affair was only for the movies. Omar Sharif could grab Faten Hamama and devour her in front of Allah and everyone. In real life, the couple would be sent straight to a mosque to get hitched and then be ostracized from society for years. Shaming their families.

Surprisingly, she didn't find herself feeling any moral issue over the thing. Being chronically sick frees you of any of society's rules and restrictions. When you know you have no life, you are free to do whatever the hell you want. The trick was not getting caught and bringing those you love down with you.

Happiness crept up from her toes as she remembered nestling her head into Jacques's chest. The security of his hug. He'd held her when she'd needed to be held. Moments like these would pop up when she was stressed, sad, or even content. Memories. Memories with him. She wanted to collect memories before heading back to the hospital, which, given her mood lately, was more and more likely. But what Jacques was asking for she had no experience in. She'd never done anything past one awkward kiss in secondary school with a wonky-eyed boy who loved insects. And biting Jacques's thumb. Her cheeks flushed at remembering that.

"What do you mean *you* win?" Hend said as she tickled a giggling Hatem. Hend insisted she didn't like kids, but Samya always thought she would make the best mother. Of course, she would never say as much to Hend out of fear her petite but strong sister would deck her flat.

Oh, Hend.

Being with Jacques was high risk. That was for sure. Maybe Samya could bribe a couple of people and sneak out. Her mind was buzzing. Was she actually entertaining this? No. It was too risky. But then she thought of her future. It was bleak. Couldn't she gather a little bit of light before the darkness took over? Samya had no idea what to do. She stuffed another piece of chocolate gateau down her gullet.

Chapter Twenty-Four

For the first time since meeting Samya Roshdi, Jacques felt relief.

He had always been calm, cool, and collected in his normal life. Nothing rattled him. Nothing was serious enough that it couldn't be fixed with a cigar, a swig of whiskey, and a sense of humor. But ever since he'd snuck behind that mantrap yelling at a shop boy through her window at night, he'd become desperate, savage, unsure, and hungry. It may have been an indecent proposal he'd given her, but Jacques had got it all out in the open, and there would be a conclusion, one way or the other, to the frustration.

As he hopped onto the curb on the way in to his hotel, he couldn't help but smile. Finally in control again.

"*Ma sa il khair, ya basha*!" The doorman said as he held the door open.

"A good afternoon to you, too, Youssef!" Jacques said with a jaunt in his step. "How are the wife and kids, my man?"

"Wonderful, *Alhamdulilah*."

"Just peachy," Jacques said with a genuine smile.

Once he got to his room he pulled out a cigar at the dinette and sat in front of the luxurious canopy bed. He imagined Samya spread out, bare, curves and all. Then contemplated if the room would be good enough for her.

A bigger suite perhaps, Jacques thought. Yes, a grander suite. With champagne and roses. Samya would laugh at that. It would put her at ease.

He loved to make her laugh.

This felt good. To have it out of the way and be done with it. He wasn't sure if she would agree. But he chose to borrow the arrogant confidence he'd received from other women having welcomed him to their beds to convince himself that Samya would do the same. Though she wasn't like anyone he'd ever met. Samya was an enigma. One he desperately wished to decode.

No, no. No time for thinking too deeply about any of this. Deciding to capitalize on the rush of adrenaline, he closed the typewriter's built-in carry case and left the hotel for Zahrat El-Bustan. It was growing dark quickly, and the warm wind was swirling through the Cairo streets. Jacques went to flag down a taxi.

"Jacques!"

Jacques's face dropped. The very last soul he wanted to see now had found him: Samya's father. Dr. Mahmoud Roshdi, with his jolly presence and kind hazel eyes, came trotting over to Jacques.

"You left so suddenly, son. What serendipity to find you here!" Dr. Mahmoud shook Jacques's hand. "Where are you off to?" He looked at the typewriter.

Jacques collected himself. "A pleasure seeing you again, doctor. I'm off to the café to finish some pages. My editor is going to tan my hide if I don't send something by the end of the week."

Why was it every time he tried to get further with Samya, some relative or overprotective friend would come from nowhere and block him? Now it was the woman's father!

"Well, I won't keep you, son." Dr. Mahmoud made to walk away but then stopped.

"You know, son..."

"Yes, sir?" What now? The nicest man on the earth was about to awaken that conscience that Jacques needed to keep dormant.

"I want you to know you are very welcome in our house. Magda adores you, and the kids, too. It gets lonely, I think, in a country like this. I, well, want you to know." Dr. Mahmoud cleared his throat. "Magda, she talks incessantly, the woman. She worries about you a bit." He chuckled. "Anyone under sixty is a child to her. Don't be offended. Oh, don't mention I told you her age. Talk about tanning hides! But she wanted— We wanted you to know you have people here. You are very welcome anytime. For a meal or a drink. Anytime." Dr. Mahmoud cleared his throat again.

"Thank you, doctor. That means a lot," Jacques said, his hopes and dreams ripping themselves into shreds.

"Well, then. Good night, and good luck with your work, son." With that, Dr. Mahmoud was off.

Jacques sighed and put his head down. And for the first time since he'd been in Cairo, it started to rain. He walked his evil, ungrateful, and drenched ass back to the hotel.

"*Ma sa il noor, basha*!" Youssef said as he opened the door, wishing Jacques a good night.

Jacques smiled, dejected, and made his way to his room.

He plopped his typewriter on the desk by the window and got a towel from the bathroom to dry off his hair. Then he fell onto the bed face first. So how was he going to berate himself tonight? A good flogging like the medieval priests of old? He was a weasel of the lowest kind. The man welcomed him to his home. Jacques had a sneaking suspicion that Dr. Mahmoud, though a mostly socially oblivious, science-obsessed man, wanted him for a son-in-law. Aside from that, Dr. Mahmoud offered him the ultimate kindness. It was genuine. The man was genuine. And Jacques had propositioned his daughter as if she were a trollop.

He winced as he poured himself a generous two fingers of whiskey. Then slumped down onto the chair in front of the bedroom window.

Mon Dieu, the blank look on Samya's face when he'd made her his offer. She must hate him. He must have made her feel cheap. He was a selfish bastard. But he was honest. She prized honesty, right?

Now he was rationalizing. He was a stupid ass. She did not deserve this.

He loosened his tie. His lust was blinding him to decency. Logic had to reign. He did not want to admit it. No, he would have to do the right thing. He would write her a letter apologizing for the ill-bred ass he was and take the first train out of Cairo to avoid Samya until the month ran out, and he was headed back to France. No more innocent detours to Cairo or gatherings he had no business being a part of. No more convincing himself that this could work. Samya was off limits, and that was that.

He had to physically separate from her because he couldn't be trusted otherwise. There may not be a relative or friend to stop him next time.

A firm knock on his door woke him from his inner diatribe. Confused, he opened it.

Chapter Twenty-Five

Samya stood in the doorway, looking into Jacques's hotel room. Cloaked in a traditional black wrap she'd borrowed from Zoo Zoo, she held the upper part in place across her face so only her eyes were visible. The wrap consisted of layers of translucent black fabric but still did its job of concealing her identity.

"Samya?" Jacques asked.

"Shhh." Samya placed a hand on his chest, pushed him back into his room, and shut the door behind them. Raindrops hit the window panes, muzzling the sounds of the outside world.

She gathered all her courage, dropped the hood of the slightly damp wrap, and let her curls pop every which way. Samya took Jacques in. His eyes were wide. His chest felt strong, pulsating up and down underneath her hand. He was in trousers and a tucked-in button down. His tie hung loose around his neck. His dark hair was in all directions.

This man in disarray. This man was hers tonight.

"Yes" was all she said.

He seemed too stunned to say a thing as she closed the space between them, slowly but surely. She placed a hand on his jaw. The bristles felt rough over otherwise soft skin. Placing her other hand on his arm, she brought him closer to her. Samya looked up at him, expecting to see him smile or make some quip. Instead, he lowered his face to hers and caught her upper lip. Wrapping his arm around her lower waist, he pulled her into him.

First, it was chaste kisses. Soft and sweet. Then he licked her upper lip and moved his tongue in between her lips. He would make a move; she would mimic. He bit her lower lip softly; she bit his. He lightly brushed his tongue against hers; she would do the same. She was caught between lust and concentrating on learning and keeping up. At a certain point, she stopped thinking, ran her fingers through his hair and simply went with the flow. It was warm, wet, and new. She liked it. A lot. The friction in the small spaces between their bodies was intensifying. More, she wanted more.

Samya pulled away, panting, and met his eyes. "I don't know what to do next."

He barked his laughter. "That entrance says different, cherie."

"Pretty scandalous, no?" She beamed.

Catching her breath, Samya darted her gaze towards his slightly bruised lips, and she leaned forward. This close she could smell his cologne and see his Adam's apple go up and down as he swallowed. And feel that thick heat between them.

Samya reached up to his face, only to have him hold her hands, and bring them down.

"Wait." Jacques let go and took a couple of steps back.

"Wait?" It felt so cold. She needed his body back to continue to melt into hers.

"Samya, I did a bad thing today. I was fresh with you. You are not a lady to be propositioned the way I did to you this afternoon." He put her wrap over her hair. "I will escort you home."

The audacity of this man. She batted his hand away from her.

"No, you wait," Samya said. "I'm not doing this for you. I'm capable of making my own decisions."

"Of course, but..."

"Weren't you the one who wanted this? Well, I've thought it over, and I want this, too. For me. Selfishly, solely, for me." And it *was* for her. Memories. She was determined to collect moments, and memories.

"I understand but..."

Before he could continue, Samya swung him around and pushed him on top of the bed. She straddled him and put her hands on his shoulders. As if he wasn't over six feet and could bowl her over anytime he wished. They just stared at each other in stillness.

Samya broke the silence. "Well, I don't know this part."

He laughed, and pulled her in to a hug. "You can't even debauch me properly. Must I teach my own ravisher how to take advantage of me?"

She scowled and then bit him on his shoulder. He stopped laughing and flipped her over, so she was underneath. His body was back on hers, where it belonged. But she was still a bit rigid. What if she wasn't doing this right?

So when he captured her mouth again, she studied what his tongue was doing. Soft circles. Then, when she started losing herself again, on a whim, she sucked his tongue. Jacques moaned and went in more aggressively. So, he'd been holding back earlier. Her heart raced. She was gasping for air between kisses. Giving her a break, Jacques broke free and licked her under her jaw. She stiffened again. Where was he going? This was agonizing. She wanted him closer and closer. Now, building a chain of kisses down her neck, he bit her shoulder.

She gasped. "Copy cat!"

Jacques wiggled his eyebrows and continued. Then he opened up the wrap she was wearing, revealing a robin blue, lace brassiere and matching knickers she had bought on a family trip to Milan.

With such care, Jacques opened her legs apart with his knee. She tensed. Jacques kissed her cheek and then whispered, "Are you sure?"

"Yes," she whispered in a voice simultaneously reticent and firm.

Jacques moved his fingers from her lips to her throat to her breast before dropping her brassiere lower to expose her breast. Samya took in a sharp breath.

Jacques paused. He lifted her brassiere back up. "We don't need to do anything. I would be happy to just lie here with you."

She shook her head and kissed him in the new way she'd just learned. She'd be damned if she let her nervousness take over. "I want you."

Samya pushed him out of the way, stood up, and dropped her wrap to the ground. Closing her eyes, she exhaled a deep breath, unhooked her brassiere, and let that drop, too. She had learned from her male friends that men liked all types of women. Jacques would like her, naked and all, she reassured herself. Shaking her head, she decided she would not miss this chance.

Samya climbed back in bed, grabbed his hand, and tried to position it where it had been before. Shoving his head back to her breast, she looked down towards him, motioning for him to carry on as if he were a server at a restaurant.

He smirked, locked eyes with her, and licked her nipple as if his tongue was a dew-sprinkled feather brushing her sensitive skin. Samya closed her eyes as her body shivered. When she was able to collect coherent thought, she surmised she was supposed to return the favor. So she unbuttoned his shirt and licked his nipple.

He chuckled. "Well, thank you, Fred."

Oh, no, a faux paus. "Don't you feel something?"

"Let's concentrate on what you feel." He went back to her face and kissed her, all the while slipping his hand underneath her knickers. His hand brushed against parts she was too timid to name aloud.

He stopped and looked at her inquisitively. "You prepared, did you?"

She thoroughly scolded herself for feeling embarrassed. "Well, I wasn't sure. Ladies sugar wax down there before their wedding night, so I thought...oh, shut up, you awful man."

He pulled his hand out, and cupped her breast while lightly circling her nipple with his thumb. Rolling over, Jacques positioned Samya on top of him. Yet again, she was straddling him. Something protruding in between her legs was poking to get inside.

"Hmm, so *he's* feeling something, then. "

"You awful woman." Jacques sat up and covered her mouth with his. There were so many sensations. Their lips moving, her gripping both his arms, his hands moving to grasp both her thighs tightly.

Then there was this raw feeling. It was as if her heart was beating in her loins. The feeling was rolling around, picking up steam. She tightened her thighs on him, squeezing, squeezing. Grabbing his arms tight, she closed her eyes and instinctively started rocking back and forth. She was rubbing herself against his mound. Then he lifted up to match her rhythm, making her moan. That thing she couldn't describe got stronger and stronger with each stroke. It was as if her insides were on fire.

There was something about him being beneath her. Like she could spend the rest of her life on top of him like this. The realization of that and looking into his hooded eyes slowed her down for long enough that she could bend down and kiss him. This time she didn't have any practiced intention. It was just soft. A reminder that they were both here with each other.

Jacques eyes widened for a second before he closed them and took a shaky breath. To her puzzlement, he gripped her hips and held her still for a long moment in silence.

Still closing his eyes, he murmured, "Mon Dieu."

Gently, he rolled her off of him. That something inside her roared in displeasure. Why had they stopped? Perspiration was gathering on her face and trickling into her hair. Her heartbeat was slowing down. All she could see when she looked over at him was his bulge practically begging to be set free of his pants. Of its own volition, her hand went to touch it. She'd always wondered how it would feel.

Jacques chuckled and stopped her hand. "I need a second, cherie." He said with his chest moving rapidly.

They were silent for a bit. She folded her hands atop each other underneath her exposed breasts, hoping they could get back to what they'd been doing. Something inside her was ravenous, and it needed to be fed. With each passing moment, it was getting slower, less wild. She didn't want it to stop. Rock, she wanted to rock again. What the hell was he thinking? With a loud sigh, she hoped to get his attention so they could carry on. But there was no response. Jacques was as still as a corpse.

After what seemed like forever, he sat up in the bed and kissed her on the forehead. "*Now*, I'm taking you home."

"What? Why?!" Samya protested as Jacques stepped away from the bed.

"Because this is a mistake."

Samya opened her mouth to go on a tirade about independence when Jacques interrupted. "And before you chastise me about how you are an adult, and you know your own mind. Consider that I am making this decision for myself."

Hurt, she took the comforter off the bed, and wrapped it around herself, realizing how exposed she was. "You don't want me?"

"It's not about what I want." He picked up her wrap from the ground. "Believe me," he muttered. "But you are the daughter of a respected colleague and…"

Samya was livid. "This is my business! Didn't you say you were an utter whore? Well, here I am willing to be a whore with you. Don't play upstanding citizen now!"

Jacques lifted up a hand for her to stop. "*You* are not a whore, but point taken. *I* want to observe some modicum of respect for you. So that *I* can look myself in the mirror without wanting to punch my reflection in. I would be putting you at too high a risk. In a societal sense, and a personal sense. Believe it or not, Samya, I like you. Very much. And my like trumps my lust."

He put her brassiere in a conveniently placed pocket inside the wrap, handed it back to her, and kissed her on the forehead.

He hesitated. "I'll be heading to Alexandria soon, so this is goodbye."

She didn't look at him. Tears were threatening to gush from her. What was so wrong with her? Had she done something wrong? She must have.

"I'll take myself home. I've made arrangements."

Once she reached the doorway, she turned around. "My lust trumps my like. I wish you would catch up to me."

He did not reply.

Humiliation, anger, hurt, vindictiveness, and a whole spectrum of other emotions were threatening to burst out of Samya. Instead, she turned and left him.

CHAPTER TWENTY-SIX

"Train to Alexandria is cancelled," the porter at Cairo train station called out.

"*Yusta*, when is the next train?" Jacques inquired.

"Not until tomorrow morning."

Jacques sighed. Of course. Of course, he would be stuck in this godforsaken place for another night. Jacques was in a foul mood, and he couldn't pin down what he was the most angry about. Himself, his behavior, or Samya, for her willingness to participate in a horrendous idea. Yesterday night had solidified the need for immediate departure. The old carousel played in his head once more; he needed to put as much distance between him and Samya as possible. The next time the consequences would be irreversible. She'd merely stepped into his room, and he'd lost himself completely.

If only her skin wasn't so damn soft. And how unabashedly she took to pleasure. She was a virgin, so he'd been forcing himself to go slow. But when she'd locked her thighs onto him, he'd been about to unbutton his trousers hastily and enter her. He'd even forgotten about safes. He hadn't been thinking.

She'd been a curious little kitten. Biting, licking, grinding. He'd been more than happy to oblige her. But that inexperienced honey had made him lose his mind. He, who had had many, *many* affairs with a variety of women. To imagine, *he* would be felled by an innocent who had likely done nothing more than hold hands up until this point.

Jacques made his way out of the train station to a curb to hail down a taxi. The call to prayer was blaring in the distance. Many drivers would be at the mosque, so he would have to wait even longer for a taxi than normal. Paris couldn't come soon enough. He needed to knock boots with someone, anyone. With no restrictions, complications, or guilt-inducing fathers. *La petite aventure* would bring him back to himself. It had to.

"Jacques?"

A man in his early fifties with a gray mustache beckoned to Jacques from the taxi line. He was wearing a rather wrinkled brown suit. Jacques recognized the man vaguely from one of the soirees he'd attended.

The pink-nosed, corkscrew-haired man extended his hand for a hearty handshake. "Khalid Routby."

"*Oustaz* Khalid, how wonderful to see you. I was headed to Alex, but the train won't resume until tomorrow at the earliest."

"Yes, yes. Terribly inefficient mode of travel. I have no further excuse to run away from the wife this evening." He chuckled. "She is at the Abaza's for dinner and was lamenting the fact that her husband must rush back to Ismailia for work. I would gladly sleep in the station if it meant avoiding those gatherings, but I'm rather starving. Are you headed for dinner?"

Jacques grinned. "I'm heading back to the hotel. I wish you a bountiful, but hopefully short-lived, meal."

"No, no. If I'm going, you must as well." Before Jacques could argue, *Oustaz* Khalid grabbed him by the arm. "You're a bachelor. I insist you get a home-cooked meal even if you have to sit through mindless conversation. It's just our family and theirs. Very informal, I assure you."

Jacques found he was too exhausted to object any further. After a couple of minutes, he was ushered into a taxi by *Oustaz* Khalid. Jacques would make an appearance and leave within ten minutes. He was in no mood for company.

***

By the time *Oustaz* Khalid and Jacques arrived at the Abaza's in their shared taxi, Jacques had learned everything there was to know about him, down to his blood type. Normally, Jacques would find this sort of quirky oversharing endearing. Tonight, he was anxious.

The Abaza's villa was modeled in a Spanish style. It was very chic, with its cream walls and dark brown trim. The exterior was especially outstanding, with several balconies wrapped around the structure for all to admire the surrounding city lights and the palm trees laid against the night sky.

Dinner had already begun, so *Oustaz* Khalid and Jaques were taken straight to the dining room. A surprise to no one, this was no small dinner between two families. Approximately twenty-five people sitting around the dining table welcomed them all in good cheer. Jacques should have known better by now. No gathering in Cairo had less than half the population attending.

There was space enough at the end of the table for one of the maids to get them chairs and place settings. Sitting towards the middle of the table were Madame Magda and Hend, Jacques saw. At least Samya wasn't there. Too tired to care, he dug into his food and avoided eye contact.

Towards the last course, he finally looked up. There was a woman sitting next to Hend who had stiff straight hair done up in an updo. Wearing a pink dress adorned with pearls, she was facing away from Jacques towards her partner, her hands neatly folded. Any other time this would have been unremarkable, but there was something about her.

The mystery woman turned towards him, and they briefly locked eyes before she pulled away immediately. Samya.

That passing moment was enough to rack up his body temperature. In between bites and conversation with *Oustaz* Khalid, he stole glances at her.

It was quite odd. She barely talked but wore a small, pasted-on smile. Her hand gestures that normally threatened anyone within arm's length of her were contained. Though once or twice he saw her about to use her hands when she spoke and then restrain herself.

"Samya, you have so much in common with Muhammad, don't you?" he overheard Madame Magda say.

Another suitor, then. He leaned closer to hear the biting comeback that Samya would have locked and loaded.

"Yes, mama." She patted her mother's hand. "We've been having the most delightful conversation." Then she looked at the man to her left and allowed him to kiss her hand.

"Jacques, are you alright?" *Oustaz* Khalid inquired.

Jacques schooled his features. "Yes, thank you."

Anger was bubbling up inside of him. It wasn't jealousy. He knew that one, he had no right to be jealous, and two, Samya Roshdi had no interest in the man she'd just let kiss her hand. The anger was on her behalf.

None of my business.

The dinner passed, and the guests were invited to mingle in the salon.

Samya unlinked her arm from the man, excused herself, ever so politely, and headed out to the balcony.

Jacques ought to have left the dinner right then and there. He'd socialized enough so that it would not be considered rude to leave early. He ought to, but his feet contrarily took him towards the balcony.

The balcony was so vast that it was more like a separate mansion unto itself. He casually, but not really so casually, looked for her. Finally, in a dark corner hidden away from the dinner guests, he found her slumped against a wall, playing with her pearl necklace and looking at the ink-black night ahead of her. Below, cars zipped noisily through the street. There was a group of old men gossiping, playing checkers, and smoking *shisha* in a cafe. Stars glittered brilliantly above the whole scene.

"Why are you dressed like that?" was the very first thing he said to her.

Sounding a bit bored and unaffected by his presence, she replied. "Because being nude at a dinner party isn't becoming."

He scoffed. "What is this?" He gestured towards her body. "And your flirting with that man in there. You aren't interested in that square."

She looked at him, incredulous. "Oof. Don't be so cliche, Jacques. Another boy is playing with your discarded toy, and now you want it back."

"I didn't say I wanted anything back. I'm commenting on whatever odd act you were putting on out there."

"Well, your commentary is not welcome, appreciated, or accepted. Leave before I really get angry." Samya turned back to the vast night sky.

A less unhinged individual would read the situation and gracefully exit the conversation that would eventually lead to a volatile mess. But Jacques's "unhingedness" was particularly high at the moment.

"Was it what Hosseni said? Is it your mother? Since when do you care what the hell they think? You've never cared what anyone thinks."

Samya did not look at him, nor did she react. He was so heated, he didn't feel the chill of the night. So he kept going.

"I hate this dress." He motioned toward her body and then settled on her face. "And I hate this hair. And I loathed that smile you had in there. It's all fake." He started pacing. "And didn't I say there was nothing wrong with you? Don't you listen? Who the hell cares what that prick says or thinks? There's not a damn thing wrong with…"

"Stop it!" Samya snapped. "It is none of your business what I wear, how I act, or who I talk to. So take this righteous tantrum and direct it towards some other woman you haven't rejected and humiliated."

"You are twisting what happened."

"That is *exactly* what happened." She threw her hands up in the air. "Ya Allah, you are frustrating. I rue the day I ever accepted cigarettes from you at my family's villa. The minute I saw you coming down the hall, I should have jumped out the window."

"Believe me, if I knew what I know now, I would have pushed you off the ledge myself."

To hell with the formalities. The pair of them were loud, and neither was backing down.

"Great! We are in agreement that we never want to see each other again. So go!" Samya said.

"I'm going!"

Jacques stayed exactly where he was. "But I will say this. You are a horrible actress, and you would be wise to think twice before going through with a sham of a marriage because you think it would somehow make things easier for Hend."

"I thought you said you were going!"

"I am. Immediately."

He was rooted to the spot. He caught whiffs of the night jasmine that always followed her as if it were a part of her soul. It only spurred him on further.

"Heaven forbid you give Hend, an adult by the way, or anyone the hell else a chance to potentially help you out. No, you have to shoulder every burden like a damn self-inflicted martyr!"

"I can't listen to any more of this. Why are you still here? Why, when you have made it entirely clear you want nothing to do with me? You don't need to worry about running away to another city in fear I would chase you down because I'm so besotted. I've moved on. Leave, Jacques."

She pushed him away from her. "I'm tired of your mercurial nature and the back and forth. Leave, and don't ever talk to me again."

"I'm leaving. I'll take your advice. I won't come back."

"It wasn't advice; it was a command. So leave."

"I will."

Jacques's body wouldn't move. He'd worked himself into a tizzy and was breathing irregularly. Samya's chest was similarly rising in a quick rhythm. Her eyes were full of unshed, angry tears.

Then his body betrayed him once more. He grabbed her into a tight hug and kissed her.

CHAPTER TWENTY-SEVEN

It was a maddening kiss, full of anger, frustration, desperation, longing. Jacques eventually ended it softly so both of them could breathe.

He leaned his head against hers. "I don't know what to do, Samya. Tell me what to do, and I'll do it."

She pulled him closer into the dark corner. "Stay."

He grinned. "But I thought you rued the day you met me."

She shrugged. "I'm not one to live in the past."

He kissed her neck. "Can you meet tonight?"

Samya looked away as if she was doing a complicated math equation. Finally, she said. "Yes, I'll slip out and come to your hotel."

"We can go to my villa in Sharah Mohammed Ali. I'll pick you up at midnight."

"No." She brushed her fingers through his hair. "I will find a way there on my own. I'll work it out. Safer that way."

He kissed her once more. "The dress is not so bad, you know. I was just angry."

"Mmhmm. Best to keep that pretty mouth shut for now," Samya responded.

He laughed. After adjusting her dress and her hair, he tapped her on the ass and told her to go back to the gathering first.

"Until tonight."

"Till tonight."

And for the first time that day, Jaques felt at ease.

***

Jacques paced the hall of his father's villa. He almost never stayed at one of his father's—well, now his own—properties. Jacques preferred the transitive nature of hotels. One where he could pick up and leave, with little to no maintenance. But he owed Samya a place big and secluded enough for them to have freedom and privacy.

His father's villa was decorated as if made for an English detective from the 1900s. Green leather chairs with brown wood frames. Red patterned rugs. Cherrywood center and side tables guarded the salon. Lamps were encased in stained glass with geometrically challenged flowers. Paintings of rural life, chickens, sheep, and donkeys were placed without nuance throughout the various rooms. It was like stepping out of the city into a Sherlock Holmes novel. In one of his father's studies, he found a case with all manner of pipes and tobacco just like what Abdo would smoke with little Jacques on his lap. He remembered that long-ago smell. The villa was full of relics like that, causing both nostalgia and confusion.

Thinking of Samya's swollen lips after their kiss and her wide hips that swayed to and fro, Jacques couldn't wait. And any sense of hesitation that he might have had a mere hour ago would not slow him down. He was not going to overthink it. He was too far gone for that. And after being with her for a couple of times and getting it out of both of their systems, he would likely do what he always did: get bored and leave.

He chose to trust. Trust that Samya knew how to handle herself. Trust that she wouldn't fall apart when he did leave. And now he was thinking too much again.

The doorbell made its sound of birds chirping, and he bolted for the door. A familiar hooded figure with molten brown eyes stood at the doorway.

"Hello." Samya grinned as she pulled her hood down to look up at him. Her hair was wet and starting to curl from tip to root.

"Hello." He put his hand on her cheek and leaned in for a kiss when he was stopped with an open-faced palm.

"Business first," Samya proclaimed and strode ahead of him. "Where can we sit?"

Puzzled but not surprised by this unconventional woman he'd chosen to entangle himself with, he motioned to the salon. A bit more conscious of the decor now that Samya was here, Jacques thought he would like to make a couple of updates, if he were to ever stay here. Which he would never do, not for the long term, anyway.

Samya sat on one of the green velvet couches, crossing one leg over the other. Her lustrous right leg peaked through the black fabric. The orange glow from the lamps showed off the luxury of her glowing bronze skin.

"Now, when we last met, you had concerns about this." Samya motioned between them. "I've thought about it, and I think they are valid."

"Do you now?" Jacques sat next to her and started nuzzling her neck. Pushing him away, she motioned for him to sit across from her, which he grudgingly did.

"I'm assuming you were concerned that due to my lack of experience, I would get too attached, which is a bit arrogant, but beside the point. I would get too attached to you and would want things you couldn't give me, namely marriage, I'm assuming?"

"Among other things, but you are correct." Jacques said.

"I've never wanted to get married. I don't plan to get married to you or anyone else. It is not a future I want. But I'm guessing you won't just take my word for it."

Jacques raised an eyebrow in assent.

"You are equally concerned about the societal implications of this arrangement."

These were the very topics Jacques did not want to think about. But he nodded.

"Which is why..." She continued. "...I want to set some rules."

"We haven't had drinks yet. Are you thirsty?"

Samya shook her head and snapped her fingers. "Pay attention! We need to get this out of the way."

He grinned like a Cheshire cat, leaned back, and put one hand on the side of his face. "Go on, then."

"One, this is for one month only. The exception is if one of us would like to cut this short earlier."

He nodded.

"Two, we have minimal to no contact and no socializing in public. We can be cordial but nothing beyond that. We will be around each other at dinners and parties in front of people, and as you so bluntly pointed out, my acting skills are not great. So the less we talk, the better. In fact, we should strategize to make sure we stagger our attendance.

"Three, I do not intend to get pregnant and so you will always wear a safeguard."

Admiring her forwardness, Jacques put his hand on his heart. "I agree."

"Not done yet. Four, when you are with me, you are with *me*. No one else."

Jacques chuckled. "I couldn't possibly handle anyone else but you."

"Is that a yes?"

"Unequivocal yes."

"Alright." She took a breath. "Here." She handed him a Cairo train station ticket. "It's a ticket in my name to Alex. I've already told one of my aunts that I'm going to be there one month from today to help with my grandmother, who's becoming a bit senile. I have created an obligation for myself that I cannot get out of. So even if I'm teaming with lust and addiction to you..." She gestured sarcastically. "I'll still have to leave, giving both of us a clean separation."

Jacques took a breath and looked at the smart woman in front of him. Her face was scrunched up, forming a line between her eyes. Her hair was shortening by the minute as it curled. He could get high merely from looking at her. No, he wasn't going back on his word, but he would give her an out if she needed it. Please God, don't let her take it.

"Sex complicates things. It tends to heighten emotion, which is great and then painful. You'll likely be hurt at the end of all of this. Are you sure you want to do this?"

"I'm not naive enough to think I'll be unaffected. I will. But I will also not die. I'm an adult. This is an experience I want to have because I will not have the chance after this. And, well, here you are offering it. So it's convenient enough."

"How flattering!" He thought about what she might mean about not ever having the experience again but reminded himself not to overthink anything now.

"You need to be taken down a peg. So do we have a deal?" She extended her hand out to him.

He clasped it and pulled her onto his lap.

"I have one more rule to add." He caressed her silky thigh. "Five, when you are with me, *you* are with me."

"Who else would you think would be here? " she scoffed.

Jacques shook his head. "I mean, I want to be with Samya. Not the society-approved Samya, just the you Samya."

"I intend to be society Samya in public from now on, you know. Straight hair, prim clothes, bad acting. I won't change that."

"So long as you are yourself with me." He kissed her on the nose. "In private."

She thought about it for a second. "I can do that."

"Great!"

She yelped as he swooped her up off the chair, over his shoulder, and jetted across the hall to the master bedroom.

"Jaques!"

"I have thirty days with you, and this one is almost over."

He put her down, yanked his shirt off, and motioned to her. "Strip. We have lessons to catch up on."

Chapter Twenty-Eight

Samya removed her cloak and shimmied out of her nightgown, which she was struggling with given an almost naked Jacques was nearby. Her lacy black knickers were the only piece of clothing she left on. For some reason she was more timorous now than she'd been during their first encounter. There was no going back at this point. They were both committed.

"Lessons?" she managed to bite out. "I came here to escape responsibility, not go to school."

"Don't worry, these are fun lessons. And I'm a great teacher. Now get over here before I have to spank you for being an insolent student."

"I'm not anyone's student!"

"Mmm." Jacques gave her a lopsided smirk. He looked equal parts big bad wolf and playful kitten. So dangerous, yet so safe.

Samya's feet clenched and relaxed on the plushy rug. The walls were an olive green, which was a nice contrast to the dark wood of the king-sized bed frame. The maroon curtains were drawn, but there was soft lighting coming from stained glass lamps. She walked towards the bed to meet Jacques. Trying to gather her soupy insides, she reverted to her comfort zone: anger.

"Listen here. I will not be ordered around for these next thirty days. Just because I don't have enough experience..."

Jacques picked her up and dropped her on the bouncy bed. Hovering over her, he leaned in and kissed her softly. Their lips barely touched. How could such a tiny movement create such inner turmoil?

These moments with this man made her want things. And she was so off balance in his presence that, for once, there wasn't any time to wonder if she even deserved them.

His body was lean but muscular. His pecs and down his arm, he felt hard compared to her plushness. Jacques continued kissing her in the most tender yet unnerving manner. When her want—no, her need—was too much, she tried grabbing him to get better access to his mouth. She wanted to practice what she'd learned last time. Refusing her request, he continued going at the slowest pace possible.

It was maddening. "Jacques!"

Heavy lidded eyes looked back at her. "Hmm."

"Stop torturing me, damn you."

His black hair was tousled. He kissed the corner of her mouth and then licked her cheek.

"I thought you didn't want to waste time." Samya huffed and tried to get back up.

He continued on as if he hadn't heard her. Trailing kisses down her stomach. Each one leaving behind an invisible symbol of Jacques's care. As frustrated as she was, she could recognize the sweetness in his touch. Touch that comforted and excited her.

Feeling more at ease, Samya sat up a bit, and caressed his jaw. He brought her hand up to his face and kissed it. They looked at each other. Samya tried to study the lines of his face. The birthmark under his right eye. His full lips. His thick brows. That familiar cedar and linen smell surrounding them. Memories. She was collecting memories. And she needed them to be as vivid as possible.

Without warning, he pulled both her legs to the edge of the bed. With care, he placed a small burgundy pillow underneath her lower back. As Jacques knelt on the floor, Samya's body became taut.

The first time they'd been intimate, he likely hadn't seen her legs. This time he was up close. He would see the scars. Samya's shame. At one of her hospital stints, when the pain was too much, she'd cut her thighs, where no one could see, in an attempt to get some relief. It was something she'd only done once in a fit of desperation. Her skin had never healed properly, and the scars left behind were noticeable. The bedroom they were in wasn't dark enough. And even if he couldn't see them, he would surely feel them. She moved her hand to cover them.

He held that hand and looked up at her with a reassuring smile. "Relax, cherie."

The embarrassment quelled a bit as she lay back down. Then she felt him kiss her scars, one by one. Little kisses that were refreshing icy tingles, soothing her. He made her feel wanted, precious. Kind, warm hands parted her legs open. She wasn't sure what would be next, but her heart started to race. The most peculiar thing happened. She felt his tongue swipe over her knickers! Just that small movement heated her insides. In the gentlest manner, Jacques grabbed the sides of the lacy fabric and pulled it off of her. With her being completely exposed, he nibbled her inner thigh and made her shudder.

It was a bit awkward as she couldn't see his face. The man was on a mission to do...something, and he was not to be interrupted. But she could feel him. His every move left an impression on her skin.

Bracing for the next move, Samya realized she was clenching her rear. As she relaxed it, another strange occurrence took place. A slight wet prod, down there! His mouth was on her. His tongue was lightly stroking the tiniest piece of her up and down. Impossibly slow. Internally telling herself to stay loose, her body tried and failed. She was unfamiliar with all of it.

Jacques abruptly stilled and then moved his tongue as if he were writing a love letter with it. Immediately, she tensed and let out a yelp.

"Jacques!"

He laughed. "Trust me, cherie."

And the strange thing was, she did. Letting him dive back down, she grabbed the sheets underneath her for support. If she wasn't so overwhelmed, she might have felt obligated to be self-conscious. But in this moment thinking was not something her body was allowing her to do. Jacques continued his hypnotic caress and gripped her rear with his hands. The pattern he chose was awakening something inside of her. There was a deep ache. The faster he went, the deeper the ache. It was as if an ocean wave was building and building and building. Gathering to an impossible height seemingly with no end. A small heartbeat started throbbing down below, getting progressively louder and quicker. Strands of her wet hair stuck to her face. Her nails were now scraping the sheets as she instinctually, and brazenly, moved along with Jacques's tongue.

Right then she could feel Jacques with her. It was *his* hands that were grasping onto her. It was *his* mouth lovingly directing her. *His* body bracing her. Making her soar. This was more than just physical sensation. Thankful, she was so thankful it was him.

The emotion of the situation overtook her. She had to close her tearing eyes to try to control herself. The little pulse got more persistent, bigger, wilder, out of control, until she couldn't take it anymore. Her eyelids were blinking rapidly. Desperation possessed her. Without thinking, her hands frantically secured his head to her, afraid he would stop before she got the release she urgently needed. Grabbing his hair, she screamed as the wave finally crashed over her entire body.

She shattered into a million pieces, falling into nothingness. For a while, she no longer existed.

Slowly, she came back together. From her waist down, she couldn't feel. Her limbs were pleasantly numb. It was as if someone had injected liquid affection into her veins. Exhaustion was taking over.

Jacques climbed back over her limp form. With a kiss on her mouth, he remarked, "That was lesson one."

Breathing heavily, she could barely hear him. "What?"

"We call it 'la petite mort.' Welcome back to earth, Fred."

The term was accurate.

She looked towards his sex, which was pointed outward. "Your turn?" she asked feebly.

He shook his head. "Don't worry. We have more lessons to get through."

Jacques gathered her up in his arms. There was no energy to question anything. So Samya allowed the angel/devil of a man take hold of her as she drifted into the deepest sleep she'd ever had.

Chapter Twenty-Nine

Other than Hend remarking on the lightness in Samya's mood, no one seemed to have an inkling as to Samya's double life.

Since the first night of what Jacques deemed their "month of debauchery," Samya's days were filled with straightening her hair, wearing pastel, out-of-date hoop dresses, speaking only when spoken to, and giggling lightly at jokes from potential suitors who had no sense of humor. Jacques and Samya did their best to spread out her societal obligations so their paths wouldn't cross. On the one hand, she was giddy. On the other, her sadness was increasing a bit. She chalked it up to fear of the future. As hard as she tried, she didn't know if her efforts to fit into society would ever be enough to save her family from her.

So her days were restrained. But her nights were anything but.

In his villa, they went through a veritable checklist that involved everything from fingers, to licking, grinding and a litany of other fun, naughty things Samya had no idea existed. During their third night together, after some play, he was inside her. That was the "traditional sex" she'd known about from medical textbooks and the whispers she would overhear from older women gossiping about their husbands's capabilities (or lack thereof). Those women were liars. It was uncomfortable and painful. She worried it would stay that way. But the more they did it, the better and better it felt. With every day, new feelings were pouring out: want, need, joy, pleasure, belonging, passion, power, indulgence.

The best thing of all was that Jacques gave Samya the space and freedom to explore what she liked and what she didn't. And what she liked was biting him. There were times where, even though they were together, she felt she wasn't close enough to him. That need to be close welled up in such intense energy that she had to bite him to fully take him in.

And he let her. He seemed to relish it. Whenever she left a mark on his neck, he would tell people it was from a pesky, ill-behaved cat he'd taken in.

Though the physical intimacy was great, what she really savored was her time with him. They talked, bickered, and laughed for hours on end. She would skip dinner at home so she could eat with him at his villa, and they could chat about their days. She learned more about his mother and how sick she'd been. How his father had left them when Jacques was a teenager and how his mother and he had struggled financially for years. As a boy, he would charm the next-door neighbors so much they would invite him over for dinner. It was an opportunity during the tougher times to sneak bread from the neighbors' table to bring to his mother. The stories that poured out of him made her understand his hatred of his father, his guilt towards his mother and, unintentionally, his hesitance about being with Samya.

His mother hadn't been sick in the way Samya was. Vivienne, Jacques's mother, apparently had days where she was happy, played with little Jacques, and would eat sweets with him until they crashed. The good times. Then there were the days she wouldn't leave her room. Not even to bathe. Screaming at and hitting Jacques became a common occurrence during those times. The unfortunate woman suffered and had thought that eliminating herself was the only way to give her son a better life. Samya could identify with the sentiment, though it may have been misguided in Vivienne's case.

Samya also shared more about her stints at the hospital. And would make Jacques laugh at her adventures in torturing Dr. Foad. It was a strange thing to be able to laugh about such dark times. This was another new plus. Being able to talk to someone so freely about her past and potential future. She did hold back some things, like the catatonia. Not because she was worried about how Jacques would take it. But she didn't want to enter such a painful thing into the new bond they were forming.

She acted in ways she never would have thought she could in front of anyone. Never once did he make her feel strange or wrong. At first she'd feared that Jacques would get bored with someone so inexperienced. That thought was quickly trampled by his unwavering enthusiasm. During lovemaking she would look at his face and see him unravel. The sight served to heighten her pleasure. Perhaps he was like that with all his lovers but at least he was entertained.

With Jacques, she got to be silly. He made her feel taken care of. The fact she allowed anyone to care for her was a miracle in and of itself. And for the first time in her life, he gave her someone to care about without having to worry she might ruin his life. This was temporary. There was no harm.

Throughout her life, Samya had been on guard. Her illness being taboo, she'd been forced to hide to survive. Often that hiding was done behind a wall of toughness. Many coined her "aggressive" as a result. Jacques already knew of her illness and never shied away from it. There was nothing to hide. She wasn't afraid he would reject her if she was too loud or picked a fight with him. He gave as good as he got.

Being with Jacques was living in unquenchable thirst. Despite herself, Samya recognized that she was getting too attached.

Her psyche constantly hacked through those weeds of wanting and hope with a sickle. She had to keep reminding herself that this would end. Their nocturnal life was a protected haven that would eventually crumble. Besides all of that, Jacques likely didn't feel the same longing she did.

So she prepared herself daily for the inevitable heartbreak that was hurling her way in a matter of weeks when things would end. There was a constant push and pull between enjoying the moment and dreading the future.

It felt like she was staring straight at the sun. She would be blinded, but what a glorious sight in the meantime.

***

One night, Samya woke to Jacques coming into the bedroom with half of a pita bread in his mouth. He looked delicious with his pajama bottoms hanging low on his hips, revealing a line of black hair that trailed from his stomach to underneath his pants. Samya was sitting at the head of the bed with her knees up. Positioning himself in between Samya's legs, Jacques sat down with his back resting on her. Instead of feeling crushed, she loved the weight of him. Instinctively, she wrapped her legs around his stomach.

"Ya, that's so disgusting."

"What?" he mumbled as he chewed.

"You eating in bed, is what."

He stroked one of her legs. "It's the one luxury I allow myself."

Samya rolled her eyes while she played with Jacques's hair. "You have multiple Rolex watches, imported cigars, expensive scotch. That's hardly the only luxury you allow."

He chuckled. "Does it really bother you?"

His hair was soft and malleable. "It's just that crumbs will get everywhere."

He shrugged. "So I'll lick them off of you."

"Then you'll get ants. And they'll crawl all over me."

He turned around to face her. "The only thing allowed to crawl all over you in this bed is me." He threw the rest of the bread onto his desk.

She grabbed his hair and pulled his head back. "So if I want you to do anything, I just have to make you jealous?" She licked his neck.

"Jealousy is a powerful thing." He shivered. "Samya, I know what you're doing."

She blew on his neck. "What?"

With a devious grin, she tickled his neck, and he jerked, laughing uncontrollably. Eventually, he broke free from her, and Samya was tearing up from laughter. Then she saw his face. The devil was dancing in his eyes.

She got up off the bed and put her hands up. "Wait, wait. Don't. That's unfair."

Rounding him, she bolted. She only made it as far as the sitting room before he tackled her onto the couch.

"Jacques!" She screamed and giggled as he pinned her down. She was sandwiched between the softness of the couch cushion and the hardness of his body.

Failing to grab his hands before they found their target, she yelled. "Truce! Truce!"

"Why should I?"

"Because I said so!"

He positioned his hand underneath her armpit.

"Okay, okay! Because I'll do that thing that I'm embarrassed to say, but you like so damn much."

He smiled. Then sat on the couch and pulled her onto his lap.

They stayed in companionable silence with her resting her head on his shoulder trying to catch her breath. And him twisting her curls with his finger.

"Jacques?"

"Hmmm."

"Have you ever been in love?"

Normally, she would never ask him a question like that. It was too intimate and implied something she didn't want him to think. But over the past week, she'd felt so comfortable around him. There was a feeling that she could ask him anything.

He paused, looked up, and then back at her. "Many times."

Samya wasn't surprised, nor was she disappointed. Part of knowing Jacques was understanding how much capacity he had for acceptance and love.

"What's it like?"

"Well, like being obsessed. Everything you see is tinted with a wash of greatness. Even their passing gas is a source of wonder."

Samya made a disgusted face, and he laughed.

He buried his face in her neck and started to kiss her. "Why do you ask?"

"Lobna always takes Hend and me to the movies. They portray being in love in the way you just explained. I always wondered if that was how it really was. It's only that in your books..."

Jacques froze.

"Yes, I read them both."

He put his hands on his face.

She chuckled and held on to his wrists. "Don't you want to hear what I have to say about them?"

"When in the hell did you read them?" he asked with his hands still covering his eyes.

She hesitated. "Don't get a big head, but a couple of days after I met you."

He pulled his fingers apart, so one eye peeked through. "And?"

She put on a look of mock pity.

"Oh, no."

She chuckled. "Look at me." He put his hands down but kept his eyes closed shut. She kissed him on the cheek. "I couldn't put them down. I read them both in a week."

He opened his eyes. "Truly?"

"Truly."

He exhaled and smirked. "I had no doubt."

"I'm sure." She laughed. "The thing is, the way Victor and Esther loved each other...what was the line? 'It was good and bad. Equal parts painful and joyful.' Well, why would anyone volunteer for pain?"

"I don't think anyone volunteers or even decides it. It just is. What they have is a different kind of love. It lasts longer than obsession." He rubbed her exposed thigh. "The first love is euphoric all the time. The second love is on a higher plane. It's more sophisticated." He kissed her hand. "Pain is a part of life, regardless of who you are or what you do. Victor has a troubled past, and Esther is being eaten up by her dark secret. They take on each other's pain. It's a commitment. And the happiness that comes with that second love is like nothing you'll ever experience otherwise. It is worth it. I'm assuming, at least. I've never loved that way, in a romantic sense, anyway."

Samya wasn't sure if she entirely believed that someone didn't have a choice but to fall into pain. Oftentimes she ruminated on how to prevent hurting others and was convinced all she could bring anyone was pain. But her time with Jacques was so new and different. It was changing something inside of her that she did not want to examine.

So she kissed Jacques and then raked herself over to the lower part of his body to do that thing he liked so damn much. Truth be told, she liked it, too.

Chapter Thirty

"Zoo Zoo!" Samya screamed up the stairs of her villa at 6:00 a.m. "Woman, we are going to be late."

It was the day of Dr. Nadia's clinic. To Samya's surprise and Zoo Zoo's displeasure, Ruqquyah insisted on joining to help at the clinic where she could. Ruqquyah had recruited Zoo Zoo against her will. She was six months along and barely showing. Her belly bump was like a little pearl hidden in several black fabric wraps. But she was glowing. Her tiny cheeks were rosy red. Her auburn hair was braided in two braids sneaking out of the wrap on her head and coming to rest atop her chest. As her little one grew, she too blossomed.

"*Khalti* Zoo Zoo is not excited to go, I think." Ruqquyah chuckled.

Samya did a double take. "Zoo Zoo, quick! Ruqquyah spoke *and* laughed!"

Ruqquyah put her hand over her mouth and chuckled again. "I can talk to you now. It's just that some people are intimidating."

Samya frowned, mimicking her beloved but ornery professor. "Like Professor Nadia?"

Ruqquyah nodded vigorously.

Samya leaned in. "I have to ask, why did you want to join today? To see me be put down by the old grump?"

Ruqquyah smiled. "I'd like to repay the favor. That 'old grump' did me an ultimate kindness. Her and a 'young grump' I know."

"Zoo Zoo! Ruqquyah made a joke!"

Both Samya and Ruqquyah laughed.

"Are you obligated to Dr. Nadia, then, because of us?" Ruqquyah asked.

"Well, yes." But if Samya was honest, she was thrilled to work at the clinic. Even if all she did was sterilize instruments, at least she'd be in that adrenaline-inducing environment.

"You'll make a great doctor one day," Ruqquyah continued. "I have to admit, I'm a bit excited. It is one thing to read the papers of Hippocrates of Kos, another to see it in action."

"Hippo-who?"

"Hippocrates of Kos. He's considered the father of medicine."

Samya's mouth hung open. It was rare for a maid to read, even rarer for one to read texts of ancient Greek philosophers.

Ruqquyah laughed. "The family I was cleaning for when I was little allowed me to join their children's tutoring sessions. I haven't stopped reading since. I'm particularly in love with ancient Greece."

"Well, I'll be!"

The two women, excited, chatted on with Ruqquyah sharing some of what she had learned from her readings.

Zoo Zoo huffed down the stairs. "Girl, if you don't stop yelling! And you, Miss *Bold*, all of a sudden, any other demands you have of me? Should I stand in front of a train, then? Or run into a pack of wild dogs? Either would be preferable to seeing that witch again."

Ignoring her, Samya and Ruqquyah looped each of Zoo Zoo's arms in theirs and skipped out of the villa to catch a taxi.

The taxi would only take them so far into Al-Qarafa, where the clinic was, before they had to get out and walk the rough terrain on their own. Al-Qarafa, or the "City of the Dead," as it was commonly called, was a slum within an enormous ancient cemetery on the outskirts of Cairo. The inhabitants could not afford housing, so they lived in the tombs above the catacombs housing the dead. The smell of decay worsened with the sun burning through the atmosphere. There wasn't any greenery or tall buildings to provide shade. Samya was glad she'd worn a loose linen shirt and pants and had her hair up in a sensible updo.

In the distance, Samya spotted a military ambulance outside the cemetery, with about five curtained tents outside where patients would be seen. There were pregnant women lined around the block.

Dr. Nadia wasted no time in greeting them. "You two organize the line of women and take this box of creams with you to hand out when they are done." This she told Zoo Zoo and Ruqquyah. "Samya, girl, you are with me."

Samya grabbed a white coat she saw lying on the counter in the ambulance and put it on. She had started sterilizing instruments on a counter when she felt Dr. Nadia place a stethoscope around her neck.

"My first year will take over here. Come with me." Dr. Nadia led her to the tents with the curtains. "You'll do intake and regular checkups up front with some of the other residents and send in the more serious issues to me. Make sure to come in when you do."

So it went. Samya got right to it. It was a bit difficult to catch the rural accent, but after a while she could wing it. Hearing multiple heartbeats, talking to mothers about what to eat as opposed to what was available. Questions abounded, from the ridiculous to the necessary:

"My mother-in-law said someone gave my child the evil eye. What can I do to repel it?"

"I've been feeling sharp pains in my lower stomach. Does that mean anything?"

"Are there any positions to change the sex of the baby? My husband says if I bring home another girl, he'll kick us all out!"

"It burns when I pee. Is there something I can take for that?"

Dr. Nadia had run Al-Qarafa mobile clinics and many others in impoverished areas in Egypt for thirty years. These women would otherwise not have access to healthcare that was desperately needed. Additionally, Dr. Nadia had single-handedly commissioned the government to fund the clinics and other medical aid for pregnant women in these areas.

It seemed like the parade of pregnant ladies wouldn't stop. In and out. In and out. In and out. At 6:00 p.m. it was nearing dark, and the line still had not finished. It was exhausting, yet exhilarating.

When Samya stopped to take a sip of water from a well next to the clinic, she heard yelling from the crowd. All of them were pointing in one direction so as not to lose their place in line.

"She needs help! She needs help!"

"Her water broke!"

Sure enough a woman with two small children stood above a puddle and was holding onto her stomach. This surely constituted an emergency. Samya and some residents carried the woman on a stretcher and brought her to Dr. Nadia. They placed the stretcher on an elevated makeshift table.

Samya had heard of strong country women who would squat a baby out in a couple of minutes and then carry on with their household chores. This didn't seem to be the case.

The woman was sweating profusely and looked like she was close to fainting. Ruqquyah came in and took the two children to occupy them while their mother gave life.

After Dr. Nadia evaluated the case, as calm as can be, she addressed Samya. "There's no time to take her into the city. The tot is in breech. Frank position. The buttocks is near the cervix, but the legs are extended. I'll need some hands."

Normally with a breech birth, a cesarean section would be the preferred method. With the lack of tools, space, and time, a vaginal birth was the only option. The risks were high: potential broken bones, brain damage, sometimes death.

Samya got on her knees with Dr. Nadia.

"I don't want him to die!" the mother screamed. "Please let my baby live. Take me instead."

"Stop being so dramatic. Focus on the task at hand." Dr. Nadia came closer to the patient. "Push when I tell you to push. You are strong enough. I've seen those enormous thighs of yours."

The mother was shocked for a second and seemed to forget her pain. These moments when Dr. Nadia was under mountains of stress but kept her cool solidified her as Samya's favorite professor.

Both Dr. Nadia and Samya gloved up all the way to their elbows. A resident was monitoring the mother's pulse.

"Now this is important." Dr. Nadia looked up to her resident who had his hand on the mother's wrist and toward Zoo Zoo, who was putting cold towels on the mom's forehead. "When her pulse is close to 90 bpm, you tell me right away."

She looked at Samya. "You'll perform the Bracht Maneuver. Easy does it. I'll take care of the rest."

Fear crept in. Samya had been away from any hands-on experiences for at least a year and a half. Surely, she wasn't qualified.

"Are you sure you don't need another resident here with you?"

Dr. Nadia looked into Samya's eyes. "You've studied this. My hands are too brittle to do this now. But you can. Breathe and execute, Samya. Breathe and execute. On my count."

Samya nodded. Dr. Nadia had to stretch and snip the mother's perineum to allow Samya's hands to go in. "Blood pressure?" Dr. Nadia asked her resident.

"80 bpm!" The resident responded next to a worried Zoo Zoo.

"Good enough. Now, Samya."

Samya's gloved hands went up the birthing canal. She could hear the undrugged mother scream but focused on the task at hand.

"Find the hips and let the contractions guide you." Dr. Nadia said.

Samya felt around for the baby's hips, which were close to the mother's pelvis. She controlled her facial expressions as the mother continued to bellow.

"Found them!"

"Now lift towards the abdomen." Dr. Nadia said in a cool but firm voice. "Gentle, gentle."

Samya was sweating as she focused on being as careful as she could to avoid any neck breaks.

"I need some help."

Dr. Nadia pushed on the area above the pubic bone to help the baby's head descend.

Feeling the head in the right position, Samya slowly took her hands out and got out of the way as Dr. Nadia coached the mother to push. The babe was out in a matter of minutes. Dr. Nadia cut the umbilical cord, and Zoo Zoo came with a warm towel to cradle the baby, now screaming at the top of her lungs. Her mother passed out from exhaustion but awoke in seconds to her bloodied little offspring swaddled beside her.

After disinfecting the perineum, Samya grabbed a needle and ran it over a fire to sterilize it. Without being prompted, she threaded it and began stitching the tear. Dr. Nadia supervised. Samya could swear she saw her former professor smile. But the day's excitement may have been playing tricks on her.

CHAPTER THIRTY-ONE

It was December, the sun was shining, and lashes of refreshing wind whipped around Cairo. Jacques walked the streets of Roxy-Heliopolis towards El-Korba. It was a bazaar with several shops embedded in old Islamic architecture mixed with Parisian-style elements. White and beige domes topped the buildings that housed several storefronts. Arches designed with geometric shapes and fine calligraphy wrapped around the framework of the structures.

Samya was coming over later to continue their "month of debauchery." They couldn't hire cooks or maids in order to maintain secrecy. So dinner was up to Jacques.

The cheese shop provided the best goat cheese he'd ever tasted. Candy shops had the sweetest delectables. The juiciest cuts of lamb were laid out at Roxy's butcher shops. Though wine was another matter entirely. He was craving a good red, and there was only one store in Roxy that imported something that was passable to his French sensibilities. After securing two bottles of this inferior beverage, he went over to the *forn*. The traditional bakery looked like an open underground cave with clay ovens. The smell was enough to make one salivate. He picked up pita bread, *eish fino*—a mini-baguette-shaped bread roll—and Danish pastries with apricots.

He had to admit the secrecy he had to keep with Samya was equal parts exciting and irritating. He'd had torrid affairs before with unhappily married women where discretion had been paramount. But this dalliance wasn't anything like those. With the women of the past, the more he'd had sex with them, the farther apart he'd felt from them. And the farther he'd felt from his own body. It was just as well. Made for a clean break.

With Samya, though, the more he was around her, the more he wanted from her. Everything slowed when they touched. He could feel her limbs, her stomach, her breasts, and her lips interacting with his body. He felt heights of ecstasy. It was both an out-of-body experience and one where he was completely present and grounded. Her smell, her touch, just her, submerged him into depths of...something. She reminded him he was here, on this earth, living. Something he didn't know he needed to be reminded of.

The same people and crowds he loved being around did eventually drain him at a certain point. Hibernation became key for a bit before he could get back to entertaining the world. Samya was allowed in during hibernation. Maybe because he didn't feel he had to entertain her. She was a performer, too, though not with him. He was honored by that.

If they hadn't had an expiration date, he would have likely pushed Samya away or disappeared. At least he'd like to think he had that control. Control was now slipping from him day by day, and surprisingly, he let it. He refused to rein himself in. Let him be lost. Let him be caught up and entangled in her essence. It was only for a couple more weeks, and then life would resume again. If the chaos took over for now, so be it.

Best not to think too much about it.

It was difficult to completely block himself off from thinking. For instance, he had seen her taking pills on a couple of occasions, when she thought she was alone. He wondered what they were for and if she were hiding something from him. What if the affair was stressing her out? In Paris, none of their behavior would have been an issue in society. Here in Cairo, it could potentially ruin multiple lives. The stakes were high. Once or twice, he tried to ask Samya if she was worried about what would happen if they got caught. She would just kiss him or change the subject, and evade the question entirely. With a mouth like that, she made it hard to think clearly.

He walked home and arranged the spread he had acquired for their tryst on the kitchen table. The dining table was so cold and big. They always ended up at the small round table for two in the middle of the night.

The familiar chirp-of-birds doorbell rang. At this point, Samya had the keys to the villa but told Jacques she preferred hearing the musical bell. Once Jacques opened the door, Samya ran into his arms and kissed him passionately. She closed the door and dragged him to the master bedroom.

She was always keen to get to their bedroom activities, but there was something different today. Life was flowing through her. Cheeks flushed, a wide smile, dimple popping, she was elated.

He pulled her back and lifted an eyebrow. "What's going on? Have you found someone to replace me?"

She was fairly jumping. "It's nothing, really. It's just I was at the Al-Qarafa clinic today."

"Oh, yes, how was it?"

"It was fantastic. I helped with a breech birth! Both the mother and daughter survived! It was like my hands were possessed. They knew where to go. It was so delicate. I thought I had forgotten everything and wouldn't be able to do it, but I did. I did." She sat on the bed and whispered it. "I did it."

"Congratulations, Fred. Why do you look forlorn?"

"Huh? Oh, no. It was a good day was all. A nice memory to have."

He knew what the issue was. Her stupid rule that she wasn't going back to medical school when that was so clearly where she belonged. The more he spoke to Samya and was around Samya, the more he understood her. She was retreating from life, partly to protect her loved ones whom she felt she was burdening, and partly because she was hopeless. She'd said as much during one of their late-night chats.

"Sometimes I wish I was a different person."

"Who would you be?"

"Someone free."

Now she was receiving hope in the form of her passion (that is, a passion other than that inspired by Jacques's bed capabilities), and she was having trouble holding on. He could fight with her as he had in the past about this issue. But her stubborn ass wouldn't listen to him. There was always some excuse as to why she couldn't go back to school. But seeing her like this, he almost wished he'd been at the clinic today, despite that he hated messes, blood, guts, et cetera.

"I know nothing will come of it, but it was such a rush. And you should have seen the mother, Jacques. And Dr. Nadia, the old bat is a seasoned professional. She was calm as ever throughout the whole thing."

Jacques let her go on and listened intently. It was clear what needed to be done.

Unbeknownst to Samya, the next day, Jacques went to El-Qasr El-Ainy Medical School, acquired the paperwork for the re-entrance exam, and purchased all the required text books. Of course, he had to pay several medical students off to help him figure all that out, but it had been done. Then he bought an additional desk to put in one of the offices in the villa.

That night he sat Samya down and told her to start studying.

Before Samya had the chance to argue with him, he gave her a chaste peck on the cheek and said, "Don't think about it. You are not particularly good at it anyways."

He went to make her tea with milk the way she liked, which was more like heated milk with a drop of tea. When he came back, she hadn't opened a book.

She placed the cup on the desk and snaked her way to his face to start a rendezvous.

"No. There'll be plenty of time for that after you study."

She made a cross face at him and plunked back down in the chair.

He set up at the desk across from her in the same room to work on his novel, which, since they started their affair, had been going swimmingly.

Jacques covertly glanced at her to see what she was up to.

She hesitated and lined the textbook with her finger. "This will lead to nothing. What's the point?"

"There you go thinking again. Just do it."

Expecting more of a fight, Jacques found he didn't get one. After a couple of minutes, all that could be heard was the flip of her pages and the "tick-tick-tick" from his type-writer.

This carried on for a couple of nights. They'd have dinner he'd gotten from outside, study and write (respectively), have sex until they were satiated, and then Samya would leave. That last part he wasn't keen on. Not at all.

"This won't do," Jacques said one night as he wrapped his arms around Samya. He put his chin on top of her head as she was writing notes on the ledger of her organic chemistry textbook.

"What now, Ginger?" She smirked.

"I'm getting awful tired of you slinking off in the wee hours of the night and leaving me naked on the bed like a used trollop."

"Well, you are a self-proclaimed slut. Who am I to contradict that?"

He pushed her head to the side and then sat on the desk and closed her textbook.

"Well, this slut is high class and at least deserves a hot meal. I want to be taken out."

"I can hardly take you out to a restaurant and maul you in full view without us both getting flogged."

"I need to travel to Tanta for business. Come with me."

Samya's face fell. "Jacques, I'm paying off Zoo Zoo's 'associates' as it is just to sneak in here a couple hours a day. I'm not sure I can keep this going for an entire trip."

"We'll need cover. Leave it to me."

Samya looked skeptical, but Jacques could get creative when he wanted something.

The next night Jacques handed Samya a flier entitled "Cairo Society of Female Physicians."

Samya read it. "I've never heard of this before."

"Strange. They are a fantastic organization that recruits up-and-coming women in the medical field. They have an annual five-day conference in Alex, which is all expenses paid. And wouldn't you know the conference is members only and takes place tomorrow?"

Jacques put his hands on her shoulders and continued. "Oh, and did I mention you were picked as one such member? And you'll be chaperoned by a 6'1 maid who will defile you daily?"

His girl beamed, and it hit him square in the chest.

"There's more. Once you get on the train, the organization will cease to exist, and you'll become Sarah, newlywed bride of Ali, and this couple will be spending their honeymoon in Tanta."

She laughed. "Who the hell spends their honeymoon in Tanta, of all places?"

"Sarah and Ali!" he responded. "Alone. Together. Out and about enjoying the sun and fresh air and then back to the hotel to enjoy other activities."

She leaped with joy. "This could work. It really could, you think? Baba would be all for it since it is a medical society outing. I've been so boring and well behaved of late that even mama wouldn't oppose me going away for a couple of days."

Before he could answer, she shoved him out of the way. "I'll need to pack. What should I pack? This could really work!"

"Woman!" He laughed and pulled her in to him. "Here, take your ticket. After two stops when we are sure it is safe, I'll come to the seat next to you."

Samya abruptly looked away from him.

He turned her around to find tears in her eyes. "What's wrong?"

"Nothing, nothing," Samya said, wiping her face with the back of her hand. "Just excited to be out of Cairo for a bit."

Jacques, who'd very rarely seen her cry, remained unconvinced.

Quick as a flash, she smiled and punched his shoulder. "You are holding me back, Ginger! I must be off to get ready for the Cairo Women's Conference."

"The Cairo Society of Female Physicians! Get it right before tomorrow, woman!" he yelled as she sprinted out the door.

Chapter Thirty-Two

To the annoyance of the elderly grump sitting next to him on the train, Jacques's leg jiggled uncontrollably. He had no idea if Samya had actually boarded the train since he'd gotten on well in advance in case they ran into anyone they knew. His left hand tapped the green, latex-lined cushion of his seat to the beat of *"Je t'appartiens,"* a song about completely belonging to someone. His right hand gripped the scarab in his pocket. Oblivious to Jacques's nerves, the train chugged along through the rural landscape.

Solayman had written days ago, calling Jacques back to Tanta. Jacques was being summoned to attend the court hearing to determine if his father's second family could keep their villa. Since Abdo had not disclosed his first marriage beforehand, he had effectively deceived the court and possibly rendered the second marriage, otherwise permissible, as illegitimate. As his father's heir, Jacques would have to affirm the claim of his father's second wife, Madame Lena, and her children to the property Abdo had bequeathed to them. Many a time Jacques had tried to skip the hearing. He told Solayman that even if the court rejected Madam Lena's ownership, Jacques would simply deed the villa back to her. Unfortunately, they couldn't rely on the court honoring Jacques's ownership of the villa as his Uncle Mostafa, who was the cause of the damn hearing, was good friends with the judge. There was a real possibility that the property would go to his uncle via some unforeseen loophole, so Jacques's presence couldn't be dispensed with.

Jacques asked Samya to accompany him for two reasons. One being he did not want to waste a day of what they had left away from her. The second was...well. How to explain it?

Balsam. He'd learned that word the other day while discussing the Ottoman era wars with *Oustaz* Khalid. *Balsam* was a healing balm that was applied to soldiers' major wounds to stave off infection and to provide a soothing effect that ended pain. The word fit Samya perfectly. She was *balsam*.

And he needed *balsam* in order to deal with the mess his father had left behind in Tanta.

After the second stop, Jacques hastened two train cars down. He didn't have to look far. Three loose curls peeked out of a seat towards the back of the train car. Samya was snoring loudly, annoying the other passengers around her.

Her leg was spread across the seat next to her, no doubt to save it for him. His eyes raked over her. Full red lips slightly parted. Smooth hands clutching her purse for dear life. A shapely bottom spilling over her seat. An alarm went off in his mind. Day fifteen. They were already halfway through their liaison.

He picked her legs up and sat in the seat before swinging them back down onto his lap. She jolted and then eased when she saw it was him. Deciding not to cause a scene, he allowed her to swing her legs down in order to sit properly. After removing the simple, gold-plated ring he'd gotten for their farce from his pocket, he held her hand to put it on. "You forgot this ring, Madame Sarah."

"Thank you, *Oustaz* Omar."

"Ali!"

She rolled her eyes and chuckled. "I know."

He pushed her head to the side playfully as he often did when they were alone. But with that fake ring, he could now do that in public. That little ring was a key to freedom for them.

"*Oustaz.*" A heavily mustachioed train station attendant held out his hand to verify their tickets. When Samya took a bit of time to fish her ticket out of her purse, Jacques crossed his arms and looked at the attendant with an exasperated expression. "There you have it. My wife, always misplacing things!"

Samya finally found the ticket and handed it to the attendant. "If you had such a problem with it, *husband*, why didn't you keep both of our tickets with you?"

"Oof." Jacques turned to the attendant who was attempting to mind his own business. "Excuse her. She's always on edge when we go to visit my family. They've never gotten along."

"They all hate me, and you encourage it." She pointed at him. "All of them think you're an angel who can do no wrong. If only they would spend a day in our home and see our lives. Me, following you day and night, cleaning up all the messes you make!"

"Lies!" Jacques yelled, and they both laughed. They hadn't noticed that the unamused train attendant had long ago left their buffoonery and moved on to other, saner passengers.

After they studied each other's faces for a bit, their hands intertwined. The little ball of joy they cultivated in his villa, under the veil of secrecy, was streaming out into the real world.

"So what is on the agenda for our grand Tanta honeymoon?" Samya asked as she traced the outline of his jaw with her finger.

Jacques snapped his head to bite her finger. She yanked it before he could catch it and laughed.

"Well, I thought we could go to Al-Khan market and get some *meshabek*, then to Sabil Al-Ahmadi for a bit, there's a charming patisserie near our hotel, go to a court hearing for a spell, then..."

Samya sat up straight. "Court hearing?"

Jacques took a deep breath. "That's the business I was talking about. Remember when I told you about my father's family?"

In fact, when Jacques had told her about his father's second family weeks ago, she'd reacted with a string of Arabic curse words he'd never heard before. It had been validating for someone else to express the anger he had bottled up for the past few months.

"He left them a villa in Tanta. That villa's ownership is being contested by my uncle, Mostafa, who by the by is completely delusional. Acts as if he never initiated the suit. Now I have to go to court to validate my father's wife's inheritance. If you'd rather not go, I understand."

"Of course, I'm going. Who would miss out on all that drama?"

"Well, as long as you're entertained. But really, I can always take care of it on my own and meet up later."

Samya looked at him. "I'm going. So who will I be then? I can't be your wife in front of people who know you."

"You will be Sarah, my secretary. You help me organize my father's properties in Alex and Cairo. You take care of paperwork and the like. Seems plausible, no?"

Truthfully, Jacques was getting tired of the sneaking around and creating multiple aliases. He was tempted to just fly them both out to France so they could walk around freely.

Jacques grabbed them a couple of the sesame sweets that Samya liked so much before she continued with her line of questioning.

"Have you met your sisters yet?"

"Haven't so much as seen them."

"Do you think they'll be there tomorrow?"

Jacques shrugged and then looked out the window, hoping she would drop it.

She craned her neck to look at him. "You should go see them. As your wife and secretary, it is my duty to set up a meeting."

He tilted her head towards the window and shushed her.

"He left them with the villa, nothing else?"

Jacques nodded. "If I've learned anything from my father, it is that people will always disappoint you."

"Well, that's true in this instance."

"In every instance. The man left two broken families behind. He didn't secure his second wife and his daughters' finances. He made sure I was kept in the dark about their existence. He left my mother and me when I was young. To hell with her getting help. To hell with us needing to eat. I often wondered if he cared if I was alive or not."

He caught himself tensing and dropped his shoulders. "Well, no matter. After tomorrow, it will all be over."

"You know, *you* are helping them. *You* don't disappoint," Samya said.

"I will. I'm my father's son." He looked out the train window where the long grass landscape was slowly transforming into cement blocks and paved roads. "Remember, I warned you now. I will always disappoint."

CHAPTER THIRTY-THREE

Samya immediately quieted upon Jacques's declaration of inevitable heartbreak. Why had he gone and reminded her of what was coming? Now, when they were finally free to do whatever they wanted? He couldn't gauge what she was thinking, mainly because, after a bit, she closed her eyes, turned towards the window, and (he was 99% sure) pretended to sleep. So he decided to follow her lead and not talk for the rest of the trip. Eventually, she turned around and leaned on his shoulder, a reset. The minute they arrived in Tanta, Samya "woke up" and started to joke again. She didn't bring anything negative up, and he wasn't going to remind her. He was content to let it go.

Once the train stopped, they hurried to the hotel, dropped their bags off, and then left to gallivant around town. It seemed both of them chose denial because their free-flowing gaiety was spilling out onto their surroundings. The lackluster concrete streets Jacques had walked so many times became vibrant and alive. The woman sitting on the sidewalk crosslegged selling vegetables seemed to smile at him. Even the open-air butcher shop with skinned goats hanging upside down didn't smell as bad.

It was mid-afternoon, still hot, and Jacques felt free for the first time in weeks. Samya and he were together outside the confines of his bedroom. Of course, he didn't at all hate their time spent together in that bedroom. But to be out with her in the fresh air made him downright giddy. He chalked all this up to the secrecy they'd been forced to employ due to societal pressure. So of course he would be smitten beyond reason. He kept reminding himself not to overthink it. This would be over soon, and he would move on to the next thing. So best to enjoy the moment.

It took a while for a taxi to come around. This wasn't the metropolis of Cairo where ten cabs would pass by every minute. Finally, Jacques whistled to grab a green-and-white taxi passing by. Sand swirled around them as the car came to an abrupt, screeching stop. The driver, a scar-faced man with a disgusted visage, looked at Jacques. "Five pounds, *basha*."

Jacques had gotten this a couple of times before. Someone would look at him, label him as a foreigner, and hike up the prices. He'd always let it go. Not worth it.

Samya, however, had other thoughts on the matter.

"Five pounds?" She dry cackled. "We pay one pound in Cairo. You are telling me it's five pounds in this little nowhere city, of all places!"

"That's what I'm telling you, madame." The driver's eyes darted toward Jacques, and he murmured. "The foreigner can afford it."

"The foreigner? My husband is Egyptian, you jackass!"

Jacques held Samya's hand to stop her from crawling through the driver's window. She refused to let up and proceeded to harangue the man on how Egyptians looked all kinds of ways due to their history, and maybe he was a foreigner if he didn't know that and on and on.

Jacques stopped paying attention to what she was saying and instead took her in. Her curls fairly begging to bust out of her coiffure. Her eyebrows crinkled together while scolding. One hand gesturing uncontrollably. All the while very tightly and protectively gripping Jacques's hand in her other.

"How dare you insinuate..." She continued on with her decimation of the taxi driver's existence.

Jacques had been alone for so long. He relied on himself for everything. He never asked for help and was never offered it. He'd learned quickly that nothing was for free. A lunch led to obligatory favors. Entrance to an exclusive club was exchanged for access to his publisher. Years and years of charm and hard work had gotten him around. Never a break from his hustling lest fate catch up to him and take everything away. His years of experience had led him to one conclusion: he was on his own.

But here she was, a storm of strength, putting down a stranger for a paltry insult. For Jacques. Protecting him. With no motive other than care. Samya was honest to a fault and did everything with a bleeding heart at the forefront. This extraordinary person, full of life, was standing up for *him*.

Jacques yanked her away when she was mere inches from biting the cowering man. "We will walk, thank you!"

He didn't stick around to see the cabbie's face turn white after learning that Jacques spoke fluent Arabic.

Jacques ran them back to the hotel.

"What are you doing? He can't talk to us like that," Samya protested.

As they entered the hotel, he ignored her and pulled her up the stairs to their hotel room, loosening his tie with his free hand. He opened their door and slammed it behind them while taking his jacket and tie off. As Samya was speaking, he grabbed her face mid-sentence and kissed her. It took her only a moment before she was wrapping her arms around him and responding in kind. He backed her against the wall. A panting Jacques pulled away and rested his temple on hers. He could smell the jasmine, sweat, and the familiar scent that was so uniquely Samya. It was like coming home. He wanted to burrow in her.

She lifted his chin up and tilted her head. "What's gotten into you, Ginger?"

There was a rush of blood to his cheeks. His heart was beating as if it wanted to break out in order to be closer to her. And for once, he was at a loss for words. He was too overwhelmed to speak. Right now, he could only do. So Jacques got down on his knees, took her tan heels off, and kissed the tops of her feet. Samya looked bewildered but didn't pull away. He continued by kissing her calf. Then he moved her dress up and kissed her inner thigh while unclipping her stockings and taking them off of her. Looking curious, Samya held onto his shoulders. He went under her dress once more and caressed the scars she was so ashamed of. They were not deep enough to cause harm, for which he was thankful. Taking his time, he felt the roughness of the scars flow into the softness of her skin. He traced them with his tongue up to her red lacy lingerie. With his teeth, he grabbed the lingerie and dragged it off of her.

Jacques got up and tried again to catch his breath. She made him breathless. His hands rested on her waist as he tried to look at her. For some reason, he was shy. It was all too much. Not waiting for him to act, Samya smiled, kissed him, and bit his lip. Goosebumps travelled up and down his body as if they had touched for the first time. This woman let him touch her. Let him in to a secret world no one knew. And he felt grateful and emotional all at once.

Seemingly wanting to drive him wild, Samya guided his hand under her dress. He entered his index and middle finger into her vagina. She was already wet. So enthusiastic, so free. And he couldn't wait anymore. He unbuttoned his trousers. The calmer of the two, Samya put her hand on his chest and motioned toward the dresser. In all the commotion, he'd forgotten. The dresser was conveniently next to them, so he grabbed a safeguard. One day he'd like to enter her without it. Just skin on skin.

With that taken care of, he grabbed her right thigh, brought it up to his waist and then thrust into her. He moved in and out, in and out and watched her face as she closed her eyes, bit her lip, and sighed. He did not want to look away from her, not for a second. That temporary shyness was gone. This was need. Desperate need. Her brown eyes surrounded by dark lashes, her button nose, her high cheekbones, her plump lips. This woman, for some strange reason, found him worthy. Fought for him. Was by his side. He let go of her leg, and she swung it around his waist bringing him closer as he pumped rhythmically. He kissed her, pinned her hands above her, and went in harder. Then he let go of one hand and applied pressure right below her stomach. She screamed and blinked her eyes fast, as she did when she was in ecstasy. She wanted him. This woman wanted him. He lost it, and with one final stroke, he orgasmed. He didn't want to exit her. He wanted to stay right there, against the wall, forever. But, eventually, they both collapsed on the floor and lay down, exhausted.

After they both calmed, Samya laughed. "Is that what you'll do to shut me up? I suppose it was effective." She wrapped her leg around him and dozed off.

He gripped her thigh in one hand and hugged her with the other.

Fifteen days. He thought. *Only fifteen days left.*

He wasn't so sure that Samya would be the only one affected when the month ended.

Chapter Thirty-Four

Samya hadn't been to Tanta since she was five when her father had attended one of his medical conferences there. The city was different now. There were half-constructed buildings pushing out the rural landscape she remembered so fondly. That was Egypt for you, in a constant state of flux. Now she stood outside of City Hall. It was sand colored and guarded by long white columns. Her heels nearly crushed a pitiful daisy attempting to grow in the grass laid around the building.

"Solly, this is my secretary, Mademoiselle Sarah," Jacques told the man they met by the City Hall steps. The lawyer had kind, honey eyes hidden behind large glasses that engulfed his thin, tired face. "She's been instrumental in helping me manage the properties, organize my novel, and other personal matters. Sarah, this is *Oustaz* Solayman, my esteemed lawyer and confidante."

If Jacques's solicitor had any reservations about the woman Jacques touted as an employee, he didn't show it. Instead, he shook her hand. "Pleasure, mademoiselle. We are waiting for one more to complete the party."

Samya decided to like him immediately. He had the look of a man who was consistently trying to recover from multiple crises. In an instant, though, his face lit up.

"Ah, there she is."

A stunning middle-aged woman wearing a modest black dress under a black shawl walked up to them.

"Madame Lena, how do you do?"

Looking away from Jacques's stare, she smiled at *Oustaz* Solayman. "Very well, considering the circumstances. Would you care to introduce me to these young people?"

Not one stray, hay-colored hair left her simple yet charming coiffure. Her blue eyes were piercing. She looked so much like the picture of the woman Samya knew Jacques carried in his wallet: his mother, Vivienne. It was uncanny. What he must be feeling. Madame Lena and Jacques took turns discreetly stealing glances at each other when the other wasn't looking.

"We should go in. The other party is inside, I believe," *Oustaz* Solayman said.

The group moved up the City Hall steps, Madam Lena and *Oustaz* Solayman leading the way, Jacques and Samya following behind. Samya touched Jacques's wrist.

He winked at her. "You still have a chance to run, you know. I can catch up and tousle you later."

At this point she could tell that behind the cool allure, he was stressed. He put his right hand in his pocket, a tick of his that Samya had discovered meant he was in distress.

"No," Samya whispered. "What kind of secretary would that make me?" She made a soldier's salute. "Ready for duty, *oustaz*."

Good, she'd gotten a smile out of him. They caught up with the rest of the group and walked down the beige hallway with beige walls and beige-tiled floors. There were beige-dressed employees who had unpleasantness etched onto their faces. One such unpleasant fellow took them to a courtroom that was the size of two small offices fused together. There was only room enough for two wood benches facing a large desk on a raised stage where two corpulent men were laughing. What seemed like young law clerks fiddled around awkwardly with files. One of the laughing men behind the desk looked to be in his sixties, had a green sash over his gray suit, a white mustache, and wore a red fez hat. The other looked to be the same age but shorter than his cohort and had kinky white hair that protruded messily from his fez hat.

"Ah, Nephew!" The kinky-haired man strode towards their group and wrapped his arm around Jacques's neck.

"*Amo* Mostafa," Jacques nodded.

Oustaz Mostafa looked over the group. "Solayman. Lena," he grunted out. Then he looked at Samya. "Who are you?"

Jacques untangled himself from the old man's grip and stood next to Samya. "*Amo*, this is my personal secretary, Mademoiselle Sarah."

Samya kept her chin up and gazed steadily as Jacques's uncle looked her up and down. "Hmm...Sarah, eh? You look familiar. Are you from Tanta?"

"No, sir." Shit and damn, what was her backstory? She didn't know where she was supposed to be from. "I'm from Luxor, *oustaz*." Phew.

"Sick of being around the pharaohs, are you?" He bellowed a laugh that no one but Samya joined in on.

"Yes, *oustaz*. I'm a mere farmer's daughter." Samya recited a scene from a rather boring novel she'd never bothered to finish. "I grew up in poverty and turmoil, true. But we survived on love and resilience. When I was sixteen, my father couldn't afford any more mouths to feed. I left to ease the burden. But where did I go, you ask? To the big city. With bright lights and cars. Oh, to be a…"

Jacques coughed, interrupting Samya's background story, which she'd thought was pretty damn good. "Thank you, Mademoiselle Sarah. Perhaps we should get along with the trial, *Amo*. Unless you've decided to do us all a favor and drop the ordeal."

Oustaz Mostafa took Jacques to the side. Samya leaned in to hear.

"Son, I'm only concerned for our legacy. The villa should remain in the family. What if Lena marries? It would go to a stranger. The easiest solution is that I marry Lena. But stubborn woman that she is, she doesn't know what's good for her. This is a necessity, my boy. Your father and I built wealth from the ground up. We must ensure that it stays in the family! Come, come, let me introduce you to Judge Hakim. Wonderful fellow!"

Oustaz Solayman exchanged a look with Madame Lena, and they both went to follow the men. Meanwhile, Samya put her hands behind her back and rocked on her heels. She wasn't entirely sure what to do. Jacques was unlike she'd ever seen him before. To an outsider, he may have looked to be a normal man handling court matters. But to Samya, her playful, imperturbable partner had transformed into a dampened shell.

Before she could inch closer to the podium to eavesdrop, the sound of a gavel reverberated throughout the space. The green-sash wearer she presumed was Judge Hakim spoke. "Order, order. Clearly this will not be solved with a quick talk. Kindly, sit on the benches in front of you and make your cases. Mostafa, I mean *Oustaz* Mostafa, you may go first."

"Of course, Your Honor." *Oustaz* Mostafa stood up at a podium in front of the Judge's stage and droned on and on about all the hard work his brother and he had put towards building their wealth.

To Samya's knowledge, *Oustaz* Mostafa was a layabout who'd contributed nothing to his late brother's wealth. In fact, if anything he was a leech. He continued with a diatribe on the dangers of a woman managing a property on her own.

"This isn't Great Britain, your Honor. Where the world is upside down and a woman is ruling the lot of them! This is Tanta. The man is the head of the family. He is the protector. He is the owner. Allah has ordained this. So has the court! This is for the woman's protection!"

Spittle was coming out of *Oustaz* Mostafa's mouth as he continued on with an unhinged rant about men, women and competency. Ironic he should speak of competency when the man hadn't held a job since his brother had made his fortune. Poor Madame Lena.

"Alright, alright, Mostafa. We've got the gist, my man. *Oustaz* Solayman, your response?" Though the Judge was apparently *Oustaz* Mostafa's good friend, even he seemed tired of his comrade's excitable nature.

Oustaz Mostafa sat on his bench while *Oustaz* Solayman went up to the podium. "Your Honor, I cannot speak to the differences between men and women, nor is it at issue during this trial. What I can say is that the late Abd El-Hameed Kamal willed the villa to his wife, Madame Lena."

Oustaz Mostafa bolted out of his seat. "His illegitimate wife! They were married under false pretenses. He was already married. She has no relation to him!"

"They were married in front of a Sheikh with a marriage document certified by Your Honor's court. We can argue over morality, but it is allowed in certain circumstances for a man to have more than one wife in this city," *Oustaz* Solayman calmly rebutted.

Samya felt Jacques tense. Ya Allah, what a mess. Madame Lena was stone-faced. It didn't look like *Oustaz* Solayman wanted to pull out an argument that defended Jacques's father's bad behavior but desperate times and all that.

"It is true, Mostafa." The Judge said.

"Yes, but as I said, it was under false pretenses! Lena did not know, nor did the court know, of Jacques's and his mother's existence. Abd El-Hameed lied to the court, Your Honor. This was not a legitimate marriage."

Judge Hakim seemed to reflect on that. He paused the hearing and conferred with his law clerks.

"Solayman," Madame Lena whispered. "If I am found to be illegitimate, my children will pay the price. Do we have a response for his argument?"

"You are protected in a legal sense, Lena. And Jacques is a good man. He showed up to fix all of this mess. After today, this will be over. You'll see." *Oustaz* Solayman patted her black-gloved hands.

"Your children will not pay any price, madame." Jacques looked at her for the first time. "Nor will you. We are in good hands with Solayman. And regardless of the outcome of this trial, you and your children are under my protection."

Samya looked up at Jacques. He, too, was stone-faced but looked so capable, in charge.

Madame Lena nodded. "Thank you. My children and I are forever indebted to you."

It was a cold exchange despite the relief it seemed to provide Madame Lena (and secretly, Samya). This was just another example of a woman paying the ultimate price for the mistake of a man. She hadn't wanted to hate Jacques's late father but was finding it increasingly difficult to find something redeeming about the man. She wasn't too keen on society, either.

Oustaz Mostafa came over to the group. "Lena, I must talk to you. Come on."

"No." Madame Lena, *Oustaz* Solayman, and Jacques spoke simultaneously.

"What is it to you?" *Oustaz* Mostafa spat at *Oustaz* Solayman.

Surprisingly, it was Jacques who answered. "She is the mother of my sisters." *Oustaz* Mostafa gasped. "I suggest you sit down, *Amo*, and await the court's decision," Jacques added.

Just in time, Judge Hakim sat back behind his large desk. "It is unclear whether the marriage was valid, but the court does not take kindly to deceit. It is my opinion that the marriage is null and void. Madame Lena, you are to give up possession of the villa at Mahmud Ali Al-Banna within a week."

Jacques looked down. Madame Lena took a sharp inhale of breath. Ya Allah, what would happen to her and her children? Jacques would take care of them. He had to. But Madame Lena would be ostracized. Something *Oustaz* Mostafa wanted to ensure in order to entrap her into marriage; that would be the only way to protect her reputation.

Oustaz Solayman was the only one without a reaction. "Your Honor, since Madame Lena is to give up possession, the property would go back to the Abd El-Hameed estate."

"About that, Your Honor." *Oustaz* Mostafa, smug, provided a letter to the judge and a copy to *Oustaz* Solayman.

"This, Your Honor, is a letter dated before the debunked marriage of Madame Lena and Abd El-Hameed. It has been authenticated to be my brother's signature. He states that the villa is intended to go to me upon his death."

"I was Abd El-Hameed's solicitor and have not seen this document. This is bad form to bring in a document all parties have not yet reviewed," *Oustaz* Solayman said in a steady but firm manner.

"It has been certified and authenticated by an officer of this court, *Oustaz*," Judge Hakim said while reading over the document.

"Even so, Your Honor, this document has been superseded by the late Abd El-Hameed's more recent will in which he bequeathed the villa to Madame Lena. If Your Honor's ruling is that the bequeathment to Madame Lena is null and void, Abd El-Hameed's will clearly states that all his remaining properties are to go to Jacques Ali Abd El-Hameed."

Oustaz Mostafa's mouth dropped. "It does not say that!"

Oustaz Solayman produced the will for the Judge.

"Furthermore, Your Honor, if the will does not stand, according to the law of this country, in the absence of a will, all property goes to the male heir. This does not include any siblings of the deceased."

"That is true," the Judge murmured. "Mostafa, you did not tell me about the will's wording."

"I didn't know! I was scammed!"

"You have had the opportunity to review the will multiple times within the past eight months, *oustaz*," Solayman said.

"I have no choice other than to rule that the villa in Mahmud Ali Al-Banna is the property of Jacques Ali Abd El-Hameed Kamal."

Oustaz Solayman wasn't done. "Thank you, Your Honor. Since we are here, my client wishes to bind over the property, certified by this court now, so there is no confusion."

The Judge assented and *Oustaz* Mostafa's unruly eyebrows rose up.

Jacques stood up. "I would like to deed the villa to the ownership of Nadine and Sophie Abd El-Hameed, Abd El-Hameed Kamal's daughters and my...sisters. The villa is to be kept in trust by trustee Madame Lena Ali, my stepmother."

Madame Lena looked up at Jacques in shock. He had publicly claimed her and his sisters as part of his family. Court be damned. In the streets of Tanta, Jacques would be recognized as the head of the family. He was taking responsibility for three individuals he hardly knew. It was bold. It was binding. It was the ultimate showing of accountability.

Samya didn't doubt Jacques capable, but she knew how difficult it had to feel to support the very family for which he and his mother had been discarded.

"So it shall be ruled. See my clerks for the paperwork." The Judge banged his gavel and looked rather annoyed at a fuming *Oustaz* Mostafa who had apparently wasted his time.

Oustaz Mostafa would not take his eyes off Jacques. Hate brewed and brewed in those olive-colored eyes. "You will regret turning your back on family, Nephew," *Oustaz* Mostafa said before storming off.

And just like that, the ordeal was over.

Chapter Thirty-Five

Awkward wasn't the word for it. Odd, uncomfortable, ill at ease. That was what Jacques had been feeling all throughout the court hearing and after, when Madame Lena invited everyone to come over to her villa for tea. "Sarah" accepted immediately, without paying any mind to Jacques. There they were: Samya sat next to him on a beige couch with multi-color flowers embroidered onto it facing Madame Lena and Solly, who sat on an identical couch. The salon was cozy. There were fresh flowers everywhere from the land the villa was on and windows abounded. It was as if they were sitting in a greenhouse. It was particularly spectacular as it was night, and all the stars were shining. Despite the ambiance, Jacques felt choked.

The plan he'd come up with Solly before court was for him to say, "I am the guardian of Madame Lena and her children." But instead he'd named them. Claimed them all publicly as part of a tribe. Stepmother. Sisters. He did not know what had possessed him. All of them discarded in some way by his father, now coming together to forge a patchwork family.

After a long silence, Madame Lena spoke. "Ah, the tea is here."

A maid came in with a tray of gold-rimmed, porcelain tea cups, sugar cubes, fresh milk, and biscuits.

"How do you like your tea, Monsieur Jacques?" Madame Lena made her way to the tray.

"Oh, no need to trouble yourself. I will prepare it." He had this niggling thought he was betraying his own mother by being in this situation.

As Madame Lena went on to prepare Solly's tea, Jacques poured milk and a quarter cup of tea into a cup and absentmindedly handed it to Samya.

Solly raised an eyebrow.

Samya chuckled awkwardly. "Traveling together so often has made us learn each other's preferences. Thank you, *Oustaz* Jacques. You really shouldn't have!"

Jacques was too guilt-ridden to notice his faux pas. After they all had tea in hand, two pairs of eyes could be seen peeking from behind the salon entrance.

Solly chuckled, and Madame Lena smiled. "Come here, *habaybi*."

Two girls, one short, one tall, trotted over to their mother. Both had the same green eyes and obsidian black hair as Jacques. They leaned into their mother's embrace shyly, never once taking their eyes off Jacques. His sisters.

"Introduce yourselves, loves," Madame Lena whispered to them.

The small one stepped forward. She was wearing a cotton dress and a bow in her wavy hair. "I am Nadine. I am nine. I go to school. Are you my brother?"

Jacques couldn't help but smile. "Yes, I suppose I am. Are you my sister, then?"

"I suppose I am. And that's Sophie, your other sister. She's eleven." Nadine walked up to him and, with her hands behind her back, said, "You look a lot like Sophie and baba, *Allah yer hamu*, may he rest in peace. I take after mama. That is what mama said when we asked about you. Do you ask about us?"

Not at all. "Well, I intend to from now on." He wasn't sure if that was true or not. But as he looked at his young sisters, he knew something inside him was shifting.

Sophie, gaining confidence from her little sister, stepped away from her mother and looked at the ground. "We were playing chess. Do you play chess?"

Nadine jumped in, her eyes wide. "Yes, baba taught us. And now we play every day to remember him. Can you play with us?"

Jacques looked at Madame Lena, and she nodded.

"I'd be honored," he said with a smile.

He motioned discreetly for Samya to come with them. She ignored him and kept sipping her tea. Dammit.

Jacques was ushered in past the hall to a large bedroom that could have belonged to a woman of seventy-five. There were lace doilies everywhere, a vanity mirror that looked like it was from the 1920s, and a morning bed. He almost laughed. Sophie caught his amused face.

"This is Nadine's room," she whispered to him. "*She* decorated it."

In the middle of the floor was a chess board positioned as if in the middle of play. He sat on the rounded carpet opposite Sophie. To his surprise, Nadine sat in his cross-legged lap as if she had done so a million times before. And it felt like he had known them for a while. He didn't want to feel like that. This is precisely why he wanted to leave Tanta. He didn't want to be charmed by two little imps who shared his blood. But they were children, and he was not going to disappoint them.

They started playing, and it was clear that neither of his sisters knew what they were doing. So Jacques joined in on the nonsense. He picked up the queen and knocked down two of Sophie's pawns, which made the girls giggle in the middle of protesting. They then started a war of the ignorant. Sophie would steal a rook, Nadine grabbed her king, and Jacques knocked down each of their bishops.

"But that's ours!" Nadine protested.

They all laughed. The kids seemed well taken care of. Happy kids. He wasn't jealous, as he expected to be. He was relieved. He hadn't wanted them to be going through what he had.

Then Jacques caught something from the corner of his eye. On the top shelf of Nadine's dresser drawer was a turquoise scarab. Nadine noticed and grabbed it before sitting back down in Jacques's lap.

"Baba gave this to me." She handed it to him, and he felt the familiar grooves in the trinket.

Sophie pulled something out of the pocket of her shorts, a light-brown colored scarab. "This one's mine."

Jacques felt out of breath. Unreal, as if he was in a different universe. His father had lived an entire life away from him. One in which he'd cherished these girls. Had his father thought of him when giving away the other two scarabs? These symbols that bound him to two precious little girls he'd never known.

Jacques pulled out his. "This one's mine." He could feel his sisters' hearts soar. And his own drop. Feeling off kilter, he excused himself.

"Will you visit us again?" Sophie said while Nadine looked on hopefully.

"Yes." And he hoped he meant it.

He walked out into the light-brown-colored hallway, rubbing his chest. Windows lined the outer side of the hallway, letting the moon creep in. Jacques was short of breath. He walked on a bit further, and to his left he found a life-size painting of his father. Father faced son. Wearing a crisp gray suit, Abdo looked to be in his forties, with deep brown skin and his signature laugh lines permanently housed on his face. The painting had Abdo looking far into the distance, away from the observer. An enigma in front of Jacques.

He did not know this man.

Jacques realized there were different and contradictory versions of this man he loved despite himself. The one that would scoop a five-year-old Jacques up into his protective arms. The one that was a shelter. Then there was the version that should have taught Jacques how to be a man but who'd left before that could ever happen. Jacques had come to resent that version, but now not completely. Not when he saw evidence all over this villa of how his father had cared for his other children. Was it age that had matured his father into becoming a somewhat responsible man? Maybe he'd viewed this family as a second chance. Though Abdo had eventually left this redo family as he had left Jacques. This time, not of his own accord. And now Jacques wasn't thinking of his father at all but of those two children who would grow up without a father who loved them. What would that mean for them?

"Ginger?" A soft voice took him out of his ruminations.

Samya walked over and stood next to him to look at the man who'd fathered him.

"He's quite handsome," Samya said.

"Mmm." Jacques could barely get out a grunt. Outwardly, he was composed; inwardly, he was overcome.

He was falling, falling, falling. How could he be responsible for a woman and her children? He was his father's son. He would leave them. He would abandon them. They would surely be better off without him.

In the midst of his spiraling, he felt a hand take hold of his. Still in a haze, Jacques looked down at Samya. They looked into each other's eyes for he didn't know how long. Slowly, she wrapped her arms around his waist and brought him into her. Her softness held him together, and he grabbed on to her, tighter and tighter, breathing into her hair. *Balsam.* A salve for all his exposed wounds. A safe haven in the violent storm of confusion he found himself in. His breath calmed. He was here. This was life, and he was here.

Chapter Thirty-Six

Jacques and Samya eventually said their goodbyes and left Madame Lena's villa with all its emotional turmoil. On their walk back to the hotel, they stopped at a small café. It was little more than a stand with three round tables out on the sidewalk. It was midnight, and the moon was full. Nothing was better than the coolness of the night to make up for the heat of the morning. Despite the lateness of the hour, the little city was still buzzing. This is what Jacques loved about this place. Even Cairo's little sister, Tanta, never slept.

The best decision he'd ever made was bringing Samya with him. As foreign as it was to have someone stand by him, he relished it. Sometimes it seemed that Samya couldn't be real. But she was solid and here with him and for him. With his father, mother, and grandmother gone, he had assumed he was alone. Objectively, he had been wrong. He now had a stepmother and two sisters who'd somehow attached themselves to him. And though he knew it was temporary, Samya made him feel less alone in the world. It was new. Maybe he didn't deserve it, but he was too selfish to give it up.

Samya tapped his leg as if he was a child. "Good job today, Ginger."

He pushed her head back. "So, when are you going to feed me, Fred? You keep talking, but all you've done is ravish me behind closed doors."

Her eyes scrunched up into half moons whenever she wore that mischievous smile of hers. The stark light from the streetlights made all the colors in her shine: the brown of her eyes, the desert rose of her cheeks, the faded red of her lips.

"You know, you are right." Samya got up. "Such a good job deserves a reward."

Samya jogged away from him. The stores that had closed had thrown water down the street to wash away the dirt that had accumulated throughout the day. So she hopped, no doubt to try to avoid the wet spots on the cobblestone road, until she reached the newsstand across the street.

After a bit, Samya came back and handed Jacques a cigarette and a pack of Chiclets gum. "Here you go."

He rolled his eyes. "I don't smoke ciggies."

Samya sat down across from him and snatched back the cigarette. "Ah, then I'll keep that. The Chiclets are banana flavored…I want one, too."

Jacques turned his nose up and quickly pocketed the gum. "It's supposed to be *my* reward. Also it's a weak one at that." He leaned in closer across the table. "When am I going to get my real reward?"

He had the hankering to kiss her in full view of everyone, society be damned.

Suddenly her smile was gone.

"Um…um…um." She stuttered and stared at him hazily. A second later, she looked faraway and confused.

"Fred?"

The cigarette dropped from her hand onto the ground. Her hands remained locked in one position. They were curled and looked stiff.

"Samya?"

Again, no response from her.

"Cherie? What's wrong?"

Tears flowed down her face as she remained frozen. He held her hands, but they wouldn't move. She looked far out into the distance. Jacques started to panic but reminded himself he had to be calm.

"Okay, mon amour, we will go to the hospital now." Before he could jet off to get a cab, she slurred the words in a bare whisper.

"No."

"Samya?"

"H…Hotel."

It was dark, so those surrounding them did not notice. He thought fast about how to get her to the hotel and ended up carrying her. Her body was incredibly taut. Her face was wet from tears. Thankfully, a taxi driver was on a smoke break outside of his car. Jacques motioned for the driver to help him get Samya in the backseat with him.

"The Grand Hotel. Quickly, please. My wife…" Jacques's heart was thumping against his chest. He pushed aside the spike of unsettling energy running through his body.

"Let me take you to the doctor, *basha*." The driver looked worried.

Jacques looked down at Samya and instinctively knew against all nervousness to trust her.

"No, just the hotel. Her medicine is there," he lied, but truly hoped that was right.

Once they got to the hotel, he carried her up the steps to their suite and sat her upright on the couch by the bed. He kneeled in front of her, holding her knees and patting her hair out of her sweat-drenched face.

"Samya, talk to me."

"Umm...umm...umm," she garbled, and then that faraway look took over, and her eyes were lifeless.

He'd seen Samya take pills before, but he had no idea what they were for. He did remember his mother had had medicine for her troubles. Though this was nothing like anything he'd ever experienced. Jacques started going through the drawers for anything that looked like a pill bottle. He opened her makeup case on the vanity. There was a small, square white bottle without a label. He shook and then opened it, his hands trembling. There were white round pills inside.

He ran to get water from the bathroom sink and held the bottle up to Samya's face.

"Is this the one, cherie?"

Her eyes were vacant.

She had left her body. Exhaling, he made the decision for her. He tried to place a pill in her mouth, but her jaw was locked; it wouldn't open. Jacques set the water and pill down on the table beside the couch. He didn't even know if this was the right medication. There was no choice but to wait. She had asked him to go to the hotel. She must know herself. He had to trust that.

He rubbed her legs and arms to warm her. He tried uncurling her fingers that had to be strained after so much tension. They kept curling back. He thought Samya's illness was similar to his mother's, but he'd never seen his mother like this. He was unaware of what was going on. Totally lost. He contemplated dashing out to take her to her family, whatever the consequences. But he didn't know if she could travel in this condition. What felt like an hour passed, and then he felt her hand extend out slowly. She looked at him and then slowly away.

"Samya." He tilted her head towards him. "Please, talk to me."

Her words were mumbled, like one who was drunk. "I'm so ashaaamed. Please, please, leaaave." Samya burst into tears.

Jacques held both her hands to his lips, relieved she was somewhat back. "Mon amour. Why ashamed? I'm so happy you are all right."

He kissed her forehead multiple times and then hugged her as she cried hysterically. "Jacques, leaaaavee. I'm so embarrassed."

"Not a chance. Not a chance. Just rest, *mon coeur*. We can talk about this later."

As her sobs became softer, he placed her on the bed. Thinking the paralysis must have scared her, and the last thing she would want was restriction of movement, he placed her on top of the comforter. He lay next to her until she finally slept.

Then he got up, left the room, leaned against the door, and dropped his head.

With his mom, he'd felt useless. With Samya, he felt helpless. What had just happened?

Jacques did not sleep the entire night. He hovered over Samya, checking to see if she was breathing. Sitting to attention at any movement she made in her sleep. He took one of Samya's smokes from the dresser and went out to the balcony to smoke. All the while, keeping one eye on the bed.

He finally settled down on the couch.

***

When Samya awoke, she looked dazed. He swept her hair out of her face. "*Sabah il khair.* Good morning."

She smiled weakly.

"Hungry? I ordered *fool wa tamaya* from outside." Jacques said. Fava beans and falafel were some of Samya's favorite foods.

Samya sat up in the bed with a dejected look. "I'm sorry about yesterday. It hadn't happened in a while. So I thought it was over for a bit. I thought I could catch it in time."

"What was that?" he asked gently.

She looked away from him. "They call it catatonia. It comes on out of nowhere."

Samya paused, and he gave her time to say what she needed to.

"I suddenly feel as if I'm being pulled behind a black screen. My mind starts to shut down. Then a wave of extreme exhaustion, of heaviness hits me. My hands are the first to go. They don't just grow numb; they become tense.

"Every body part succumbs until I completely freeze. I cannot speak. My mind is trapped inside. I'm trying to break through, past my body, past my brain and to the outside. At the same time, the outside world tries to come in and overwhelms me. Light bulbs, the colors of the room, anyone talking to me, their skin, the bumps on their skin. It hits me all at once, and I have a hard time processing it all together."

Jacques did not dare interrupt. He was trying to understand what she was describing.

"It's as if...instead of you looking at an artist's painting on a canvas, he throws the paint, the brushes, and the feeling of the painting at your face all at the same time."

She looked defeated. "With time or intervention, I'm able to move again."

Samya looked at the pill bottle still unused on the table. "I have barbiturates that I have to take immediately when I feel it coming on. It happens so fast that oftentimes I don't get to the pills in time. I'm so frozen, I can't swallow a thing. In the hospital, they would just inject me. Though even when they did, the only thing that ever really helped was time. As you saw."

He tried to take that information in.

"It's not physical; it is part of my...sickness...the sadness...psychotic depression, some say." She looked down at the bed.

"Are you sad now?"

"I'll always be a little bit sad. I can't remember a time I wasn't." She crawled on the bed towards Jacques and held his hands. "But, Jacques, I've also never been so happy."

"Then why? Is it the sneaking around? The guilt maybe?"

"I've never felt guilty about us, and I don't regret a thing. They don't yet know why it happens, but it's been happening to me since I was nineteen. This and the sadness is why I am in and out of the hospital. It is safer for me to be in a contained space away from prying eyes until the bouts stop. So, they'll stop for a couple of months or even years, and then there's a resurgence."

She smiled while rubbing his cheek. "It has nothing to do with us or what we've been doing."

He didn't believe her. He'd never truly appreciated how an affair of their kind would be so out of the norm for someone who'd grown up in Egyptian culture, where such things were taboo. Mon Dieu, he was an idiot. He was hurting her. And he had no idea how to care for her. To protect her as she'd protected him.

Chapter Thirty-Seven

Jacques's face was pale, he had dark circles under his eyes, and he looked drained. Samya had drained him.

She wanted him to believe her, that this had nothing to do with them. The worry carved on his face told her he didn't. In all honesty, she didn't know if the stress of potentially getting caught hadn't contributed a little to the recent episode.

All she wanted to do was jump in his arms and bury him in her. But he could see everything clearly now.

She hadn't prepared him for it. Likely because she'd been living in denial about her circumstances. She had started taking the barbiturates a couple of days ago because she'd felt tingles. She'd been hopeful the pills would merely be precautionary.

How scary it must have been for him to experience that, with no prior knowledge of her catatonia. The episode had hit faster than any she'd gone through before. She hadn't even had a minute of warning so she could hide.

The catatonia served as a reminder. It broke the spell she'd been under with him, that she could possibly be carefree and in love. Because she loved him. And as much as she wanted to lie to herself, she couldn't anymore. And she couldn't put one more person she loved in peril.

"I know it doesn't make a lot of sense. There is no logic or reason to it."

That was the thing about it that drove her wild. There weren't enough words, hand signals, or gestures to clearly articulate what happened to her. She hated that she didn't know if he understood her or not.

Disheartened, she pulled away from him and got up from the bed. "I do need to go home today. As soon as possible."

He nodded. "Of course."

Jacques had to stay in Tanta for business, but he insisted on riding the train all the way to Cairo to drop her off. They were silent while Samya packed her bag, throughout the taxi ride to the station, and on the train.

To his chagrin, she insisted on moving to another train car once they hit Menouf in order to avoid detection. Before she left, she held his worried face. "Thank you for letting me debauch you in public."

He smiled but looked so very sad. "Please, let me take you home."

She kissed his lips lightly, to which he had no real response. "I promise I'll be fine on my own."

She handed him the ring he'd given her for their faux marriage and left.

When she reached home, she avoided her family and Zoo Zoo, went straight to her room, and closed the door. Samya knew her illness would be the death of her relationship with Jacques. She only wished they could have held on to what they had for another two weeks. So she could squeeze every minute they had together.

There was no way of coming back from what they'd just gone through.

***

The next day she sat on her bed, hiding from the outside world. Hend was off on a trip with her friends, so there was one less person to avoid. Wanting to prolong her time out of the hospital as much as possible, Samya decided not to tell her father of the recurrence of the catatonia. The pattern from her past told her she would have a couple of weeks before it would become a dire situation, and she would have to go to a hospital. No need to alarm her father if she could put it off for a bit.

In her bedroom, her curtains were closed. Her thoughts ran wild in the pitch-black darkness. The only sound that could be heard was the fan buzzing to and fro.

Erasing Jacques's forlorn face from her mind was near impossible. How she wished it hadn't ended the way it had: traumatic and abrupt. She would have been heartbroken either way. She could admit that to herself now. But why couldn't she have had just a few more days with him?

It was her fault. She'd given in and secretly started hoping that the arrangement could keep going. Though what did she realistically expect to hear from Jacques after he'd seen her illness in action? "I love you no matter what." No, that was not the person she was to him. He wouldn't want to be involved with a mess like her. She was a screwup, a mental case. She wouldn't let him be with her, even if he wanted to. He was probably looking for a convenient exit, anyway. And he'd gotten it.

She closed her tear-stained eyes and started to feel her feet tingle.

Hope was a killer. If she didn't know what life could be like, what love was, perhaps she wouldn't be hurting this much. Gone were her dreams of going back to school. The only institution she would be headed to now would be a mental one. How could she have allowed herself to believe otherwise? Stupid, stupid, stupid. Now things were infinitely harder than they needed to be. The little tingles in her feet crept up to her thighs.

Ya Allah, it was happening again. *Why me?* she thought. She didn't care that she should be grateful since others had it worse than her. *Why me, Allah? Why me? What have I done wrong?*

The tingling came up to her waist. She was now losing coherent thought. The ability to string sentences together was a thing of the past. But she was angry, so angry. Normally, she would accept it, the hopelessness. But something had changed in her over the past couple of months. Yes, she knew things were bad, but dammit, why did they have to be? She didn't want to simply acquiesce. Determined to rebel, she made herself fall off the bed and accidentally hit her head on the dresser on the way down. Something wet flowed down her face. Meanwhile, her lower half was completely paralyzed.

"No. No." She tried to yell, but it came out in slurs. "Not again. No."

Hysterically, Samya cried as she dragged her body towards her bedroom door. She didn't have a destination, but she was sick of it. Move, move, move, she had to keep moving. She stopped feeling her body as her right arm froze in place.

"No!" she screamed. The rest of her body followed suit like a row of dominoes. The paralysis hitting her left arm, then hands, and neck. She couldn't speak. Finally, she stilled completely. She was facing the door. Suddenly she couldn't understand the concept of the door, or where she was, or what was happening.

Time during catatonia was arbitrary. Sometime during the episode, she could see the door open. Slippers shuffled in, and she heard what might have been a scream. Then they left, and another pair of slippers came in.

Someone was speaking to her, or at her. What were they saying? Where was she again? That someone picked her up. Gray mustache, long sleeping frock: her father, she supposed. He wiped something red from her nose. She could barely hear it, but someone said, "*Habibit albi*, my heart, my daughter. I'm so sorry." Samya couldn't feel but knew someone was holding her.

Then her eyes came into focus on that door, and she saw an older woman in a silk nightgown clutching her mouth and silently crying: her mother. As they made eye contact, her mother turned and left the room.

Her father's voice came more into focus. "We'll take care of this, *ya rohy*, my soul. I promise you we will find a cure. Be strong, *habibti*. Don't stop fighting. Please, don't give up."

After everything that had happened, Samya didn't know if she had the energy not to surrender.

CHAPTER THIRTY-EIGHT

Jacques assured himself that Samya got home safely by following her into Cairo, unbeknownst to her. Then he went back to the train station, hopped back on the train, let the Tanta stop pass him by, and rode until Alexandria. He would go back to get his belongings from Tanta later. Disturbed, he didn't want to go back and see the couch where Samya had sat frozen for an hour. Jacques didn't want to go back to the room where he'd been completely useless to her. Yes, he fled. When he got off in Alexandria, he checked into the first crappy hotel he saw and didn't leave.

Jacques kept remembering Samya paralyzed like that. He'd been aware she was sick, but he'd had no idea the severity of it. It was such a shock. How had she even got through the schooling she had with her illness? She would be safe with her family, at least. Though that didn't quell his fears. What if she was walking by herself on the streets of Cairo alone? What if she was overtaken by the illness then? What would happen to her? He needed to see her. And he couldn't just waltz over to her home without exposing her and her family to scandal. That would place her in even more harm. Besides, there was a niggling thought that he might be the very last person she needed to see.

He couldn't help believing that he had triggered something in her. What if seeing him had been the cause of her inner chaos? They'd become too close. Too intimate. The affair had put her under so much stress. The sneaking around, the possibility of getting caught, the risk they'd taken being out in the open. All things to which he'd exposed her. She deserved so much better, and he'd robbed her of it.

Racking his brain, he tried to find moments during their time together that might have hinted at her illness flaring up. Aside from having seen her take pills, there were times Samya had been quiet or would leave his villa early. He'd noted but never questioned her behavior. As much as he'd thought she was comfortable with him, she'd still been hiding.

She suffered alone. She didn't trust him. Why should she? He'd reinforced his lack of trustworthiness by his recent behavior. At the first hint of strife, he'd run away.

He couldn't face the fact that he was a coward.

This had been more than just a mere fling for him. It had been more than just sleeping with her. He wanted more of her and wanted her to want more of him. And now, he was going to lose her.

Suddenly, he wanted to move his flight back to Paris up to that week.

Thoughts cycled through his head incessantly. Images of his mother flooded him. He kept remembering how he'd disappointed her. He hadn't known how to take care of her, and she'd up and killed herself. What would he do to Samya? What had he already done?

He needed to get back to France.

After a couple of hours of spiraling, Jacques headed back to Tanta to gather his belongings. When he got back to the hotel, he threw his clothes haphazardly into his suitcase. He left word with Solly that he would be by the office later that evening to wrap everything up, and then he would be off. That would be best for everyone.

There was a knock at his door.

A bellboy with disheveled hair but wearing a crisp white garb handed him an envelope on a silver platter. Jacques thanked him and closed the door to read the letter in peace.

Monsieur Jacques,

I would like to invite you to lunch tomorrow, before you leave Tanta. The girls very much wish to see their brother. Lunch will be served at 2:00 p.m., if that suits you.

Sincerely,

Lena

He put the letter down and slumped onto the desk chair. Exhaling deeply, he contemplated this. He was irresponsible, yes. Completely good for nothing. But he would not disappoint those two little girls. So he decided to see them before he left for wherever he decided to go.

***

Jacques was back sitting in the greenhouse-like salon that belonged to his stepmother. The girls were washing up from their trip to the *nady*. So it was just Jacques and Madame Lena drinking tea in silence. Several times she put her tea and saucer down as if she was about to say something but then thought better of it and continued sipping tea.

Jacques cleared his throat. "This is excellent tea. Is it imported?"

Madame Lena looked at him in shock. "Oh, no, it is from some local farm here." She proceeded to put her tea and saucer down and exhaled. "Monsieur Jacques..."

"Really, you can call me Jacques."

"Ah, Jacques." She smiled at that. "Jacques, I would like to talk to you about myself and your father, so you can understand."

He waved his hand. "Not necessary."

"Regardless," she said in a firm voice. "I would like to share my story with you. If you will listen."

He couldn't handle much more turbulence, but he nodded out of respect.

"Egyptians tend to take their secrets, hopes, and truths to the grave with them. I am going against culture to tell you these stories, but I feel I owe you answers that I know you are too polite to seek. If you were my son, I would want you to know."

She took a deep breath and began. "I grew up in Tanta. I was orphaned at a young age, and the family that took me in was...not nice. I dreamt of the day I could go to a women's college in Cairo to escape them. But I did not have the funds or courage to do so. Through happenstance, I met your *Amo* Mostafa, and we became engaged. He promised that my dream of going to college would not be postponed. But that promise and many more were broken. I met your father when he came to Tanta to visit his family one day. Over the months, every time he visited, I fell more and more in love with Abdo."

193

Madame Lena looked down at her hands, wistful. "He was sharp, quick-witted, handsome. A warm, safe hug personified. I took college and Mostafa completely out of my sights and wished fervently to marry and build a life with Abdo."

She looked at an enthralled Jacques and continued. "Despite the protestations and resentment from his brother, we married."

Jacques interrupted her. "When?"

Madame Lena looked away and sighed. "You would have been ten."

He slumped into the couch. Even though his father would still visit home when Jacques had been that age, his father had already mentally "left."

Madame Lena took Jacques's silence as a signal to continue.

"He didn't want to have children. For years, we argued over it until I gave up hope. Abdo would travel for business all the time, per usual. So my life became about the months he was home. There came a time where he slowly started pulling away more and more. You see, I knew Abdo well. I could tell when he was hiding something. It took me years to have the courage to confront him. Then he told me about you and your mother."

Jacques tried to ignore the ringing in his ears and listen to the rest of the story he desperately wanted to hear. He shifted in the couch, trying to find a comfortable position.

"I was livid. I threatened to leave him. I felt betrayed by him. I felt that I had betrayed your mother, a woman I didn't know. But my family wouldn't take me back, and I had nowhere else to go. And despite my dignity, I still loved him deeply. Regardless of what my reality was, I still had a choice. We slept apart for months, but I didn't leave. It took a while, but we rebuilt our relationship, and I tried to accept the flawed man in front of me.

"When he opened up more, I learned your mother had passed, and you were completely on your own. I begged him to take you in. He dismissed me. Not because he didn't love you. Because he truly did, as much as he came to love Sophie and Nadine when they came along. But you have to understand, you were the son. He wanted you to find your way on your own, just like he had. To have the world make a man out of you. That is why he didn't come get you. Not because he didn't love you. He thought he was doing the right thing. He found confirmation in your literary success. I disagreed wholeheartedly with his thinking, but I had to respect a father's wishes for his son. Jacques, he talked about you a great deal."

"I have a hard time believing that. No need to rewrite history, madame." Now Jacques was incensed.

Madame Lena got up and sat next to Jacques. With caution, she put her hand atop his.

"Jacques, I'm not saying this to make him look good. He made a lot of mistakes. A majority of them with you and your mother. I represent the man as he was."

She removed her hand. She was done talking and looked like she expected him to ask questions. But there it was, all laid out before him. The carcass of Jacques's relationship with his father.

"Did he tell you why he left my mother and me, then? It couldn't possibly have been to make a man out of me."

She shook her head. "I don't know. The answer to that died with your father."

She paused for a bit.

"Your father was a flawed human. He loved you, but you certainly don't need to accept his actions. Love isn't always enough, especially for a child. I don't think Abdo wanted to deal with your mother's issues. I selfishly lay awake many a night worrying he might leave me if I had any such issues. But he made his choices. And I, a flawed person as well, chose to accept him. He eventually came around to the idea of having children. I had Nadine and Sophie late in life, when you were well into adulthood. These are not ideal circumstances, but I've always wanted you and your sisters to know each other. You never have to accept me as your family, but Jacques, I am here. Of course, you have Sophie and Nadine. They are in love with you already. But you also have me, if you need me."

"Jacques!" Nadine ran to Jacques. Other than her matching pink blouse and skirt, she looked like she'd come fresh out of the shower with her long, wet hair.

Sophie, in a similar outfit in yellow, followed her with a small smile.

Nadine leaned on him. "Are you ready to play chess now? Mama, can we?"

Madame Lena looked at Jacques with so much concern in her eyes. It was ten times harder that she looked so much like his actual mother.

Jacques had been a punching bag the last couple of days, taking hit after hit. There was hardly time to process. But he saw those eager faces and collected himself. "Yes, you little imps. Let's go!"

He picked Nadine up and took Sophie's hand, and they retreated to Nadine's room. There were thoughts banging about in his head, but at this very moment it was about

Sophie and Nadine and playing fake chess. So they did. He made them laugh and scream with glee. They asked him about memories of their father.

"I used to sit on his lap and line his face with my finger as if to draw him. He would throw me up in the air so high, my mother would yell at him." Jacques felt a sharp pain in his gut. Because that had been his father, too. He had loved Jacques. It just hadn't been enough.

The siblings were then called for lunch. Nadine went on and on about her best friends and enemies at school. Sophie quietly told him that she'd read one of his books. He grew nervous.

"I didn't understand it, but I liked it."

That made him laugh.

After lunch, Sophie took him to the library where they had an entire shelf filled with copies of his novels, translated from French to English and from French to Arabic.

"Baba brought all these from his business trips. I want to be a writer, just like you." Sophie said while her hands were clasped behind her back.

He looked at this shy kid filled with so much possibility. She had the right to grow up with support and nurturing for all that possibility. It was easy to fall in love with these kids. But what they needed was someone to be there when things were rough. Someone to be there at all. They needed consistency. When fake chess and throwing them up in the air and small gifts from different business trips weren't enough. Right then he decided Sophie would want for nothing. Both those girls would want for nothing. And it wouldn't just be financial support. He vowed to give them something more precious: time. Jacques couldn't be a father to the girls, but he could try to be a brother.

Sophie followed the call of a yelling Nadine, leaving Jacques behind. His fingers ran along the tomes, feeling the rough texture of the sturdy spines. There were more than fifteen of his first two books in hardcover. Each likely purchased from a different location. More evidence of love, but not enough of it. He took out the black scarab he'd carried with him around the world, through every event in his life, and set it atop the shelf. With one last look, he left.

CHAPTER THIRTY-NINE

Five days had gone by since the loveliness and horror of Tanta. Samya had lost sleep. She'd started crying profusely, wildly, howling even. The pain, seemingly from nowhere, was rooted so deep inside that her body was desperate to get it out. The sadness was somehow worse than the catatonia because she was present to every bit of it. Thankfully, the catatonia had paused for a few days, so she didn't need emergency care. She would, however, need long-term care. There was a doctor in a new hospital in Alex who specialized in a different shock treatment technique. Both she and her father thought it was worth trying something new to tame the beast. But it would be at least a week before said doctor came back from a speaking tour in Europe. There was no sense in her entering the hospital before he arrived. She was holding that off as long as possible. She hated the damn hospital. So in the meantime, she hid in her room, riding out the ebb and flow between normalcy and depression. Smoking became more prominent in her daily routine. She tried to accept her circumstances. Tried to forget Jacques and let go of all she had lost.

As for Samya's mother, she never mentioned the episode she'd witnessed. They would pass each other in the hall. Madame Magda would say something about Samya's disheveled look and then shuffle away. It was as if she was avoiding a jinx. She seemed to believe that if she acknowledged what happened, it would happen again. Denial appeared to be a shield for her mother. Samya felt a mixture of hurt and pity. She wanted to be angry with her mother, but she couldn't muster the effort. Seeing your adult child sick in such a shocking way couldn't be easy.

Dr. Mahmoud wasn't as forgiving. Though he never said a thing, it was evident that Samya's father was irritated with his out-of-touch wife. He avoided her like the plague. One night, Samya saw him coming out of a guest bedroom with his pajamas on. So he was sleeping apart from her mother now. But ever the peacekeeper, he would probably never confront his wife directly.

One afternoon, Samya heard her mother screaming at no one in particular. Curious and looking for any distraction, Samya left her room and headed towards the salon. There she found Madame Magda plopped down on a settee, her sequined blue wrap falling on her face. Samya cautiously pulled the wrap off of her. "Mama?"

Madame Magda sat up. "She's a menace, that Iman! The heifer spent the night comparing everything to my last dinner party. 'Oh, I have five courses as opposed to your three, Magda.' 'I thought it best to have cigars for the men handy after yours had none, Magda.'"

Samya sat next to her with a smile not quite reaching her eyes. "You know she's jealous. Both of you are of each other. It's sort of the foundation of your friendship."

Not entirely listening, her mother threw hands up in a huff. "She insulted our veranda!" Madame Magda stared straight ahead, avoiding eye contact with her daughter.

Samya held her hand, and her mother gave a bit of a jolt. Tears fell from Madame Magda's cheeks and rained down on their joint hands.

"She's awful and careless! And doesn't give a damn about anybody but herself." Madame Magda nestled herself against Samya and started wailing.

Samya, confused, put her arms around her. It was hard to imagine that Madame Iman had wreaked this much havoc.

"What are we going to do, Samya?" Madame Magda muffled into her daughter's shoulder. She was clinging so tightly her hands were digging into Samya. With a whimper like a distressed child, she looked up at Samya. "What can I do?"

Taking a deep breath, Samya refused to cry. Her mother was heartbroken; she just didn't know how to communicate it. It was unlikely her mother would ever acknowledge reality. This was the best she could do. Samya held her mother tighter and kissed her on top of her head. Her mother's breakdown was another reminder of what Samya was doing to those she loved. Merely thinking about how much of a burden she was made losing Jacques a tiny bit less painful. Maybe she could distract her mother and relieve her during the few days she had left before going to the hospital. After holding her mother for several minutes, she let go.

"Maybe throw a party to rival all parties? Come on, Magda." Samya smirked at her teary-eyed mother. "Are you going to let a two-faced simpleton like her take you down?"

Her mother sniffled. "I don't think I can."

"You can do anything you put your mind to. Isn't that what you've always told me...or yelled at me, rather?"

Her mother chuckled and held Samya's face. "You are beautiful, you know...if only you straightened that hair."

Samya laughed.

"Will you come to the party? Hend is out of town still, and your father is useless when it comes to hosting, honestly."

Samya hesitated. She wasn't really up to seeing anyone after everything that had happened.

"Of course not. That's alright," her mother said, downtrodden.

"I'll be there," Samya said before she could take it back.

Madame Magda beamed and kissed her cheek.

She could do it. Just one night where she would give her mother the illusion of normalcy. She could put on a mask for a couple of hours if it helped her mother cope.

Not two days later, the servants were in a flutter, hanging up last-minute decorations, making food, and cleaning the villa top to bottom. Madame Magda shouted and ran around like a chicken with its head cut off.

Despite the fact that the last thing Samya wanted to do was be around the Cairo elite, she decided to do this one last thing for her mother. At the last minute, Samya convinced her father to attend although he still refused to talk to her mother.

With that settled, she dragged herself to take a bath. Zoo Zoo picked out a burgundy, sleeveless, silk dress with a sweetheart neckline for her. Too tired to straighten her hair or any of the other silly things she'd been doing over the past month to appease society, Samya kept her curls in place. She put her red lipstick on. There, she'd tried. Zoo Zoo looked worried and kept asking Samya what was wrong. Samya feebly joked around with her to get her off her back.

When the time came, Samya's society mask went up automatically. She greeted the guests downstairs with her parents. It was scary how easy it was to compartmentalize. Like Cinderella's carriage, she knew she would turn into a pumpkin in a couple of hours, but for now she could keep it together.

Dr. Hosseni and the entire Waqab clan attended. Samya didn't have the energy she normally would to spite him. So she moved out of the way and pretended to consult the cook in order to avoid greeting that family altogether.

The soiree went off without a hitch. Madame Magda alternated between charming her guests, looking smug in front of her arch nemesis and closest friend, and scowling at the maids. Samya mostly stayed in the corners of their ballroom. Since Hend was gone, and Omar was avoiding her, she was able to keep to herself without anyone commenting too much.

It was around 10:00 p.m. when Jacques showed up. Of course, he looked handsome as ever to the untrained eye, but Samya could see how wrung out he was. She quickly averted her eyes as both of them had practiced when they were in public, but she could feel his stare. As if connected by an invisible rope, he headed straight to her.

Jacques was feet away from her when he stopped. Feeling she had no other choice, Samya looked up. His breath was erratic. Ya Allah, he looked tired. There was an insurmountable sadness in his eyes.

Within seconds, Lobna sidled up next to him. "Monsieur Jacques! How naughty of you to show up when you were unexpected!"

Jacques continued to look at Samya. Samya answered for him before Lobna could comment on his odd behavior. "Jacques was telling me he came the minute he heard you were attending, Lobna."

Samya smirked at him conspiratorially to remind him of the game they often played.

He smiled brightly at Lobna. "It is lovely to see you, Lobna. I'd like to talk to Samya privately, if you don't mind."

With pursed lips, Lobna left. Samya darted her eyes back and forth but supposed since there was nothing between her and Jacques any more, she no longer had to hide.

"How are you?" he finally said. He searched her face as if wanting to communicate much more.

"All right." Samya deflected. "You look like hell."

His smile was fleeting. He continued to look at her, to bore into her with his eyes. She let him. She had missed him. It was a small miracle that she was getting to see him again before...well, before they would part forever. Her eyes roamed over his face, the birthmark under his right eye, the rakish waves of his hair, committing all of him to memory.

Something like desire or desperation flashed in his eyes. It seemed that they'd both tuned out their surroundings. Jacques inched closer and closer until he had all but cornered her against the wall.

"I'm sorry..." Jacques started.

From the corner of her eyes, Samya could see they'd attracted a couple of onlookers.

"Not here," she whispered.

He stepped back.

Then they both heard it. It was Hosseni's arrogant voice talking to a group of men nearby.

"I've just come from Tanta, where I was visiting a friend who was unfortunate enough to end up there. Actually, funnily enough, I met a man who said you were there at the same time, Jacques. He said he's a relation of yours. Mostafa Kamal?"

Samya stilled. Jacques turned towards the group, inadvertently shielding her.

"Yes, I was there a couple of weeks ago for business. My father had several properties in the area."

"Now that you mention it, I may have seen you in front of a café." Hosseni looked sharply at Samya, who was peeking from behind Jacques, and curled his lips upwards.

"Odd," Jacques said, unfazed. "I was trapped in my solicitor's office the entire time I was there. No time for outings, I'm afraid. Must have mistaken me for someone else."

"Perhaps. Though it is difficult to confuse you. Being a tall, green-eyed, fair skinned man in a sea of brown. No, it must have been you. In fact, I think you had a lady with you," Hosseni said.

Samya's heart hammered, begging to burst out of her chest. She was relieved to see that her parents were completely engaged in conversation on the other side of the ballroom.

Another man clapped Jacques on his back. "Surprised it was only one."

The group erupted in laughter.

Hosseni cut through the laughs. "You looked quite cozy together. You and the woman, or floozy, if you prefer."

"I don't prefer," Jacques said lightheartedly, but Samya saw his fist curling up.

She'd never truly appreciated how formidable Jacques was until now. When they were alone, he always teased her and acted silly and self deprecating. It was easy to forget what a dangerous and intimidating presence he could be in public. He was a playful kitten with her, but he could be a lion when he chose to be.

"Was surprised. I didn't think you cavorted with such types. I thought your tastes were more refined than that. How disappointing."

That creature, Hosseni, was goading him.

Jacques raised his eyebrow, and he spoke in a languid tone. "I would ask how your trip was, but it seems all you had time for was stalking others' whereabouts. May I recommend a couple of spots in the city? That way you could sightsee and not carry on gossiping like an old woman. I'm a pleasant enough fella, but not many others would be so forgiving. Just looking out for you, *ol' boy*."

With the exception of a snarling Hosseni, the rest of the men looked amused. Hosseni leveled a threatening look at Samya. Jacques turned back to her, covering her from Hosseni's gaze.

Her ears were ringing. Her cheeks were hot. She wanted to scream. It was over. Everything was done with. It felt like someone had sliced a huge gash at a newly healing wound.

"Thank you for the company." Jacques smiled at her. He looked as calm and charming as ever. As if their world wasn't falling apart. "I look forward to our paths crossing soon."

After carefully avoiding Hosseni and praying that every single guest would just leave, Samya was able to sneak out of her villa around 2:00 a.m. In the black of night, her heels click-clacked on cement as she sprinted to Jacques's villa. Before she could use the key he'd given her, the villa door swung open. Jacques grabbed her by the waist and held her. His breath tickled her ear. Warmth, she'd missed the warmth of his body. She enclosed her arms around his waist.

"How are you really?" Jacques said while kissing her neck.

"Peachy." She smiled.

Jacques pulled away from the hug and held her shoulders. "Really, tell me."

Samya sighed and looked down. "Not good. It's escalating. I'll be going to a hospital for treatment. There are moments when I'm alright, though."

"When will you go, and where is it?"

"Not sure yet."

He nodded. She knew he didn't believe her, but he didn't push.

Abruptly, he gave her a peck on the lips and then disappeared into the bedroom. Samya followed him as he shrugged on a coat.

"Where are you going?" Samya asked.

"To a registrar I know."

"At this hour? Why?"

"To get a marriage license."

Samya looked at him in horror. "I don't know who you think you are using it with, but it won't be me."

Jacques pulled open his drawers, pulling out money. "We don't know when this idiot will strike, but he will, and I'm not waiting around for him to do it. We are getting married." He paused. "Be reasonable."

"Jacques, I told you before I'm not getting married, period, full stop. Did you think I was just saying that? *You* said you never wanted to get married."

"It doesn't matter what I said now. We don't have a choice." The circles under his eyes were so dark compared to his pale face.

"Of course, there is a choice. We'll pay him off or...I'm leaving soon, anyway. Gossip won't have much intrigue if the subject isn't there. It will be old news."

"You are comfortable with a ruined reputation, then? What about your parents? What about Hend?"

Samya stopped him from leaving the bedroom and held his face. "Look at me. I'm *not* forcing you to marry me." She breathed slowly to quell her emotions. "We can figure this out without anyone's reputation being ruined. Just think with me. You are being obtuse."

He stepped away from her. "What is there to think about? Mostafa ratted on us, Hosseni saw us, or both. I'm not going to let you take the fall. Because that is what will happen. This is not something you need to worry about on top of everything else you have going on. Just let me handle it."

Her shoulders tensed; she was livid. "Oh, so you're the savior, are you? I don't have a choice, I suppose? Are you even listening to me? We are not getting married. I'm not going to trap you."

"Believe me, it's the other way around," he murmured while he hurried to reach the door. "These are the circumstances. I'll put up with it. So can you. We'll do it before you go to the hospital, so you don't need to think about it."

He went to hold her hand, and she shrugged him off.

Jacques sighed and looked away from her. "We can divorce in a year, or if you are lucky, we can do it after a couple of months if things die down."

Struck, tears spilled from her eyes. Her heart shattered, and she felt every shard cut her inside. This man, who'd just held her like she was his anchor, who she felt so at peace with, was now resigned to being stuck with her. Reason was clearly out the window. All he was focused on was fixing an immediate problem. There was no consideration for what being tied to each other would really mean. Well, he could do whatever the hell he wanted. She'd go it alone.

Busting the door open, she threw his key behind her back and left the villa, and Jacques, without ever looking back.

Chapter Forty

Jacques picked up the key Samya had thrown on the ground and hesitantly pocketed it. After wallowing in self pity for a couple of minutes, he reasoned that there was no sense in staying, so he left the villa. The emptiness of the street was eerie. Jacques walked fast to get to the main street where some straggling taxis likely waited.

He hadn't meant to come off as authoritative. Hell, he'd been anything but his entire life! But picturing Samya, catatonic, vulnerable, and also having to deal with the ire of society—it had scared him. Samya was the strong one. She took on so much and held back a lot. Even this very night, when their world was going to be devoured by flames, she acted like she was the healthiest person in the world. But he knew her now. He knew all the tricks and masks she used to put up a facade of normalcy.

Jacques stopped at a shawarma joint encircled by men smoking outside their taxis.

"*Yusta*, want to give me a ride?"

A man with a long, blue-and-white traditional frock and wrinkled skin motioned him over to a taxi that looked like it would break if you slammed a door too hard. With not much choice at this hour, Jacques got in.

"Where to, *basha*?"

Jacques hesitated. Samya would not marry him. That was clear. But he could still help somehow, and he knew where to start. "Cairo train station."

After a fifteen-minute ride, Jacques departed the taxi, giving the driver a generous tip, and walked up the stairs to the station. He cut a ticket to Tanta, got a Turkish coffee at a newsstand, and sat on a bench nearby. The next train wouldn't leave for a couple of hours.

While he waited, his erratic thoughts overtook him. The night Jacques had gotten back to Cairo, he'd waited in his villa by the door. Although he knew Samya would avoid him after what had happened in Tanta, he'd hoped she would forget herself and come to him.

She hadn't showed. He'd known he couldn't go over to Samya's home uninvited, so he'd frequented the cafés in order to find Dr. Mahmoud to try to charm an invite to the villa to see her. But he'd had no luck.

Then earlier tonight, he hadn't been able to take it anymore. He'd found himself headed straight for the Roshdi villa. He had no idea there was a soiree in full swing. This would have surprised him, given Samya's situation, but he knew she would figure out a way to pretend all was well. His girl knew how to keep everything together for others, to her detriment.

When he'd seen her, everything had rushed back to him. He was not worthy. He would hurt her. All those thoughts remained stuck to him like barnacles on a ship. Despite that, he couldn't stop trying to take her in. Living through every memory they'd had together and realizing all the new moments he was going to lose.

Jacques knew what being alone was. That had been the majority of his life prior to Cairo. Samya was alone. That is what he'd seen in the Roshdi ballroom. She had looked brilliant, with a dress that hugged her curves perfectly and jewelry that anyone in Cairo would be jealous of. But what he'd seen was the woman underneath who was suffering in silence. She was shouldering everything on her own. Jacques doubted Samya even shared what was fully going on with her with her father, her lone confidant when it came to her illness. And now, when she was at her loneliest, Jacques had managed to push her away.

Shaking his head, he came back to the present. Finally, just before sunrise, the train opened for seating. Jacques walked his weary self to the first-class cabin, holding on to the seats along the way for support.

The minute the words had left Hosseni's foul mouth, Jacques had known what had to be done. He was almost relieved not to have a choice. No one in Cairo society would judge him. He was a man. A foreigner with different morals. But Samya was one of them. She would be cast out as a slut, a whore. She would have no future and be forced to run and hide. This was someone's life. Someone he cared about immensely. More than just cared about. He had to make things right.

***

After the train arrived in Tanta, Jacques walked on foot to his uncle's apartment. The only people out were fruit and vegetable vendors just opening up their storefronts. Jacques walked into the apartment with a key he had and slipped into the dark library. It was deathly silent. There were no windows, and the place had a suffocating air. The plush tangerine chair he sat in matched the rugs and light wood shelves. There was a stale smell to the library as if it hadn't been used for decades. Considering its inhabitant, that did not seem far-fetched. Jacques was wired yet inexplicably calm for having been awake for twenty-eight hours. He heard the door creak.

"*Amo* Mostafa. Please sit."

Jacques's uncle, wearing a long, white nightshirt and a matching linen nightcap, jumped with fright and apprehension. "What? How did you get in?"

"You should really lock your doors, or my doors, to be specific."

His uncle composed himself and chuckled awkwardly. "I wasn't expecting you is all. You should really call ahead, son. That way I can receive you properly."

Jacques leaned back, clasped his hands together on his stomach, and smiled. "I'm very well aware of how you receive people. I'd rather an impromptu visit. You've been talking to some of my friends in Cairo, I've heard."

The old man hunched and played at being confused. "Well, son, so many people come from Cairo to Tanta, it is hard to tell."

"Let's skip the part where you stumble over your words, and let's get to the truth of the matter. You are using a conduit to threaten me. Is that right? If you had fought fairly and only directed your anger towards me, I would have dealt with you differently. But you've involved an innocent in your quest to get back at your dead brother and his living wife. Your mistake lately is you've involved those who are my responsibility and in my care."

"I would never do anything..." His uncle started to tremble.

"Did you talk to Dr. Hosseni Waqab? "

"Well, yes."

"And what did you talk about?"

"I mentioned you visited and came with your secretary. I merely described her, and he seemed to know the young lady. Look, son. You are unaware of the culture. The young lady you were with was likely out to trap you. Someone has to look out for you."

Jacques was disgusted by the man in front of him. He couldn't stomach the lies and deceit.

Jacques held a hand up. "Let me get to the point. You will not come anywhere near my sisters or their mother. If they are walking the same street as you, you will turn around and sprint, or limp quickly in your case, to the opposite side of the street. You will not get an *irsh* from them or from me. Madame Lena, as a wise woman, has rejected your proposals, and she *will* be left alone."

Jacques then stood up and walked slowly to his uncle. He didn't stop advancing until his uncle fell back into a chair.

"As for the young lady, Samya Roshdi, who you want to drag through the mud. You will call Dr. Hosseni and tell him you are a delusional, decrepit shit, and you never saw her with me in Tanta. In fact you've never seen her in your life. You said those venomous things to besmirch your nephew because you are a rat and you will apologize profusely. And after that call, you will *never* mention that woman's name in any circle. Consider those four people as fire that will burn you if you come anywhere near them."

"How dare you talk to me like that? I'm your elder!"

Jacques ignored him. "If I find that you have any association with Mademoiselle Samya, Madame Lena, or my sisters, or if you even breathe in a way I don't like, I'll turn you out on your ass so fast you'll forget your own name. Oh, yes. The deed for this house is under my name. I bought it months ago, just in case something went wrong with the court case."

His uncle's eyes widened.

And the nice little check you get every month is from my account. I will cut that off, and you will understand what real deprivation feels like."

"But I can't control what Hosseni says. He pressured me into it. I swear I didn't mean to..."

"I've told you the consequences. How you accomplish your salvation is up to you. I want a confirmation that you've talked to Dr. Hosseni and cleared up your misstep."

He raised his hand, and his uncle flinched. Jacques dusted his uncle's shoulder.

"My dad was a bastard, to be sure. Not just to you, but to all of us. But I will not allow you to exercise your frustrations on others. You have until tomorrow."

With that, Jacques strode out of his uncle's house.

Six months ago Jacques thought he had lost his last family member. Now, in a matter of weeks he'd gained two sisters, one stepmother, and he wasn't sure what Samya was. But she was possibly the biggest thing he'd acquired in his life. Though he had no practical or legal right to have her, she had somehow imprinted herself onto him, and he wouldn't let go.

They were four people to care for, and if he allowed himself, four people to care for him.

Chapter Forty-One

Anger helped Samya push down the hurt as she ran from Jacques's villa and snuck back home. Once she entered her room, she stuck her face in a pillow and expelled all the hurt and sadness in screams and tears. After crying herself exhausted, Samya sat up, eyes red rimmed, and took two barbiturates from her vanity drawer. It was difficult. The sadness was increasing by the day. She was holding everything in until next week when she could get to the hospital and get shock treatment.

She hadn't had an episode in days and hoped the trend would keep long enough for her to figure out how to shut Hosseni up. Oh, how she'd wanted to smack Jacques before she'd left his villa. He was uncooperative. That was men for you. Just go, go, go without a thought for nuance. The way Jacques had talked so callous-like about their potential future as man and wife. "*We can get divorced...*" Not that she ever would have agreed to marry him and subsequently ruin his life, but still. And if she wasn't sick... She didn't have that option, so it didn't matter, either.

She needed to think about how to defeat Hosseni. But her thinking was clouded, and she was depressed. Although she always did everything on her own, this time was different. Though it was against every fiber of her being to ask for it, this time she needed help.

***

It was early morning at the *nady*, and Samya found herself sitting across from an apathetic Omar. The café she'd chosen was tiny and discreet, hidden within a flower garden and covered by tall trees. She hadn't seen Omar since their fight over Jacques in downtown Cairo. At least he'd shown up when she asked him to.

Omar ordered Turkish coffee and then crossed his legs and arms. He was wearing a smart tan suit with a red tie. He was likely headed to court after his meeting with her. She sipped on her tea with milk and then crossed her arms. They were at a standoff.

He would revel in how right he'd been once she told him about her affair. She was preparing herself for the put down that would have hits such as "I told you he was out to get you!" And "You are so naive." And "You know, the women are the ones to suffer in these situations." But she had to remind herself not to fight back. She needed a favor, and now was not the time to debate who was right (Omar) and who was wrong (Samya). And she was so damn tired and sad. And angry with herself and Jacques. Omar was her best hope in finding a solution to the mess that was hurling her way. So, against her own nature, Samya prepared to grovel and come clean.

She took one big breath. "Omar, I need your help."

His eye twitched, and he didn't say anything for a bit. "What did he do?"

Dammit, why did it have to be so obvious to him? Samya sighed and looked down. "So you know. Well, all the less I'll have to catch you up on, then."

"Start from the beginning." Omar leaned in as if he was going to pull out a pad and paper and take notes.

"I've been meeting Jacques in secret for a bit. A week ago, we went to Tanta together under the guise that we were husband and wife. He was closing out a family issue."

Samya could see that Omar was doing everything in his power to hold back a lecture. And for that, she was thankful.

"We were likely spotted."

"By whom?"

"Dr. Hosseni. Well…Jacques's uncle who hates Jacques."

"I don't blame him."

She ignored his retort. "His uncle somehow figured out who I was and clued Hosseni in. Hosseni all but announced a threat during the soiree at my parents' yesterday night. It's clear he wants to expose us."

Omar pinched the bridge of his nose and took a breath. He didn't talk for a while. This was a habit of his, and she was never sure if it was prosecutor behavior or just Omar. Omar would take in information and then analyze it in his brain to find every possible outcome. He needed the utmost silence.

Finally, Omar spoke. "There's only one solution, Samya."

"No."

"He may have been a dalliance, but your reputation is on the line. Look, all I know of Hosseni is he is from the Waqab family, and judging by his behavior last night, I hardly expect him to act mercifully towards you. Jacques acted dishonorably and must pay the price. I'll see that he honors his duty."

Samya laughed. "Well, you'll love this. He's already asked me…well, told me, more like. I rejected him, and I don't plan on marrying him or anyone else, Omar, before you offer that up. I came to you because I know there is another way. Can't you have one of your detectives at the police station dig up some dirt on Hosseni so we can blackmail him?"

"Why not just pay off a bunch of thugs to frame him for murder?"

Samya's eyes widened. "Can we do that?"

Omar sighed and rubbed his face. "I'll see what I can find out. In the meantime, I suggest you stay out of sight. I'll update you when I have something."

Omar got up to leave but then turned around. "Samya, the man is repulsive to me, but you clearly have some sort of affection towards him. This could be easily fixed if you married. Why not?"

"I won't let it happen."

"Is it because you regret the affair?"

Just then, tears she didn't give permission to flowed down her face.

Omar sat back down, concerned.

Ya Allah, she was so tired. The depression was constantly at her heels. Never letting up. Never giving her a break.

"No. I don't regret a thing. I don't regret spending time with him. Unfortunately, this incident hasn't wisened me up like you would want."

She tried to keep her breathing even and went for a watery smile. "There's so much you don't know about me."

Omar leaned in. "Tell me. I'm here."

She really wanted to. It was at the tip of her tongue, everything she wanted to say but couldn't. Out of fear. The pain of watching Omar's expression as she told him that she'd been to the mental hospital and that she'd be going back would be too much. The disgust or, worse, the pity in his eyes would be unbearable. It had been so easy with Jacques. He hadn't judged her. And she'd never had to hold herself back. He knew all of her. As much of an ass as he was being, she missed him fiercely.

"It is not the time."

Omar touched her hand. "Samya, is something else going on?"

She looked at him. "Just discover what you can and come find me."

Chapter Forty-Two

Dar El-Qadaa El-Ali was as silent as a crypt. It was close to 9:00 p.m. and most employees of the High Court of Justice had already gone home. With Kareem following him, Jacques knocked with urgency on one of the prosecutors' offices. The door was bubbled glass with the name "Omar Khaled Nabil" etched on it. Omar opened the door for them and flared his nostrils.

"Bringing Kareem here won't protect you from me. If it weren't for the catastrophe you put Samya in, I would have decked you flat by now."

Despite this welcome, Omar left the door open when he went back inside his office.

The office was organized, not a speck of dust to be found. Certainly not the mountain of papers Jacques had seen at Solayman's. A plain but polished brown desk, chairs, drawers, and a two-person couch occupied the space. It smelled of coffee with cardamom and books whose decaying pages were constantly being rifled through.

Jacques spoke as Omar sat behind his desk. "I brought Kareem to help. You'll have plenty of time to beat the hell out of me later. For now, please tell Samya to come here. We can fix this, but I need her here."

Omar crossed his arms. "You need her? You don't get to need anything anymore. She came to me. But for the blood that runs through our veins, that girl is my sister. If you have business, you can say it to me directly."

Kareem sat down in the chair facing him. Omar was one of the few people from the elite that Kareem spoke to. "My friend, the situation is what it is. We all want the same outcome, that Samya come out of this unharmed. Four brains are better than three."

Tightening his jaw, a cross Omar eventually left and, not half an hour later, came back with Samya in tow.

Despite the circumstances, Jacques had missed her intensely. She wore a white linen shirt tucked into beige cigarette pants. Her lips were the red Jacques remembered kissing off of her night after night. But his girl looked weary with a glazed expression and a less assured stride. The dramatic, confident, chaotic air that embodied Samya was nowhere to be found. Some force she couldn't control was deflating it all out of her.

Samya eyed Kareem, and Jacques interjected, "This is Kareem Waqab."

She raised her eyebrow. "Waqab?"

Kareem stepped in. "You don't know me, mademoiselle. Yes, Hosseni is a cousin, but I did not grow up with him, nor do I have any allegiance to that family."

Jacques appreciated his kind friend's presence. "He's akin to my brother. You can trust him."

As if Jacques hadn't spoken, Samya looked at Omar and relaxed a fraction when he nodded. The dismissal stung.

"Everyone is flawed. Always a hidden secret or two. Hosseni must have something," Kareem said.

"I'm waiting for a thorough background check. Not much I could find on him on my own. Samya." Omar looked at her. "There's a possibility, our last resort, that you'll have to marry."

Samya made a slicing movement with her hand. "Absolutely. Not. The only reason I agreed to come here was to come up with an alternate solution."

Jacques stayed quiet. He had done enough damage regarding this topic. Now was not the time to debate her. Besides, who would want to be forced into marriage under these circumstances?

Kareem leaned in. "I'm unclear about the reason for Hosseni's animosity. Did anything happen between you three?"

Samya looked at the couch and unraveled a thread. Jacques looked up at the ceiling.

"I put bleach in his shampoo." "I put itching powder in his boxers." Both said at the same time.

They looked at each other, and she gave him a small smile.

Kareem held back a smirk, but Omar paced the room. "Well, what a pair you are! You're smiling, eh? You are proud of yourselves, are you?"

"Omar, he deserved it. He was nasty to me," Samya said.

"So you play a prank on him? How old are you?"

"Twenty-nine." "Thirty-one." Samya and Jacques said at the same time.

After shaking his head in amusement, Kareem looked at the pair. "Though the elite are narcissistic, block-headed, arrogant..." His friend was getting progressively worked up over his clear distaste for the privileged. Jacques motioned his hands for Kareem to move on from the tirade.

Kareem sighed. "They are a difficult bunch is the point. Still, I doubt small pranks would make him threaten someone's entire reputation. There has to be something more. What's not being said?"

Samya slightly rocked back and forth, likely not aware she was doing so. The truth, Jacques suspected, was that Hosseni's problem was Samya. Her illness, her personality, her very existence offended him.

Jacques unglued his eyes from Samya. "I'm a foreigner and grew up poor besides. I'm not exactly Hosseni's favorite person. As for my uncle who exposed us, I messed up his plan to marry my stepmother and get her inheritance. This fiasco is my fault."

Kareem squinted his eyes as if he was not entirely convinced, but he let it drop.

Samya stopped rocking and looked at Jacques. There was sadness in her eyes. What Kareem and Omar didn't know was that this woman was dealing with a crisis within a crisis. He knew she was repressing the illness as much as she could in order to handle this on her own. That she'd asked for any help from Omar was evidence that she was struggling badly. Jacques would have done anything to change that. If she would just let him in. He needed to earn it, though, and he wasn't sure if he had done enough for that.
Omar continued to pace, acting like he was hanging onto his sanity by a thread. "How about...?"

A knock swiveled their heads toward the door. A young officer with a thin mustache came in.

Omar brightened. "Yes, what have you found, man?"

The officer handed him a paper and then left in haste. Omar scanned it, blew out a breath, and then handed it to Kareem.

Jacques and Samya leaned forward. "And?"

"He's clean. Medical license is up to date. No debts. No complaints. Unfortunately, there's no crime against being an arrogant bully," Omar said.

Samya got up. "Then we'll pay him off."

"His family is well off. He doesn't need anything from us."

Jacques racked his brain, trying to keep the hopelessness at bay. He couldn't think of a thing to get Hosseni off their backs. The man was old money. He had the education, the riches, the women, anything he could ever want. What they needed was a miracle.

Samya threw up her hands in exasperation and sat back down. "Can't you pay one of your officers to rough him up a bit?"

"Ya Allah, Samya," Omar sighed.

"There are tons of corrupt police in the news all the time. Where are those guys?"

"Well, I'll just take out an advertisement in the paper: 'Seeking crooked police officer to disappear a rich person seeking revenge for bleached hair.' Problem solved!"

A soft knock sounded. With a huff, Omar went to the door.

With Omar gone, Jacques leaned in towards Samya. "How are you?"

She smirked. "Well, I'm about to shame my entire family. So, just peachy."

Kareem thankfully got up and pretended to be interested in the legal literature on Omar's bookshelf. Good man.

Jacques leaned in, so only she could hear. "How are you really? How are the episodes?"

"They're fine. They said to say hi." She looked away, frowning. "This is not your fault, you know. I chose this. No need to feel obligated. Either way, this won't harm you. Omar and I will figure something out."

Jacques shot up and sat next to her on the couch. "So, this doesn't concern me?" He forced himself to soften his tone, reaching for her hand. "When will you understand? What concerns you, concerns me."

"Samya, you're needed at the door," Omar said before looking down at Jacques's hands on hers. He shook his head.

Samya looked thankful to get out of the conversation. Who could possibly have needed Samya at this hour, at the High Court, no less? When Jacques went to follow her, Omar blocked his path.

"I said '*Samya.*'"

Samya went to the door, leaving Jacques and Omar locked in a stare down.

Omar seethed. "I told you all those months ago. I told you to stay away from her. But the rules just don't apply to you, do they?"

Omar's berating wasn't pleasant, but Jacques couldn't blame him. Jacques had placed Samya in the situation they were in.

In an attempt to defuse the situation, Kareem stepped in between them. "He's here to make things right. Besides, this wasn't just a lustful mistake. Omar, you see how they are together. As tense as this situation is, you can't deny what you see before you."

"I wish I didn't."

Taking Omar's bait would do nothing to improve the situation and would stress Samya out. Besides, Jacques was glad Samya had someone like Omar watching out for her even if the man did hate Jacques.

After a couple of minutes spent in awkward silence, Samya came back. She was accompanied by a petite young woman wearing a traditional black wrap with two auburn braids that fell to the middle of her back. The young woman was looking towards the ground and shaking.

Samya held her hand, smiled at her in a maternal way, and spoke to her alone. "You don't have to do this."

The young woman shook her head vehemently.

Samya sighed and addressed them. "Gentlemen, this is Ruqquyah. She used to work for Hosseni's stepmom. She has important information to share with us."

A tear streamed down Ruqquyah's cheek, but she placed both her hands on her slightly swollen stomach, breathed out, and proceeded to become their salvation.

CHAPTER FORTY-THREE

Ruqquyah, Jacques, and Samya waited in the shadows across the street from the Egyptian Automobile Club. It was an exclusive social club reserved for the Cairo elite and, once upon a time, British patriots. Dr. Hosseni was likely forced to migrate to it when the Muhammad Ali Club closed down. That was where majority of nobility and old money families used to belong pre-revolution.

When Ruqquyah had come the night before, Samya had thought the visit had something to do with her health.

"Are you hurt, *habibti*?"

Ruqquyah shook her head. "*Khalti* Zoo Zoo told me you were here. Please don't be upset with her, but I heard you were going through trouble with the Waqab family. She knew I used to work there."

Samya had told Zoo Zoo about her dilemma to see if, as a last resort, her maid could hire ruffians. Zoo Zoo had been a sourpuss to Samya for half the day afterward for having thought she would be associated with such types. It turned out that the well-meaning old gossip had great instincts.

Ruqquyah had given them enough to make a plan.

Omar was a member of the Egyptian Automobile Club, and he'd been able to take Kareem in as a guest. They would go through the front entrance and lull Hosseni to an upstairs parlor room with promises of rare cigars and courtesans. Meanwhile, Jacques, Samya, and Ruqquyah would sneak in through the service entrance, courtesy of a maid they'd bribed.

Samya was feeling a bit ill about having Ruqquyah involved at all. She'd rather face the consequences than expose the nineteen-year-old to Hosseni's nastiness. Said nineteen-year-old wouldn't have it. The girl too shy to talk to Samya during their first meeting was obstinate.

Ruqquyah wore the traditional club's maid uniform: a navy blue blouse and matching skirt. She added a shawl to hide her pregnant belly. Jacques and Samya wore veils so that no one from the hundreds of the elite inside would recognize them. It was hot underneath the layers of the black dress and veil Samya donned, which only revealed her eyes. She wondered how Jacques was faring. Hopefully, it would be dark and smoky enough inside that no one would notice the 6'1 lady wearing an abaya that only reached the top of her hairy ankles.

Wearing the face veil was in sharp decline these days. Once the trend for urban elite women, it had been de-popularized in 1923 when feminist Huda Sha'arawi tore hers off in the middle of the Cairo train station. Nowadays, only those clinging onto tradition and those seeking to hide their identity wore them.

Plan or not, Samya regretted coming. She and Jacques should have stayed behind; it would have been less conspicuous. But Ruqquyah had wanted Samya to be there and Jacques wouldn't leave Samya to face Hosseni alone. Apparently, Kareem, Omar, and Ruqquyah accompanying her did not count.

Pulling up the sleeve of his black frock, Jacques looked at his Rolex watch. "It's past midnight, and the servant's entrance door still hasn't opened. I say we rush in."

"Why would you wear a Rolex watch underneath that? No one will see you," Samya said.

"It is still a social club." Jacques's eyes crinkled up.

Being around him was a reprieve from the mess they were in though, even so, it was harder and harder to concentrate on the present with the depression escalating. Only sheer will had got her out of bed and dressed this evening. In the dark alley they were in, she put her hand on her fast-beating heart. Droplets of cold sweat were dampening the interior of her veil. Tingles started populating her legs. She breathed slowly, and tilted herself away from the others. This was not the time for an episode. The barbiturates she had taken earlier should be working. But they were so inconsistent; she was constantly on edge. It could be the start of an episode, or it could be extreme nerves; she wasn't sure.

Samya felt a hand hold her upper arm and squeeze. These days, her body wanted to stray and disconnect from her mind. But Jacques's firm grip served as an anchor, helping her focus. That grasp reminded her she was here. She curled her toes in her shoes until they strained. She dug her nails into her wrist, the pain breaking through the numbness. Then she slowed her breathing. She resisted the urge to close her eyes and completely float away.

Finally, whatever it was subsided. She wasn't sure how Jacques had known to hold her so securely. Normally, she hated when people touched her during episodes, where she had no autonomy. But his touch was a reliable chain back to earth. When she looked at him and nodded, Jacques moved his thumb across her arm in a reassuring caress before letting go. Moments like these made the burden of leaving him that much greater.

The service entrance door swung open, letting out light, music, hustle and bustle. A young woman in a club uniform with her black, coily hair wrapped in a bun motioned for them to come in quickly.

They ran across the concrete street and stepped inside the warmth of a busy kitchen.

The maid looked at Jacques and Samya with her mouth hanging open. Samya supposed it was strange to see the veiled entering a men's social club.

"Thank you. Leave now, so you don't get in trouble," Samya said.

The maid nodded her head. "It is on the fourth floor, your third door to the right. May Allah be with you!"

The trio made their way out of the kitchen to the service stairs that ran behind a humungous stage where belly dancers were twirling to a ten-piece orchestra. The theme was apparently something like "Arabian Nights" since all the performers were dressed in lavish colors with gold coins bouncing off their hips. Samya could make out hundreds of men smoking cigars and drinking, seated at small round tables facing the stage. Accompanying them were, ahem, ladies of the night.

Being later than the appointed hour, they had no choice but to run. Ruqquyah leaned on Samya as she went up the stairs. It wasn't easy for a seven-month pregnant woman as petite as her to go up even one flight of steps, let alone four.

They finally reached the top, only to be stopped by a butler. He was an older man with wisps of white hair on his head, and he wore an English-styled, black-and-white uniform.

"Girl! Who are those things with you?"

Ruqquyah tensed.

"Are you deaf? We don't allow those kinds of people in this establishment. Shoo, now. Go."

Samya stepped in as she was still trying to catch her breath. "Oh sir, we are not *those* kinds of people." Not knowing exactly what he meant. "You see...me and my very tall sister were burnt in a terrific fire set by a drunk man who hated my father. We are very scarred and ashamed to show our faces. If only you could have seen us, sir. We were such beauties in our time. Well, not my sister, but I was. And now? What do we have...?"

The butler squinted his eyes. "What does this have to do with anything? Don't think you could come in here and stir up all kinds of trouble."

"*Yusta* Hamdy!" A male voice called from down the stairs, distracting the butler. "Do you have the whiskey yet?"

The butler huffed and looked toward Ruqquyah. "Get those two con artists out of here."

She nodded, and he disappeared down the stairs.

With the hallway clear, they hightailed it to the third door and knocked.

An excruciatingly long minute later, Omar swung the door open. "Where were you guys? We've had to entertain this fool forever."

The three of them walked into a cozy parlor. It had a small but full bar to the right, and lush maroon-and-gold curtains served as a barrier to the cars, pedestrians, and palm trees outside. The low lighting created an atmosphere of anticipatory sin. Cigar smoke floated from where Kareem and Hosseni sat on large leather couches. Kareem, who was a giant, kept fidgeting in black and whites that didn't quite fit him.

Hosseni smiled lazily and hiccuped. "Ah, I see the entertainment's here. I didn't know you had such traditional tastes, Kareem."

Hosseni froze when his eyes landed on Ruqquyah. Jacques, ever the showman, took the opportunity of the shocking moment to uncloak. He was wearing a crisp three-piece suit, all in gray, his hair somehow in perfect place.

Hosseni put his whiskey down and straightened up in his chair. "What is this?"

"Why, your comeuppance, old chap," Jacques said with a smile.

Hosseni made a clumsy run for the door but was blocked by Kareem.

"I think you'll want to sit down," Omar motioned towards a couch.

"Or what?" Hosseni spat. His eyes were a bit red, his tie askew, and his hair slightly ruffled. Although Samya could smell strong liquor from across the room, the ambush seemed to sober Hosseni up some.

"Well, that's what we are going to talk about. Of course…" Omar put his hands on Ruqquyah's shoulders. "We could do this out in the open if you'd like."

"What is she doing here?" Hosseni slurred slightly at Ruqquyah.

Samya had to fight the urge to shield her, but to her surprise, Ruqquyah spoke.

"Hosseni." It came out as a shade louder than a whisper.

"It's Dr. Hosseni." He looked around nervously at the others.

"Dr. Hosseni, I…" Ruqquyah was trembling. She looked at Samya, who nodded reassuringly. Then, Ruqquyah fisted her hands and dug them into her sides. "I have a story to tell that I think many in your community would be interested to hear."

"Well, I don't give a damn what she has to say. No one will." He seemed to address the men in the room.

Omar gave Ruqquyah's shoulders a squeeze before stepping back from her and giving her space.

"I think some will," she said. "It's about a maid working for the Waqab family. When you came from England, the maid was infatuated with you, from afar, of course. You were handsome, well read, and distinguished. But you knew that, I think. You used it to get close to her. When you saw her read Timaeus, you didn't mock her or act shocked that a lowly maid was literate. You debated philosophical theories with her. You and she became closer, and you told her of your troubles with your ex-wife. 'If only she were like you' is what you told her more than one time while she was falling deeper and deeper in love with you. Then she gave herself to you, thinking you would marry her."

Ruqquyah's voice broke then. Her pale cheeks burned red, as if to broadcast the shame she felt from that statement.

"You touted her as the ideal woman so many times, she foolishly thought marriage was a foregone conclusion. But then she was fired without explanation and told to leave the villa immediately."

Hosseni didn't bother to look Ruqquyah in the eye. He sighed as if she was reading him the table of contents of a textbook.

Ruqquyah wavered but kept on. "She saw you with another girl from the house when she came back to try to speak to you. Then it all made sense. You got what you wanted, and you were done with…her. Unfortunately, you've given her something she'll never be able to forget."

She let down her shawl and revealed her bump.

Chapter Forty-Four

Hosseni stared, looking horrified. His shock vibrated off of him as he plopped down into a chair. As if he'd just remembered he was in a room full of people, he collected himself.

Looking down at her unborn child seemed to fuel Ruqquyah's slow growing confidence. "After I was kicked out, I vowed to leave and never let my child know their father. But circumstances have changed."

He shot up out of his chair. "How do I know it is even…? She's a slut. Lowly girls like her are broken in when they're fourteen and even younger. She's probably had lots of men. I'm not claiming her bastard."

Ruqquyah, a soft, sweet soul, widened her watery eyes. "You were my first." She looked down. "My only."

"She's clearly lying," Hosseni said to Omar.

"I believe her." Jacques stepped forward.

"So do I," Omar said.

"Me, too," Kareem affirmed.

Jacques stood next to Ruqquyah. "And so will the men of the elite downstairs when we expose you to them."

"They'll never believe her," Hosseni said firmly.

"Sadly, that may be true. But they will believe three respected men from amongst their kind."

"Besides that, there are two other maids who will testify against you in public," Ruqquyah said, standing her ground. Her voice was now fully audible. "You did the same with them."

Hosseni, the man Samya had thought of as substantial, respectable, and formidable mere months ago, was now acting like a cornered wild animal, waving his hands as he yelled. "You wouldn't dare spread such lies about me. The other men will know it is dishonorable."

Omar looked down at him. "What's dishonorable is seducing very young women under your family's home and protection and then abandoning them. One of whom is bearing your child."

Hosseni opened his mouth and then shut it.

He seemed to contemplate the situation. Samya could see the moment defeat claimed him. He wiped his face with his hand, his pinky ring glinting against the light. "What do you want?"

"For you to stop."

"And a sum of 10,000 pounds for Ruqquyah, along with an official document stating you will not come for the child," Kareem added.

"And to leave Samya Roshdi and her family alone," Ruqquyah added.

Hosseni stilled as if he was internally calculating something. Slowly, he twisted his features into a grimace. "Oh, so this is what it's really about, is it?" He looked at Jacques. "You're out to cover for your whore?"

At the sound of the word "whore," Jacques launched himself towards Hosseni. He was stopped by Kareem and Omar, who pulled him back by the waist.

Shaking his head, Hosseni cackled. "I'm surprised she isn't here with you, seeing as she has you by the balls."

"Here I am...sans balls." Samya flipped open the veil over her head so the vile man could see her smiling face. Jacques wasn't the only dramatic one.

For the first time during this entire fiasco, Hosseni looked genuinely disgusted. "You caused all this trouble." He pointed at her. "Did you think I didn't know what you did? You burnt my scalp! I had to wear a hat for weeks, you bitch."

Good, she thought. Samya walked up to Jacques, who was boiling. He looked down at her with his hardened emerald eyes, his chest moving up and down rapidly. She placed her hand on his heart, and he seemed to ease. It was her turn to confront the man who'd threatened so many. Who was turning her world upside down.

She turned to face him, but before she could get the chance to speak, Hosseni raised his voice. "She's insane, you know. I mean looney bin crazy. She's been to several asylums.

I have a psychiatrist friend up in Alex who will verify it. And now they've released her on unsuspecting, decent people."

Struck, Samya didn't dare turn around. She didn't dare see her friends' faces. The absolute silence in response to Hosseni's declaration was a slap in the face.

She felt someone slide past her. In a blur, Jacques grabbed Hosseni up by the collar and slammed him into the wall. Kareem and Omar must have let go willingly because each now flanked either side of Samya.

"Apologize. Now," Jacques gritted out.

Hosseni was not a slight man, but the effects of his drinking were still evident. He flailed unsuccessfully to get Jacques off of him.

"What are you—? Ya Allah." Hosseni stopped struggling. "You knew." He laughed. "You knew and still fucked her."

"Stop!" Samya screamed before Jacques could get a hit in.

It clicked. Samya understood now. Hosseni hated *her*. When the nobility had been taken down by the revolution, families like Hosseni's were forced to socialize with the non-noble—albeit rich—masses. Exclusivity and money were the last things he could cling onto from his old life. Samya wasn't a person to him. She was a pollutant.

"You are right. I am crazy," Samya said in a soft tone.

Omar placed his hand on her back. Keeping her eyes steady on Hosseni, she refused to look at her best friend's face and the expression of concern he almost certainly wore.

Words she had no control over started pouring out of her. "And this crazy whore will occupy the same social circles you do. Will be dancing at the same soirees you frequent. Will be drinking the same champagne, breathing the same air as you. And someday soon, this crazy whore will be your colleague, and you'll have to call me doctor. All the while, you'll know that everything I am, everything you hate is on *exactly* the same level as you."

It came out of her so assuredly.

But she didn't know if she believed it. She hadn't needed the affair with Jacques to ruin her reputation. She'd become unacceptable the moment she went to the hospital at age nineteen. Hosseni was not an anomaly. Most would not fully accept her. Amongst the elite, she would have to live in the margins. The chill of loneliness crept up her body. Still, her pride wouldn't cede to Hosseni's bullying. Maybe pride inspired her, and some little fleck of something inside her begging to be lit up.

Lie or not, her monologue shut Hosseni up.

Omar cleared his throat. "To the matter at hand. Let's get this over with."

He pulled a briefcase out with a contract he and Kareem had worked on the night before. Jacques slammed Hosseni back into the chair.

Before he signed, Hosseni paused and looked up at Omar. "How could a prosecutor like you condone blackmailing one of us?"

Jacques jumped in. "Don't think of it as blackmail. It's vigilante justice."

Samya was relieved that he'd cut in to give her strait-laced friend an escape from answering.

Hosseni signed the document, almost puncturing a hole in it with his force. In the end, Hosseni's threat of societal shame to break Samya had broken him.

With the contract secured, the triumphant heroes left the villain to lick his wounds in the parlor alone.

Chapter Forty-Five

Jacques, Samya, and Ruqquyah came down the service entrance and ran across the street from the club. They waited in the same alleyway they'd been in earlier for Kareem and Omar to come out of the main entrance. The chilly night air cooled Samya's sweat from the run. The light of a street lamp from the main road illuminated the alley just enough that they could see each other. The sounds of people from the open air café next to the club were muffled at this distance.

Samya could feel Jacques watching her, biding his time, but she wasn't ready for him. Instead, she held Ruqquyah's hand. Though Samya was hesitant to speak given the way Hosseni had exposed her in front of everyone, she pushed the memory down. "*Habibti,* you saved us. Thank you. You have no idea how much..."

Ruqquyah's doe eyes were dancing with apparent happiness, and she was smiling from ear to ear. "I should thank you! I thought it would hurt seeing him again. Of course, it did. But, with all of you there, I don't know. I feel lighter than I have during this whole pregnancy."

That was a relief. "I'm so glad for you. Will you now come to live in my family home? We would love to have you, and you'll be near Zoo Zoo. There will be plenty of people around to spoil the little one."

"Well, I've just decided something crazy." Ruqquyah took in a sharp breath, likely noticing her unfortunate choice of words.

Samya only smiled. "What?"

Ruqquyah's shoulders relaxed. "I think I'll move to Greece." She bit her lip.

Letting a pregnant nineteen-year-old venture out to an entirely different country gave rise to several anxieties in Samya's mind.

Ruqquyah pressed on in the face of Samya's silence. "I want my child to have a chance. I can't have that in Cairo. Maybe I can study one day when my baby is bigger. Either way, I want to start new. It's what is best for both of us."

Ruqquyah was glowing. The girl, no, the woman, was one of the bravest, most intelligent people Samya had ever seen. "I know it will be wonderful. I have cousins there. We can find you a place to live with their assistance. Can you at least let me arrange that?"

The short woman jumped and gave Samya a big hug. "I would love that!" She held Samya's hands. "And I know things will get better for you." Ruqquyah looked in Jacques's direction and then back at Samya. "You have many people who care about you. I hope you will let us do so one of these days."

"Little sister!" Omar and Kareem entered the alley, and Omar pinched Samya's cheeks. "We're free! You're a right pain, but you know how to hold your own."

Samya smiled, rubbing her cheek. Omar's cheeriness was a respite before the barrage of questions she knew he'd be bombarding her with soon.

Kareem loosened the tie that was likely choking him. "I'm glad this worked out. But we shouldn't stay here too long. Ruqquyah, I can take you home."

The group made their way out onto the street, with Ruqquyah and Kareem breaking off to head to his car. That's when Jacques held on to Samya's hand, pulling her back.

Omar looked back at them sternly. "Do you want all our hard work to go to waste?"

"One minute," Jacques said, looking at Samya.

Omar indignantly went about fifty yards away, where he was close enough to shield them from discovery but far enough for them to have privacy.

Samya broke the silence. "Well, it's over," she said breathlessly.

Jacques nodded, his eyes crinkling at the beginnings of a smile. He brought her in for a tight hug.

"You were brilliant," he whispered in her ear.

"We were brilliant," Samya whispered back.

A loud Omar-sounding "tut tut" reached them, and Samya slowly pulled away from Jacques.

He pulled a curl from her coiffure. "I've missed you, Fred."

She huffed a laugh and rolled her eyes. "Well, of course you did, Ginger. I will miss you."

Jacques looked taken aback and patted his chest. "What am I, dying?"

She pushed his head to the side. "France. Have a couple of crepes for me when you go back."

"What if I don't go back?" He looked at her, almost nervously so.

She ignored the question. "I'll be going to Alex to see my grandmother. She's a meanie of an old woman, and needs a calming influence."

At this point, Samya knew his looks. The tilt of his head indicated he knew she was lying.

He moved his thumb over her cheek once. "I have so much to say to you. First, I'm sorry. You should never have been put in this situation, ever. I put us in this position. And the way I initially sought to deal with this? I'm sorry. It wasn't meant to be a last resort or…" Jacques put his hand on his heart. "Nothing is going as planned, and maybe I'm going about things a bit backwards." He chuckled. "I'm tripping on my words." Jacques gave that crooked, unsure smile Samya would miss dearly.

"I love you."

She took a breath and exhaled. "I know."

He laughed. "You know? This woman," he said mockingly to no one in particular. "Her answer to a declaration of undying love is: 'I know.'"

"Ah." She rolled her eyes, trying to keep things light and held back the tears that were threatening to pool. "Virgin deflowerers can be so needy."

He didn't respond. She reached up, touched his cheek, and then dropped her hand.

"I love you, too, of course. I only admitted it to myself after Tanta. You just caught on recently, I'm guessing. Slow, as usual."

His eyes widened. "Then…"

She shook her head. "Then, nothing. Nothing has changed. You should know that as awful as this ordeal was, I don't regret having been with you. I didn't have hope that anyone would tolerate, let alone love, me the way you do, you did. Meeting you has been the greatest privilege of my life."

Jacques stood there woodenly.

She could feel the sting of tears behind her eyes. "But you understand, don't you? You've only witnessed one of my episodes, and I completely drained you. I can't do that to anyone, especially not to someone I love so dearly. But Jacques, isn't it great? I loved, and was loved right back."

Holding his hands, she smiled at him, and it took everything in her to hold it together and not feel the pain that was peeking from the corner, waiting to pounce on her. "You are free now, *albi*. Thank you for the adventures and the memories I will treasure. Thank you for you."

He broke free of her hands and stepped back. "Thank you? Thank you?! This isn't a charity, dammit! You are being a martyr that no one asked for. You are not protecting anyone by doing this!"

Samya's tears were now falling. Because he was fighting a losing battle. Soon he would be better off, she told herself.

"*Habibi*, I am not trying to protect you. I am protecting myself." She looked at his handsome, distraught face. "I won't be the reason you hate your life. I won't have a caregiver as a lover, their life revolving around my health. Every couple of months dropping me off at the hospital, and who knows when I'll be coming back out. That's no life."

"So you are just making a decision for both of us, then? No. I don't agree."

"You deserve a normal life."

"I don't want normal; I want extraordinary, and that's you!"

"So will you be moving into the hospital with me? Holding my hand through the shock treatments? Having to deal with me on days I'll forget your name?"

Jacques stepped forward with gusto. "You are joking, but I'm not. If that's what it takes, dammit, then yes."

He sighed then and looked downcast. "You are dealing with something bigger than both of us. But I need you to trust me. I know I need to earn it. Give me a chance, mon amour. Give us a chance. That's all I'm asking."

She closed her eyes, opened on an exhale, and spoke softly. "I'm already a burden to my family. My father doesn't know what to do half the time. My mother is going mad trying to figure out how to handle me. And Hend's reputation is inextricably linked to mine. I don't want to add to that list. This is not me giving up. This is me not letting my circumstances trap those I love."

He gestured with his hands, palm up. "I know the circumstances. Hell, we all have circumstances. You accept me, don't you? There's ups and downs, good and bad. But we'd be together. Don't pull away, please."

"Samya," Omar shouted from the distance. "Hurry up."

"I'm begging you." Jacques cupped her face with both hands. "Please."

She wiped her tear-stained cheeks with the sleeve of the black frock she wore. "Let's end on good terms, yes? It was lovely. You were lovely. And I'm better for having met you. I truly love you, Jacques. I want you to be happy. Be happy."

He pulled his hands away from her, his eyes glassy. She took a gamble, melded into him and then kissed his cheek one last time. His arms came around her, and he wouldn't let go.

"No," he whispered.

Silent tears left his eyes and landed in her hair.

"Ya Allah, Samya!" Omar yelled.

She gripped Jacques's arms and pushed herself away from him. Not trusting herself to stay any longer, she turned around and walked quickly towards Omar. There was a persistent pounding in her head. Her body felt it. The moment she walked away from her heart.

Upon seeing her, Omar frowned. "What happened?"

She shook her head.

They walked in silence to his car a street over. There were the honks of one or two car horns from night owls who hadn't gone home yet. Tall palm trees lining the concrete street stood strong and tall. But Samya was in a tunnel. All sounds were dampened. The cold of night forgotten. Nothing existed anymore.

When she and Omar got into his black Volkswagen, he paused. "You can't keep doing this. How long have we been friends, and you haven't told me something so big about yourself? Talk to me. Tell me anything."

Samya covered her face and burst into noisy tears. Omar reached over and cradled her in his arms, tightening as if shielding her from the monsters outside. She clawed on to his arms, so he wouldn't let go. She didn't want to be alone. She didn't want to feel the depth of this loss. Every time she tried to stop, the crying would rise up and spill out all over again. The catatonia, the sadness, dropping out of medical school, all those heartbreaks didn't compare to the hurt she was feeling now.

Jacques didn't know. He didn't know what he had done for her. For years she'd been living at the very bottom of a glass jar, trapped, gasping for air. Jacques had come along and, with gentle ease, put his hand through the top and made her realize there'd never been a lid. She could crawl out and seek freedom. There would be many days, like today, where she would be back in the jar, barely breathing. But now she knew the jar was open.

Yes, she'd known their relationship would eventually end. And she knew she'd just done the right, responsible thing. But she hadn't been prepared for the despair, the grief of knowing she would never again be held by that man.

Omar rocked her in his arms as if she were a child. "Shhh, shhh, shhh."

Samya buried her face even deeper into her friend's embrace.

She had the memories. She would see Jacques when she closed her eyes and when she smelled men's aftershave or fresh cigars. That was enough. That would have to be enough.

Chapter Forty-Six

Samya started packing behind Zoo Zoo's back. Her episodes and bouts of crying were getting worse and more acute. She stayed in her room more and more as the days passed by, and her mother tried busying herself with other pursuits. The sense of dread in the villa was palpable. The hospital couldn't come soon enough.

Jacques was out of her life but constantly on her mind. The image of his face when she'd left him haunted her. The empty pit in her stomach made her feel as if she'd made a colossal mistake. But no matter how she worked it out in her mind, she always came to the same conclusion. She couldn't hurt him. And being with her would hurt him.

Hend was finally back from her vacation with her friends. The day before Samya was set to go to the hospital, Hend knocked on her door. She was dressed in a gorgeous pastel pink skirt with an Audrey Hepburn-like white button down, tucked in. So effortlessly elegant and beautiful was Hend. Samya, in comparison, was sitting on the floor, still in her nightgown well into the afternoon. She hadn't taken a shower in two days, or perhaps it was three.

Hend looked warily at Samya. "Sim Sim, would you be up for going to the *nady* with me?"

"No, *habibti*." Samya mustered all the energy she could to act normal for her sister. "Have fun, snatch a couple of bachelors for us, and report back."

Likely taking the hint that she was being dismissed, Hend smiled small and started to head out. Samya heard the voice of the man she loved in her head. *You underestimate her, you know. She can handle more than you give her credit for.*

"Hend?"

Hend turned around. "Yes, *habibti*?"

"Will you sit with me?"

She ran to Samya and just enveloped her. That was all it took for Samya to bawl. Hend sat on the floor and held her sister until Samya felt wrung out and tired. Then, pulling away, Samya forced herself to look at Hend.

"There has been so much I haven't told you. I thought I was protecting you, but I'm a fool. Please forgive me. I wasn't in Greece all those times, you know."

Hend got her a tissue and sat back down on the floor next to her. She chuckled. "Give me some credit, Samya. Of course I knew."

Puzzled, Samya looked at her.

"The minute you went on your 'trip,' I rummaged through your room and found your passport in the box at the corner. I have a friend who works in the airline who confirmed that you never purchased a ticket. And one night, I tailed baba all the way to Alex and found he was going to the hospital. I then bribed an orderly to confirm you were in there and then a nurse to find out for what."

Samya laughed.

"You're not angry?"

Samya shook her head. "I'm more impressed than anything. He was right."

"Who was right?"

"Jacques told me that I was underestimating you and that you were cunning."

"He was right." She paused. "He knew?"

"We actually met the first day he came to our villa. He saw my bruises and deduced what they were right away."

Hend nodded and then tilted her head to the side. "Is there more you want to tell me?"

Samya took a breath and told her about Jacques, their tryst, and how wonderful it had been. She told her of the glorious couple days in Tanta and the plot against them by Hosseni and Jacques's uncle, and how she, Jacques, and their friends had banded together to solve the issue.

"That family is insufferable!" Hend exclaimed.

"Indeed."

Then she told Hend about her catatonic episode in Tanta and how distraught Jacques had looked then and after, and how she could never do that to anyone.

"May I borrow a line of his? You underestimate that man. He is cunning in his own right," Hend said.

They paused, and said nothing for a while. Samya felt lighter, if possible. And ashamed of herself for ever having doubted Hend's insurmountable strength.

"How long do I have with you?" Hend asked.

"I leave for a hospital in Alex tomorrow. The doctor who specializes in a new electroshock technique will have finally come back from a tour in Europe."

"This time, will you let me visit?"

There was hesitation on Samya's part. Familiar voices reminded her not to stress out her beloved sister. But a louder voice was drowning it out. One wondering how it would be to not be alone for once.

An exhausted Samya fairly beamed. "Hend, I need you to visit, so yes."

Chapter Forty-Seven

Jacques looked out the plane window at the whipped clouds and clear blue sky. A blond flight attendant came by and asked him if he wanted a glass of champagne.

"Non, merci."

Mere months ago, he would have smirked, winked at her, and within hours of landing have been leaving her bed before heading to a lounge for a cigar.

Now? Well, now he was tired. It was expected, he thought. He'd get over Samya, his father, and Egypt in general once he arrived in Paris and was around his familiar surroundings again.

But when he got to Paris, he found he was restless. Jacques had already submitted the first draft of the new novel to his eager editor. In short, he had time to spare. So he went to Le Club Saint Germain to listen to jazz and dive into debauchery as much as possible. That day he drank heavily, avoided going home until he was piss drunk, and then collapsed onto his bed. He was outrunning himself, knowing if he just kept busy and didn't dwell, he could survive. Like a fast-moving river, if he kept moving, he wouldn't be able to see what was in the water.

The next day, he sent letters to Tanta to check in on his sisters, whom he assured he would visit in a couple of months. He arranged to send them and Madame Lena tickets to visit him in Paris before then. Later in the day, he went to Saint-Germain-des-Prés to meet Kareem, who was on his way back from Belgium to see his sister and nieces.

Saint-Germain-des-Prés looked like a medieval village occupied by modern artists and intellectuals. There were hills and layers of streets that all led to a church at the very top. Jacques and Kareem sat outside of a small café to have dinner. The neighborhood was buzzing around them with chatter, music, and cars passing by. The throaty voice of Juliette Greco accompanied by an accordion blared out of the radio. After months of deprivation, Jacques was finally able to enjoy a good glass of Pinot Noir. The two men ate, and Kareem told Jacques the news from Cairo, seemingly careful not to mention anything about a certain former lover of Jacques's.

After dinner, Kareem pulled out a small, yellow paper box: Chiclets. "Want one?"

Jacques stared, and he finally allowed himself to think of her. It hit him like a violent wave.

"What happened?" Kareem looked alarmed.

"I lost her."

Kareem sighed. "I'm sorry, brother. But you're home now, aren't you? Just give it a little time, and things will go back to normal."

"What's normal?" Jacques's shoulders dropped. "I...I don't even know how to be."

"Well, she refused you, no? Not much you can do now." Kareem repositioned himself on the tiny, ornate metal chair. "I have never been in your position, but maybe she is right. There is a lot of difficulty in her life right now. It may be for the best."

Samya's refusal had spurred self-doubt. Jacques's long-held belief that he'd failed his mother. And that he was just like his father. That he would ultimately let Samya down.

But was he like his father, really? Abdo was less of a mystery now. He'd been a flawed human being, and he'd made his choices. He'd left his wife and only son to fend for themselves. Jacques had stayed with his mother. Abdo hadn't made provisions for his second family in Egypt, where Jacques had stepped in and taken care of them. In time, he would allow them to care for him. Those were choices he'd made. He wasn't perfect by any means, but with time, he could keep growing into a person he would be proud to be.

"No."

"No?"

"No. It won't always be good times with Samya. There are truly tough times ahead. But I've committed to that. Those are my tough times, as well. She can't rob me of them."

There would be many ups and downs. But wasn't that all of his life? The past few years hadn't been any better; he'd simply chosen to ignore life by numbing himself. For the first time, he'd gained the courage to live, and it was because of Samya. Being with her was true living.

"I've made a mistake."

His mistake with Samya had been not fighting harder. Not thinking he was worthy enough of her and letting her leave. She'd said she loved him, hadn't she? He had to show her that she wasn't a burden but a guiding light. She had no clue what she was, not only to him, but to everyone around her.

Kareem sipped his coffee. "You are sure?"

"Life will go on. I won't die. But I have found something and someone very few have the privilege of finding. I'm not going to give up on either."

Kareem shrugged. "You are a better man than I am."

Jacques shook his head. "No. I may not be worthy of her, but I'm selfish. She's isolating herself from this mistaken sense of preserving everyone else's sanity. I need to get to her before she is lost to the abyss she created for herself. I…"

"You are going back to Cairo," Kareem finished.

Jacques smiled. "Care to drop me off at the airport?"

Kareem smirked. "You didn't give me a chance to give you one of my famous inspirational speeches."

"When have you given one of those? You were about to talk me out of going back to the love of my life."

Kareem laughed and patted his friend's back. "Ya Allah, I've missed your dramatics, you jackass."

Jacques's presence wouldn't cure Samya. The experience he had with these type of illnesses made him know better than to think love would solve everything. But care might help Samya fight more fervently. And right now, she needed to fight.

***

From Cairo International Airport, Jacques went straight to the Roshdi home.

Zoo Zoo opened the door with a duster in hand. Jacques didn't know what the hell she was doing dusting. Samya had told him the family didn't allow Zoo Zoo to clean that much anymore since she'd gotten older. She was supposed to rest. Now was not the time for all that, though.

"Zoo Zoo, where is Samya?"

"Well…" She looked at the floor.

"Take me to Dr. Mahmoud, then." Jacques looked over her shoulder. It wasn't hard to do with her 5' frame.

Hend walked up to the door. "Jacques, what a pleasant surprise. To what do we owe this pleasure?"

Zoo Zoo let Hend deal with him.

Jacques was growing impatient. "I want to see Samya."

Hend smiled. "She's not here."

Jacques felt his chest tightening. She was at the hospital, then. He unwittingly ran his hand through his hair. He had to figure out where the hospital was and go there.

"I need to talk to your father."

"I don't think you need to do that. Please come in, and I'll grab some tea."

"Hend."

"Humor me, Jacques."

They walked into a sitting room, and he reluctantly sat down. His leg was vibrating uncontrollably. Likely Dr. Mahmoud was out. Samya was definitely gone. He may have already missed his opportunity. He knew from his mother's experience how disoriented someone would become after shock treatment. Samya might not want to see him. But he had to try.

Hend brought a tray of tea in and closed the door. She served herself a cup but didn't prepare one for him. Uncharacteristic, for a society darling.

Hend wore pearl jewelry, a stylish pink dress, and a disingenuous grin. "My father is not here. My sister is not here. What do you want with her?"

Jacques held steadfast. "My intentions are honorable."

"I'm finding that hard to believe as you put her in a rather precarious position only a bit ago."

So, Hend knew everything then. Good. "Where is she, Hend?"

"I am startled by your lack of suaveness, Jacques." She sipped her tea with excruciating leisure. "What will you do if you do see her?"

Jacques let out a frustrated sigh. "We need to finish a conversation we started before I left. I need to talk to her immediately."

Hend put her pointer finger on her cheek as if she was thinking. After taking a very long pause, she spoke. "What will you say to her ?"

He leaned forward. "That's between me and her."

"She is my sister, and anything you choose to say to her, you can say right to me."

Jacques rolled his eyes and grinned. "Are you sure you aren't Omar in a dress? Listen, I love your sister. My intention is not to interfere, but she needs to know that I'm with her."

"She is recuperating and needs time to herself."

Jacques huffed, trying to be patient but failing miserably. "I will not stop any progress she is making. I won't burden her or stress her out. But I need to talk to her. I need her to know that I am here, especially now. Your sister is—there's no way to say this politely—a stubborn ass who fancies herself a martyr. She is being unfair. So I need to see her, throttle her, kiss her, and care for her, in no particular order.

"Hend, if you don't tell me, I'll go find out where your father is and hound him. If he doesn't tell me, I will scour every hospital from here to the south of Africa to get to her. You'd be saving me some time, but make no mistake you are superfluous here."

Hend eyed him for a bit. She set her tea down gently on the table.

"How much money did you say you make?"

Chapter Forty-Eight

"Lie here, mademoiselle," Dr. Aman instructed Samya. He was in his late forties with a mahogany complexion, brown eyes, and he wore a white lab coat.

The hospital she was in was smaller than the one she'd gone to earlier in the year. It was by no means a significant upgrade. It still had the same flavor of barren white walls, cold tile floors, screaming patients, and disorderly orderlies. But this hospital touted updated procedures and experimental treatments for severe mental illness. She knew she could only come here because her family could afford it, and for that she was thankful. It was no use imagining what her life would be like if she hadn't come from money.

She was feeling drowsy from the medication that had already been administered. Leaning on the bed for balance, she rolled onto it, avoiding the straps she was unfortunately familiar with. As a former medical student, she understood the practicality of the straps. They would hold her body down to prevent injury, which she was thankful for since she'd broken her arm during a session the last time she'd been hospitalized. As a patient, she'd felt trapped.

Samya shivered from the chilly, sterile hospital room, and possibly the situation she was in. "Are these still necessary?"

"In theory, no." Dr. Aman said. "But it is a safety precaution. I promise it will only take a couple of minutes, and you won't feel it too much this time."

Dr. Aman was a half Sudanese, half Egyptian psychiatrist on the cutting edge of electroshock treatment. He was one of the first doctors in Egypt to introduce a new technique of administering anesthesia and relaxants to patients before inducing a seizure. There was excitement in the international medical community about a more humane and effective way to treat severe depression and, in Samya's case, catatonia.

A couple of nurses buckled her arms and legs down onto the bed. Her breathing quickened. One placed a leather strap in her mouth to bite down on. Inner anxiety was competing with her numb and chemically relaxed body.

"Be calm, mademoiselle." Dr. Aman patted her shoulder. "Be easy. That's it."

The kind man's words were becoming garbled as her eyes started closing of their own volition. Samya felt the cool touch of circular metal on her temples. Before she could react, she'd drifted away.

"Oof." Samya wiped her mouth after hurling what was left of what she'd eaten at breakfast, which wasn't much. True to Dr. Aman's words, she had not felt the electric current nor the causal seizure at the time. However, the aftereffects were in full swing. She got up off the bathroom floor, where she had been for an hour, and rinsed her mouth. Then she headed back to her stiff bed, praying that sleep would come and relieve her of the hammer banging aggressively in her head. True to her history, the crying and sadness were swallowing her up as the days went by. The catatonic episodes had become persistent and had been lasting longer by the time she'd gotten to the hospital.

The treatment should work this time, hopefully. Normally, she would want the days to go faster so she could reach the other side of this hell, when the fog in her mind would clear and the episodes would peter out. But now, her hope was dwindling. She lay with her arm across her eyes and applied pressure. She certainly wasn't in a rush. And though the hospital was her least favorite place, time seemed to stop here. The outside world couldn't pierce through the building that now housed her. Nothing came in, but she could still see it all. Everything she'd lost was on display in her mind. Dr. Aman reminded her of the education and the bedside manner she would never be able to obtain or carry out. And then there was *him*. Her drowsiness clouded things often, but he would come to her in dreams. Her face would be wet when she awoke. But she wasn't bitter; she wasn't mad or upset. Her conscious self was apathetic.

"Mademoiselle." A nurse in a white uniform came into her doorless room. "Dr. Aman suggested taking a walk. How about just down the hallway today?"

Samya shook her head, pulled the blanket tighter over her body, and closed her eyes to feign sleep.

"You haven't had lunch yet. Perhaps some *tamaya*?" The damn nurse just wouldn't give up.

Yes, it was childish, but Samya made a snoring sound. She heard a sigh and the clicking of sensible heels moving away from her room.

Maybe Hend would come in a couple of days. Samya really did not want anyone seeing her like this. Well, she didn't have a mirror, but she could only imagine the mess she portrayed. But she refused to shut Hend out again. She'd made a commitment to be honest with her sister, and she could at least do that much. She'd made no such commitment to her father, though. She was feeling so ashamed because this last hospitalization had really taken a toll on him. He'd been so sure the last time would be enough to cure her. Her capacity to handle seeing her father's worn face had disintegrated as had her overall resolve.

It had been a week, and Samya was recovering from her third treatment. Tears flowed down her face without her permission. At least in the hospital, everyone expected you to fall apart. Here there were no alarmed faces or looks of pity.

She had no idea what time it was, and she was too tired to look at the clock outside of her room. So she lay on her side in the bed. She gathered her hair, damp from sweat, and knotted it onto itself. Her body couldn't decide if it were hot or cold.

An orderly came in her room and handed her a note. "Mademoiselle Samya, a foreigner would like to visit you. He said to give you this."

A strike of lightning hit Samya at the mention of a foreigner. Of course, she didn't have to ask; she knew who it was. She got up slowly and took the note. The rough texture and cream color of the paper reminded her of the sketchbook he carried around. How had he gotten into a place this secure? Ya Allah, was everyone in Egypt that bribable? Maybe she shouldn't open it. She unwrapped the note anyway.

Fred,

I humbly request your presence for a Turkish coffee at the commissary downstairs. I come bearing Melachrinos. Please come quickly. A ninety-five-year-old nurse has been pinching my ass for the last half hour. She is disproportionate with her pinches, and my left cheek is numb.

Hurry.

245

Yours,

Ginger

Chapter Forty-Nine

In the cafeteria, Jacques eagerly waited for a sprig of curls to bounce through the doorway. Instead, the young orderly he'd bribed came back alone.

"She's not seeing visitors, *basha*. She said to please leave and not come back."

Jacques's face fell. But he'd figured as much. And it was fine and dandy with him. He was just as stubborn as she was, if not more so.

The next month proceeded with a cascade of offerings from Jacques, at least one every day. He brought the first the day after his first visit. It was a doodle of what looked like a naked Lu Lu looking down between his legs, with a word bubble that read, "It's not small, it's European-sized!"

The day after that, he sent her a box of chocolate gateau with a note attached.

From your favorite patisserie. I told them I'd be feeding a monstrous cat with an insatiable appetite, and a horrible attitude.

Gros bisous,

Jacques.

The day after that:

Fred,

I've decided to take up poetry to fill my days. Tell me what you think.

Her bottom is as big as her heart.

Her asthmatic laugh is my favorite part.

The way she sneezes is an art.

Oh how I miss that bloody tart.

What do you think? Your man is an accomplished author after all!

With all my love,

Ginger

The day after that, he slid her pages from the first draft of his novel with a note:

The day after that, he sent her a small package of Chiclets and cigarettes. For a couple of days after, he sent her lewd and ridiculous drawings. Then one day, a drawing of a feral kitten with curly hair, hissing, and a dog with a beret licking it. It was accompanied by a note.

Did you notice I didn't write you? I was ignoring you because you were ignoring me. I choose to forgive you since I am a very generous individual. Lulu says hello.

A couple more pages from his novel. Then some short stories. Doodles.
And then some random musings.

I miss you, woman. So much, dammit.

- Jacques

Each time he sent something, the orderly would come back and only confirm that he'd dropped it off at her room.

She never responded. Not one day in an entire month.

Eventually, Samya's father heard of Jacques's behavior, and confronted him at a café. "What is the meaning of this?"

"Doctor, I wish to marry your daughter. I don't deserve her. But I will do everything I can to."

Dr. Mahmoud relented. "Son, she is..."

"I know of the circumstances she has had to endure. I just ask for the privilege to endure with her, so she knows she is not alone. Respectfully, Doctor, look at me. I'm a lot to handle, and there is no one else for me but your daughter. And you've met your mulish daughter; I think there is no one else but me for her. We fit. I just need her to see that. I wish to marry her. But I will not pressure her. I beg you to not even tell her we spoke if you see her. She will come out of this. I'm sure she will."

"She will not see anyone but Hend. Not even me."

"Doesn't bother me. I'll wait. She'll come out stronger, you'll see."

Dr. Mahmoud looked skeptical but shook his head and chuckled. "Alright then, son. We'll see."

CHAPTER FIFTY

Samya was living in an ocean wave. Everything was muffled, and her mind bobbed up and down with no particular aim. It was difficult to do much of anything. And she was ignoring Dr. Aman and the hospital staff's instructions to take on the smallest tasks, like leaving her room. It wasn't merely that she wanted to give up on life; a big part of it was exhaustion. Her activities were as follows: wake up, smoke, sleep, treatment, sleep, throw up, sleep, smoke, sleep.

Jacques's letters, notes, and gifts arrived every day, without fail, at 4:00 p.m. sharp. He was consistent. The first couple of weeks, she was too disoriented to read or look at anything. But she wouldn't throw anything out. They were all kept in a box under her bed. When she was able to make out words again, she read the notes and got angry. One of them he'd sprayed with his signature cedar and linen cologne, that bastard. Why would he do this to her?

One day, when she was particularly low, she reread the short notes. Some of them made her laugh. Others made her cry and ache so fervently for a life that wasn't hers. Her heart wavered. With each delivery, a little piece of her thought on the possibility that maybe…just maybe… But then she would fall in the hallway from an episode or practically vomit her lungs up from treatment and retreat to her bed to sleep her thoughts away.

She kept one note in particular under her pillow:

You are strong. You are brave. You are wild. You will get through this.

Yours, whether-you-like-it-or-not,

It was wrinkled and tear stained. She held it while treatment was being administered. She would be lying if she said it didn't get her through many hard times. The memories were hard to hold onto in her current state, but the hope those daily treasures provided was something she hadn't known she needed.

As the days went by, she realized she needed to look forward to something because hopelessness was creeping in every day that the treatment didn't work. But there were times it was futile to fight against despair. Because what did she have to look forward to? More hospitals and needles and treatment that were seemingly going nowhere?

An orderly knocked on the doorless entrance to her room. "Mademoiselle Samya, someone is here to see you."

"I am not seeing anyone." If it was Hend, he would have announced her as such. Samya couldn't bear to look anyone in the eye right now. Especially since she'd spent the last couple of hours crying her eyes out.

The orderly looked nervous. "I'm sorry, but she won't take no for an answer. And she has a cane!"

Samya widened her eyes. It couldn't be. Embarrassingly, she fell out of bed, but she stumbled up before the orderly could get to her. Adrenaline shot through her, aiding her as she ran out the door. The run made her dizzy, but she made it to the commissary. Sure enough, there, in all her glory, was Dr. Nadia. Samya could see all the frown lines on this paragon of a woman she idolized. Of course, she would never say it to her in fear of getting whacked with the cane, but her former professor looked rather adorable. Her white hair in a bun was tucked into a black pill box hat, and she wore a navy jacket dress, pinned with a golden broach consisting of two snakes wrapped around a staff.

"Girl, come over here. Don't keep me waiting, for Allah's sake. Do you know how old I am?"

Samya got a hold of herself, rubbed her red eyes, and sat across from her old professor.

"Hmm." Dr. Nadia looked her up and down. Samya must have looked a fright. Her hair was in all kinds of directions, she was wearing a hospital gown and paper slippers.

"You've gotten too thin again. You need to run a comb through your hair once in a while. You are still a woman."

Samya attempted to pat her hair down. "Doctora, it is good to see you. May I ask what brings you here?"

"Why did I take an uncomfortable train, whose chairs crushed my arthritis-riddled bones, for two and a half hours? Why do you think, girl? To see you, of course."

Samya just stared at her mentor, trying to hold back the tears that were banging on the door of her eye ducts to get out.

"Well, offer me tea, at least!"

"Oh, sorry." Samya motioned for a young boy, the cook's son, to come over. "Hamouda, two teas with mint, please. And can you go outside and get some *basbousa* and a half kilo of sunflower seeds?"

"No, boy."

Hamouda, who had slip-on sandals and a traditional white frock, trembled at Dr. Nadia's booming voice.

"I'm watching my sugar. No *basbousa*, and make the half kilo a full one. Run along, now. Go."

"Yes, madame." The boy couldn't have run off any faster.

"Now. Both Dr. Aman and your father called me. So, you are choosing to flop around like a fish and give up on life?"

Damn gossips. "Doctora, I'm only dealing with the situation I've been dealt the best way I know how."

"*Bala, bala.* Do you know how lucky you are to receive the treatment you are? A couple of years ago, you'd be thrown in a cage. Hell, even now, those poor souls who can't afford the cup of tea we're about to sip get locked away for being an inconvenience."

Samya looked down at her lap. She was ashamed of herself, but she already knew what the woman was saying. "I am trying."

"No, you are not." Dr. Nadia dug through her utilitarian black purse.

She plopped a black-and-white picture of a family on the table in front of Samya. Samya picked the photo up. It showed a rural family: a man, a tall woman, two small children, and a baby. It was the woman with the breech delivery and her family.

"She wanted you to know she named the baby after you. If you are into sentimental crap like that."

Something was crawling up Samya's throat. "I...thank you so much." And then tears, and snot, trickled down her face.

Unfazed, Dr. Nadia carried on. "I had them take this picture, so I can bring it to you. You made this possible."

"It wasn't me. Any one of your residents could have... You did most of the work."

"Stop. You delivered that child. And you will leave here and deliver more children. Because families like these need you."

"I know, Dr. Nadia, I'm fighting, I swear," she lied.

"Don't fight this."

Samya furrowed her brow. "Didn't you just say to?"

"Don't fight what you can't change. Accept it. Work with it. Then fight for something worth fighting for. Look, girl. Accepting your situation doesn't mean giving up. With illnesses like yours, medicine and treatment will never be enough. Your heart has to be in it. You have to push forward, as much as your nature is pulling you back."

Hamouda came back with two glasses of tea and handed Dr. Nadia her sunflower seeds. Samya was so embarrassed that she had no money on her. Luckily, Dr. Nadia pulled out a couple of coins and gave them to the young boy, whose smile broke out despite the tremors caused by Dr. Nadia's abrasiveness.

Dr. Nadia started cracking shells and nibbling on the seeds. She batted at the steam coming off the tea. "Who the hell makes tea this hot?"

Samya sighed. "Doctora, I'm just going to fail school again and end up back here."

"If you keep thinking that way, you will. Do you think I came here for your engaging conversation? No, I am here because you have skill and talent. I can't make you do anything, though the world would be a much better place if I could control everyone in it, I'll tell you that much.

Dr. Nadia held onto Samya's wrist. The human contact startled her.

"People out there need you. You and I have been given the opportunity to have an education. The least we can do is serve those who don't."

And that hit Samya in the chest. Zoo Zoo, Ruqquyah, the women at Al-Qarafa. What would they have done without Dr. Nadia's expertise? They had no other access to medical care. In an instant, Samya realized what was at stake. But she didn't know if she was strong enough to be that person for them.

"It doesn't take someone special to get out of what you're in. It takes someone willing. Your father, Dr. Aman, myself, your young man, yes, I've heard of him and his antics. None of us can make you do anything. You have a choice. You can play dead before your time is up, or you can confront your circumstances. Understand your limitations and battle what you can. Your father told me not to guilt you, but I've never listened to anyone else, and I'm not going to start now. Your life is not the only one affected here."

Dr. Nadia got a felt pen and paper out of her purse and started scratching something on it that resembled a spider web.

"You see this? This is life. We go round and round and repeat patterns over and over. But everything is connected."

Samya put her elbows on the table and her palms on her forehead, attempting to cover the tears that simply wouldn't stop. "I'm so tired and sad and broken-hearted. I hate that I don't want to do a thing. I didn't choose this."

"Of course, you didn't choose this! You are in hell."

"Then what can I do?"

Dr. Nadia surprised Samya by speaking in a soft tone. "Do what you can. Little by little. It will be painful. But nothing stays the same.

"*Walla!*"

Samya jumped as Dr. Nadia yelled in Hamouda's direction. He sprinted over to the old woman's side. Samya would make sure to give the boy several packets of Chiclets when she got back to her room.

"Help me up from this blasted chair." Back to her ornery self, Dr. Nadia got up, leaning on Hamouda. Before leaving, she looked at Samya.

"Think about it, girl."

The next morning, Samya sat up in her bed and put her feet on the floor. The quick movement made her head spin. She put her face in her hands, with her elbows on her thighs. Waiting until her breathing evened out, Samya finally got up. Then, for the first time in weeks, she looked at the clock outside her room. She leaned against the doorway. Her body ached something fierce. The nausea was churning her stomach over. Sweat dripped from her brow.

Little by little.

Taking a deep breath, she held on to the wall, and walked down the hallway. One foot in front of the other. She made it ten steps before she had to shuffle back to her room to throw up.

***

Samya walked further and further each day. She forced herself to talk to anyone, even if it was once a day. She read anything. First it was only Jacques's notes. Then she went on to read a paragraph of anything she could get her hands on in the hospital. Soon, she was reading books instead of moping around in her bed. There were days where it seemed like she wasn't making any progress, or even going backwards. But she allowed herself to rest and then kept going. She created routines for herself. Jacques's deliveries would be her treat for whatever accomplishments she'd made in the day.

It took extreme effort on Samya's part and more aggressive treatment, but in two months she became more lucid, the sadness was manageable, and the episodes titrated out. Samya was also on a new blend of medications.

A gaunt, spent, but more assured version of Samya took her first step outside of the hospital. And though she was terrified, she welcomed the outside world.

Her father, who teared up when he saw her, took her home to Cairo. She was welcomed heartily by her mother, Hend, and Zoo Zoo.

Zoo Zoo showed her pictures of Ruqquyah's sweet baby boy. They'd immigrated to Greece and were living in an apartment close to Samya's cousins. Ruqquyah was having a hell of a time taking care of the young one, but Zoo Zoo said she was ecstatic.

Samya was disappointed yet grateful that Jacques wasn't there. She didn't know what she would have said to him.

Interestingly enough, when she got to her bedroom, she saw a small box in the middle of her bed.

Hend smiled. "He insisted. The French are ever so dramatic." She chuckled and closed the door behind her.

Samya opened the box, which contained a smaller box, which she opened to find an even smaller box inside. She laughed and opened the last box. Inside was a neatly folded piece of beautifully textured paper.

Congratulations, I knew you'd make it. I will reach out to Hend every Thursday.   When you are ready, tell her, and we can take a walk in the nady. Can you believe it? In public, no less! As an incentive, I will stop the gifts until I see you in person.

Lovingly yours,

Jacques

Chapter Fifty-One

It had been an agonizing week since Samya's release from the hospital. Essentially, Jacques had to sit on his hands and wait. Finally, he found a letter under his villa door.

Dear Jacques,

If you think that I shall tell you how lovely and life-saving, heartening, and comforting your gifts have been and how much they've meant to me, you would be mistaken. How bothersome of you to send me all those bawdy pictures of big-breasted women. Did you have to remind me of my physical failings?!

I humbly request your presence at El-Fishawy tomorrow at 5:00 p.m. if you are available. And if you are not, make yourself so. I hope your left butt cheek isn't too sore from being pinched by that nurse (her name is Fatma by the way). I'll be happy to catch your right one up tomorrow, so it doesn't get jealous.

Until then,

There wasn't an "I love you" or "I'm yours" or "I've missed you like crazy" in the letter. But reading those words and knowing the hands that wrote them and the mind that came up with them existed caused a flood of hope to rush through him.

Chapter Fifty-Two

Samya stood outside El-Fishawy. She decided to wear her high-waisted pants and her favorite short-sleeved blouse with a collar. Her hair was tamed with a small tie at the back, and she wore bright red lipstick and eyeliner. This was nerve-racking. The hospital had been brutal. It had taken an extraordinary amount of time and patience to crawl out of the hole she'd been in. And now that she had a better grip on life, she wanted to give herself the best chance to succeed. Dr. Nadia's talk had affected her. There were so many who didn't have the opportunities she had and who needed help. It was her responsibility to serve them. So she was going back to medical school if it killed her. She was still recovering, though, and she could only handle one thing at a time. But there was Jacques, who was fast becoming the most important person in her life. He was also her biggest dilemma. It would be selfish to ask him to wait for her while she secured a medical degree. The dedication pouring out of his daily deliveries to the hospital filled her heart with so much love and showed a devotion she wasn't yet sure that she deserved. Though the evolution of Samya's ability to participate in life was slow going, she kept reminding herself...*little by little.* She wouldn't ask him to wait for her, but she really hoped he would.

So nothing substantive would change today, but it was imperative that she thank Jacques for the hope he had given her. And why not look nice while she was at it? Perhaps they could be dear friends. And that would be enough for now, she told herself. Digging her nails into her palms, she prepared herself against getting confused.

She'd picked El-Fishawy, a café in the heart of Khan El-Khalili marketplace, for a couple of reasons. First, it was the busiest place she could think of. Tourists and locals alike frequented the smoke shop and café. Being surrounded by hoards of people would make it easier to say what she had to say without throwing herself at the man she still very much loved. Second, the café was an artist and intellectual hub. It was a hotspot for some of Egypt's esteemed writers, and she wanted to introduce Jacques to another place he could write. Third, they had the best *shisha* in Cairo.

In order to have somewhat of an advantage and shed some nerves, she arrived a half hour earlier than she'd told Jacques. But when she stepped inside the café, she saw him already sitting there. Lazily leaned back and talking to Rezan, the fifty-year-old server who resembled a gangster maven. Rezan stood at 6', was wearing a bandana with fuzzy multi-color balls attached, and a black *galabeya*. Jacques was making the unmovable, unassailable Rezan laugh because, of course, he was just that genuinely charming. He looked magnificent in a shirt tucked into tan slacks. His obsidian hair was mussed up in all directions, making him look like the lovable rogue he was. His long legs crossed one over the other, and his hands and long elegant fingers were gesturing.

Feeling choked up, Samya walked towards them, but Rezan came up, blocking her view. The woman crushed Samya in a huge hug and gave her a million kisses on each cheek.

"You horrible girl. Why haven't you come to visit me in so long?" Rezan asked, her voice raspy from a lifetime of smoking.

"I needed you to miss me enough to give me a free *shisha*."

"You awful mooch. Just for that, I'm going to throw in a free coffee as well." She gave Samya another kiss on the cheek and gave Jacques a smirk before she trailed off.

Jacques stared at Samya, and she could swear she heard him breathe. It was tough to make out, though, over the crush of people and her own violent heartbeat. Taking in a breath, she sat down in front of him in a nonchalant manner. She picked up his finished Turkish coffee inquisitively and then flipped the cup upside down.

"Think very hard about what you want to know about the future." She quickly held a finger up. "Don't say it out loud. Close your eyes and think."

Dutifully, he obeyed but cracked one eye open. "I would ask how you are, but I see that you are back to your old self: bossing me around."

She gestured. "Eyes closed, dammit."

Samya took the opportunity to study his face, afraid because she didn't know how long it would be before she would be able to look at that face again.

With a serene expression, his eyes remained closed. "Samya, I know I'm pretty, but stop ogling me."

She laughed. "I see you are back to your old self: conceited."

He opened his eyes, and she turned the cup over to study the pattern of the coffee grounds.

"Oof. Oh, my."

"What, what? Tell me, woman!" He leaned over towards her. His familiar, luxurious smell wrapped around her like a warm hug.

"I see a one-legged dog, who's balancing a one-eyed cat on his head, and the cat's balancing a one-eared rat on his head, and the rat is balancing a one-winged flea on his head."

"What in the hell does that mean?"

"It means you have a long lost soulmate in your future that you're destined to meet shortly...and a name...I see a name..."

He smirked and put his hand over his eyes.

"Yes, yes. Do you perhaps know a Lu Lu?"

He playfully pushed her head to the side, but his hand lingered a bit before he pulled away. She wished so badly for him to envelop her in one of those actual warm hugs. But for so many reasons, one of which was they were in public, that couldn't happen.

Rezan brought over two Turkish coffees and a fresh *shisha* for Samya.

When Rezan left, the noise of the shopkeeps yelling hiked-up prices at tourists and older men talking loudly and playing checkers seemed to fade away. Jacques looked at Samya with a giddy smile. His body radiated trapped energy. Little sparks were exploding inside of her. There was a pull to bring them closer to one another that was threatening to crush the wooden table between them. Ya Allah, she'd missed the crinkles next to his eyes and his laugh and his, well, basically everything about him. Looking away before she reached out to touch his face, she took a swig of her bitter but rich coffee.

Jacques cleared his throat. "I heard you are applying for medical school again."

Samya inhaled smoke from the *shisha*, making the water bubble up inside, and exhaled. She was grateful for a subject she could actually handle. "Yes, I'm taking the reentrance exam in two weeks. I've only a year left in school. So, hopefully...no..." She shook her head. "I *will* graduate this time."

Jacques's broad smile was infectious. "There's no doubt about that."

"It was so hard inside," she blurted out. "In the hospital. And your gifts and notes...they were like a string connected to the outside world reminding me it was still there. That you were still…well." She laughed to cut off anything that seemed close to a confession. Though she desperately wanted to scream, "Don't leave me! Wait for me!"

She took another puff from the *shisha*. "Who would have thought a naked cartoon Lu Lu would be my salvation?"

Jacques seemed to skip over her attempt to deflect with humor and leaned towards her. "I've missed you. It's hard to believe you're really here. Tell me how you are."

"Better." And she meant it. "Things were really tough. I gave up for a while. Then I suspect someone told my father to call Professor Nadia to knock some sense into me."

Jacques looked away to sip his coffee. "Really?"

"Yes, really. And I owe him a lot. I don't know what I did to deserve that sort of care, but I'm thankful for it." She continued in a careful tone. "I've learned a lot these past couple of months. Mainly, I should take things slowly."

He nodded. "Of course."

"Studying for the exam will take up a lot of time. Then there's school itself. And I have to manage the depression, too."

"You'll do it all."

How had she gone through life without his assurances? Nervous, she looked to the side.

"I was surprised you stayed here. I'd thought you would have left for Paris a while ago."

Jacques shrugged. "I did, but I couldn't stay away for long. Besides, we have this invention called the airplane. I've decided to split my time between Paris and Cairo. The people I care about are here."

Ya Allah, this man. Samya took in a breath. "Everything you did meant so much to me. You are so kind."

Jacques frowned. "I don't want to fight with you in public, but I will if necessary. Believe me, my intentions were anything but kind."

"Even so…" Samya made to reach for his hands and stopped midway on the table when she realized where they were. "You gave me hope in a hopeless situation. I don't think you know the impact of your actions."

Jacques put his hand on the table and discreetly extended his pinky to touch hers. "Well, you taught me that I wasn't alone. I wanted to return the favor."

She smiled and then, with reluctance, moved her hands to her lap. This was it. She had to be clear.

"My situation is fragile now. I can only handle friendship at this point. And I can't ask you to—"

He looked her over, and his face went from indignant to relaxed. "Friends." He seemed to mull the offensive word over. "Alright, Fred. We are friends."

***

True to her word, Samya passed the entrance exam, and got back into El-Qasr El-Ainy medical school with a recommendation from Dr. Nadia. For the next couple of months, Samya barricaded herself in the school library with one goal: get that degree. There were times where Hend would force her to outings at the *nady*, or Omar would pick her up to play tennis. She didn't fight too much because she needed balance in her life. Samya and Jacques saw each other but only in group settings. Always in public, never alone. Jacques didn't so much as kiss her hand the entire time she saw him. Embarrassingly, she often looked at Jacques with longing. She was very careful to make sure he never caught her as he was sure to make fun of her relentlessly. Though she was appreciative of the space, she couldn't say that she wasn't a bit stung by the fact that he hadn't so much as given her a pat on the back. Samya couldn't complain, though. Not when she was the one who'd set the tone. This was good, she assured herself. Right now, she needed to focus on her studies. She was going to get that damn degree.

CHAPTER FIFTY-THREE

After hardwork, sweat, studying, humility, new medication, and tenacity, she did it. Doctora Samya Mahmoud Roshdi graduated from El-Qasr El-Ainy with a medical degree in hand. Her father wouldn't let go of her for an hour after her graduation.

"*Habibti*. My hero. You are my hero."

This time he was crying tears of joy.

Dr. Nadia lectured her about getting through the rest of her career just as diligently as she had school because she had more work to do. But she did give Samya a half smile when she handed her the diploma. There was a lot more to do before she could help people on a professional level without supervision. Residency in obstetrics was next up on her journey if all else went smoothly. But she had completed this crucial first step.

"Sim Sim, you haven't stopped smiling since the graduation," Hend hugged her big sister.

Samya rubbed at her cheeks. "I can't stop! I look like a fool. And my face hurts."

"Don't worry. I'll just do it, too."

Hend insisted that she they go to a party at a club ballroom to celebrate. Normally, Samya would rather be at an open air café, smoking *shisha*, and sipping on strong coffee. But she wanted to dress up. She wanted to show off. Many wouldn't know how big of a deal it was to have graduated, but those she loved knew. Hend did. Omar knew. And Jacques. She needed to find him and tell him. He likely already knew, but she hadn't seen him in a couple of weeks, and he was the first person she'd thought of to celebrate this with. She wanted to see his face when she told him. In a way, he'd got her started by encouraging her to study for the reentrance exam during their month of debauchery. It was his win, too.

Hend wore a beautiful, pastel-blue swing dress and swept her long, elegant reddish-brown colored hair in an updo. She wore pearls and matching blue gloves. Samya, by contrast, wore a black, off-the-shoulder wiggle dress with a sweetheart hem. A thin gold necklace adorned her throat. Her hair was well behaved but loose. The sisters were so different and therefore complemented each other.

The ballroom was filled with a crush of well-dressed young people laughing, drinking, and dancing. There were glittering lights strung along the walls, and large glass doors were open to an outside garden. A large orchestra played traditional Arabic music with a *tabla* to keep the beat.

Aside from celebrating her graduation, today was a very important one for another reason. Jacques didn't know, but Samya had been fighting for the both of them day after day. The plan had always been that once she secured her degree, Jacques would be next on her list. She'd used the year to build enough strength inside herself to trust that she deserved Jacques. That he deserved a right to choose to be with her or not. Nerves tickled her insides. She hoped, but didn't know, that Jacques still loved her. Tonight, she would try to convince Jacques to be with her.

Hend ran off to find Lobna, leaving Samya to look through the crowd for her man.

"Doctora!" Omar strode over and pinched her cheek.

She rubbed at her already tense face. "Ay! That hurt."

He laughed. "Who are you looking for?"

"Never you mind."

He raised an eyebrow.

She tensed. "What? Are you going to tell me to stay away from him and how bad he is to be around, and on and on?"

He gave Samya the crook of his arm. "No, but do me a favor. Do things the right way, so I don't have to save your behind again. I don't want to become prematurely bald like my uncle."

Samya grinned. "That's fair."

In the distance Samya smelled that certain cologne with the clean and spicy scent that she'd come to know so well. Hend, Lobna, and Jacques were laughing together by a high table. In a svelte black suit with a black tie and his midnight-black hair slicked in a neat part, Jacques emanated charm and confidence.

"Samya!" Lobna waved.

Samya waved back to her friend, who wore a red, ruffled gown with gold bracelets, earrings, and necklaces–multiple in fact.

Omar made a face and whispered to Samya. "I cannot stand her. I don't know why Hend insists on making her a fixture at outings."

Under his prim and proper facade, Omar was the most caring and dependable person Samya knew. But the history of his birth and how his uncle, who eventually adopted him, had treated him always made him feel like he was inferior. Samya thought that Omar's still-secret fiancée, Sawsan, was not the best for him. Omar needed someone who would challenge him, shake him out of his prissy ways, and show him he was good enough as is.

Samya smiled. "You should get to know her before judging her so harshly. If we hadn't grown up together, you may have felt the same about me."

Omar chuckled. "You tore down every wall I had up against you. I had no choice. Besides, no matter what, you'll never catch me voluntarily conversing with Lobna Ayoub."

Samya tsked. "You underestimate her, you know. She's incredibly impressive."

Omar smirked as he looked ahead. "Well, Jacques certainly seems to think so."

Samya whipped her head so fast she could hear it snap. She saw that Jacques now had his hand placed at the small of Lobna's back. Heat rose up Samya's cheeks. She wanted to peel those hands off and then peel his fingernails off one by one. Jacques motioned over to them, and then greeted Omar with a handshake and Samya with a nod.

Lobna double kissed Samya on each cheek, while Omar decided at that moment to excuse himself.

"Sim Sim, is it true? Should I call you Doctora Sim Sim now?" Lobna giggled.

Samya had to hold herself back from slapping the girl she'd just been praising a moment ago. She started to become livid even as she internally told herself to calm down. She had no ownership over Jacques, and Lobna had done nothing wrong.

"Yes, *habibti*. I've finally graduated." She looked at Jacques to see his reaction.

His eyes filled with warmth, and Samya felt her cheeks redden. It was a private moment in the midst of a sea of people and noise. Ya Allah, she missed being held by that man.

A foreign man with blond hair and blue eyes walked up to Jacques.

Jacques cleared his throat. "May I introduce you to my friend, Jean Luc?"

The pale-skinned man, who looked a bit overwhelmed, tilted his head.

Jacques continued in French, a language all the girls knew, being from the elite class. "He is my editor. Jean Luc, you know the fabulous Lobna." He winked at her, making Lobna sigh audibly. "The lovely Hend, and that's Samya."

"What, I don't get an adjective?" Samya put her hand on her hip.

Still at Lobna's side, Jacques chuckled. "Yes, yes, how about the handsome Samya? The homely Samya? The dependable Samya? Anyways, congratulations are in order." He switched back to Arabic. "What are your drinks, ladies?"

Hend chimed in nonchalantly, "Champagnia for me."

"And you, *habibti*?" Jacques addressed Lobna.

"Champagnia as well, *habibi*," Lobna said in a saccharine voice.

"*Habibti? Habibi*?" Samya mouthed with a disgusted face.

Samya glared at Jacques, feeling like she wanted to rip him to shreds. Jacques turned on his heel, and Samya found herself stalking after him.

"What in the hell was that?" she whisper yelled.

"Whatever do you mean?"

"Calling Lobna '*habibti*.' Where'd that come from?"

"Oh, that. Did I not tell you? Being around my sisters has domesticated me. I'm looking for a wife. Well, it is about time, you know. I took your advice. Lobna is a doll."

"You want to get married?" Samya said slowly while silently reminding herself she had no right to be this irate.

"Yes. Does that bother you?" He spoke without looking at her as he strode up to the bar.

"Of course not. You are free to do what you want, obviously. I just think you are laying it on a bit thick. You and Lobna don't exactly match well."

"Hmm." He pondered, still staring ahead. "Who would match well with me, do you think?"

"No one comes to mind," she snarled.

"I guess we'll see what happens with Lobna, then."

"Fine, but I don't think she'll want you if she ever finds out you and I have a history."

"Oh, she knows I was smitten with you once."

Samya felt as if she'd just been slapped in the face.

He smiled. "She's fine with it. Actually, I'm glad you pulled me out separately. I need your advice as a friend. I want to get her a gift. What do you think I should get?"

"A scorpion," she murmured.

"What'd you say?"

"Nothing. I don't know. I need a damn cigarette." With that, she stormed off.

CHAPTER FIFTY-FOUR

Samya was stewing, stark raving, earth-shatteringly, murderously angry. She avoided everyone during the soiree, and in turn, everyone was content to leave her to her childish response. Samya went home early and face planted onto her bed. Then she got up, faced the vanity mirror, paced, and rehearsed all the put-downs she could think of to hurl at Jacques.

Calm was nowhere to be found. But she had no right to be upset. Jacques had every right to seek a companion. Though he had adamantly claimed that he would never marry. What a liar! Well, she could see now that she'd made a mistake. Ya Allah, she'd waited too long. She might very well have lost her chance with him. She hadn't thought a year would be enough to erase her from his mind, but she'd been wrong. And *Lobna*? It made no sense. Regrets flooded her mind. She'd been overconfident. The right thing would have been to tell him to wait for her whether he damn well liked it or not.

Well, the hypocrite might think he knew what he wanted, but he was mistaken. As much as she wanted to kill him, she was not giving up on him. Lobna was Hend's dearest friend, and though not so dear to her now, she was Samya's friend, as well. She had to find a way to separate the mismatched couple without throwing Lobna off of a cliff. Right now, though, she had to calm down.

The next day, Omar picked her up in his Volkswagen to play tennis. The distraction was a relief. He was droning on about some corruption case or other; Samya wasn't entirely paying attention.

Omar furrowed his brow as he looked at her. "Who put salt in your tea this morning? What's wrong?"

Samya rolled the window down to let out the steam still coming off her head. "Hmm? I'm handling it."

"What happened to not keeping things from me?"

Samya sighed. "You can't use that all the time, you know." She crossed her arms. "Did you see him last night? Fawning all over Lobna like he was a dog in heat. Despicable. He wants to get married all of a sudden."

Omar rolled his eyes. "Better him than me."

"We are talking about me now."

They turned into the *nady* parking lot, and a man off the street began guiding them to a parking spot.

Omar threw his hand up. "There's no one else here. Who are you waving in?"

The situation brought Samya out of her mood, and she laughed. "Don't be so hard on the man. He's just trying to make a living." Samya went into her purse to pull out money. Omar blocked her and motioned the man over to the driver's side to give him a tip.

When they got out of the car, Omar carried their tennis equipment, and they walked through the *nady* entrance towards the courts. "You never told me. What is it about the French fool that inspires this much emotion?"

Samya dropped her shoulders. "First, he's also an Egyptian fool. Second..." How would one describe a love like hers for Jacques?

"For so long, I thought I didn't have choices. But he came into my life, and I didn't just go to him. I ran to him, and it was all my choice. I've now seen what I can feel when I allow someone in. He showed me that I can live bigger, that I can be on this earth, and people won't leave or be crushed under the weight of me. I only have to allow it. And he was the person who made me feel safe enough to allow in. And I love him for it."

Samya had learned a lot in the past year. Though she knew deep down Jacques loved her as-is, she couldn't ask someone to accept her if she didn't accept herself. Fully, with perceived flaws: being loud, contrary, misbehaved, curious, and yes, ill.

"I won't be outside looking in. I want him. Because choosing not to be with him is retreating and living small. I want more. I'm petrified, but I want more."

Omar was silent, seeming to contemplate her speech.

They reached the tennis court gates and were stopped. "Omar!"

Jacques looked irritatingly beautiful with his long muscular limbs in tennis shorts and his lean torso in a fitted shirt. He leaned against the gate by the closest court to the entrance with both legs crossed and had Lobna beside him. Both of them had tennis rackets.

Lobna wore a billowy white dress, large sunglasses, white heels, and the largest brimmed hat Samya'd ever seen. How Lobna expected to play tennis in that, Samya didn't know. Omar grabbed Samya's hand, pulling her back, but she stood firm.

"How wonderful to see you both!" Jacques jogged towards them. "Dearest Lobna and I fancied exercise this morning and thought this was the perfect thing."

Dearest. He'd never called *her* "dearest." Samya glowered.

Omar stepped in. "Well, Samya and I can settle for drinks at the café while you two finish your game. *Ma'a salama!*" He tried to bid them an abrupt goodbye.

"Nonsense, my man! We'll play doubles." Jacques intertwined one arm with Omar's and the other with Samya's, dragging them both to the court Lobna was waiting in.

When they reached her, Lobna was powdering her face looking at a compact mirror. Samya exhaled. Lobna was her friend for a reason. Her unconventional quirks were the best part of her. Samya realized then that her ire shouldn't go towards Lobna, but Jacques. She did love him. But she hated him. Logic be damned.

She pulled away from Jacques and hugged Lobna fervently, hoping her inner apology transmitted to her friend. "*Habibti*, how are you?"

Lobna, in true Lobna fashion, said, "Oh, the makeup, darling, the makeup."

Omar rolled his eyes.

Lobna then smiled at Samya and gave her two air kisses on each cheek. "I'm so glad you are here, Sim Sim! Jacques wanted to play this dreadful game but anything for *rosy*."

He was her soul now? Oh, this was simply too much.

"Let's play doubles. I know who I want to be my partner." Jacques wiggled his eyebrows at Lobna.

Samya wanted to singe those eyebrows right off his face.

"Lobna and I will play you and Omar," Samya spat out.

"But...But..." Lobna's lips wobbled.

Jacques held her hand. "I will miss you immensely, but we'll reunite once this bloody game is done with."

Samya wanted to retch.

They started the game. Lobna and Samya lost every set. Jacques kept suggesting that they switch partners for a more enjoyable game, but Samya ignored him and continued to serve. Omar had not objected. Samya knew he cared more about winning than anything, no matter how unfair.

Somehow, Lobna had found a chair (who knows when that happened) and sat at the back of the court swinging her racket with the least amount of effort possible if a ball came her way. Meanwhile, Samya was running up and down and side to side on the court, swinging with all her force and missing nine out of the ten serves being lobbed her way.

At one point, she grabbed her knee right after hitting a serve lobbed her way. "Ay!"

Jacques ignored the ball coming toward him and jumped the net to get to her. She turned to ensure that the ball had landed in bounds and celebrated.

She could have sworn he smirked before walking back to the net. He was met with Omar's annoyance on the other side.

"How could you fall for that?" Omar gestured towards Samya. "She's a horrific actress."

Jacques retrieved the ball. "It was one point out of the hundred games we've won, Omar. It'll be fine."

"It's the principle of the thing."

"Lobna, we got a point!" Samya rejoiced.

Lobna waved a feather-filled fan in a congratulatory manner. "Let's get drinks at the café to celebrate, darling!"

***

Since it was so early in the morning, there were no other patrons in the café. Once an elderly waiter sat them at a table inside, Jacques and Lobna began making eyes at each other.

Samya tapped the table impatiently. "Lobna, how's the farm?"

Lobna had been given a small plot of land from her grandfather's field. She hired laborers in the community to sweep the brush and plant crops fitted for that particular soil. The plot turned a good profit. Only Hend and Samya knew that Lobna spent the money on people in her farm community. She'd just paid for a big wedding for a farmer and a widow shopkeep. Another reason Samya couldn't hate her, dammit.

"I just came back from there, Sim Sim. Did I tell you we've started on guava? You'll need to visit some time and have jam!"

"I, for one, would love to try it." Jacques interjected.

"She wasn't talking to you," Samya snapped. "It is rude to invite yourself where you are not wanted."

"It's not an imposition at all, Sim Sim." Lobna assured. "I'm sure he won't need an invitation soon enough."

Samya had had enough. She shot out of her seat. "Enough! Omar, say something!"

Omar looked shocked but didn't say anything.

"This." She pointed at Lobna and Jacques. "It's not happening! He is a scoundrel, Lobna."

"Oh, Sim Sim. I'm so touched by your concern, but if there is anyone who can handle him, it's me," Lobna said.

"You don't understand. He's awful!"

"What does he do that's so awful?"

"He...he..." Samya's mind was blank because he wasn't awful. He was far from it. "You aren't suited; we'll leave it at that."

"But why ever not?"

"Just take my word for it."

"I don't think she can." Jacques folded his hands on the table and turned his attention to Samya. "If you want to sully my name, at least give a reason for it."

Lobna nodded. "Yes, darling. I know he is quite smooth, but why ever do you think we shouldn't be together? I think we will make a great family. In fact, we are planning to travel to Paris soon. Won't that be fabulous?"

Samya closed her fists.

"Perhaps we should go," Omar said, but Samya was too riled up to be placated.

"Why are we not suited, Samya?" Lobna asked.

"Because he's mine!" The words hurled out of her before she could shove them back in.

CHAPTER FIFTY-FIVE

Samya looked mortified. Omar put his hand on his face.

Finally, Jacques thought.

He kissed Lobna's hand. "It's true what they say; you are vastly underestimated. I will add acting to the list of your many talents."

Lobna smiled and looked at Samya. "I care about you, Sim Sim. But if you don't snap this man up, a more cunning woman than me will snatch him from you. You." Lobna pointed at Omar. "Come escort me to a taxi. We are no longer needed here."

"Who are you to...?" Before Omar could finish, Lobna grabbed him by the arm and led him away from Samya and Jacques.

"What?!" Samya screamed. "You tortured me on purpose?"

Jacques leaned forward in his chair towards her. "It was very bad of me, mon cherie. But I had to get your attention somehow."

"So you wanted to anger me?"

"I needed you to see that you and I are not just friends."

Samya collapsed on the chair. "Well, I was going to...oof. I need to calm down. Did you not trust me to come to you?"

There was no one at the café, allowing Jacques to hold her hand. "I knew you would." He shrugged. "But I wanted to speed things up."

Samya raised an eyebrow. "Tell me what you're thinking first."

He kissed her hand. "I'm thinking we make each other laugh. We can talk about anything or nothing at all. I keep you from killing most people; you keep me from being scammed. You forced me to meet my sisters, and as a result, I have gained a family that a year ago I didn't have. Before you interrupt, do you agree?"

She relaxed in her chair. "Yes. And my illness?"

"I'm glad you mentioned it. Do you expect anyone who is sick or has a hardship, for that matter, to just give up on life in order to appease others? Do you know how much you affect those around you? Hend loves you. Omar needs you to keep him from being the snob and ass he is. Your mother and father are enriched by your presence. Everyone who meets you falls in love with you. And I…"

He leaned in closer to her.

"Have gained something I never knew would fill me so completely."

"You know I feel the same about you. The last year has been absolute torture for me." She folded her hands in her lap. "But life won't be easy, you know. Things will be difficult."

"And neither of us will go through it alone. No one knows what will happen in the future. I do know I want to spend it with you." He continued as she looked at him with her watery yet gorgeous almond eyes. "And if anything, you can make me laugh when we're both old farts."

She chuckled at that and then took a breath. "Okay, my turn."

Samya looked scrumptious. He'd missed her so much. The self-control he'd exercised over the past year had been extraordinary.

"Please hear me when I say this. You have been and are the most important thing in my life. I needed time to prepare myself to be fully ready for you. I don't just love you, Jacques," she began. "I want something strong. I have the audacity to want a life with you. Something we build together. I'm terrified: I'll slip up. You'll run away. We'll fall apart. Despite it all, I'm fighting for you, for me, for us. Are you willing to fight with me, alongside me? It will be tough, wrought with complications and…"

Jacques looked around to make sure no one was watching. Then he interrupted her with a peck on her cheek. Because she was real, and here, and had come to this decision on her own.

"Yes."

"After all that, all I get is a yes? From an acclaimed writer, no less!"

He shrugged. He was speechless. This woman, this person, was accepting a piece of his soul and giving him a piece of hers. No words could capture the feeling of that.

"Well?" He looked at her.

"Well, what?" She laughed.

"I told you a while ago I would never ask you. So go ahead. Ask me."

"We don't have to, you know. We can figure something out. Maybe move to Paris and just live.

"Is that what you want?"

"Well…"

He leaned back in his chair. "What do you really want?"

Samya brightened. "I want to be with you."

Jacques motioned with his hand for her to keep going. "Mmhmm."

"I want to continue my residency in Cairo and help Dr Nadia expand her outdoor clinics. Maybe open some permanent ones. I want to be able to see my family and yours."

"Easy. I can write from anywhere, so we can live here, and then Paris on your off time."

She cracked a smile.

"As for the thing," Jacques said. "Well, we could continue on in sexy sin, but I don't want to hide anymore. Besides, I'll make sure we end up in the same place regardless of where we live. And, you owe me."

"I owe you?"

"Yes, for all the waiting and the plotting I had to do with Hend and Lobna. And I haven't eaten in my bed for a year!"

"Hend was in on this? I'll kill her."

He brought her face down to him. "Focus."

Emanating warmth, she looked into his eyes. There were so many things he wanted to do at this moment that even in France would be deemed indecent in public.

She plopped onto his lap. In the middle of the *nady* cafe, in front of the world. Well, the world was now only the elderly waiter who was cleaning the cafe. Jacques might have seen the old man gawk if he hadn't been so focused on the warm body that he'd missed holding.

"Jacques Ali Ginger Abd El-Hameed Kamal, since you are so desperate and won't let it go, I suppose we should go ahead and get hitched."

Jacques's heart opened up. Blood rushed to his face. Happiness, just pure joy, exploded within. "That wasn't an ask."

She shrugged and hopped off of him, then dragged him up on his feet, grabbed the collar of his shirt, and kissed him. A scandalous, juicy, electricity-shooting-through-your-body sort of kiss.

When she let him get some air, he panted, his forehead against hers. "Yes, you heathen. To protect my modesty, I'll marry you."

Tears formed in her eyes. All composure lost, she hung her arms around his neck and kissed him again.

Samya whispered, "About the wedding…"

He smiled into her hair. "It'll be a big one. For Hend and Lobna to meet the poor souls who will take those two on."

She smiled widely. He pressed into her dimple with his pointer finger. There was excitement, peace, relief, and love in his heart. Together, they would take on the world and all problems thrown their way. And it would be good, and bad, but mostly good. Because he wasn't alone. And Samya wasn't alone. They had each other.

Jacques kissed her again even as the waiter shooed them out the cafe with his broom, cursing.

Acknowledgements

Prior to finishing this book, I went through the toughest couple of years of my life. Illness temporarily took away my ability to read, or write. Gone were my ambitions, dreams, and hopes. They were replaced with bitterness, confusion, and anger. I lost years of my life to an illness. One that I had to hide from the world. I found I couldn't relate to many. The loneliness was visceral. Eventually, like Samya, little by little, I pulled myself out of the dark hole I was in. With the help of many who've extended their hands out to me, I got up off the ground. When I could read and write again, I wrote this book.

I am eternally grateful to my family, and friends. Cat, TJ, Yvonne, LeeAnne, Elizabeth, Tyne, Sherouk, Nouran, you held me up when I lost my balance. Thank you. Mama and Baba, though you don't quite understand your emotional, crazy daughter, you still support me. Thank you. Nada, my favorite person in the world, nothing is possible without you. Christine and Dr. Saah, my guardian angels, you never gave up on me, even when I gave up on myself. Thank you. Tayta Kefaya Soad, my grandmother, your life is a wonder to me. You have saved my life more times than you know. And now, you've given me something to look forward to. Thank you.

ABOUT THE AUTHOR

YASMIN YOUSSEF is the author of the Cairo Sirens series, of which there are three books. Her writing focuses on the stories of people of color, mental illness survivors, and yearning romantics. She is dedicated to providing happy endings, especially for those with severe mental illness, to replace the tragic narratives pervasive in media. She lives with her cat, Lulu Youssef. He is a menace, but the light of her life.

COMING SOON

Cairo Sirens, Book Two, Hend and Kareem's story.